Quest for Magic, Books 1–3

# QUEST FOR MAGIC

## BOOK 1

## Song of the Unicorns

by Rachel Roberts

# Prologue

The centaurs, half man, half horse, stood on a ledge overlooking a gorge. Long shadows fell across an ocean of mist. The bloodred sun dipped at their backs. Eliath, the first was called, shook the clinging damp from his hide and glanced north, then south.

The proud centaur lifted the silver amulet that hung from his neck. Beams of light shot from the object, casting a circular web of stars over the thick clouds that covered the open maw.

"I told you not to make that last jump," the other one, Corinth, complained. "We're not supposed to be here."

"I'd agree with you if I knew where 'here' was." Eliath studied the fairy map carefully, pinpoints of light reflecting in his wide, humanlike eyes.

One light blinked more brightly than the others. It meant that a portal lay a short distance ahead, but the only way to get there was to cross the gorge.

"There's another portal on the far side," Eliath observed.

"We can't trust the map," Corinth said, long tail swishing nervously. "The magic has been too unstable all along the web."

"You forget how important our mission is," Eliath said, nodding toward the wagon behind them. Inside the wagon, bursts of mournful wails like a wounded orchestra wafted over the lonely and desolate place.

"Are you sure the bridge is here?" Eliath asked.

Eliath altered the bubble of light, honing it to a sharp beam. It revealed a series of interconnected flat stones twisting their way across the gorge and then vanishing into the mist-shrouded far side.

"There," Corinth said, pointing. "The Demon's Crossing."

The wide stones floated precariously, moving and shifting to the silent rhythm of ancient magic.

"That bridge goes completely across?" Eliath asked.

Corinth stamped his forelegs to keep the icy chill from seeping up his thighs. Glancing to the covered wagon behind him, the centaur frowned. "We have no choice. We can't go back."

"Let's just move on," Eliath said sharply.

Corinth sighed and adjusted the shoulder

straps that hooked to long leather reins connecting to the large wagon.

The two centaurs moved carefully to the edge of the outcropping and stepped upon the floating bridge. It was solid as rock.

Mist curled over the stone like smoke as the wagon jostled forward. The centaurs could barely see their hooves.

"What was that?" Corinth shuddered, looking out across the bottomless chasm.

"There's nothing beneath us, all around us, but mist," Eliath answered. But something tingled across his shoulders, inched down his back—fear.

"I swear something is moving out there," Corinth insisted, craning his neck to look more closely into the swirling void.

Corinth was right. In the vast mass of clouds, something coalesced into a dark shape, moving—no—*swimming* through the mists.

"Let's move!" Eliath commanded.

But their steel horseshoes slipped on the damp rocks. The wagon staggered. A cacophony of screeches and whines rose from inside.

"Quiet!" Corinth hissed.

The centaurs moved quickly now, the wagon only narrowly avoiding the bridge's blunt edges and the perilous drop into nothing.

Suddenly, Corinth lurched backward, his hind

legs almost slipping over the edge. Eliath released the reins from his shoulder straps and trotted to the back of the wagon. The left rear wheel was wedged in a deep crevice that had been eaten away by centuries of icy wind.

The centaur lowered his shoulder and pushed against the wagon. Again, his cargo reacted with another chorus of angry and frightened sounds.

Muscles cording tight, Eliath strained. Sweat began to pour freely down his rich brown hide.

"Pull, Corinth!" Eliath yelled. "Harder!"

Then, a mass of something black flew across the wagon's path.

The wagon rolled forward.

Breathing hard, Eliath ran to the front of the wagon. He froze.

"Corinth?" He called out, looking left, then right. Torn reins fluttered in the wind. The other centaur had disappeared into the thick mist.

Snorting, Eliath tried to shake off the panic creeping into his chest. He quickly snapped the reins to his harness and pulled.

Black shapes swam all around now, skimming through the mists with terrifying speed. A sharp beam suddenly pierced the top of the wagon from within, sending splinters of wood flying. Jarring sounds screeched and squealed.

"No!" Eliath called over his shoulder. "You'll only make it worse!"

But it was too late. Like sharks to fresh blood, the mists roiled with huge black beasts. Too many! Eliath thought.

From the depths of the gorge, a razor fin sliced though the surface, coming right toward them.

With a mighty effort, Eliath pulled the wagon forward.

Bursts of light sent fireworks trailing as the wailing cries from the wagon turned to panicked screams.

Eliath tried to close his ears to the powerful forces building behind him. He swept the silver amulet from the chain around his neck, crisscrossing its light into a wide, blunt shield.

The monstrous creature erupted from the void, huge jaws gaping, revealing rows of long black teeth. It missed the wagon by inches, smashing into the shield and exploding to angry tatters of mist.

Eliath pulled with every ounce of his strength, trying to gauge where the next attack might come from.

The far side of the gorge was just ahead!

Eliath stopped short. Something stood at the end of the bridge, blocking the path. A figure covered in black armor, faceplate drawn, stepped forward. In a black-gloved hand, the dark knight held a staff of power. The jewel upon its tip glowed dangerously.

Eliath drew the sword strapped to his back. Ancient Elvin magic coursed up and down its fine edges.

The dark knight raised his staff, sending its foul magic into the mists.

A mistbeast sprang from the gorge, sinking teeth into wood. With a vicious shake of its massive head, it ripped out the rear wheels. The wagon fell backward, crashing to the stone and sliding half over the edge.

Eliath instantly threw the amulet. The glittering shield expanded, wrapping around the wagon.

The startled centaur suddenly felt his neck locked in an iron grip.

Eliath desperately struggled to stand his ground, but the knight was too strong. With a cry, the brave centaur was thrown into the void.

The wagon lurched, teetering perilously on the edge of the bridge.

The knight's armor-clad hand grasped only mist as the wagon tumbled into the gorge.

Blinding light exploded, spreading into a wide circle inside the clouds.

With a last burst, the light vanished, taking the terrified screams with it.

# Chapter 1

The mistwolf's howl rang across the bright examination room of the Stonehill Animal Hospital. Dr. Carolyn Fletcher dodged the pup's thrashing tail as she handed the syringe to her thirteen-year-old daughter, Emily. The wolf turned and snarled.

"Watch your manners!" Adriane scolded. The dark-haired girl, Emily's friend, was struggling to hold the squirming pup in place.

Adriane had a special bond with the young mistwolf; she was his pack mate. His name was Dreamer. The mistwolf locked his emerald gaze into Adriane's dark eyes. The image of a long, sharp needle entered Adriane's mind.

"I know, but it's for your own good," Adriane read Dreamer's mind and reassured the mistwolf pup.

"Good boy, you're almost done." Dr. Fletcher ran her hands over his lustrous fur, checking for abrasions or marks.

Dreamer wriggled under the vet's touch, his front paws sliding off the examination table.

"Emily, help Adriane get him on the scale."

Emily deposited the syringe in a disposal bin and put her arms around Dreamer's midsection. "Easy, Dreamer, this won't hurt. I promise." Emily's rainbow healing stone set inside her silver bracelet pulsed soft blue as she sent waves of calm at the growling pup. She and Adriane wrangled him onto the scale.

"Stop being such a big baby," Adriane said gently.

"Big is right," Dr. Fletcher said, adjusting the weights.

"Thirty pounds already?" Emily's hazel eyes widened. "He's only three months old."

"Hand me his chart, Emily," Dr. Fletcher studied the scale.

A small, furry paw pushed the folder toward Carolyn's outstretched hand.

Emily grabbed the chart and glared at the golden brown ferret standing on a stool behind her mother.

*"Just being helpful,"* Ozzie said, smiling. His paw rested proudly on a bright golden stone secured to a leather collar. Though most people believed he was just a remarkable ferret, Ozzie

was actually an elf. He had been sent to Earth disguised in a ferret's body by the Fairimentals, the guardians of his magical home world of Aldenmor. Since receiving the ferret stone from the Fairimentals for his bravery, he'd been using it nonstop to chatter telepathically with his friends who had their own magic jewels.

"With all that special puppy chow *someone's* been ordering via e-mail," Carolyn said, eyeing her daughter. "It's no wonder Dreamer's not full grown by now."

"E-mail orders?" Emily gave Ozzie a glower.

*"Er, they had a special on beef bits and liver snaps,"* Ozzie said.

"Dreamer will need another immunization in six months," Dr. Fletcher told Adriane. "He's perfectly healthy, and a magnificent animal."

Adriane smiled. "Hear that?" she asked, attaching Dreamer's collar, a black leather and turquoise band she had made to match the one around her wrist.

"He's going to be well over 100 pounds," Dr. Fletcher continued, her brow furrowed in concern.

"And he's like nothing I've ever seen before."

Dr. Fletcher was more right than she realized. This was no ordinary wolf. Dreamer was a mistwolf, an animal native to the magical world of Aldenmor. No longer was he the scraggly, scared orphan he had been just a short time ago when Adriane, Emily, and their friend Kara had found him. Under Adriane's care, his jet-black coat gleamed like velvet, rippling over streamlined muscles, built to run. Green eyes that had been dark with fear now shone like twin emerald pools. A snow-white star gleamed on his chest, and each paw was banded in white, as if he ran on clouds.

"Adriane's been working really hard training him," Emily said.

"Even with the best of training, he's a wild animal, and at some point might need to be cared for by specialists, for his own safety as well as yours," her mom advised them.

As if trying to prove her right, Dreamer made a break for it, nails screeching against the metal scale. Adriane grabbed and held him.

"You've both been doing a great job with Ravenswood, but it's my job to monitor the animals for the town council. We still don't know what's become of Stormbringer," Dr. Fletcher said.

Emily caught the quick flare from Adriane's golden wolf stone along with a sharp wince of pain. Stormbringer had been a beautiful silver mistwolf bonded to Adriane. During the battle with the Dark Sorceress, the evil half-animal, half-human magic master, Storm had sacrificed herself to save all of Aldenmor's mistwolves. The pain of losing her former pack mate was still very fresh, and Emily worried constantly that Adriane was keeping too much inside.

"And you!" Dr. Fletcher swung around and grabbed Ozzie, plunking the startled ferret on the scale. "You've gained six whole ounces in less than a month!"

"Hee-hee."

"I'm putting you on a strict diet!"

*"Gah!"* Ozzie exclaimed, and was about to protest when Emily quickly covered his mouth.

"Mom, it's your fault for giving him lasagna." Emily poked Ozzie's round belly.

*"Lasagna! I need that!"* the ferret squealed.

"From now on, it's diet lasagna." Dr. Fletcher smiled, patting the ferret's head. "Who's the best ferret in the world?"

Ozzie pointed to himself, cracking Carolyn up. Emily sighed.

"Oh, and Emily," Carolyn said seriously, "you need to call your dad back and let him know what you've decided about winter break."

"Yeah, I know,' Emily mumbled, her long curly hair falling over downturned eyes. Her dad had asked her to join him and his new wife on a vacation out west. She had tried not to think about it.

"Come on," Adriane said, slipping into her vest. "We have some hungry animals that aren't as lucky as the chubby ferret."

*"Hey!"* Ozzie said. *"I resemble that remark!"*

❧   ❧   ❧

Patches of snow glinted white in the noonday light, making Emily squint as she crunched down the frozen path through Owl Creek Bird Sanctuary, one of her favorite spots on the Ravenswood Preserve. She watched diamond flakes drifting to and fro between thick, towering trunks of maples and oak. Rows of pine, hundreds thick, resplendent in their winter greens, lined the distant ice-crested shores of the Chitakaway River.

The comfort she normally took from this place had little effect today. She was upset with her dad for marrying a woman she didn't even know. But there was more to what she was feeling. Emily and her two friends, Adriane and Kara, were mages, users of magic, but they were young and inexperienced, with profound responsibilities placed upon them. Emily was a healer, Adriane a warrior, and Kara a blazing star.

During their battle against the Dark Sorceress, the mages had released healing magic from Avalon, the hidden home of all magic. They hadn't heard anything from any of their friends on Aldenmor in weeks. The portal in the Ravenswood field had just seemed to vanish, leaving only nagging questions.

What did it really mean to be a mage? How long could they keep the secret? What were they supposed to do now?

"Over here, slowpokes," Adriane called out. She was hoisting a bag from a wooden shed, one of many feed stations set among the trails of the preserve. Already several hawks, peacocks, and white-tailed deer had gathered, waiting for the young caretakers.

Emily marveled at Adriane's strength and courage. A healer could only fix things after they were broken. She wished she could take action, be a warrior like her friend.

"You know, it's seventy degrees in New Mexico today," Ozzie said, snuggled in the deep front pocket of Emily's parka.

"Maybe you'll like her," Adriane said, spreading the feed into several wide troughs.

"I hate her!" Emily blurted before she could think. "They eloped and didn't even invite me to the wedding."

"They probably didn't want to make a big deal about getting married," Adriane guessed.

"I already have a mom!" Emily swallowed, suppressing the hot ache in her throat. "I don't need some *stepmom* telling me what to do."

Before Adriane could answer, Dreamer sent a mental image of forest underbrush and a pair of big ears.

Adriane frowned at the interruption. "You're a mistwolf, not a dog. You can talk if you want to tell me something."

"*Rabbit!*" Dreamer said impatiently.

"This is an animal preserve. You can't eat rabbits!" Her dark eyes flashed with exasperation.

"Just have a little patience with him," Emily said soothingly, instantly forgetting her own problems.

"I've tried! Your mom is right, Dreamer's just getting wilder all the time. Storm never acted like this."

Emily's heart ached for her friend. Adriane's bond with Stormbringer had been deeper than they could have ever imagined. That was the way with magical animals. Once bonded, it was a true friendship meant to last a lifetime.

In response to his pack mate's distress, Dreamer leaped onto the path, scattering the animals with a loud growl.

"Dreamer, no!" Adriane shouted. "They're not hurting me."

Emily tried to calm the frightened animals as Adriane settled Dreamer down.

The mistwolf sat and projected an image of the needle, as if its medicine could help Adriane.

"It's not the same thing," the dark-haired girl tried to explain as she knelt to stroke the wolf. "Sometimes you just hurt inside."

Dreamer gave her face a lick.

She smiled. "Thank you, yes, that's better." Adriane rose and faced Emily. "Sometimes I wish I could be a healer mage like you."

Emily took Adriane's hands in hers. Blue light from the rainbow jewel mixed with sparks of golden fire from Adriane's wolf stone, reinforcing the bond between healer and warrior.

*"Hoooo!"*

A white owl barreled from the sky right toward Emily's head. The red-haired girl instantly stretched her arm out—and the bird made a perfect landing, wings shimming with gold, turquoise, and lavender.

"What is it, Ariel?" Emily asked.

*"Come quickly,"* the owl said. *"Blazing star out of control."*

"I left her in the library," Ozzie said. "How much damage could she possibly do?"

# Chapter 2

"*GAH!*" Ozzie ducked as a flying book smacked into the library wall. The Ravenswood Library was a whirlwind of motion as dozens of books careened in all directions at once. Adriane and Emily swung the door fully open, knocking the ferret onto another diving leather-bound tome. Ozzie was whisked high into the air.

Dreamer dashed inside and chomped a low-flying journal. Shaking it furiously, shredded pages fluttered around him like snow.

"Dreamer, no!" Adriane ran inside, dodging a large bookend shaped like a dragon. She raised her arm, instantly releasing a wave of gold from her jewel. She spun the light into a broad shield to protect herself and Emily from the myriad of flying objects.

Under a wide table, a large gold leopard-spotted cat, Lyra, huddled next to a pegasus called Balzathar. The cat had unfurled magical golden wings to cover Ronif and Rasha, two ducklike quiffles.

"Mage gone wild," Balthazar warned, swatting a book away with his tail.

"Thank goodness we're rescued," Ronif said, popping out from under Lyra's shimmering wing. His mate quickly caught the quiffle as he was lifted in the air by the magical forces.

"Kara?" Emily shouted, shielding her face as a screaming ferret whooshed by.

"Up here!" a voice called out.

Hunkered under Adriane's golden shield, Emily made her way past the huge mobile hanging from the domed ceiling. Suns, moons, and planets swung in concentric circles.

The spacious library occupied several top floors of Ravenswood Manor and was lined with racks of shelves to store the wealth of books. High atop the tallest bookshelf sat a blond-haired girl with a crystalline jewel sparking erratically from her necklace.

"How did you get up there?" Emily asked.

Kara pointed. The tall, rolling ladder was making its way around the far side of the library, barreling straight for the mages.

Adriane whipped the shield into a rope, ensnaring the ladder and pulling it to a stop next to Kara.

"Thanks, Indy." Kara daintily climbed down,

holding the book she had retrieved, oblivious to the chaos.

"Kara!"

"Yes?" She looked up, blinking her light blue eyes.

Adriane and Emily each extended an arm, indicating the magical mess.

"Oh, that." Kara closed her eyes and held up her unicorn jewel. The flying objects suddenly crashed to the floor in crumpled heaps. Dreamer yelped and dove under the table, scattering the other animals like bowling pins. Ozzie's book skidded atop the table, sending the ferret flying into a furry heap on the couch.

"Fascinating." Kara Davies's blue eyes sparkled happily as she read from the book. "Did you know that amulets and talismans date back to cavemen?"

"A monkey couldn't have made a bigger mess," Adriane said angrily.

Kara rolled her eyes.

"I could use a protection amulet," Lyra complained, green eyes glinting as she stretched her lithe body.

Kara stuck her tongue out turning it green for a split second. She had absorbed her new shape-shifting abilities from one of the Dark Sorceress's minions, a skultum, after defeating the fairy creature in a battle of wits.

"We're supposed to practice together," Adriane warned. "You know what happens when you use magic, everything goes crazy!"

"Oh, this is nothing. I'll fix it in a jiffy," Kara said, raising her sparkling jewel.

"No!" Everyone in the room yelled at once.

"Whatever." Kara slumped in a chair and read from her book.

"Kara, you know you have to be careful with your jewel," Emily lectured. "We have no idea what it's capable of."

"How am I supposed to find out if I don't use it?" Kara pouted.

"It's obviously very powerful, so we should all be together when you do—just in case, okay?" Emily reminded her.

"Okay, okay."

Ozzie scampered to a leather chair and used his jewel to open a secret sliding bookcase. Hidden behind was the Ravenswood computer. The computer stored all sorts of magical information and allowed the mages access to their website. Ozzie immediately began pounding away at the keys, sorting the latest e-mails for the girls to answer later.

"So what's with the long faces?" Kara asked, peering over the top of her book.

"Emily has to decide if she's going to New Mexico," Adriane answered.

"You can't avoid meeting her forever, you know," Kara said to Emily. "She'll think you don't care."

"She obviously doesn't care what I think," Emily shot back. "I'm not dropping everything and going all the way cross-country just to meet her."

"Isn't your dad going, too?" Kara asked, eyes twinkling.

"Funny!" Emily scoffed. Then she added, "Yeah, I really want to see him."

"So, there you go."

"It's not that easy."

"Yes, it is. Three simple words: Get over it." Kara rolled her ice-blue eyes.

"That is *so* not helpful, Miss Overachiever," Adriane said.

Kara extended her fingers into claws and morphed her face into a horrid image of a wizened banshee.

"Keep it up, princess," Adriane laughed. "Maybe your face will freeze like that."

Kara's eyes widened, and she quickly morphed back, checking her face in the wall mirror to make sure.

"Here it is, Emily," Ozzie called out. "The Four Winds Resort, located in sunny Carlsbad, New Mexico."

Emily and Adriane walked to the computer and glanced over the ferret's head.

"Wow, check out these desert pics!" Adriane exclaimed, hitting some of the links. "And right next door is the Happy Trails Horse Ranch. It would be so awesome to ride horses for a whole week!"

"If you think it sounds so great, you go," Emily muttered. She stopped short, her own words giving her an idea. "Hey, you *should* come with me."

"I dunno," Adriane responded. "How would I afford it?"

"I'll ask my dad," Emily said excitedly. "I'm sure he'll cover it."

"What about our chores here?"

"Balthazar, Ronif, and I can handle that," Rasha quickly put in.

"Well, what about Dreamer?"

"He's still small enough for a transport cage. Pleeeeeeze, Adriane!!! You've got to go. I'm not going unless you do," Emily insisted.

Adriane thought for a minute, then turned to Kara. "What about you, Goldilocks?"

"Send me a postcard. As of today, there're only two weeks left before the Valentine's Day dance!"

Kara began counting off on her pink-polished fingers. "I have to get the band, arrange for the decorations, find the perfect dress, get my hair done, a manicure, a pedicure, a—"

"Fine," Emily said, hitting a link on the screen. "We'll check out the spa without you."

Kara's blue eyes opened wide. "What spa?" Dropping her book, she leaped to her feet and crammed between Adriane and Emily, reading the computer screen.

"The Fours Winds is home to the world-famous health and beauty spa . . . ," Kara read, suddenly radiating with enthusiasm. "Honey-infused facemasks, exotic kelp wraps, mud baths, complexion massages! I'm in."

"What about your ball, Sleeping Beauty?" Adriane asked.

"After a week at the Four Winds, I'll totally be the belle of the ball!"

"Nature hikes, desert tours, horseback riding—they have it all!" Adriane added.

"Girl, we are going to have so much fun!" Kara squealed.

"I'm shocked," Adriane suddenly stated.

"Why?" Kara asked, checking her sweater for stains.

"This might be the first time we've agreed on

anything," Adriane laughed, and gave Kara a high five.

Looking at her friends' eager faces, doubt gnawed at Emily. "Guys, what about the . . . you know." She held up her wrist, the rainbow jewel catching glints of light. "What if we're needed on Aldenmor?"

"We don't know what's happening on Aldenmor!" Kara jumped away from the computer. "We did our job, so let the Fairimentals do theirs. It's time for us to get back to our normal lives." She wagged a long purple finger.

"Normal, huh?" Adriane arched an eyebrow.

"Oops." Kara quickly changed her digit back. "Besides, the Fairimentals have a knack for finding us if there's an emergency."

Emily realized her friends were right. With the Ravenswood portal closed, there was nothing they could do for the Fairimentals for the time being.

She'd have to meet her dad's new wife sometime, and she'd rather have her friends by her side when it happened.

"All right," the red-haired girl said. "I'll let my dad know."

"Wait a minute!" Ozzie shouted, nose plastered against the monitor. "New Mexico is 'the Land of Enchantment.' Are there wizards there?"

"That's just the state motto, silly," Emily laughed.

"Yeah, the only thing you have to worry about are aliens," Adriane said, pointing to the Roswell link.

"Aliens?" the ferret gulped.

"Those are just stories, Ozzie," Kara said, "like dragons and trolls and, uh, okay, so we've actually *seen* all of those."

Ozzie narrowed his eyes and looked at each of the girls in turn. "Somehow I get the feeling this is going to be quite an adventure."

# Chapter 3

*Help! TooPH! It's dark in here—CroooOP—You*
*stepped on my tail! Where are we?—EEEooo-*
*eeoop—that smells!*

A jumble of sounds and voices echoed in
Emily's mind. She shut her eyes, blocking out the
mental barrage. She seemed to be picking up a
magical transmission. But what could be calling to
her in New Mexico?

She paced outside a big red barn as crowds of
happy tourists gathered inside. The Happy Trails
Horse Ranch was a series of stables, corrals, picnic
grounds, and low-rise buildings sprawled across
several acres of desert. Emily shaded her eyes as
she scanned the Four Winds Resort about three
hundred yards up a dirt road. The complex glis-
tened like a glass-and-chrome oasis complete with
landscaped gardens and fountains.

She watched Dreamer and Adriane running
along the dusty road leading from the resort to the

ranch. The wolf, ecstatic finally to be outside, was sniffing and exploring everything in sight.

"I still don't hear anything," Ozzie said, his eyes squeezed shut as he gripped his jewel. He was sitting in Emily's backpack. "What's it sound like?"

"It's weird, like a jumbled radio," she admitted. As soon as they'd landed, she'd heard it: tingling snippets of sounds rippling through her mind.

Her senses always increased exponentially by the magic of her healing stone. Like her past experiences, these feelings were unfocused, like a half-remembered melody echoing across the desert. At least she didn't get sick anymore.

"I can't get Dreamer to calm down. Can you help?" Adriane called, approaching as Dreamer pulled and chewed on the leash.

Emily kneeled to rub Dreamer's head. At her touch, he instantly calmed, looking deep into the healer's eyes. Waves of sparkling colors floated across Emily's mind. "You feel it too, don't you?" she asked the mistwolf.

A low growl slipped between Dreamer's teeth.
*"Magic."*

"Magic? Out here?" Adriane asked, startled. "You sure?"

Dreamer nodded. He was a natural magic

tracker, and Adriane had worked especially hard honing the mistwolf's skills.

"I think an animal is in trouble," Emily explained.

Adriane examined her amber wolf stone. "I don't sense any danger."

"Gather round, cowpokes!" boomed a deep voice from inside the barn.

"Any sign of your dad yet?" Adriane asked.

"No." Emily was almost glad her dad was late. She needed time to pull herself together before dealing with her new stepmom.

"Come on, we're going to miss the welcome speech," Adriane said, hitting the retractable leash, pulling Dreamer close.

The three walked into the cool shade of the large barn. Inside, guests gathered in the wide center, about twenty-five kids, teens, and adults. On the far side, Kara stood chatting away with a dark-haired woman, well dressed in an expensive Western skirt, silk shirt, and jacket.

Kara laughed and chatted with the woman as if they were old friends.

Leave it to Kara, Emily thought. Making friends already with a mannequin from some well-dressed Western fashion catalog.

"Whoo-hoo!" A tall, burly man stood in the

center of the barn, whooping. He was dressed in full cowboy gear, from his hat, boots, and bolo tie down to a big brass belt buckle with a bucking bronco. "Lemme hear you, now! Come on, let's do some whoopin'!"

The group gave a cursory whoop.

"Naw, that's a city slicker whoop. We need a real Texas whoop!" He smiled.

The group whooped louder. Dreamer threw his head back and howled, startling everyone.

"Dreamer!" Adriane hissed, struggling to untangle the wolf from his leash.

"That's the ticket. Name's Texas Slim. And I welcome ya'll to the Happy Trails Horse Ranch. For the next five days you're gonna be livin' the life of cowboys and cowgirls. Ridin' horses, explorin' the desert, cookouts . . ."

*PhoooBB! Move over! Faaahtooot!*

Emily looked sharply around her. "Ozzie, did you hear that?"

"No, I can't get my stupid stone to do anything," Ozzie whispered, shaking his ferret stone.

Emily moved away from the crowd to try to get a sharper impression from the strange sounds. Shining saddles sat on stands, and bridles hung from wall hooks as she walked past a row of stalls. An image of carrots suddenly popped into her mind. Where did that come from? She looked at the nearest stall. A black-and-white-splotched pony stared at her with beautiful liquid eyes.

Emily petted its velveteen muzzle, half listening to Texas Slim's speech.

"Some of y'all might be in the Southwest for the first time. It's prettier than a painted peach, but there's an old sayin' 'bout these parts: Everythin' in the desert is gonna try to bite, sting, or scratch you, and sometimes all at once . . ."

Emily scratched the pony's soft ear. "I'm sorry, I don't have any carrots for you."

"How'd you know carrots are Domino's favorite?"

A pretty teenage girl with short, dark brown hair and dark eyes slipped out of the neighboring stall. She quickly latched the wooden door before a white-and-reddish-brown-spotted pony could follow her out.

"I'm Sierra Sanchez." The girl took a carrot from the pocket of her brown suede vest and handed it to Emily.

"Hi, I'm Emily Fletcher." The healer took the carrot and smiled.

"You're from the Ravenswood Preserve," Sierra said as Domino eagerly devoured the carrot from Emily's palm.

"Yes, how did you know?" Emily was startled.

"Ravenswood is *so* cool. I've been to your website," Sierra said excitedly. "When I saw your name on the guest list, I practically freaked. We have a lot in common. I'm a guide here."

"My friends Adriane and Kara are here, too," Emily said. "And Ozzie."

The ferret leaned toward Sierra and pointed to his mouth.

"He's adorable!"

*"And hungry."*

"She's a beautiful paint pony," Emily quickly said, stroking Domino's head as she gave Ozzie a stern look.

"You know your horses," Sierra said approvingly, feeding another carrot chunk to the pony in the stall next to Domino. "I've ridden paints my whole life, mostly this gelding here. His name's Apache . . ."

Sierra's words faded. Loneliness, fear, and confusion filled Emily's senses.

Something felt so familiar—

". . . beautiful bracelet. Are you all right?" Sierra asked, glancing at Emily's wrist.

"Just a little jet lag," Emily smiled weakly, covering her glittering jewel with her shirtsleeve.

*"Emily, twelve o' clock,"* Adriane's voice popped in her head.

At the barn doors, a man stood waving.

"Excuse me, Sierra, I see my dad," Emily said.

Forgetting about everything, she began running—and stopped short. His wave had not been for her.

*Oh no!* The woman talking to Kara was waving back to her dad.

Emily watched in horror as he walked to the woman and gave her a kiss. She stood frozen as she watched Kara point right toward her.

David Fletcher's hazel eyes, the exact color of Emily's, widened as he caught sight of his daughter. "Em!"

He ran over and caught her in a big bear hug, just like he used to do.

"Daddy!" Emily hugged him back, tears leaking from her eyes.

"Emily, sweetheart, look how you've grown." He held her at arm's length, eyes also damp. "You're so beautiful!"

Emily smiled self-consciously, trying to tame her long red curls. She and her dad hugged again. She felt the familiar comfort from his presence, and her heart soared.

"You look good, too, Dad," Emily said truthfully. He *did* look good. He had thinned down, and his warm, friendly eyes and strong brow were framed by neatly trimmed curly hair.

"*Gah!*" Ozzie had wedged himself firmly between Emily and her dad.

"Oh, sorry, little guy!" David let Emily go and patted the ferret. "This must be Ozzie! A little chubbier than I thought."

The ferret covered his stomach with his paws and scowled.

"You missed the orientation," Emily told him.

"Sorry, Em. I had to register and get the bags to the rooms," he explained, smiling at the dark-haired girl who had joined them. "You must be Adriane. I've heard so much about you, I feel you're a real part of the family."

"Thank you," Adriane said, beaming. "This is Dreamer."

"Hey Boy." David leaned to ruffle the pup's scruff.

Emily saw the dark-haired woman straighten her suede jacket and step forward. Edging past Dreamer, she pushed her flowing hair into place with perfectly manicured nails.

"Emily, this is Veronica," David began.

"Emily, darling!" Veronica grabbed Emily in a hug, then looked her over as if appraising a piece of furniture. Her smile revealed faultlessly white teeth framed by glossy red lips. "Your dad has told me so much about you."

"Hi," Emily muttered. She felt Veronica's eyes

canvassing every part of her, from her wild curly hair to her denim shirt and jeans.

Emily felt woozy.

"Em, are you okay?" her dad asked.

Focusing on the dark auburn of his hair, she nodded. "Just a little tired from the trip."

"I've had the most precious time with your friend Kara. She is just the best!" Veronica's pale skin seemed too white.

Emily nodded mutely, watching Kara's beaming smile.

"I just *love* those boots, Veronica!" the blazing star said, admiring the woman's stylish beige suede boots. "Where did you ever find those?"

"Paris, hon." Veronica winked. "Perks of being a curator. The galleries I represent send me to Europe a few times a year."

"That is *so* cool!" Kara gushed. "Isn't it, Em?"

Emily managed a faint smile thinking: Someone get me out of this nightmare.

Dreamer sniffed Veronica curiously. She frowned, brushing mistwolf slobber off her purse.

"Hey!" David said excitedly. "Guess what, girls? I managed to reserve a cabin just for the three of you."

"A cabin!" Adriane beamed.

"A *cabin*?" Kara wailed. "We're not staying at the resort?"

"Veronica and I are. We figured you girls would have more fun at the horse ranch. Isn't that great?"

"Cool! Thanks, Mr. Fletcher," Adriane said.

"Yippee-kay-yae," Kara said sarcastically.

Veronica pulled a slip of paper from her purse and smiled. "I have a pass to the spa for you, Emily. I thought we could spend some quality bonding time in the mud bath."

Mud bath! I'm not a flobbin! Emily thought, aghast.

"I'm not big on spas," she managed, clenching her teeth. "Kara might like it, though."

Kara was practically salivating.

"Well, if Emily doesn't feel like using it, you can certainly join me instead, Kara."

"Giddyyup!" the blonde whooped.

"So how you fine folks doing?" Texas Slim asked as he approached, grinning broadly. Sierra was at his side.

"*Ooof!*" Veronica stumbled as Dreamer sideswiped her.

"That's some hound dog you got there."

"He's a dingo," Kara said quickly, earning a sharp look from Adriane.

"Your daughter's already met my niece Sierra," Texas said to David and his new wife. "Best darn horse wrangler in four states."

Sierra's eyebrows rose at the sight of the huge "dingo."

"I'm Kara and I love your pendant," the blond girl said, stepping forward and smiling. "Turquoise is always *so* in."

"Perfect accessory for any outfit," Veronica added, smiling at Kara.

Emily looked at the beautiful gemstone that hung from Sierra's neck. Why hadn't she noticed that before?

"Thanks. It's been in my family for generations." Sierra touched the bright turquoise oval suspended by a thick silver chain. "Your gems are really cool, too."

Kara proudly held out her sparkling unicorn jewel. "I found mine in a little place over the rainbow—"

The unicorn jewel suddenly popped with diamond light. Startled, Kara jumped back.

"Kara, where did you get such an outrageous fashion statement?" Veronica giggled in delight. "I love it!"

Emily looked at Kara's jeans. The blazing star's belt had turned into a pink feather boa.

"Never did understand fashion." Texas Slim shook his head.

"Um, it's the latest thing," Kara explained quickly. "Belts that change from casual to casual-er. They're still working out the bugs—"

Sierra's brow furrowed suspiciously.

"Listen up, everyone!" Texas Slim waved his hat in the air. "I'm gonna be leadin' a hike to the Arrow Rocks drawings just a yodel south of the resort, and Sierra's leadin' a trail ride to Echo Ridge, a holler or so up north. That's a lot of beautiful country to see. So let's get crackin'."

"Emily, come on my trail ride," Sierra pleaded. "Domino would love it."

"Okay, I guess."

"Great, see you guys later," Sierra said, heading back to the stalls.

"We're going to check out the hotel. Dinner's at six," David said, giving Emily a hug. "It was great to finally meet everyone. Have fun!"

Veronica's hand slipped into David's arm, pulling him away.

"Your stepmom is so awesome!" Kara raved.
"What?"

Adriane glared at Kara. "What are you doing?!"

Kara squeezed her eyes shut and changed her belt back into brown Gucci leather. "I didn't do anything!"

"Keep your magic in check," Adriane warned the blond girl sternly. "We've got a situation."

"I'll say. I'm not sleeping in a log cabin."

"You can sleep in a tree if you want, but I was referring to Emily."

Kara noticed the tight lines of distress on her friend's face. "Emily, what's wrong?"

Taking a deep breath, Emily told the blazing star, "I think there's a magical animal in trouble."

Kara looked around. She'd been through enough with the mages to trust Emily's intuition about animals and magic. "Here?"

Dreamer barked in agreement, sending an image of the desert.

"Somewhere out there," Emily said.

"What do we do?" Kara asked.

"Okay, huddle up," Adriane ordered. The three mages leaned forward, heads touching. Ozzie scrunched in between with Dreamer in the center.

"Here's the play," Adriane said. "I'll go on Texas Slim's hike and let Dreamer do some scouting. You ready for that?"

Dreamer nodded affirmatively.

"Good boy. Emily, you go on Sierra's trail ride and canvas the area. You find anything, you let us know right away."

Kara clutched the free pass in her hand like it was a magic gem. "And I will check out the spa!"

"Fine. But no one goes near anything unusual without the others. Okay?"

"Hike!" Kara exclaimed as the three mages clasped hands, fuzzy ferret paw on top, wet wolf nose underneath.

"And no more magic, Dorothy!" Adriane said to Kara.

"Okay, okay," Kara bit her lip and fingering her stone nervously.

"Don't you worry, Emily," Ozzie said. "We'll find whoever it is."

"I know we will, Ozzie," Emily whispered, her senses reeling. That was just what she was afraid of.

# Chapter 4

The group of eight riders marveled at the sun-bleached desert stretching to the horizon. Contrasting starkly with the panorama of muted yellows, browns, greens, and silvers, the brilliant azure sky soared overhead.

The riders had stopped at Echo Ridge lookout to view the perfect picture postcard vista.

"We're in the Guadalupe Mountain Range," Sierra said, pointing to the bronze mountains rising like majestic towers. "In the middle of the Chihuahuan Desert. Although it looks dry and parched, it's teeming with life if you know where to look."

As if in response to Sierra's words, a gaggle of twittering quails skittered between nearby cacti.

"Easy, girl," Emily said, patting Domino's neck.

The mare shifted anxiously, sensing Emily's concern. Something was definitely reaching out to her, drifting across the wide-open space like tumbleweed. Even Ozzie's ferret stone was reacting, flashing erratically with golden light. The ferret sat in front of Emily, braced against the saddlehorn. With one paw to his brow, he surveyed the land while holding his stone out in the other paw like a homing beacon.

Sierra moved among the group, offering advice to the novice riders, tightening stirrups and bridles.

Although Emily hadn't ridden in years, Domino seemed to make it so easy for her. She closed her eyes and took a deep breath. Her senses filled with sweet, dry, desert air, the smell of leather, and the heft of Domino's strong smooth muscles beneath her.

*I'm hungry! FooB! I'm scared. I'm itchy. I'm more itchy!*

Who said that?

Startled, Emily turned to a canyon running about a mile east of the lookout. The reds, beiges, browns, and purples of the ridgeline swept into the enclosed space.

"Ozzie?" She nodded her head toward the voices.

He swung his ferret stone toward the canyon walls, and it glowed deep gold. "Yes, definitely over there."

"I'm going to try to contact whoever it is."

"Right!" Ozzie held his ferret stone close to the healing stone upon Emily's wrist.

She closed her eyes and reached with her mind. *"Hello. Can you hear me?"*

*PooT?*

*"My name is Emily. I'm a healer mage."*

*PHHOOOOLLL! BoooF-FrOOOth! PaWOooO!*

Emily's mind was bombarded with overwhelming noise. She gasped, covering her ears.

"Are you all right, Emily?"

Emily opened her eyes to see Sierra swinging Apache around beside her.

"Er, yes, I'm okay," she answered. "What's that canyon over there?" Emily pointed east.

"That's Pecos Canyon. It's part of Carlsbad Caverns which run throughout these mountains. They're world famous for deep caves. Just don't ever go inside without an experienced spelunker."

"A what?"

"A cave explorer," Sierra explained. "You could wander about for days and never find a way out."

Emily eyed the canyon worriedly. "You'll probably think I'm crazy, but I think there's an animal in trouble there."

Sierra's eyes widened. "How do you know that?"

Emily frowned, not wanting to say too much. "Something doesn't feel right to me."

Instead of questioning Emily further, Sierra called to the others, "Everyone stay here. Emily and I are going to check something out."

The group, grateful for the chance to ease their sore behinds, cheered.

Apache snorted and took off at a gallop.

Domino followed, allowing Emily to adjust to a canter before breaking into full gallop. The paint moved in perfect harmony with her rider.

The two horses sliced a wake of dust as they made their way down the sloping trail. They soon found the entrance to the canyon.

"Hold up," Sierra called, slowing Apache to a walk.

Brown and red desert sands of the canyon floor stretched before them, surrounded by high-striated walls. They reminded Emily of sand sculptures she had seen, layered with pastel colors.

"We'll do a quick pass through and head back," Sierra said.

"Thank you," Emily said gratefully, letting Domino lead the way.

"You've always had a way with animals?" Sierra wondered.

"I grew up around them. My mom's a vet."

"Ah, that explains it." She nodded toward Domino. "I've never seen Domino so taken with a rider before."

"She's the best, Sierra. I just love her," Emily said, patting the horse's neck.

Domino nickered, radiating waves of pleasure.

"What about you, Sierra? I mean, you seem so in touch with the land."

"Before I left Mexico to live with Uncle Tex, my grandpa gave me this jewel." Sierra fingered her turquoise pendant. "He said it had special powers that only I could use."

Emily could have sworn the turquoise jewel pulsed just then. It must have caught a reflection of sunlight.

"Emily, I wanted to ask about your jewels."

The healer stiffened.

"Each of your friends has one. Even Ozzie. I read on your site that sometimes jewels have . . . properties."

"Yes, that's true. They focus different types of energy."

"Sometimes mine helps me see things, feel things . . . differently. I can sense things about the desert," Sierra said as her attention was drawn to a solitary dune rising from the center of the canyon floor.

"What is it, Sierra?" Emily asked, eyeing the strange mound.

"I don't know. But it wasn't here last week."

*"Emily, look,"* Ozzie said, pointing to the ground.

Splintered wooden planks littered the sand as they approached the mysterious mound.

They were practically on top of it before they realized what they were looking at—the wreckage of a fancy carriage. The size of a bus, it was face-down, half buried in the sand. The rear axle was broken, one back wheel ripped to pieces. Broken wood surrounded a gnarly hole in its side where a large chunk of the wagon was missing.

Sierra pulled back on Apache's reins and slid effortlessly to the ground. Emily dismounted, set Ozzie on the sand, and joined Sierra by the wreckage.

A burst of wind made the single whole wheel creak in a slow circle.

"There's nothing inside," Emily said peering into the open hole.

She looked closer. Deep rents scarred the richly grained wood—teeth marks. Running her fingers over the serrated slashes, Emily shivered, suddenly feeling cold in the bright afternoon sun. Whatever had made those marks was big.

"And there are no tracks." Sierra swept her arm over the surrounding area. "It's as if the thing just fell from the sky."

*"Emily, look at this!"* Ozzie was digging into the dirt where the front of the wagon lay submerged.

It was a section of polished wood. Ornate symbols were carved in a brass plate.

*"It's some kind of academy crest,"* he explained.

*"You mean this is like a school bus?"* Emily asked.

*"Yes, I think so."*

*"Then what kind of students was it carrying?"*

*Mage? Are you there? Shhh, quiet! How do we know it's a mage and not a werebeast? Oooot, you're right—gimme that—No, that's my last sunbeam cracker!*

The magic hit Emily like a fist. She gasped, eyes drawn to the sheer canyon face in front of them. Several cave openings riddled the base. It was coming from inside one of them. And now she had no doubt.

*"Ozzie, it feels like unicorn magic,"* Emily told the ferret.

*"Unicorns? You sure?"*

*"Yes. I think there are unicorns here—and I think they are in trouble."*

Ozzie knew as well as the mages that unicorns were the most powerful of all magical creatures—and the most coveted by those who desired magic. The mages had fought for them before, rescuing a unicorn named Lorelei from the Dark Sorceress and saving the unicorn jewel that had eventually become Kara's.

"We have to get the others and head back," Sierra said, scanning the desert skies. "There's a sandstorm coming, a bad one. If you've sensed an animal here, it's probably a lost bobcat or cougar. They make quite a racket."

The horses pranced nervously as they, too, sensed approaching danger.

"Let's go, Emily," Sierra called as she mounted Apache.

*"You start back with Sierra,"* Ozzie said. *"I'll look in the nearest cave, see if I can confirm a sighting."*

Emily bit her lip. She couldn't risk saying anything else to Sierra. *"Okay. Five minutes, and be careful!"*

The ferret scrambled away and disappeared into the desert.

🌀   🌀   🌀

Ozzie crept against the rocky wall near the entrance to a large cave. The ferret kept an eye on his surroundings to make sure nothing was following him. The high sandstone was ribboned with rich earthy shades from pale peach to bright rusty red. Scraggly prickly pear cacti sprouted in clumps, with spiny, paddle-shaped leaves.

"Ahh!" Something bit him! Ozzie leaped and spun around, putting his paws on his ferret stone. Grimacing, he carefully extracted a cactus needle from his fuzzy bottom.

A strong breeze blew through the canyon, sending small pebbles and bits of sandy dirt flying in the air.

"Pa-tooeey!" Ozzie shielded his eyes as the wind grew stronger.

At the far end of the canyon, a whirlwind shimmered into existence and began to take shape. Ozzie blinked—was he really seeing that? Or was it a mirage? But it was no trick of the desert.

The spiral grew larger, pulsing with brilliant colors like a rainbow twisted around itself. The twister touched down on the desert floor, twirling forward like a tornado. Ozzie watched in amazement. Wherever the whirlwind touched, the ground buckled and warped like soft clay.

The dazzling tornado danced over the half-buried wagon. The effect was amazing—brilliant lights shimmered, morphing the wagon into *glistening blue-white ice!*

The whirlwind then wobbled—and headed right for the startled ferret.

*"Gah!"* Ozzie dove for cover behind a rock outcropping.

The twister coiled overhead in a flurry of color. Inches from his head, the rock morphed into a strange, marshmallowy mass.

An instant later, the whirlwind disappeared, specks of colored magic dissipating like mist.

Ozzie's paws flew to his golden ferret stone. *"Emily! Come in, Emily!"*

*"I'm here, Ozzie,"* the mage answered. *"Did you find something?"*

*"Did I?!? You're lucky I'm still a ferret! A weird magic whirlwind just changed a cactus and a rock and the wagon. It nearly got yours truly in the process!"*

*"Slow down, what are you talking about? A wind?"*

*"Actually, it was an elemental shift in paramagical forces, to be precise,"* a new voice broke in.

*"GAAAHH! Aliens!!"* Ozzie screamed. *"Emily, warn the others, I'l—"*

🌀  🌀  🌀

Emily was almost at the sloping trail that led up to Echo Ridge when Ozzie's frazzled voice vanished.

"Ozzie? Ozzie?" Emily called frantically.

There was no answer. Heart thudding, she looked toward the canyon. "Sierra, Ozzie's gotten loose. I need to go look for him."

The brown-haired girl brought Apache up sharp. "Okay, but hurry. I'll round up the others and meet you back here on the trail, but whatever you do, don't go into the caves."

"Okay, I'll be careful," Emily promised.

Domino sensed the mage's urgency and broke

into a gallop, racing back into the canyon. Fear pulsed through Emily's veins. If anything happened to Ozzie, she didn't know what she'd do.

She was halfway across the canyon floor when she realized the wagon was gone. In its place was a large pond of water. Leading Domino to the canyon wall, she searched for Ozzie.

"Give me back my stone or you'll never see your spaceship again!"

Emily turned toward the sound of the ferret's voice. She saw Ozzie hopping up and down on what looked like a pile of twigs.

"Ozzie," Emily said, sliding off Domino and running to her friend, "what are you doing?"

"Interrogating him." Ozzie waved a paw at the twigs. "This alien attacked me!"

Emily looked closer at the mass of twigs, desert grass, and shrubbery. "Ozzie, wait a minute."

The pile suddenly spun and formed into a little wobbly whirlwind.

Crackling and rustling, the tiny whirlwind took another shape before it came to a halt. Slightly shorter than Ozzie, it looked like a little stick figure, made of twigs, dirt, and bushes magically held together. A gray-green clump of sagebrush served as its torso and another as its head. Sparkling eyes of quartz looked at her curiously. Hanging around its neck was a small silver-and-blue gemstone on a chain woven of desert weeds.

"You're a Fairimental!" Emily gasped.

"This thief took my jewel!" Ozzie yelled. "Huh? What the—"

Fairimentals were very powerful and mysterious magical creatures who protected the magic of Aldenmor. Made entirely of elemental magic, they took their physical forms from water, fire, earth, and wind. This one was an earth Fairimental.

The little twig figure stared at Emily's rainbow gem. "You are the Healer?"

Emily nodded. "Yes."

"Oh, thank goodness. I found this mookrat impersonating a mage—does this belong to you?" A spindly branch held out a golden stone.

"That's Ozzie's ferret stone," Emily said.

"Gimme that!" The ferret grabbed his stone and attached it back onto the setting on his collar. "I've met Fairimentals and *they* never robbed me. How do we know you're one?"

"I'm an E.F., and my name is Tweek," the creature said.

"What's an E.F?" Emily asked.

"Experimental Fairimental. I'm the first ever of my kind. The Fairimentals made me at their lab."

"The what from the where?" Ozzie demanded.

"It used to be a place called the Shadowlands,

but now it's a magic preserve and research facility called The Garden. I'm designed to stay on Earth for long periods of time." Fairimentals had visited Emily, Adriane, and Kara on Earth in the past, but their particular magic could only be sustained in this world for minutes, sometimes seconds, before falling apart.

"What are you doing here?" Emily asked.

"I was sent here to find the three mages." Tweek's quartz eyes eyed Ozzie. "*You're* not one, are you?"

"Maybe I am." Ozzie crossed his arms angrily.

"I have a very important message!" Tweek cried, waving his arms so dramatically that a few twigs flew off.

"What is it?" Emily asked worriedly.

Tweek's twiggy features settled into serious lines. "Something terrible has happened. Avalon has lost its magic."

Ozzie pressed his paws to his head. "What!?"

"Can you tell us anything else, Tweek?" Emily asked.

Twigs and branches fell to the ground as the E.F. shuddered. "This is my first assignment," he said, picking up pieces of himself. "Maybe I didn't get everything just right, but I know I have to find the missing magic—AHHHHH!"

Mage and ferret stared at the E.F.

"Look out behind you, it's a—"

*BANG!* Tweek exploded into a cloud of twigs and brush .

Emily whirled around, her rainbow gem pulsing a deep green warning light.

Four sparkling tornadoes were touching down on the far side of the canyon.

The desert floor bulged and undulated as if it had suddenly turned liquid.

Domino neighed, stomping her hooves, ready to run.

"Let's get out of here!" Ozzie cried.

Grabbing Ozzie, Emily sprang into the saddle as the pony bolted. She had to warn Adriane and Kara. This was no ordinary sandstorm.

"Go, Domino!"

The horse ran at breakneck speed, slaloming around the first whirlwind. The tornado spun like a giant colored top, roaring over rocks and melting them to vile black sludge. Another wind engulfed several cacti, twisting them into horrible thorned monstrosities. Emily leaned left as Domino raced between a pair of oncoming tornadoes, missing them only by a few feet. Stinging edges of dark magic whirled past Emily as her jewel blazed upon her wrist. She stifled a scream. Nature itself was being twisted and bent into unnatural forms. She leaned forward, urging Domino to outrun the fourth wind, leaving the twisters spinning against the canyon walls like pinballs.

Within seconds they were safe, out of the canyon.

Emily looked over her shoulder. Behind them a huge jagged fin rose up and then disappeared beneath the sands.

# Chapter 5

*E*mily walked into her living room. Ghostly beams of light played over what used to be couches and chairs, now twisted into bizarre shapes.

"Emily," Carolyn said, standing in the hallway watching her daughter. "Your new mother is here to see you."

Facing the hearth stood a tall woman, long dark hair falling down her back. The woman turned, and Emily's voice locked in a silent scream.

The woman's porcelain white skin matched the streak of white lightning in her jet-black hair. And her eyes, the vertical slits of an animal, pulsed with a feral glow.

"We're family now, dear," the Dark Sorceress said, beckoning Emily forward with a long silver claw.

Vampire fangs appeared at the edge of her thin lips as the Sorceress embraced Emily, pulling her into darkness—

"Emily, are you in there?"

Emily opened her eyes to find two noses, one furry, one damp and cool, in her face.

Dreamer gave her a lick as Ozzie dropped a tangle of curly hair back over her face. Wiping sleepy eyes, Emily let the nightmare fade.

"We brought you something to eat," Adriane said, standing by the bunk bed. She handed Emily a covered tray and a container of juice.

Suddenly feeling famished, Emily swung her legs to the wooden floor and opened the tray. "Thank you," she said, biting into the most delicious tuna sandwich she had ever tasted. "Why didn't you wake me earlier?"

"You were exhausted," Adriane said. "The social butterfly mage covered for you at dinner."

"Hey, kids," Kara said, bounding through the screen door and flouncing on the bed next to Emily. "Veronica invited me to the Moonlite Mudbath at the spa tonight."

"Yeah, great," Emily mumbled over a pickle.

"Look, Emily, I was just trying to be friendly," Kara said. "You should give her a chance."

"Well, thanks for keeping her busy."

"No prob." Kara popped open two matching floral suitcases. Their contents immediately spilled out. She started sorting through shoes, pastel bandanas, silk shirts, jackets, and assorted outfits.

Emily pulled her hair back, taming it with a scrunchy.

"Can you still hear them?" Ozzie asked, ferret face full of concern.

"Not now."

"Ozzie filled us in," Adriane explained. "Dreamer and I checked the grounds. No sign of unusual whirlwinds or any magical activity. We think it was isolated to that canyon, drawn to the magic of whatever's in the caves."

Emily nodded.

Kara was neatly laying out several outfits. "Well, you can go out tomorrow morning and look around all you want."

"No," Emily said. "We have to go *now!*"

Kara put her hands on her hips. "You're going to go wandering around in the desert *now?*"

"We can't wait," Emily said, slipping into her hiking boots. "Whatever animals are in there could be hurt."

"Emily says we go, we go!" Adriane said.

Dreamer paced the room and sent an image of the moon.

"Come on, you can say it," Adriane urged.

*"The wolf hunts at night."*

"That settles it," she said, looking to Kara. "Four against one."

"I'm not going to miss the mudbath to go wandering around in the dirt!" Kara glared, and her hair stuck out like a porcupine.

"Nice," Adriane commented.

"It's at least three miles. How are we going to get there?" Emily asked.

"The Bride of Frankenstein here was kind enough to secure us a ride." Adriane pointed through the screen door. A shiny new golf cart sat in front of the cabin. FOUR WINDS RESORT was stenciled on the sides in looping turquoise.

"No way! I'm not walking, like, way over there." Kara headed to the cabin's bathroom and yelped when she saw her hair in the mirror.

Dreamer huffed, the equivalent of a mistwolf laugh.

With a brilliant zap, Kara tamed her hair back to normal. Satisfied, she cleared Emily and Adriane's toothbrushes off the shelf and started carefully arranging her lipstick from palest to darkest pink. "Maybe I'll just keep it like Veronica's." As Kara spoke, her blond tresses twisted and shimmered into Veronica's flowing black mane.

"Don't do that!" Emily said angrily.

Kara gulped and shut her eyes in concentration. Her hair turned blond. "Sorry."

Emily paused on the woven Southwestern rug. "It's not funny."

"It's not a fashion accessory. Get your jewel under control!" Adriane ordered.

Kara fretted, twisting the unicorn jewel in her hand. "I am, I'm trying . . ."

Emily saw a glint of fear in Kara's eyes. "Okay, you stay here, Kara," she said, plucking the jean jacket from her suitcase.

"Let's move out," Adriane ordered, zipping her down vest. "Anything happens, you call us right away," she said to Kara.

"Check." Kara saluted.

Adriane, Dreamer, Emily, and Ozzie barreled out the cabin's screen door.

"Your carriage, m'lady." Adriane bowed formally, gesturing to the golf cart.

"Thank you, kind knave," Emily giggled, stepping into the front passenger seat. Dreamer and Ozzie climbed in back.

Adriane swung into the driver's seat and started the ignition, Dreamer and Ozzie hanging anxiously over her shoulder.

"Hey, no sweat, I've been driving lawn mowers since I was seven."

The cart jumped backward.

"Okay, eight." The cart lurched forward, crunching along the gravel-covered path that wound between clusters of cabins.

"The trail starts beyond that big rock," Emily pointed.

Adriane swung the cart off the main road, jostling over small rocks and brush.

The last golden glow of sunset had disappeared, swallowing the desert in darkness. Adriane switched the headlights on, projecting a bright circle of light. They rode in open desert for thirty minutes, Emily and Ozzie directing them by landmarks spotted earlier that day.

"There's Echo Ridge," Emily said, pointing to a shadowy wall looming in the distance. "Follow the ridgeline east." She moved her finger. "The canyon's about a mile . . . over there."

Adriane steered the cart toward the canyon. The rising moon cast its ghostly white glow over the land, making everything stand out in stark relief.

At the wide entrance to the canyon, Adriane brought the cart to a stop.

Mages, Ozzie, and Dreamer sat listening to the night sounds of the desert. Insects chirped and buzzed, a coyote brayed in the distance.

"There's a big cave on the far side of the canyon," Ozzie said.

The warrior looked at her jewel. It lay quietly on her wrist.

Dreamer raised his nose in the air and sniffed. With a bark, he leaped from the cart.

"What you got?" Adriane asked.

*"Magic."*

"Okay, but stay close."

With Dreamer leading the way, eagerly sniffing the night air, Adriane drove the cart into the canyon.

*"Mage?"*

A soft voice crept into Emily's head.

*"Yes, I'm here."*

*"Are you really a mage?"*

*"Yes."*

*"Then what's my name? Quiet, Clio! Don't speak to strangers!"*

*"Clio,"* Emily answered.

*"Ooo, you hear that, Riannan? She heard me say that, you bubblebrain!"*

"Another message?" Adriane asked, sensing Emily's thoughts.

"Yes, let's hurry."

Emily's jumbled thoughts settled on the memory of a beautiful white unicorn.

Lorelei was her name. The Dark Sorceress had captured Lorelei and cut her horn off in an effort to steal the unicorn's magic. Emily shuddered, not wanting to think about what they were going to find. It was her job to feel that pain and heal it.

"Emily!" Adriane whispered, holding up her wolf stone. It blazed with a warning golden light.

The healer's hazel eyes shone, reflecting the deep green light of her pulsing rainbow gem.

"Where's it coming from?" Ozzie looked all around, his stone also ablaze with a magical warning.

Dreamer sent an image of sand.

Adriane held out her arm, focusing a beam of light across the surrounding sands. Nothing moved in the silvery desert dreamscape. "I don't see anything."

The mistwolf's hackles rose, and he whirled around, growling.

The golf cart suddenly rose and lowered as if cresting a wave.

"Whoa!" Ozzie called out, "Look!"

Behind them, the desert floor billowed and rolled like a stormy sea.

Emily held on tight, then stood, her jewel radiating light. The threat was all around them. "Faster, Adriane!"

"We're going as fast as we can!" Her foot was flat against the cart's front plate.

"I think I see—"

Emily landed on the ground, face first in sand. She twisted around and looked up. The cart careened into the air. Spinning head over wheels, it landed with a blunt thud.

Pushing to her knees, she frantically looked for Adriane.

The blaze of golden light caught Emily's eye as she saw the warrior whipping circles of fire from her wolf stone.

"Emily! Are you all right?"

"I think so." She tried to clear her head and squinted. The sands swelled with movement. Something was *swimming* in there. Something dangerous. A sharp fin rose, slicing its way toward her. She couldn't outrun it, it was too fast.

A monster erupted from the sands not three feet in front of her! For an instant, Emily saw its massive sharklike head and maw of stalactite teeth.

Dreamer crashed headfirst into it, viciously ripping at the thing's throat

The shark twisted and leaped, its full body rising out of the desert sand.

Adriane aimed her wolf stone, and golden fire flew in the night, striking fast and hard. The beast exploded in a cloud of sand and stone.

"It's made of sand!" Emily shielded her eyes from falling debris.

Adriane cut the stream of magic, sharply pulling the fire back to her wrist.

Behind the dust, flashing lights suddenly appeared in the desert sky.

"Spaceships!" Ozzie yelled.

A whirlwind spun into existence. Bright reds, greens, and purples cast an eerie glow across the sand.

"Another magic whirlwind!" Emily cried.

Like a snake, the whirlwind burrowed into the ground. Amid the roiling desert, eight sharp fins materialized.

"Where's the cave, Ozzie?" Emily shouted.

"Er . . . this way . . . no over there . . . *Gah!*"

A huge dorsal fin burst from the sand, sending the ferret skidding to a stop.

"Dreamer! Cover our backs!" Adriane ordered, honing the glowing golden beam from her gem into a light saber. "Emily, take the right! Ozzie, the left!"

"We can't hold them, Adriane," Emily cried. "Run!"

But it was too late. Sharklike fins dove in and out of the sands, circling them. The mages were completely surrounded.

# Chapter 6

The desert churned as the creatures swarmed, sending rippling waves of sand against the four defenders of magic. Emily, Adriane, Ozzie, and Dreamer stood back-to-back, gems drawn. The mistwolf bared his teeth, growling low and dangerously.

"Steady, stay sharp," Adriane said, wielding her sword of wolf light.

"Look out!" Ozzie screamed.

Sand erupted as an enormous beast attacked. Its huge body surged from the desert, long teeth gnashing.

Adriane sliced the beast in half, sending sand raining everywhere. Dreamer tried to block another sand shark, but he accidentally barreled into Adriane's legs, almost knocking her over.

"Dreamer, stay behind me!" the warrior ordered.

The second beast lunged. Silvery moonlight reflected off crystal teeth as the creature's gaping maw stretched wide. Adriane fired a bolt of fire down its throat, exploding the thing into a cloud of sand.

Several more creatures came at the group from all sides.

"There's too many!" Ozzie smacked his ferret stone, trying to make it do something.

A shadow swirled across the ground as a dark shape swooped from the sky.

"Incoming!" Ozzie cried.

With a fierce growl, the flying creature dove right into the attacking monsters, razor claws flashing. The beasts were ripped to bits of sand and rocks in a matter of seconds.

"Lyra!" Emily cried.

*"The way is open, run!"* the flying cat called.

"Go, go, go!" Adriane yelled. She leaped and spun, lashing a stream of golden wolf light at another beast.

Dreamer barked and growled.

Another whirlwind materialized, this one much smaller. Adriane landed in a fighting stance, ready to unleash her fire.

"Adriane, wait," Emily yelled.

Veering crazily, the tiny whirlwind wobbled to a stop, revealing a small, twiggy figure.

"Tweek!" Emily cried.

"The magic's gone wild!" the E.F. squeaked, quartz eyes spinning in his head. "Took me forever to get . . ."—he found himself eye to quartz with another sand shark—"baaaaaaack!"

The shark swallowed Tweek whole.

Adriane lassoed her golden light into a fiery rope and closed it around the thrashing beast.

The little twig figure freed, fell to the ground in a cloud of sand. "Fascinating! This elemental magic is like nothing I've seen before."

The desert rumbled ominously.

"Everyone into the cave!" Adriane ordered, herding the group across the remaining distance.

Stumbling over the undulating sands, Ozzie grabbed the E.F.

They entered the dark cave. The mage's jewels wove gold and blue light across the interior, illuminating an immense chamber.

Lyra landed inside, and Emily ran to hug the big cat.

"I am *soo* happy to see you!" she cried.

Lyra nuzzled her sleek head against Emily's face, her bright green cat's eyes dancing. *"I couldn't let you go on an adventure without me."*

Adriane scratched behind Lyra's ears. "Would never be the same. How did you ever find us?"

*"I just looked for magical mayhem,"* Lyra purred playfully as Adriane rubbed the cat's neck. *"Of course, I was expecting to find the blazing star."*

Staring into the black depths of the cavern, Tweek, still in Ozzie's grip, spoke quietly: "Adventure? Is this a normal day for you mages?"

"Tweek, this is Adriane, Dreamer, and Lyra." Emily introduced her friends.

"Pleased to meet you. I'm an experimen-*geek*!"

"Yeah, we know," Ozzie said, shaking a few loose branches from the E.F. "Why do you always show up when something bad is happening?"

"Ozzie!" Emily scolded. "Put him down."

"It's not my fault," Tweek said, losing a few stray twigs and scrub. "Someone is using fairy magic to twist elements of nature."

"Who?" Ozzie asked, arms crossed over his chest.

"I don't know. Only Fairimentals are supposed to use elemental magic."

"I knew that," Ozzie replied.

"Someone is after the lost magic," Emily guessed.

"Yes, yes!" Tweek waved his twiggy arms.

*HOoooo! Teeeeooo! SQuoooooK!*

Mournful sounds echoed from the depths of the dank cave.

"What was that?" Tweek asked.

Emily stood as still as a statue. The noises

pulsed in a rhythm strangely familiar to her. "I think that's your missing magic—unicorns."

"Unicorns? Tweek gasped. "Sounds awful!"

Adriane spread her golden light across the back walls, revealing a series of tunnels running in several directions. "Which tunnel leads us to the magic, Dreamer?"

More strange out-of-tune noises echoed through the cave.

Dreamer barked excitedly, pointing his nose to the tunnel on the far right.

"Lead the way," Adriane told her pack mate.

The tunnel snaked through honeycombed caverns, the mages' magic gems illuminating eerie limestone fingers on either side. It was if they had wandered into a subterranean universe. They passed extraordinary natural sculptures that looked like frozen waterfalls and melted castles. Along the ground, weird lacy rocks twisted crazily and disappeared into the dark. Emily could sense they were going deep underground.

*TOOT! BLAARP! LAA!*

"That way." Emily pointed as the tunnel ended in several other offshoots. She edged in front of Dreamer, moving quickly. The noises were getting more agitated.

"It's getting stronger," Emily said.

Dreamer agreed, growling low in his throat.

"Be careful." Ozzie walked in front of Emily protectively, his stone emitting a faint golden glow.

They passed a huge chamber. Enormous stalactites hung like icicles from the ceiling. Trails of iridescent water dripped along their ghostly lengths and onto spiky, yellowish stalagmite spires surging from the cavern floor.

"It's got to be right around here!" Emily said, continuing down the tunnel, her stone now pulsing bright blue.

"I don't see anythi—*agHp!*"

*TWONK!*

Ozzie bounced off . . . nothing!

"Ozzie, are you all right?"

"Perfect!" The ferret leaped to his feet, whiskers springing back in place.

Reaching over the ferret, Emily's fingers bumped up against an invisible barrier. "There's something here," she said, running her blue and lavender jewel light over the area. Wherever the light hit, a shimmering silver shield was revealed.

"A protection shield!" Tweek said excitedly "Ooo, Gwigg was right, you are good!"

"They're in there," Emily whispered. Placing both hands against the shield, she leaned in close. "Can you hear me?"

*Go away! Leave us alone, you snarkmoose! There's no one in here! Shhhhh!*

"We're not going to hurt you," Emily said, trying to send calming vibes through the barrier. She looked to Adriane and nodded.

The black-haired mage summoned a thread of golden magic and directed it carefully at the shield. It bounced off, ricocheting over Tweek's head.

"Now what?" the warrior asked.

"The HORARFF!" Tweek exclaimed.

"Bless you." Ozzie patted the E.F. on the back

"No, no, the HORARFF: *Handbook of Rules and Regulations for Fairimentals!*" Tweek held the little turquoise gemstone at his neck. "This might tell us how to get past the shield."

Tweek's quartz eyes sparked in concentration, and a glowing orb blossomed from the gem. Strange symbols and images flashed rapidly through the little sphere, casting shifting shadows upon the rocky walls of the cavern.

"It's like a fairy map!" Adriane exclaimed.

"Something like that," Tweek said, studying the symbols.

"The HORARFF is tuned to me, so I'm the only one who can operate it," Tweek explained. "Ah, here we go. This barrier is a unicorn shield. The only way to get through it is to use unicorn magic. I don't suppose anyone has some lying around?"

"We don't, but—" Emily started.

"We know someone who does," Adriane finished.

"You'd better call her, Lyra," Emily said to the cat.

Lyra nodded.

"Who, who?" Tweek asked excitedly "Another mage?"

"The pink one," Adriane answered dryly.

"Tell her to get the dragonflies to open a portal," Emily continued. "It's the only way to get her here. We took her golf cart."

The cat closed her green eyes to send the message telepathically to Kara. Lyra's face scrunched, and her brow furrowed as if she was arguing.

"Wait!" Tweek exclaimed, jumping excitedly. "The blazing star, right?"

"Bingo," Adriane muttered.

Lyra opened her eyes and grimaced. *"She's not happy, but she's coming."*

*Pop! POP! Pop! POP! Pop!*

Suddenly, bubbles of bright light like starbursts popped into the cave, each bearing a brilliantly colored flying mini dragon.

*"Dee Dee! Emeee!"*

Purple Barney, red Fiona, blue Fred, orange

Blaze, and yellow Goldie flew about the mages excitedly.

"*Ozooo!*" Barney flopped onto Ozzie's head.

"Gah! Get off me, you pest!"

"Hi guys," Emily said, scratching Fiona under her little neck.

The dragonflies immediately brushed against the shield, cooing and oohing.

"Yes, we need to get in there, but we need Kara."

"*Oooo!*"

The five minis hooked wingtips together and formed a circle, spinning and whirring, creating a swirling mass of color. They were forming a portal.

The tunnel walls rumbled and shook as if a train had passed underneath.

"I don't like the feel of that," Adriane said, glancing at her wolf stone.

"You think whatever attacked us outside has followed us in?" Emily asked worriedly.

Tweek's quartz eyes started spinning. "Something awful is coming!"

"*Kee kee!*" Goldie squeaked.

In a burst of diamond light, a figure stepped from the portal's center and into the cave.

"AHHH!" Tweek screamed, barreling into Ozzie as he tried to flee, twigs and sticks flying.

Kara scowled, cracking the thick brown mud mask plastered to her face. Her plush white terrycloth robe and matching towel turban only made the brown mask stand out more.

"Try not to let her beauty blind you," Adriane cracked to Tweek.

"This better be good!" the blazing star fumed.

"We found the source of magic, but it's behind a shield," Emily explained, pressing her hand against the barrier. "Tweek says we need your unicorn jewel to get past it."

"I can't!" Kara said adamantly.

"What do you mean you can't?" Adriane asked. "Your jewel is the only thing that can open it."

"Kara, what's wrong?" Emily asked, sensing the dread in Kara's words.

"I . . . well . . . you know . . ." Kara twirled the belt of her robe with trembling fingers and looked away.

The mages stared at her.

"My magic is all *flooie!*" she burst out.

"Flooie . . ." Tweek quickly began looking up "flooie" in his brightly glowing jewel.

"Would you turn that off? It's blinding me!" Ozzie yelled at the E.F..

"Kara, we know you've had some problems with your jewel," Emily said gently.

"I'll say! I turned the mudbath into Jell-O!"

"We'll help you, okay?" Emily said soothingly. "Trust us."

Kara looked at the faces of her friends. "Fine," she said, holding up her unicorn jewel. "But if I change you into a brimbee, I'll blame you."

Adriane and Emily stood on either side of Kara holding up their jewel.

Kara stretched her arms wide. "Do you mind?" she asked the pile of twigs at her feet.

The E.F. moved away to give her some room.

Kara gingerly raised her unicorn jewel. "Okay, let's do this—my mud is caking."

Emily and Adriane touched Kara's hands. Shaking, Kara pointed her jewel at the shield.

Sparkling magic spilled from the gem, completely surrounding her. Only it didn't have the desired effect. With a brilliant burst, her robe sprouted into a hairy red pelt!!

"Does it come in black?" Adriane asked.

Kara's face flushed.

"Try again," Emily encouraged.

Unsteadily, Kara released another blast.

"Your face!" Adriane clapped her hand over her mouth.

This time, a rainbow of feathers had sprouted from Kara's mud mask.

"Fantastic!" Tweek exclaimed.

Adriane and Emily touched Kara's hands, sending gold and blue light spiraling up and around the blazing star. Scowling with frustration,

Kara tried one last time. Crystalline light beamed forth, melting the invisible barrier. The shield glowed, then shrunk into a small, flat silver object that plopped into Kara's hand.

"Hey, cool, a protection amulet—I was reading about these," she said.

But no one was paying attention to Kara. The blond girl turned around to see what everyone was staring at.

Thirty pairs of wide eyes looked back in silent terror.

# Chapter 7

"Ooooo, ponies!" Kara squealed.

A herd of beige and white creatures with lanky legs and flowing manes trembled against the cave wall.

Tweek hopped up and down, loose twigs flying. "Those aren't ponies, those are unicorns!"

*Help, it's a fuzzy muckle! EeoooPP! No, it's a werebird! FhoooB!*

*WWAAAAAAAAHHHHHHHH!*

The terrified unicorns burst into tears, pushing and stumbling over one another to get as far away from Kara as possible.

Wild unicorn magic erupted uncontrolled. The cave shuddered as fireworks sparked across the ceiling. Stalactites shattered, sending jagged shards flying.

*"Keee KEEaaaaa!!!"*

The frightened dragonflies dodged falling rocks and disappeared in bursts of brilliant bubbles. The unicorns wailed louder.

*Help!!! OOOaaaaHHHHH!*

Rainbow arcs of unfocused power swirled and flashed. A huge stalactite plummeted and crashed to the floor.

*"HowwUUUU!!"* Dreamer howled, racing about in circles as the wild magic pummeled his senses.

*WWWAAAAAAHHHHH!*

Diamond light streamed from Kara's unicorn jewel, forcing her backward. The magic swung over the unicorns' heads, slamming into the walls. "I can't control my jewel!" she screamed.

Lyra roared, leaping to Kara's side to keep her from falling. Ozzie frantically waved his paws.

Emily had never felt such strong magic. The panic and pain of these creatures crashed into her senses, wild and raw. Falling to her knees, she fought to keep from fainting as the room spun around her.

"Help me, Ozzie," she gasped.

"Emily!" Ozzie cried, his ferret stone exploding in bright amber light. "*Stop* it!" he yelled to the unicorns. Amplified by his jewel, his voice thundered over the chaos. "You're hurting her!"

The unicorns looked up, startled into silence. Their magic faded.

"Thank you," Emily said, catching her breath.

Adriane ran to Emily's side, helping her up.

"Easy," the warrior said.

Fighting past the unicorns' fear, Emily reached into the calm, bright center of her healing powers.

"It's okay," she said, sending a shimmering wave of blue-green magic over the terrified creatures. "We're not going to hurt you."

The unicorns looked wonderingly at the red-haired girl.

*What about the fuzzy muckle?"* a unicorn sniffled.

"I am not a fuzzy muckle!" Kara scraped at her plumed mud mask and took the towel turban off her head. Her blond hair sprang up in long spikes.

The unicorns looked at one another, squeaking like out-of-tune bagpipes.

"I'm Emily," she said softly. "I heard you calling to me."

Tweek walked among the lanky legs, counting. ". . . twenty-eight . . . -nine . . . thirty. . . . It's the entire class of unicorn trainees!"

"But where are their horns?" Kara asked.

"Their horns haven't grown yet, thank goodness," Tweek explained. "They're babies."

*Am not! I'm almost one!*

"How'd you get here?" Emily asked the little unicorns.

*SQEeeOONK!! TOOT! . . . couldn't find the portal and . . . BEEP! SQUooooK! . . . we fell over the bridge . . . pHloop . . . I bumped my head!*

All the unicorns brayed at once in a combination of screeching sounds and jumbled thoughts. The chaos unleashed bursts of wild magic again.

Emily gasped.

"Gah!" Ozzie yelled, stone pulsing. "One at a time!"

The unicorns turned their heads into a protective huddle. A hoof rose up as one unlucky unicorn was booted from the group. He landed on his rump in front of the mages. He had very large ears, a bulbous nose, and a forelock that stuck straight up. Realizing it was up to him, he took a deep breath and blurted his story.

*"My name's Pollo, and we were on our way to Dalriada, but the monsters found us and we must have fallen through a portal and landed here. Then we ran into this cave and used the amulet shield to hide us."*

*Honk!*

Another baby unicorn, taller than the others, with a beautiful flowing mane and tail, peeked out. Realizing Pollo wasn't going to get eaten, she pushed him out of the way and took over. *"How'd you get past the shield?"*

"This is Kara," Emily explained, pointing to the blazing star. "Her unicorn jewel opened it."

*Oooo!* All the unicorns looked at the sparkling jewel dangling between Kara's fingers.

*"I demand you take us out of here,"* the tall unicorn said adamantly.

"*Riannan, it really is a unicorn jewel!*" Pollo said.

*What!?* The unicorns looked at one another.

"*Who are you?*" Riannan demanded.

"*I'm your brother, Pollo.*"

"*Not you!*" Riannan stamped a sparkly hoof. "*You!*"

"This is Adriane, Lyra, Dreamer, and Ozzie," Emily said. "We're from Ravenswood."

"*Just because they say they are doesn't mean anything,*" Riannan sniffed, swatting her golden tail against Pollo's skinny flank. "*Everyone stay back.*"

The unicorns all pushed past Riannan to examine the girls and magical animals.

"Hey, you know I rode a big unicorn," Kara said with a brilliant smile.

*She's a blazing star! Wowhoot!*

The babies piled around her.

"May I see that?" Tweek asked Kara, reaching for the protection amulet in her hand.

She handed the amulet to the twiggy guy.

Tweek ran a beam of light from his own jewel over the silvery object. "This is a very powerful amulet. And it's been tuned to the unicorn jewel. Someone sent the unicorns to you."

"Here?" Adriane asked, incredulously.

"*Gah!*" Ozzie hopped with surprise as a unicorn butted him. The baby's sleek hide was covered with polka-dot spots.

*"I'm Ralfondiz. What are you?"*

"Watch it, Ralfie," the ferret answered.

"Ozzie's another mage," Emily explained. "He's an elf."

*"Are all elves as fuzzy as you?"* Ralfie asked, cocking his head.

"No, I'm extra fuzzy!"

*"I'm Snowflake. Are you a mistwolf?"* A snow-white unicorn asked Dreamer shyly.

*"Big mistwolf,"* Dreamer huffed.

*"I'm Calliope."* A beige unicorn with big blue eyes sidled up to Kara. The creature's hide twinkled as if coated with fairy dust. *"My hair is all dirty."* She hung her head.

Kara ran her fingers through Calliope's tangled silky mane. "Not to worry; a little herbal conditioner and you'll look amazing!"

The unicorn beamed.

*"Thank goodness we're rescued!"* another unicorn exclaimed, tripping over her big feet and falling on Lyra. *"Hi. I'm Electra."*

*"Easy there, Electra."* Lyra nudged the lanky unicorn to her feet.

An ominous noise rumbled through the cave, dropping bits of rock and dust.

A little unicorn whimpered against Emily. *"Are the monsters still after us?"*

*"Violet, you're such a worry wommel,"* Riannan said, rolling her beautiful dark eyes.

Adriane moved to the cave opening, her wolf stone glowing, warning of imminent danger.

"What attacked you, Violet?" Emily asked.

Violet squeaked and hid her head between her long front legs.

*"Big monsters made out of mist,"* a unicorn with a sock marking on each foot told her.

*"I saw better than you, Clio!"* another one scoffed. He had a pale blaze on his forehead. *"They were mist monsters."*

*"That's what I just said, Dante!"* Clio stamped her hooves.

"Whoever made those creatures has powerful conjuring skills!" Tweek exclaimed. "Only a magic master could use fairy magic like that."

"We have to leave this place now," Adriane said decisively.

*"Just get us to our wagon and take us to Dalriada,"* Riannan ordered.

"I'm afraid the wagon is gone," Emily said, understanding now how they came here.

*"Well, now what do we do?"* Riannan groaned.

A howl of rushing wind echoed eerily in the cavern.

*BLEEEEEEAAAAAHHHH!*

Everyone jumped as a little unicorn blasted a noise like an air horn.

*"Spruce, can that honker!"* Dante scolded.

*"Something bad is coming!"* Spruce said, shivering.

A wet, slithering sound echoed down the tunnel.

"Of course, a very powerful fairy creature could be using elemental magic. There are some from the Otherworlds capable of it," Tweek mused.

"How do we fight it?" Adriane asked, looking over her shoulder, down the dark tunnel.

"Fight it? That's quite impossible. You're only Level One mages."

Kara, Adriane, and Emily stared at him.

"I thought we were full mages," Adriane said slowly.

"How many levels are there?" Emily asked.

"Didn't you guys read your HORARFM?" Tweek sighed with exasperation. *"Handbook of Rules and Regulations for Mages!* Your mentor should have given you that."

"We don't have a mentor," Adriane said.

"What?!" Tweek shuddered, losing more twigs. "You mean to tell me you've been wandering around with magic jewels all by yourselves?"

"Hey, what am I?" Ozzie interjected. "Chopped-liver snaps?"

An eerie metallic swishing whispered up the tunnel, getting closer.

Dreamer growled, his hackles standing straight up.

*"You won't leave us, will you, Emily?"* Violet asked, trembling against the healer's side

"Of course not," Emily said as the unicorns huddled against her and Kara.

"Can't the unicorns open a portal, Tweek?" Kara asked.

"Absolutely not! Their magic is completely unreliable."

"Kara, call the dragonflies back," Adriane said, glancing into the inky tunnel. "Get them to open a portal and we'll go through it, take the unicorns with us."

"Where?" Ozzie asked. "I think Texas Slimbob might notice thirty extra equines hanging around the ranch."

"The empty stalls by the feed room in the barn," Emily suggested. "No one will see us there this time of night."

"Twighead," Ozzie handed the E.F. a branch. "Get the protection shield back up."

"I'm afraid I can't. It has to be recharged,"

Tweek said, looking over the object in his twiggy hand.

"We have our own protection shield," Adriane said, turning to the mistwolf. "Dreamer, turn to mist and cover the cave opening."

The young mistwolf shuffled back and forth, unsure about how to use his special magical abilities.

"You can do it," Adriane ran her hand over the wolf's thick black fur. "Just like we practiced."

"Okay, Kara, let's do it. Hurry!" Emily ordered.

"Oh, all right." The blazing star closed her eyes and called for her mini friends. "Hey! D'flies! Front and center!"

Colored bubbles popped over surprised unicorn faces as a quintet of mini dragonheads carefully peered out.

"*Oooooo.*" Goldie surveyed the situation.

"Goldie, open a portal back to the ranch," Kara ordered. "Get us in the barn."

"*Okeee-dokeee.*"

Squeaking industriously, the pint-sized dragons locked wingtips in circular formation and created a shimmering portal.

Dreamer stood, eyes squeezed tight. His body began to shimmer, and his head suddenly disappeared into a swirl of hazy smoke.

"Concentrate," Adriane urged. "Let the magic run through your body."

Dreamer's head reappeared—but his legs had vanished. The pup whined.

A high-pitched scream filled the tunnel as the slithering sound came closer.

The minis had spun open their portal and were stretching it wide.

"Okay, that's enough. Lemme see." Kara stuck her head through, then stepped back. "We're good to go. Move it, everybody!"

*I'm not going first! No way! I hate portals! I threw up!*

"Listen up!" Ozzie marched back and forth in front of the little unicorns. "The sooner everyone goes through, the sooner we'll be in a safe barn filled with hay, oats, grain, carrots—"

*"Blech, we're not horses, Fuzzy!"* Ralfie stuck out his tongue.

"Ozzie. All right, all right, whatever you want to eat, I'll get it *personally*." Ozzie started pushing Ralfie toward the portal. "Now, who's first?"

Dreamer had managed to spread his misty body over the cave opening. His head floated in the center, wide eyes looking none too pleased.

"Not bad," Adriane said. Tight circles of golden fire spun around her wrist and up her arm.

Something huge skittered by the opening. Through the mist, a long body snaked past them.

"*Ahh-!*"

"*Shhhh!*" Riannan swished her tail in Clio's mouth.

"*Ooooooooo.*" The dragonflies were shaking as the portal quivered in and out.

"Go! Someone go first!" Emily hissed.

Without warning a giant creature punched through the mist. Multiple eyes looked everywhere from stalks reaching out of a bulbous head covered with needles. The color of bruised purple, the grotesque centipede creature advanced on dozens of noisily scissoring legs. Thick, oily armor plated its huge body, needles protruding everywhere. Tentacles twitched as its mouth stretched wide in a fetid hiss, revealing rows of sharp, needle teeth.

The unicorns stampeded. Six babies tried to jam themselves through the portal at once. The dragonflies yelped, squashed by the struggling mass.

*Lemme through! SPLLARRP! Ow! My nose!*

Emily and Ozzie pried the babies apart and pushed them through one by one.

"Keep that portal open, no matter what!" Emily instructed the dragonflies.

Lyra roared, protecting the portal with her shimmering wings.

Adriane was already in motion, whipping a ring of golden wolf light at the monster. Squealing like a ferocious pig, the thing convulsed, armor rattling. Gooey tentacles writhed as the warrior danced out of reach from their twitching grasp.

Kara stepped forward, pointing her glowing unicorn jewel at the creature. A flare of white light shot straight up, slamming the cave ceiling. The blond girl stumbled back, face flushed.

Shrieking, the creature lunged, trying to swallow the unicorns whole.

Adriane struck again, wolf fire hammering the monster's head, forcing its snapping jaws away from the portal.

"Lyra, get everyone through!" Adriane yelled. "We're right behind you. Move!"

Ozzie and Tweek crammed the last two frightened unicorns through the portal and raced in. Nosing Kara and Emily through, Lyra leaped and disappeared.

"Dreamer, go!" Adriane looked around frantically. "Where are you?"

*"Pack mate! Go!"*

Dreamer stood in solid wolf form right in front of the monster.

The thing swung its massive head, mouth gaping.

Moving with lightning speed, Adriane raced past the creature and shoved Dreamer into the portal. The dragonflies squealed as the warrior dove through.

Shrieking, the monster charged in after them.

# Chapter 8

Adriane and Dreamer tumbled onto the barn's floor, the monster's foul breath hot on their backs.

Needle teeth gnashing, the creature thrashed its head through the portal.

The warrior rolled into a fighting stance, crossing her wrists in front of her face. "Dreamer, behind me!" she commanded as wolf light surged from her jewel.

*GrEEP! Hide me! Snoooop! Run away!*

The unicorns scrambled through the barn, diving into stalls. Horses neighed, surprised at their visitors as Lyra nosed the stragglers out of harm's way.

Adriane swung her wolf stone, releasing a fury of magic.

With a fierce growl, Dreamer leaped at the monster—right in the path of the bolt.

"No!" Adriane wrenched her jewel away. Light

arced wildly, wrapping the warrior in sparking golden fire.

The monster lunged, closing its massive jaws completely around Dreamer.

*ZZZZAP!*

In a brilliant flash, the portal vanished, severing the gruesome head. Slime-covered skin and twisting eyes morphed into a pile of green guck that splattered to the floor. Unharmed, Dreamer shook drops of goo from his fur.

Five dragonflies peered from a floating bubble. *"Kaakaa!"*

"Good job, D'flies!" Kara called out.

*"Get off me, Ralfie!"* Dante complained, crawling out of a stall.

*"Where are we?"* Ralfie asked, bits of hay stuck to his forelock.

"It's okay, you're safe now," Emily said, sending a wave of calming magic over the frightened horses. She shut the barn door before Electra could stumble outside.

Ozzie ran about, herding the babies to the stalls.

Adriane picked sticky muck out of Dreamer's fur. "You have to learn to listen to me! Next time we won't be so lucky!"

Dreamer's eyes were downcast.

Gently, Adriane raised Dreamer's head, looking deep into his emerald eyes.

*"Pack mate."*

"Yes." Adriane hugged the wolf close. "What would I do if I lost you?"

"Looks like my grandma's creamed spinach." Kara wrinkled her nose at the gob of goo splattered across the floor. "What *was* that thing?"

"Elemental, my dear mage." Tweek plucked something from the guck. "A prickly pear needle, I believe."

"So it was what, a cactipede?" Kara asked.

"All this magic isn't supposed to be on Earth," Tweek fretted, wringing his crackling twig hands as he looked at the unicorns.

*"We have to get to Dalriada,"* Riannan said, stamping her feet.

The others squeaked and tooted like a broken carousel.

"Okay, everyone settle down," Emily said, herding Snowflake and Pollo into the stall. "You have to stay here until we can figure out what to do."

"If that elemental magic found them in the desert, it will find them here," Adriane pointed out. "The unicorns are sitting ducks without the protection shield."

*"What's a duck?"* Electra asked, flopping over a hay bale.

"How do we recharge the amulet, Tweek?" Emily asked.

"You'd need real unicorn magic," Tweek said.

*PhoOOT!*

"But that's out of the question," the E.F. continued. "Without their horns, there's no way for them to focus their magic. It'll just go wild like it did in the cave."

"What if *we* could focus the unicorns' magic?" Emily asked.

Tweek eyed her suspiciously. "How would you do that?"

"You said it was tuned to Kara's unicorn jewel," Emily said. "Maybe we can help the unicorns."

"That might work—" Tweek began.

"Nuh-uh." Kara closed her hand around her jewel and sighed. "Okay, you guys, I admit it, I don't know what I'm doing with it."

"We'll help you, Kara," Emily pressed.

The unicorns sat up listening.

"It's worth a shot," Adriane said.

"Let's all form a circle," Emily instructed.

Scuffling and bumping into one another, the babies managed to form a ring in the center of the barn. Ozzie marched around, pushing or pulling a unicorn here and there to make the circle even. Tweek stood in the center holding the amulet containing the shield in his twig. "This is highly irregular."

Radiant gold arced from Adriane's wolf stone, surrounding the amulet. Summoning a dazzling beam of pure blue, Emily's healing magic swirled around the warrior's.

Holding out her gem and pointing it at the amulet, Kara shut her eyes. Blazing white magic exploded from the unicorn jewel, engulfing Emily's and Adriane's steady light.

Kara shrieked—her hand had morphed into a giant hairy goblin hand!

*Ewww! That's gross!*

The blond girl coiled huge stubby fingers around her jewel, her face tense with determination. In a flash she had her hand back, with a bonus: freshly polished pink nails.

"The unicorn jewel is completely flooie," Tweek announced.

"Unicorns can use music to focus magic," Emily said excitedly to her friends, remembering she had helped heal Lorelei with a special song.

"Spellsinging," Kara finished Emily's train of thought.

"That's strong fairy magic," Tweek said, astonished. "How do you know about— Never mind, I don't want to know."

Emily faced the herd. "I'll hum a note, and you follow. Ready?"

*Yay! Oooo, fun! Me, me, me first!*

*"This is silly! I'm not singing!"* Riannan stamped her hoof down.

*"Riannan's a 'fraidy corn!"* one of the others teased.

*"Am not!"* she shot back.

Emily pressed her lips together and hummed a single pure note.

A deafening racket of blaring noise rattled the barn.

"Stop!" Ozzie yelled.

*BlaaRp?*

Emily smiled. "You have to follow the music. Let it flow." Remembering the beautiful song she and Lorelei had sung together, she hummed the first verse. Pollo's little squawk joined her, wavering an octave too high, but in tune.

"Good. Now you try it." Emily nodded toward another.

*"WEEEEAHHHHHHH!"* Spruce blasted in an abrasive tenor.

"Concentrate on singing together," Emily told the unicorns. "Listen to everybody around you."

Clio and Snowflake started tooting.

Violet added a soft, shaky note.

"That's nice, Violet," Emily said.

"Easy there, guys," Kara said nervously, watching her jewel pulse with light.

Dante, Electra, and Ralfie tootled and honked. Not to be outdone, Calliope joined in with a bell-like tinkling. Soon every unicorn jingled, jangled, yodeled, and yelped. Except for Riannan, who stuck her nose in the air and huffed.

Power flared from Kara's jewel, enough to make the amulet pulse radiant silver.

"Look!" Tweek said. "It's working."

"*FLEeepBaaarrG.*" Spruce unleashed a blast of off-key noise.

Dante and Pollo sang louder, each trying to outdo the other.

Calliope tried to drown out the boys.

Kara's magic undulated strong and bright, threatening to burst free of her control. Emily and Adriane twined their streams of magic around Kara's white-hot beam, holding it steady by creating a braid of liquid diamond, amber, and topaz.

In a bright flash, the unicorn amulet projected a small, shimmering bubble hovering in the air.

"Holy HORARFF!" Tweek exclaimed.

Everyone watched as the glowing lines encircled a network of stars. A fiery pulse swept along one line intersecting with a series of shining points.

"You've unlocked a fairy map!" Tweek explained.

"We've seen plenty of those," Kara said, making Tweek jumble. "Each one of those stars is a portal."

"That's where we started from," Pollo said, pointing a hoof at a blinking light at the edge of the map.

"So then," Emily said, following the bright line to a last blinking star, "there is where you have to go, Dalriada."

"Inconceivable!" Tweek blustered, twigs flying. "They can't open a portal without their horns. Besides, with the web all crazy, we can't trust this map to be accurate anymore. Who knows where you'll end up?"

"We'll worry about that later. Right now we need to get the shield over the entire ranch," Adriane said, guiding Kara between herself and Emily.

Dreamer and Lyra stepped closer. The unicorns closed their eyes in concentration.

Emily reached out with her magic. She could *feel* her power coursing through the map. "I add the protection of healer magic," she called out.

Adriane's amber wolf magic pulsed bright. "I add the strength of a warrior!"

Now it was up to Kara. She took a breath and lifted her jewel high. "I add the fire of the blazing star to bind it together!"

The fairy map was replaced by a glittering dome hovering in the air.

"That's it!" Tweek yelled.

The mages stepped back, allowing their magic to stretch the shield wider and wider. It floated to the ceiling in shimmering blue, gold, and white magic, passed through the roof, and vanished.

"I can't believe my quartz—you did it!" Tweek yelled, handling the amulet back to Kara.

"How long's it good for?" Adriane asked.

"Few days, maybe," Tweek said, pacing wildly. "O' me twig!"

Emily plopped down in the hay, exhausted. Clio, Spruce, Violet, Pollo, and Snowflake piled over her, snuggling close.

*"We rock!"* Ralphie brayed proudly.

"What's Dalriada?" Kara asked, carefully draping a blanket over the hay so she and Calliope could sit without getting dusty.

*"That's where the Unicorn Academy is,"* Calliope responded, nudging the others away from the blazing star.

*"I'm going to run the web!"* Dante snorted

*"I'm going to run it faster!"* Ralfie said.

Dante and Ralfie began tussling, rolling over Ozzie.

"GarG!"

"I'm going to run with a blazing star!" Calliope eyed Kara lovingly.

"We have to get these unicorns to Dalriada before their horns sprout." Tweek stumbled over the mages to examine each of the unicorn's foreheads closely.

"What do you mean, Tweek?" Emily asked.

"The first thing they're trained to do is tune magic with their horns. Without proper supervision, it would be disastrous—O' me Twig!" Tweek's quartz eyes began spinning wildly.

"Whoa," Dante went cross-eyed as Tweek stood on the unicorn's nose, brushing away his forelock.

"This is awful, just terrible!" the E.F. wailed.

"What's wrong?" Emily asked.

"Look!" Tweek shuddered uncontrollably, pointing a twig at Dante's head. "His horn is about to sprout!"

"That's right, I'm bad!" Dante proudly displayed a small nub protruding from his forehead.

"OOOOO!!" The unicorns all started concentrating, trying to make their horns sprout.

"AHHH!" Tweek was in a frenzy.

Ozzie grabbed the distraught E.F. "Keep yourself together, man!"

"There're thirty unicorns. It's an almost inconceivable amount of power! If they can't control their horns, it could throw the *entire* web off balance!" Tweek cried, shuddering dangerously. "I'm just a rookie!"

*BANG!* The E.F. burst apart in a huge explosion of twigs.

"Not much for good-byes, is he?" Ozzie commented.

Violet brushed shyly against Emily. *"You can teach us how to tune our horns, Emily."*

*"Pleeeezzzzz!"* the others pleaded.

"We'll see," Emily said, rubbing her eyes. "But right now we're tired. It's been a long night. Ozzie, I want you to stay here."

"What?" The rest of the ferret's protest was lost as the unicorns nuzzled up to him.

*"I'll stay as well,"* Lyra said.

*"We're hungry, Fuzzy,"* Clio complained, dancing on her socked legs.

"You did say something about feeding them, as I recall," Emily said, smiling.

*Food! Food! Food! Food! Yea, FuZZY!*

"The name's 'Ozzie'!" the ferret protested. Then, throwing his paws up, the ferret gave in. "Fine, I'll get you some . . . uh . . . what *do* you eat?"

*"Unicorn food, what else?"* Ralphie laughed, making his spotted coat jiggle.

"Er, remind me again what's in it."

"*It's easy,*" Dante said.

"*Pure morning dew,*" Riannan began, swishing her beautiful tail.

"*And a handful of starlight,*" Spruce honked loudly.

"*Don't forget fresh honey!*" Electra pushed clumsily to the front of the group.

Licking his lips so enthusiastically he lapped his big round nose, Pollo chimed in: "*And you have to stir it exactly nine times under the light of the moon.*"

Ozzie gaped in disbelief. "How much of this stuff do I have to make?"

"*I could eat two whole batches!*" Snowflake exclaimed.

The others squawked and tootled in agreement.

Leaving Lyra with Ozzie, the weary mages walked back to their cabin. This day had been like nothing Emily ever could have predicted.

She looked at the star-filled sky and thought about what Tweek had told them. The babies had already attracted strong magic. If their horns sprouted, there might as well be a neon sign over New Mexico advertising thirty baby unicorns.

A simple protection amulet wouldn't do much good, then. And, according to Tweek, the mages' combined Level One powers didn't even have a chance against whatever evil was out there.

Emily had to get these unicorns to safety. Their lives depended on it, and somehow she knew Avalon depended on it, too.

# Chapter 9

Glowing golden sunlight crested the horizon over the Happy Trails Horse Ranch. The mages and Dreamer walked quietly but quickly past the cabins. They'd awoken at dawn to check on the unicorns while the rest of the resort was still sleeping.

"So, what's the plan?" Kara asked the healer.

"I don't know, okay?" Emily said, more grouchily than she meant. "I'm sorry. All I know is, we have to get them to the academy before their horns appear."

Adriane agreed. "We'll just have to chance using the fairy map."

"You heard Twighead. Without their horns, they can't open a portal," Kara reminded them.

"Then we're going to need as much unicorn power as we can get," Adriane eyed Kara's gem.

"Don't look at me, I can't even turn my nails pink without making my head green." Kara bit her lip. "What if I have to give it back?" she wailed, clutching her jewel. "Maybe it was a mistake!"

"Kara, the jewel was meant for you," Emily reassured her. "It attracts magic like you do. It just has to be tuned a little differently."

"Absorbing all that fairy magic didn't help, Rapunzel," Adriane commented.

"It's making it worse!" Kara conceded, looking looked at her friends.

"We won't let anything happen to it, or to you," Emily pledged.

"We're in this together—, got it?" Adriane concluded.

"Okay," Kara said meekly.

As they entered the barn, the horses nickered in their stalls, but otherwise it looked empty.

For a split second, Emily thought it had all been a bad dream.

"How does this taste?" Ozzie's voice wafted across the barn.

*Yuck! PhooeyPhooie!*

Inside the feed room, a gaggle of unicorns huddled around a big bucket overflowing with a white, bubbly, pudding-like concoction.

The ferret held a large ladle, offering a dripping sample to Clio and Spruce.

*"Emily!!"*

All the unicorns gathered around the mages.

Dreamer sniffed the bucket and shook his snout.

"No luck making unicorn food?" Adriane asked, trying not to laugh.

*"I'd rather eat a stinkberry!"* Riannan complained.

"Well, I think it's delicious." Ozzie tasted a mouthful—and gagged.

Emily took a quick survey. "Ozzie, are all the unicorns here?"

Ozzie looked around. "Front and center," he ordered, pushing Violet and Snowflake to the center of the barn. "Roll call. Just like we practiced."

The unicorns scrambled around the ferret as he called out each of their names. "Riannan, Spruce, Violet, Clio . . ."

As each one answered "Here," the ferret nodded his satisfaction.

"Daphne, Kalinda, Ruby, Snowflake, Lysander, Phoebe, Boodle, Harvard, Mailai, Beowulf, Dulcinea, Barnabus, Pierre, Sibby, Quincy, Cromwell, Elvis, Windmill, Zoey, Riccardo, Celia, Electra—"

There was no answer from Electra.

"Where's Electra?" asked Adriane.

*"Hey, where are Dante and Ralfie?"* Spruce asked.

*"And Pollo and Calliope?"* Violet looked around.

"Well, that's only five missing," Ozzie said, shrugging.

"Where's Lyra?" Kara demanded, closing her eyes to contact her friend.

"Everyone *stay* here," Emily told the unicorns. "We'll find the others."

The three mages and Dreamer ran to the barn door—and right into a startled Sierra.

"Sierra!" Emily exclaimed. "What are you doing here?"

"I work here," the brown-haired girl said, trying to peer over the mages' shoulders.

Adriane and Kara shifted to block her view.

The sounds of scuffling and giggling were heard along with a "Gak! and a "GarG!"

"What are *you* doing here?" Sierra wanted to know.

"We got up bright and early to help with the chores," Adriane said quickly.

Sierra gave them a puzzled look as she strolled into the barn. "Well, that's unusual for guests, but thanks."

"Ahh!" Kara screamed as Electra trotted up to the door, right behind Sierra.

The mages scrambled to block Electra from Sierra's view. The unicorn tried to poke her nose between the girls' waists.

The brown-haired girl stared at Kara. "Are you all right?"

"I get, like, totally excited by a good . . . chore," she stammered, looking over her shoulder for the unicorn.

Sierra shook her head as she walked to Apache's stall, Electra trotting right behind her.

Adriane made a grab for the unicorn, but Electra stumbled forward, bumping into Sierra.

*"Hi."*

Sierra gasped. "Where did this filly come from?"

The girls shuffled, looking at each other.

"Her hide." Sierra bent to examine Electra. "It's practically sparkling! Where did you come from, you sweet thing?"

*"Palenmarth, on the north side of the web."*

Sierra cocked her head. "Funny, I thought she said something."

"Look, Sierra," Emily began. "Remember I thought an animal was in trouble?"

"This is it?" Sierra raised an eyebrow. "She looks perfectly healthy."

"Yes, well, good thing we found them, er, her," Adriane said.

Sierra furrowed her brow. "She must have wandered away from the Triple A Ranch about ten miles east of here." She reached in her pocket and pulled out a shiny red apple. "Here you go, sweetness."

*"Ooh, thank you. I'm very hungry."* Electra chomped happily on the apple.

A dozen unicorn heads peered from the stall.

*Hey! We want apples too!*

"What's going on here?" Sierra asked, turning to the stalls.

The unicorns quickly stumbled backward, squashing another. *"GaH,"* from Ozzie.

"Sierra, wait!" Adriane said. "We can explain."

"We can?" Kara asked.

"How many others are in there?" Sierra asked slowly.

"Oh, just a few," Kara said.

Twenty-four unicorns tumbled out of the stall, flattening the ferret to the floor.

Sierra's mouth opened in shock. "I have to call Uncle Tex right away!"

"No, *wait!*" the mages cried in unison.

"We have to get them back to the Triple A!"

"You can't tell *anyone* about them, Sierra!" Emily blurted out.

"Why?"

"Because . . ." Adriane looked to Emily.

"You know that we're caretakers for all kinds of animals at the Ravenswood Preserve," Emily explained carefully.

"You mean like Dreamer?" Sierra asked crossing her arms. The girls exchanged glances. "I know a wolf when I see one," Sierra declared, "but I've never seen a pony like this!"

"Sometimes we deal with, well, unusual breeds," Adriane said.

"We've handled animals like these before, and we want to make sure they get home safely," Emily finished quickly.

Sierra seemed unconvinced.

"You have to trust us on this," Emily pleaded. "Promise you won't tell anyone, it's *really important*."

Sierra considered. She seemed to deliberate for a long time. "Okay. I can close off the barn for the day, but you're going to have to muck the stalls if no one else can come in here."

"Thank you, Sierra," said Emily, relieved.

Sierra nodded. "Meantime, I'll get a barrel of apples in here."

*YaY!*

Sierra looked at the unicorns and giggled. "I swear they're talking. But that's so silly, isn't it?"

"Hysterical," Kara said.

Sierra shook her head and left the barn.

"Oh, this is just great!" Kara cried. "Now I have to muck!"

"She's cool, Kara," Emily said. "And a little cleaning work won't hurt you."

"Sierra may be cool, but others won't be," Adriane pointed out. "We'd better round up the escapees."

"Lyra's spotted Pollo and Calliope out back by the corrals," Kara reported.

"Okay, Adriane, you take those," Emily said. "Kara, you check the spa."

"Right."

"And the rest of you," Emily ordered the unicorns. "Stay *here!*"

❂　❂　❂

Emily raced between the cabins, almost missing Ralfie's spotted rump. His head was poking into an open window.

"Emily, there you are!" Veronica's smooth voice rang out. The step-monster.

The healer stopped in her tracks. "Uh, hi."

"I've been looking all over for you." Veronica walked up, Pollo trotting alongside.

*"Hi, there."*

Emily's eyes went wide.

"Look what I found," Veronica said. "Isn't he just adorable?"

"Has anyone else seen him, I mean, where— what—"

Emily caught Dante trying to push Ralfie in the window.

"I brought him to you right away," Veronica said. "I think he's lost."

Emily smiled, relieved. "Oh, good—I mean, I'll take care of him."

"Say, I'm going to an art gallery in town. Would you like to go with me this afternoon?" Veronica's red lips curved in a hopeful smile.

"Um . . . I'm—" She was about to say busy, but managed a more polite, "I have my friends and everything." Emily caught Ralfie's long legs flailing. "I really have to go now."

"Yes, of course," Veronica said. "You know, Emily, maybe I'm out of line here, but I really hope we can be friends. You're the whole world to David, and I can understand why." She smiled.

"Thank you," Emily mumbled, slightly embarrassed.

"Tell you what, meet us at the barbecue later. It'll be fun."

"Okay," Emily agreed.

"Great. See you then." Veronica sauntered off.

Emily caught Pollo smiling at her. "What?"

*"What's a barbecue?"*

"It's not for you. Come on, help me get the others."

❁   ❁   ❁

It was late afternoon when the girls finished

cleaning the stalls. When they were sure all the unicorns were accounted for, they put Ozzie in charge and left the barn.

"There you are, girls!" David exclaimed as he and Veronica marched toward the mages. "What have you been up to? You haven't been at any of the activities, Em."

"We were—um . . . ," she stammered.

"They were helping Sierra round up some stray ponies, David," Veronica explained. "You know how good Emily is with animals."

"Yes, she certainly is," David agreed. "Come on, I'm starved. Texas Slim promised the best barbecue this side of Memphis."

The mages followed, the sudden thought of barbecue making their mouths water.

The cookout was behind the ranch near the corrals. A huge barbecue pit sizzled with ribs, burgers, hot dogs, and chicken. Resort guests sat on bales of yellow hay ringing a crackling campfire. Everyone was chowing down and chatting merrily.

Texas Slim carried a few mesquite logs from a nearby woodpile and tossed them in the pit. "Come on, fill up them plates, girls!"

"How's it going?" Sierra stood near a long wooden picnic table laid out with biscuits, iced pitchers of lemonade, beans, salads, and condiments.

Emily filled a plate with salad, beans, and a burger. "Okay. Thanks for covering for us."

"Someone is bound to find them," Sierra noted. "We can't keep them hidden in there."

"Yeah, I know. We'll get them home soon," Emily said as she went to sit next to David and Veronica around the campfire. "I hope," she added quietly.

Sunset streaks of bright orange, soft purple, and glowing pink shone with vivid clarity, set off by the dark blue sky. Stars danced overhead, reminding Emily of the magic web. Unicorns were the only animals that could actually run on the web, keeping magic under control and flowing to the right places. Without them, what would happen to all the magic from Avalon now flowing wild?

"Hey, now! What's a cookout without some stories and singing!" Texas Slim crowed.

Sierra picked up a guitar. "I'll start off with an easy one to get us all in a campfire mood." She adjusted the blue woven shoulder strap before placing her fingers expertly on the frets.

Emily's dad smiled and she grinned back, knowing he was thinking of the fun they'd had playing music together in Colorado—when they'd been a real family.

"She'll be comin' round the mountain when she comes," Sierra sang. Soon, everyone joined in.

Emily noticed David and Veronica holding hands and laughing. To her surprise, she wasn't upset. Her dad seemed genuinely happy. For the first time since she'd arrived, Emily began to relax.

"She'll be comin' round the mountain when she—"

*SQUONK!*

Emily bolted up, startled.

*"Emily, we have a problem."* Lyra's voice popped in her head.

"She'll be comin' round the mountain when she—"

*TOOOT!*

Sierra looked at her guitar strings, puzzled, then continued.

*"It wasn't my fault!"* Ozzie yelled.

"She'll be coming round the—"

*BeeP Beep*

"She'll be coming round the—"

*floohonk*

"She'll be—"

*Pffoooping*

"round the—"

*toOOtle*

"when she—"

*BwAAP!*

What the—! Emily looked around at the chuckling guests. Those sounds weren't just in her head. Everyone heard them!

*LAAAA! LAAA!*

"Whooo doggies, coyotes must be gettin' hungry out there," Texas Slim said. Something green scuttled behind the guests on the far side of the campfire. What was that!? Something *orange* moving the other way caught Emily's eye.

Holding her jewel, Emily sent a telepathic SOS. *"Adriane!"*

*"I'm on it."* Adriane dashed after the green thing, Dreamer close on her heels.

Emily wondered why Dreamer wasn't in the barn watching the—*uh oh*.

A glittering silver animal followed the mistwolf.

"Wonderful—Anyone else have a talent they want to share?" Tex called out.

*ZZZZAP!*

Kara yelped as diamond-white magic sparkled in the night like a miniature fireworks display. When the glittering light faded, her hair was a mass of curling purple ringlets.

"Cool, a magic act!" one of the guests exclaimed amid appreciative applause.

Gulping, Kara bowed. "And now for a disappearing act." She dashed off, shaking her colorful head at Emily.

"Okay, we had a song and a—whatever that was—but now it's time for ghost stories!" Tex announced.

Emily excused herself and ran to the barn. Pulling open the door, she gasped.

The unicorns were huddled in a big mass tootling and hooting up a storm.

"What's going on?" Emily asked.

Something sparkled in the middle of the group.

Emily pushed her way through the unicorns. There in the center stood Dante, Boodle, and Spruce. No longer beige, their coats were sparkling silver, green, and orange. And upon their foreheads, swirling crystal glittered.

*Oh no!* Their horns had sprouted!

*"How cool is this?!"* Dante crowed.

The unicorns proudly displayed their new horns.

A hay bale flew across the room. Adriane ducked for cover just in time.

A bright light surrounded Ralfie. When it cleared, his hide was a deep green, with bright brass-colored spots. His new horn shimmered with rainbow magic.

*"I'm so handsome!"* Ralfie puffed his chest proudly.

A perplexed Domino rose a few inches off the ground.

"Everyone! Stop!" Emily shouted. "Listen to me, do *not* use your magic."

The unicorns all stopped.

"What happened to you?!" she asked, shocked. "You're all silver and orange and green!"

*"These are our real colors,"* Ralfie explained. *"They appear when our horns grow in."*

"I thought unicorns were white," Adriane said.

*"How many have you seen?"* Ralfie challenged.

"Two," she admitted.

*"Well, there you go."* Spruce said.

Suddenly bright lights flashed—horns were popping up like popcorn!

"Where's Kara?" Emily was looking about frantically. "Kara?"

*"Hey, where's Calliope?"* Dante asked. *"And Mailai and Violet? And Electra? And Snowflake?"*

"Roll call—" Ozzie shouted.

"Not now, Ozzie!" Adriane yelled.

Hiding thirty baby unicorns that looked like colts and fillies was one thing. How long would it take for people to notice thirty bright rainbow-colored unicorns with real sparkling crystal horns?

*"Come to the cabin!"* Kara's voice popped in Emily's mind. *"Hurry! We have an emergency!"*

"Everyone just *stay* here!" Emily shouted, running toward the barn door. "Let's go, Adriane."

# Chapter 10

**H**igh-pitched squeals split the air like a strangled trombone as Adriane and Emily barreled through the cabin door.

"Kara, are you all right?" Emily called out.

"*Hi.*"

Electra, Daphne, Phoebe, Kalinda, Ruby, Dulcinea, Sibby, Zoey, and Celia were lolling about on the beds, pillows, and rugs, looking dazzling in shades of mint greens, ocean blues, lilac lavenders, and sunset reds. Their crystal horns twinkled with magic.

"Oh!" Emily stared.

"What's the emergency?" Adriane asked.

"We need those extra towels," Kara called from the bathroom.

"I think she means these." Emily lifted the pile of towels set on the dresser and opened the bathroom door—into a storm of bubbles. Violet and Clio were in the tub, splashing about in a bubble bath. Snowflake and Mailai were preening in front of the mirror.

Kara sat on the edge of the tub, comb in her mouth, styling Calliope's mane and tail. The room was littered with plastic bottles of conditioner, shampoo, mousse, and hair gel. A blow dryer hung over the sink. Unicorn hair was piled on the floor.

"Cool, set them down over there." Kara ran the comb through Calliope's mane, carefully trimming the silky hair.

Emily gasped. "Calliope, you're . . ." The unicorn's hide had turned an incredible shade of pastel green, iridescent and absolutely gorgeous.

"Green!" Adriane finished.

"And so beautiful!" Emily added.

Calliope beamed. Her crystal horn swirled from her forehead, pulsing with a bright pistachio light.

"Stay still!" Kara ordered. The blazing star's jeans and tank top were covered in shampoo, bubbles, and brightly colored unicorn hair.

Violet and Clio barreled out of the tub and started primping next to Snowflake and Mailai.

"Your horns!" Emily exclaimed, examining the unicorns' foreheads. "They've all grown! And look at you!"

True to her name, Violet had turned a beautiful shade of lavender, her crystal horn glowing upon her forehead. Snowflake had become a dazzling snow white, Clio an aqua blue, Mailai a sunburst orange. The rest of the female unicorns crowded in the bathroom door, proudly showing their sparkling horns to Emily and Adriane.

"You're all so beautiful!" Emily exclaimed. "But what's all this?" She swept her hand over the mess that started in the bathroom and now spilled all over the cabin.

"They can't show up at the academy without looking their best!" Kara said, smiling.

*"Kara would never let us jump across the web all dirty!"* Electra declared.

"First impressions are very important." Kara held Calliope's head to inspect her handiwork.

*"Absotootly!"* Calliope agreed, nodding.

*"Oh Emily, we're so excited!"* Snowflake exclaimed. *"We going to make magic!"*

*"We're really going to run the web!"* Mailai squeaked.

Kara sniffled. "I'm so proud of my little girls, all grown up so fast!"

*FloooB!*

Clio's horn burst with sapphire light as her magic sent a swarm of bath bubbles all over Kara.

"Well, don't just stand there," Kara said to the other mages. "This is a par-*tay*! We're styling!"

Adriane and Emily couldn't help themselves.

They got into the spirit and joined right in. Each took towels and started drying and brushing the shampooed and conditioned unicorns.

Laughing and giggling, the unicorns and three mages took over the entire cabin. Each unicorn was beautiful, horn blinking like a Christmas light.

Suddenly, Kara put her hand up. "Wait!" Stroking her chin in deep thought, the blazing star surveyed the group. "There's something missing."

*"What?"* The unicorns checked themselves over.

"I know!" Kara leaped to the dresser and began riffling through her clothes. She pulled out several silk blouses. "These will do." Holding up the scissors, she closed her eyes tight.

Emily and Adriane were shocked.

As they watched, Kara cut up her prized possessions into long strips.

"Now I've seen everything," Adriane said, laughing. "Her jewel has driven her completely over the edge!"

"Didn't hurt a bit," Kara said, tying silk ribbons and bows in the unicorns' hair.

"Oh, my *GawD*! *Kara!*" Emily howled, rolling on the bed and doubled over in laughter. Violet, Dulcinea, Clio, Electra, and Phoebe fell over the healer, squealing in delight.

A knock at the door brought the group up sharp.

"Who's there?" Emily asked, giggling.

"gAh!"

"Come in, Ozzie," Emily called.

The door burst open—but the ferret was not alone. Fifteen boy unicorns tumbled over him, hooting and hollering.

"*Hey!*" Clio said. "*Girls only!*"

"*Wow, Clio,*" Dante said. "*You look . . . nice!*"

Clio blushed. "*Really?*"

"It was a mutiny!" Ozzie stood up and kicked Ralfie.

"It's okay, Ozzie," Emily said, breaking up in laughter again.

"*Check it out, ladies!*" Ralfie pranced about, proudly displaying his deep green hide with bright brass-colored spots.

"*Ooo, Ralfie!*" Daphne, Zoey, Mailai, and Dulcinea crowded around, admiring his gleaming spots and new, shimmering horn.

"Well, don't you all look just incredible!" Emily said, walking about the room, inspecting the new horns. She caught movement out the window. "Where's Riannan?" she asked, looking about the group.

"*She won't come in,*" Clio huffed.

"*Party pooper!*" Spruce blew a raspberry noise.

"Say, you could use a little trim." Kara ran her hand though Pollo's silvery blue scruffy forelock.

"*I want a mullet!*" Ralfie tooted.

Emily nodded to her friends. "I'll be right back."

"Right this way to Kara's unicorn beauty parlor!" The blazing stylist motioned to the bathroom. Ralfie and Dante took a flying leap right into the tub, splashing water everywhere.

*"Boys!"* Clio huffed.

Emily walked out into the cool night and breathed in deeply. The air smelled fresh and clean. Stars winked across the sky like diamonds. Luckily their cabin was set apart from the others, so no one could hear the party going on inside.

A unicorn peered around the cabin, head lowered, mane and forelock covering her face.

"Riannan?" Emily called softly. "Don't you want to join us inside? We're having a lot of fun."

The unicorn turned her hornless head away. *"No!"*

"Then is it okay if I sit here for a while?" Emily asked.

*"I guess . . ."*

Emily sat on the front step. "What's wrong, Riannan?"

*"Everything!"* The unicorn sobbed, dark eyes glimmering. *"What if my magic isn't good enough?"*

"When you get your horn, I'm sure you'll sound beautiful," Emily reassured her.

*"You don't understand!"* Riannan swished her

nearly golden tail. *"Everyone thinks I'm going to be the princess!"*

"Princess?"

*"One unicorn in each generation is a prince or princess,"* Riannan explained.

Emily was startled into silence for a moment. She'd never heard of unicorns having princes and princesses. "You don't know if it's you or not?"

*"Nobody knows until our horns are tuned."* Riannan flopped down next to Emily. *"What if I'm not really special? I'm scared, Emily."*

The healer looked into Riannan's deep liquid eyes. Gently petting the unicorn's neck, she began, "Not long ago, I found myself in a whole new place, with no friends. I was scared. More scared than I've ever been in my whole life."

Riannan regarded Emily closely.

The healer smiled, then continued. "Then I met Adriane, and Ozzie, and Dreamer, and Lyra, and Kara. Through their friendship, I found strength I never thought I had. I love them so much, there's nothing I wouldn't do for them."

Riannan leaned closer to Emily.

"And you know what I'm scared of most?"

*"What?"*

"I'm scared I'll let them down," Emily's voice was almost a whisper.

Riannan hung her head.

Emily gently raised the unicorn's chin. "But I know they also love me, no matter what I do or what mistakes I make. So I just keep trying to be the best healer I can be.

"It's okay to be scared," Emily continued. "But you'll never know how good you are if you don't try."

Riannan nodded and pawed the ground.

"Princess or not, it doesn't matter." Emily hugged the unicorn. "We all love you just for who you are."

Riannan thought for a moment, then stood and faced the cabin.

*"I won't let you down, Emily,"* Riannan said softly.

Emily smiled. "Now, come on. Let's get inside before Kara shampoos the entire ranch."

Opening the door, they faced a tooting, bleating, cacophonous mess.

*"Watch this!"* Spruce yelled. *"BeeHoobWaaHH!"*

Pillows flew across the cabin, raining feathers everywhere.

*Laa LAAA!* Others joined in. *SqEEONK! BleeeaH!*

*"That sounds awful!"* Riannan shouted.

Everyone stopped and stared at the unicorn.

*"If we're going to tune our horns, we have to work together,"* she said.

Emily walked between the unicorns. "Riannan's right." She held up her rainbow gem. "Girls?" She nodded toward Adriane and Kara.

The mages each held up their jewels. Her wolf stone glowed bright as she hit the note.

"Nice, Adriane," Emily turned to the unicorns. "Now you try."

*TOOOOT! BeeeBOP! DOoWaaa!*

Magic shimmered and flowed up and down the unicorns' horns.

"Very good!" Emily praised them. "But technique is only one part of playing music. You have to feel the music from here." She touched Riannan's chest, over the unicorn's heart.

"What you guys need is your own song," Kara suggested. "One you can all sing together to focus your magic."

*"Hey, yeah!"* Spruce blared a line of bouncing bass notes.

Dante and Clio added a flurry of syncopated toots.

Adriane pounded out the rhythm on Kara's suitcases as she sang the first verse.

*"You're the rhythm that rocks*
*To the beat that never stops*
*Be the tick, be the tock*
*Be the rain as it drops."*

The unicorns cheered as Kara took the next verse.

> *"You're the melody that soars*
> *Fairy's wing, ocean's roar*
> *Sing it low, sing it high*
> *Let's go dancing on the sky."*

Emily stepped in and sang the third verse.

> *"You're the harmony that shimmers*
> *Like a star, be the glimmer*
> *As the sun gives moon light*
> *Lift the song into flight."*

The unicorns all tooted and hooted, Emily conducting as everyone sang together.

> *"When rhythm, melody, and harmony meet*
> *It's music by heart,*
> *The magic complete."*

"Work it, girls," Kara shouted. She raised her arms and shimmied as Clio, Electra, Dulcinea, Snowflake, and Violet danced alongside, shaking tails and manes.

"Okay, now the boys!" Emily called out.

Dante, Ralfie, Pollo, and Spruce slid across the

wooden floor, spinning and jumping, stomping and hooting.

The cabin was filled with the magic of music and laughter.

Notes wavered and settled into perfect harmony. For a split second all of the unicorns' horns lit at once, perfectly in sync, voices all in tune. A rainbow arc of magic swirled above them, twinkling like stardust.

"Bravo!" The mages clapped.

*KNOCK! KNOCK! KNOCK!*

The cabin door rattled as the magic faded.

"Who could that be?" Adriane asked, getting up to open the door. She looked outside and shrugged.

"Hey! Down here!" a voice called.

Adriane looked at the ground. "Tweek!" The stick figure marched over her hiking boot and into the cabin.

"I can't believe this is happening!" Tweek's arms flailed in despair. "I was out there floating in the astral planes trying to coalesce my earthly elemental particles into material matter—"

"English, Tweek," Kara ordered.

"The web is in worse shape than we'd thought. Someone released all the magic from Avalon! Can you believe it?!" the E.F. wailed. "It's, like, flowing all over the place. Who could have done such a stupid—!?" Tweek looked at the mages. "By the great tree! Don't tell me you did that, too?!!"

"We were *supposed* to release magic," Emily told him.

"Not that much!" Tweek barked. "I just learned nine power crystals were washed away from Avalon when the magic started flowing. And now they're all missing!"

"Well, that doesn't sound good," Adriane said.

"Good? It's positively awful! Those crystals anchor the magic around Avalon. The entire web is going to spin off its axis if they aren't returned."

"Where are they?" Kara asked.

"Nobody knows." Tweek smacked his head so hard, one of his twigs went flying. "These unicorns have to be trained—and fast. They're needed on the web to control all that wild magic until those power crystals can be found."

Emily looked at the other mages, determination flashing in her hazel eyes. "I think the unicorns can open the portal."

*Pooobahh! BROONK! Ooahhhh! MeeMEE!*

"We have no choice now," Tweek said, shuddering.

"So how does it work?" Kara asked, taking the silver amulet from her pocket.

"This is a fairy map of portals to the Unicorn Academy. The map has been tuned to unlock only with special magic, including your unicorn jewel," Tweek explained. "If the unicorns can open the right portal, it should lead them along the web to the U.A."

"We'll have to go into the desert," Adriane said. "Portals can get pretty big."

"It's still risky. The portals are all flooie," Tweek fretted. "Without an experienced unicorn, traveling the web will be very dangerous."

*"We can do it!"* Pollo said.

*"Yeah, we can open the portal,"* Dante added.

*We sure can! TweeP!* The group began tooting, lights flashing in their crystal horns.

"Well, we can't risk keeping them in the barn anymore," Adriane said.

Emily nodded. "They can stay here tonight. First thing in the morning we leave for Dalriada."

Unicorns piled into a heap on the floor, snuggling close together as they settled down for the night.

Violet scrambled under Emily's bunk and curled up happily while Calliope lay on one of Kara's pillows.

Emily huddled deep inside the covers, listening to the soft toots and honks. Ready or not, the mages had to try and get the unicorns home.

*"Good night, Clio."*

*"G'nite, Violet."*
*"Good night, Dante."*
*"G'nite, Emily."*
*"Good night, Snowflake."*
*"Good night, Calliope."*
*"G'nite, Fuzzy."*
"Good *night*!"

# Chapter 11

*L*ight broke into fragments, rippling along towering crystalline walls. Frozen spider webs shivered, draped like delicate glass sculptures.

Emily wandered into an immense chamber of black
ice.

She wasn't cold. She didn't feel . . . anything.

Flashes of light silhouetted a large block rising
from the center of the chamber. She moved carefully
across the smooth floor, trying to see inside the block.
But murky smoke ran through its icy surface.

Emily placed her hands on the block.

"She's only a girl!" a surprised voice shattered the
silence.

"Do not forget these girls are mages." Now a familiar voice floated across the chamber. "They are smarter
than you think."

Emily slowly turned.

Several cloaked figures—creatures—sat upon a
raised podium, studying her.

"Who are you?" Emily called out.

*"She knows we are watching," the familiar voice hissed.*

*"It's only a dream," the first voice answered calmly.*

*Emily spun around and dug her fingers into the murky ice, desperate to see more. Parting the smoky blackness, she glimpsed what lay inside—bodies.*

*She shut her eyes, seeking the familiar sensations of healing magic from her stone. She tried to feel something, anything—but she couldn't. Her heart was numb.*

*Light flashed. She moved behind the block to find the source. Wild light played like fire from thirty crystal horns piled high.*

*Emily stifled a scream. She whipped around to the black coffin. The bodies inside— No!*

Emily opened her eyes and winced. She had no sensation in her right arm. Turning to her side, she found herself buried under the warm bodies of Clio and Violet. Gently pushing the unicorns aside with her left hand, she slid her numb arm free, rolled out of bed, slipped into her jeans, and pulled on a sweatshirt.

Squinting in the early morning light, she took in the room. It was jammed with bodies. Panic shot through her as she flashed on her nightmarish image. She let out her breath as she saw the unicorns stir, awakening from their sleep.

"Emily," a voice called softly from outside the cabin.

Adriane heard it too. She jumped from the top bunk, awake and ready in an instant, Dreamer by her side.

"Emily, are you in there? I need to talk to you!" Sierra's voice pleaded from the other side of the cabin door.

"Shhh." Emily held a finger to her lips as she climbed over the pile of groggy unicorns.

"Emily, are you all right?" Ozzie flailed and dug his way out of the pile, shoving Spruce's hoof aside.

"BLLEEEAHHHHH!" The startled unicorn complained.

"Where's the snooze button?" Kara's hand waved in the air and bonked Spruce's nose.

Emily carefully opened the cabin door and slipped outside.

Sierra's sweet face was lined with worry. "The barn is empty!"

"It's okay," Emily reassured her. "They're safe."

"Look, Emily, I know you three are involved in something," Sierra said anxiously. "You have to tell me."

Emily searched Sierra's deep brown eyes. She made a decision. "Okay, but you can never tell anyone about this. I'm trusting you with their lives."

Sierra nodded gravely.

Emily's rainbow gem and the turquoise jewel around Sierra's neck pulsed with a sharp light. "All right." The healer called into the cabin. "Adriane, Kara, I'm bringing Sierra inside."

Sierra's eyes went wide, and her mouth opened in shock as the herd of multicolored unicorns with shimmering crystal horns stared back.

"What ... I mean, who ...!" Sierra could barely form words. "What's happened to them?"

*"We grew our horns."* Snowflake proudly displayed her shimmering horn.

"They're not ponies," Adriane said.

"They're unicorns," Kara explained.

"What?! But that's impossible! Unicorns aren't real." Sierra looked closely at Clio's pistachio horn, pulsing with soft light. "Right?"

*"We could use some apples."* Pollo yawned and stretched, sending a flurry of magic up and down his crystal horn.

"They're so beautiful!" Sierra trembled as she walked among them, absently reaching in her vest pocket for a few apples.

*"Thank you,"* Electra said, stumbling over Pollo to take one.

"I feel like I'm dreaming." Sierra rubbed her wide brown eyes as the dazzling blue unicorn munched from her hand. "Where did they come from?"

Emily grasped Sierra's arm. "I can explain everything later, but we have to get them out of here right now. Do you want to help?"

"We need to take them to a secluded area," Adriane said. "No one can see them."

"The Arrow Rocks," Sierra suggested, though she still seemed dazed. "It's about three miles south of the ranch."

"Any idea how we can sneak them away?" Adriane asked.

"I'm scheduling the trail rides this morning. I can make sure everyone heads north. The path through the riding arenas will be all clear." Sierra said thoughtfully.

"Sounds good," Adriane approved. "Dreamer and I know the way."

Sierra shook her head in amazement. "I knew Ravenswood was special, but I never realized just *how* special."

"Welcome to the club," Kara said.

❦   ❦   ❦

The unicorns marched single file past the cabins and riding areas. Just as Sierra had promised, no one was around to see the strange herd as they left the ranch grounds, crossed the dirt road, and made for the desert.

Adriane took the lead as Dreamer scouted the perimeter, keeping a nose out for trouble. Kara walked alongside the group, while Emily took position in the rear. Ozzie and Tweek, riding Ralfie, scanned the desert. Lyra, her elegant magical wings spread wide, circled overhead, watching from the skies.

*"You think we'll like school?"* Calliope asked, sticking out her tongue.

"Of course you will," Kara answered. "I love school. You get to hang with all your friends and look cool."

"And you can even learn things, too, Kara," Emily pointed out.

"Oh yeah, that," Kara conceded.

"You're going to be the best class the academy ever had!" Emily smiled.

The unicorns proudly puffed their chests and marched faster.

Emily's smile faded as she looked around nervously. The vast desert stretched in front of them, empty and quiet. It felt so open, vulnerable to attack from anywhere. But they had the all-clear from Dreamer and Lyra. They could make it. They had to.

"Everyone's looking terrific this morning," Kara said, walking up and down the ranks inspecting the group.

Calliope tooted in agreement, head held high. But no one could deny the cloud of despondency and worry among the group. Last night had been sheer joy; now, the unicorns were scared.

After a while, the group wound down a trail that led past a series of rolling, scrub-covered hills. Up ahead, a cluster of tall, red rocks stood in a giant circle.

"There it is," Adriane said. "The Arrow Rocks."

The strange dream nagged at Emily's mind again. She felt the need to hurry, as if they were running out of time.

The ring of rocks pointed to the wide, blue sky like rough fingers, surrounding an area about half the size of a football field.

"Quickly now, I want everyone in the center!" Emily called, the minute they reached the Arrow Rocks.

The mages herded the group through the tall, wide spires.

"Okay," Emily instructed. "Let's get into position."

Inside the circle of rocks, the unicorns made their own ring around the healer.

"Dreamer?" Adriane called out.

*"All clear,"* Dreamer's voice popped into Adriane's head.

*"Everything's quiet up here,"* Lyra reported, gliding overhead.

The warrior nodded to her friends.

"Okay, Kara, open the fairy map," Emily said.

Kara took the silver amulet from her pocket and stood between her friends.

Adriane held up her wolf stone. Emily raised her healing gem. The unicorns prepared to unleash their magic, lights pulsing from their horns.

Kara held her jewel, closed her eyes, and concentrated. "Open sesame!"

"A magical incantation!" Tweek's quartz eyes spun in his twigs. "Fantastic."

A bubble of light blossomed from the center of the amulet, forming an intricate web of lines and lights. Kara stepped back. The fairy map floated before them.

Everyone watched in awe as bright star points glittered and sparkled, reflecting off the crystal horns.

Emily pointed to the brightest light amid an arcing strand of stars. "That one?"

"That's the one that opens to Dalriada," Tweek said, hopping up and down. "Hurry now!"

"Focus on that portal," Emily directed. "Are you ready?"

The unicorns nodded their heads in unison.

"Okay," she raised her arms as Adriane and Kara held up their jewels. Together, they hummed a clear note, jewels pulsing in sync.

*BLLeahHHH! DiNG! LaaaaAA!*

Horns blinked as notes wavered in and out of tune.

"Eeeek!" Tweek squeaked. "That's awful."

"Easy now." Emily tried to hide her anxiety. "Try again."

Bright magic flashed from their horns. But the notes were all off-key.

"Let it flow naturally," Emily called out, trying to sync the wild lights from the horns to her pulsing healing gem.

The unicorns sang louder, trying to get their music in tune. Magic zipped up and down their horns, sending bursts of fireworks into the air.

Kara grasped her jewel tightly but the fairy map began to dissolve, warping into wavering lines.

"Hold it together, Kara!" Adriane ordered.

"I'm trying!" The blond girl clamped down harder.

The unicorns hooted and honked. Wisps of rainbow magic twinkled above them, shimmering in the wind. Emily fretfully tried to conduct the music but the unicorns seemed to have reached the limits of their untrained magic.

"Ahh!" Kara screamed. The unicorn jewel flared. The fairy map burst apart! Fragments snaked away, and the amulet burst into light and vanished.

"What happened?" Adriane demanded.

"Are you all right?" Emily grabbed Kara's hand, inspecting it for burns.

"I don't know, it just overloaded," Kara said, examining her jewel. "I'm okay."

"Oh no!" Tweek cried. "The amulet is destroyed."

The unicorns went silent, heads bowed sadly.

Then Violet squeaked, *How are we going to get home?*

Emily didn't have an answer.

*We'll figure out another way, Emily,* Riannan said reassuringly.

Emily tried to smile, but inside, she felt the first tingles of panic crawling in her stomach. This was all her fault. She'd said they could do it, but they just weren't ready. What were they going to do now?

A flash of rainbow lights popped in the air. To the group's shock, a small portal split open in front of them.

"Look!" The E.F. gasped. "They must have opened it after all."

"It's a lot smaller than the Ravenswood portal," Emily noted. Still, she was hopeful.

The shimmering circle stretched to the size of a large door, trails of mist spilling to the desert sand. Inside, a grid of dark purple gleamed amid glowing black lights—this was nothing like the glittering magic web the mages had seen before.

"That doesn't look right. What is *that?*" Kara pointed at dark shapes slithering and skittering inside the portal.

Dreamer ran past the rocks, skidding into Adriane. *"Magic. Bad magic."*

"Everyone, stay together!" Golden wolf fire sprang from Adriane's jewel, spiraling up her arm. "Kara, Emily, by me!"

Emily and Kara assumed positions back-to-back against Adriane. Lyra landed next to Kara, teeth bared.

*"BLEEWaaWWW!"*

*"Shhh, Spruce!"* Riannan whispered.

*"Something's coming!"* Spruce wailed.

*"I'm scared! Emily! Don't let them hurt us!"* The unicorns trembled, their warbling notes squeaked and peeped.

"Steady," Adriane said, whipping her magic into a lasso, ready to defend her friends.

Without warning, a ball of green light sprang from the portal.

Kara's jewel exploded with bright magic, sending the blazing star rolling backward. She struggled to control the power as Lyra leaped to protect her.

"Kara!" Emily yelled.

In a flash, the light opened. A tangled mass of strands expanded into a giant net.

Adriane tried to deflect it, but the net flew over her head, ensnaring the unicorns.

*"AGHHHH! Get it OFF! EmilYY!! HELP!"* The unicorns erupted in screams, light bursting from their horns.

Emily ran to the unicorns, clawing at the glowing green net. "Adriane!"

The warrior and mistwolf ripped and tore at the net, but it wouldn't budge.

The unicorns were trapped inside, defenseless.

"Stop using your magic—You'll only make it tighter!" Tweek cried.

"How do we get it off?" Emily shouted to Tweek.

"It's goblin magic. You need the reverse spell— in goblin!"

"Stay calm, we'll get you out!" Emily cried, though panic threatened to overwhelm her.

"Oh me, me, *mee!*" Tweek was on the verge of exploding. "If these unicorns are taken, it will be the end of the web as we know it!"

The portal pulsed before them, billowing like a

balloon. Magic burst forth, spinning violently into a tornado. A wild whirlwind lifted the goblin net, filled with screaming unicorns, into the air.

Adriane flung her whip of golden fire, trying to hook the net. But more tornados of sparkling fire spun from the portal, bouncing off the tall rocks and leaving molten scars. Spinning wildly, the tornados bore down on Emily and Adriane.

"Emily!" Ozzie ran to the healer.

"O' me TwiG!" Tweek shook, twigs flying in all directions as he pushed Ozzie away from a wild magic wind.

Ozzie fell facedown in the warping sand. A whirlwind spiraled right over his upturned rear. *"GARG!!"* When the wild magic spun away, the ferret had a huge beaver tail where his short ferret tail had been a second before.

*Oh no! Fuzzy! AHHH!*

Adriane shoved Emily behind her as she and Dreamer faced the oncoming tornadoes. The warrior fired a stream of golden magic. Several whirlwinds smashed into the rocks, exploding in colored rain. Emily tried to add fuel to Adriane's fire, but the other tornados were coming too fast. Adriane barreled into Dreamer, knocking the wolf aside as the wild magic closed in. In a blinding flash, the whirlwinds slammed together, trapping Emily and Adriane inside.

"Adriane!" Emily shrieked. She felt twisted and dark power rip deep into her magic.

Through the blinding storm, she saw a dark figure appear in the portal.

In one giant stride, a dark knight stepped out. At least seven feet tall, his midnight black armor swallowed the sunlight and leeched the heat from the air. Red light glowed from the eye slits of his horned helmet. In his right hand he clutched a staff crowned with a glimmering green crystal.

Emily felt the screams of panic from the unicorns.

The knight raised his staff high in the air, green jewel pulsing. Closing his hand into a fist, the knight pulled the net toward him.

"No!" Emily screamed.

*AHHH! EmilY!! HELP!*

The memory of Lorelei tore through Emily's mind like a bolt of lightning. The unicorn had suffered horribly when her horn had been brutally cut off. *"You have to give up your magic,"* Emily shouted frantically at the baby unicorns. It was their only chance.

*AHH! We just got our magic! NOOO!*

*"Unicorns can give their magic to whomever they wish. You have to give it up, please!"* she pleaded with all her heart to the unicorns. *"It's the only way!"*

Amid the terrified unicorns, Emily heard one

high soprano voice soaring above the cries and screams.

*"I won't let you down, Emily!"* Riannan promised.

The knight stepped into the portal, dragging the unicorns with him.

# Chapter 12

In the center of the cyclone, Emily felt herself caught in a whirlwind of spinning lights. Her senses careened, as if the magic was out of her reach.

"Emily!" Adriane shouted, reaching out for her friend. Long dark hair flying, she clasped Emily's hand. The girls held on to each other, trying to steady themselves in the eye of the twister.

"I can't make my jewel work," Adriane screamed, trying as hard as she could to fire her golden magic at the maelstrom. But her wolf stone would not obey. It sputtered out chaotic magical fragments.

*"Pack mate!"* Dreamer's desperate howl pierced the air.

"Dreamer, stay away!" Adriane called.

Lyra and Kara scrambled outside the whirlwind. The blazing star tried to use unicorn magic from her diamond gem, but she was no match for the terrifying tornado that had trapped her friends.

The wind increased in its strength, squeezing the two mages in its crushing power.

"Your unicorn jewel is only making it worse!" Tweek yelled, hopping up and down.

"Well, do something!" Kara screamed back at him.

"You need to disrupt it with elemental magic!" Tweek shouted, twigs flying.

"Where do we get that?"

"The mistwolf," Tweek cried. "He can change his physical properties."

From inside the tornado, Adriane called to him. "No, Dreamer, it's too dangerous!"

But Dreamer knew what he had to do. His lupine form twisted into mist and shot straight toward the swirling wind. Like a piece of string caught by a spinning top, the mist whipped around, winding tighter and tighter into the wild magic.

"Where is he?" Adriane clutched Emily's hands tighter. "I can't see him!"

Patches of black suddenly appeared hurtling around the cyclone.

"He's trying to take his wolf form inside the wild magic!" Emily cried.

The whirlwind shuddered and sparked.

"He'll be ripped apart!" Adriane screamed.

With a fierce howl, Dreamer's wolf body materialized, flying around the rim of the cyclone in a blur of speed.

Shaking violently, the whirlwind spun off its axis. With a final convulsion, the wind exploded, sending wild magic shooting into the skies. Dreamer was thrown clear, landing in a spray of mist at the base of one of the rock towers.

Adriane and Emily fell to the sands, miraculously unhurt and seemingly unchanged by the wild elemental wind.

"Emily! Adriane!" Kara's worried scream cut through the desert as she ran to her friends. "Are you guys okay?"

"I think so," Emily answered, springing to her feet. She felt surprisingly agile, so perfectly balanced.

"Dreamer!" Adriane made for the injured mistwolf, but stumbled forward. Steadying herself, she ran to her pack mate

"Emily!" Ozzie lumbered over. "Look what happened to me!" The ferret bent over, pointing to his bottom. A wide, flat beaver tail thumped against the sand.

"Oh my—"

"Dreamer!" Adriane's anguished scream tore through Emily's heart.

The mistwolf lay on the ground, gasping for breath. He shimmered in and out of mist.

"He can't return to wolf form!" Adriane yelled frantically. "Come on, Dreamer!"

"Dreamer, you can do it!" Kara cried.

*"I'm fading, Adriane,"* Dreamer rasped, his voice a ghostly echo.

"Emily!" Adriane grabbed the healer's arm, pulling her down close. "Do something!"

Emily knelt by the injured wolf. Trails of mist snaked away like blood spilling across the sands. The healer raised her jewel. She tried to release her magic, but instead of healing power, the gem erupted wildly.

Kara screamed and ducked as a bolt of magic zigzagged like lightning, ripping a smoking trench across the sands.

Ozzie fell back, but his huge tail sprung him forward—headfirst into a gopher hole.

*"Wild magic!"* Lyra called out, leaping into the skies.

The cat was right. Wild magic had splintered off from the whirlwinds and seeped into low-lying clouds, twisting them into dark shapes. The shapes came to life. Wide wings angled out over giant batlike bodies, as four flying monsters screeched and dove to attack.

Lyra was ready. Snarling, the fierce feline hit the first one head on, ripping it to tatters. But the others swooped down on the mages.

Adriane fired her magic, but wasn't fast enough. Two cloud creatures skimmed overhead as she dove clumsily out of the way, tripping and sprawling to the sands.

"Adriane!" Kara ran to help the warrior.

"I . . . I lost my balance." Adriane spit out sand and pushed herself up. "Something's wrong with my magic!"

"Hold on, Dreamer," Emily said, trying to reach into the mistwolf's pain and fear. But it was as if the connection to her healing magic had been severed. "I can't feel my magic." Emily barely heard her own words.

Shadows fell across the sands as two huge monsters dove from the air.

"Emily!" Ozzie rolled over, bouncing up protectively in front of the girl, but his tail made it impossible for the ferret to keep his balance.

Aiming her wolf stone, Adriane fired. A thin stream of warped blue light shot harmlessly into the air.

Easily dodging the weak magic, the flying

cloud monsters lunged for Emily. But she rolled out of the way, amazed at her agility.

With a ferocious roar, Lyra knocked the bats from the air. One smashed into a rock tower, the other skidded into the sand. The big cat was on the downed monsters in a fury of claws and teeth.

"I don't know what's wrong with my jewel!" Adriane cried, sending another blast of unfocused magic.

Dreamer whined, gasping for breath. *"Wrong magic."*

"Dreamer's right," Emily exclaimed, suddenly realizing what had happened.

"Emily, look out!" Adriane scrambled out of the way as the two remaining bats swooped over her head.

Without thinking, Emily rolled and came up in a kneeling crouch, aiming her rainbow gem. A blast of golden light erupted from her jewel. But it arced wide and missed, ricocheting off the rock towers.

Emily stared at her gem. That wasn't her magic. "Adriane!" she cried. "The whirlwind switched our magic!"

The dark-haired girl clumsily scrambled away from one of the bats. "Then you have to fight!"

Raising her rainbow gem, Emily summoned a wavering bolt of golden magic. The strange new power flooded through her senses. It was wild, raw, filled with a crackling fury that she had never felt before.

The monsters dove again.

Emily struggled to control her jewel's new power, golden magic firing wildly.

"Take a breath, let it out slow, and fire," Adriane advised.

Emily spun around, firing at the oncoming creature. A direct hit exploded the monster into shreds of cloud.

The last bat dove over her head. She rolled out of the way, and fired another bolt of warrior magic, sending the monster banking to the right.

Lyra was right there waiting, ripping it to shreds.

Carefully, Emily pulled the magic back to herself.

"Emily!" Adriane knelt by Dreamer, her face pale with worry. "Save him!"

"Adriane, you have the healing power now," Emily said gently. "It's up to you."

The dark-haired girl nodded, swallowing her tears. Placing her hands uncertainly on Dreamer, her fingers slipped through mist and into the sand below. "I can't do this!" Panicking, she looked to Emily for help

"Reach out with your senses," Emily instructed, kneeling beside her friend. "You are connected to mistwolf magic."

Adriane closed her eyes, concentrating. Her wolf stone glowed faintly blue.

"Reach into the magic and feel it," Emily said urgently.

Bright blue-green coursed through Adriane's wolf stone. Opening herself completely, the warrior reached the fallen mistwolf.

*Pack mate in danger.* Dreamer's thoughts echoed in her mind.

*Dreamer, young and strong, depending on me.* Adriane let her own thoughts and fears flow freely, mingling with those of the fallen mistwolf.

*Monster will take her away, like wolf mother and wolf father.* Dreamer called.

*Loneliness clawing at my heart.* Adriane cried.

*With her I am warrior wolf.*

*One day will he leave me, too?*

*Without her, I am lone wolf.*

*Abandoned again by the one I love the most.*

Adriane threw back her head and howled. The desert seemed to fall away, as she let herself be swept into the wolf song, connected to the ancient spirits of the pack.

She ran, strong and free. Her body was a shimmering outline, trailing starfire. The endless forests came into focus around her, timeless and full of life.

*Run with us, warrior!*

Adriane was surrounded by mistwolves, thousands strong, the thunder of paws pounding the earth.

One wolf broke from the pack to run by her side. The wolf's silver fur rippled over powerful muscles, golden eyes shining bright.

*"My heart soars to see you, warrior."*

Adriane was filled with joy at the sight of her beloved lost pack mate. Stormbringer.

"Storm, is it really you?"

*"Run with me, pack mate."*

There was no past, no future. Only the moment as mistwolf and warrior ran the spirit trail together. Adriane felt the ancient mistwolf magic flowing through her.

*"Stay focused, warrior. Open yourself to those who love you."*

Wolf and warrior arrived at the edge of the forest. Two trails ran in opposite directions, shrouded in mist.

"I want to run with you." Adriane knelt and hugged Storm, tears streaming down her face. For an eternal moment she felt the warmth and strength of her friend, the smell of the forests in her soft fur.

*"Stand strong with your friends. Your destiny still lies ahead of you. I am with you, now and forever."*

"I love you," Adriane whispered, her hands clasping soft fur.

She opened her eyes, her hands in Dreamer's thick coat. His body was solid and whole, black fur lustrous and shiny. Bright emerald eyes stared back at her, full of love.

"How many times do I have to tell you to listen to me!" she scolded, then smiled, hugging her pack mate close. "Don't you leave me ever again."

Dreamer's emerald eyes danced. *"I am with you, now and forever."*

"You did it!" Emily embraced both the wolf and the warrior.

"That was incredible!" Kara joined the group hug, Lyra by her side.

*"Gah!"* Ozzie was grabbed and squeezed into the hug, wide tail flapping.

"I must say, you mages certainly make interesting magic." Tweek stood to the side.

"It's called a hug, Tweek," Emily explained. "You should try it."

"I have enough trouble, thank you."

Dreamer stood, proudly stretching his lithe body.

"How do we switch our jewels back?" Emily asked Tweek.

The twig figure looked through images in his gem. "I think you're stuck."

"I never could have healed Dreamer alone," Adriane confessed.

"I could never be a warrior, never like you," the red-haired girl admitted.

"Hey! Being a blazing star isn't exactly a trip to the mall!" Kara huffed.

"Well, actually it is," Tweek said, looking up "mall" in his HORARFF.

"You think its easy being a ferret *and* a beaver?" Ozzie asked, flapping its giant beaver tail.

"A berret," Kara commented.

"It's all my fault," Emily said, frowning. "If I hadn't pushed the unicorns to open the portal, this never would have happened."

"This is bad," Tweek rattled. "We have to report to the Fairimentals somehow and tell them this dark knight captured the unicorns."

"What was that thing?" Ozzie asked Tweek.

"My guess is a hunter, hired to kidnap the unicorns."

"Hired by whom?" Emily asked.

"I don't know," Tweek answered, inspecting Ozzie's new tail. "But the dark knight carries a powerful jewel."

Adriane folded her arms. "We're going to have to work with the magic we've got."

The desert rumbled ominously, shaking the tall rocks.

"What was that?" Kara asked.

On the far side of the rock circle, the air twisted and split apart. A glowing portal opened. Instantly, something hurtled out, crumpling onto the red desert sand.

The goblin net. Inside, the unicorns lay still, as if in a trance. Their once vibrantly colored bodies were pale and washed out. No lights blinked or shone from their horns.

"Oh no!" Emily ran to the unicorns.

Riannan's head fell listlessly against the net, a dulled, lifeless horn protruding from her head. *"Emily,"* she rasped.

"Riannan!" Emily cried. "What's happened?"

*"Our magic . . . it's all gone."*

# Chapter 13

"**H**oly root rot!" Tweek shuddered, threatening to fall apart. "Where's their magic?"

Emily tried to determine if the unicorns were hurt. But her healing gem flared with warrior magic. She swiftly pulled her wrist away.

"*My horn,*" Riannan smiled weakly. "*I got my horn, Emily.*"

"Yes," Emily whispered proudly. "You did." But what should have been exquisite crystal was just a dull colorless horn, completely without magic.

"*Kara,*" Calliope whimpered. "*My hair got all messy.*"

"Shhh, it's okay." Kara's jewel blazed furiously. "We'll get you out!"

Dreamer growled as the portal pulsed with green light.

"What trick is this?" boomed a voice from inside the swirling portal. Jewel pulsing wildly, the dark knight stepped out.

Lyra and Dreamer leaped in front of the net, blocking the knight from his prey.

The knight turned his horned helmet toward the mages. Red eye-slits pulsed in rhythm with his green jewel.

Scrambling to her feet, Adriane faced the knight.

But Emily pulled her back. "No, Adriane. You can't fight, not now."

The knight raised his staff. A beam of green light began scanning the desert. "Where is the unicorn magic?"

"He doesn't have it!" Emily whispered.

"But if he didn't capture it, then where did it go?" Adriane asked, looking looked around.

Emily and Adriane held their breath as the knight's magic fell over the rainbow gem and the wolf stone. It slowly passed over the unicorns' horns without even a twinkle.

*"Riannan gave her magic away,"* Electra said, shuffling into the cramped net.

*"We did, too,"* Ralfie added.

*"Riannan said it was okay,"* Violet sniffled.

*"I gave it up so the knight could never get it,"* Riannan told Emily.

"Where did it go?" Emily asked.

*"I don't know."* The unicorn hung her head. *"I couldn't focus it."*

Dreamer and Lyra growled as the green light moved over them.

Emily felt frantic. She had been entrusted to keep the unicorns safe, and now their magic was missing. She'd failed miserably. "Tweek, how do we get them out?" Emily's voice was tight with panic, realizing the knight could easily pull them away at any moment.

"We need a goblin spellbook. Anyone got one?"

"No!" Ozzie thumped his tail.

"Oh wait, I do." The E.F. held up his HORARFF. "If only we had a jewel that wasn't all flooie so we could focus goblin magic."

"What about this one?" Ozzie held out his ferret stone.

The knight's magic edged toward Kara.

"Hurry!" Adriane urged.

Tweek started riffling through images, letters, and documents. "I have over three hundred different dictionaries in two hundred languages stored in my HORARFF, plus local street map directions," Tweek said proudly.

"Gah!" Ozzie sputtered.

Suddenly, the knight's green beam fell over Kara. The jewel upon his staff flared as it scanned her unicorn jewel.

"You think to hide the magic in this jewel," he hissed. "Give it to me!"

"Kara's got the unicorn magic!" Emily gasped, realizing where it had gone.

"Makes perfect sense," Tweek said, studying his HORARFF. "Magic attracts magic."

"Stay away from them!" Kara's voice rang out. She stepped toward the edge of the ring with Dreamer and Lyra, drawing the knight away from the net. Gleaming diamond magic blazed in her jewel.

The unicorns mashed together as they scrambled to watch the blazing star. *"Yay, Kara! Go, blazing star!"*

Kara bowed to the cheering unicorns, jewel blazing with power. "I'm back!"

A bolt of green magic shot from the dark knight's jewel.

"Ahhh!" The blazing star screamed as the foul magic encased her. Shimmering in green light, her body twisted into a haggard, green-skinned banshee.

The unicorns gasped. *"Boooo! Hissss!"*

Lyra roared, ready to strike the knight.

"Lyra, stay with me. I need your help," Kara commanded, flicking a tress of greasy hair away with gnarled fingers. Her blue lips scowled. "Nobody messes with my accessories!"

The unicorn jewel blazed, slamming a bolt of diamond-white magic back into the knight. Kara transformed herself into a twinkling pointy-eared sprite with flowing turquoise hair. "That's better."

*"Whoohoo, Kara! Yay! Oooo, pretty!"*

"Twingo!" Tweek projected a series of symbols and letters in the air. "Ozzie, try this. 'Plithree floob.' "

The ferret held his jewel and called out the translation:. "Feel my beard!"

With a fizzle, Ozzie sprouted a long beard. "What the—?!"

*"Fuzzy got fuzzier!"* the unicorns shouted. *"Yay! Not yay! Oh, yeah."*

"That's not right," Tweek mused.

"You're telling me, you, you, *you*—!" Ozzie flapped his beaver tail and pulled at his beard.

"Give me the magic!" The dark knight growled, his murky green power smashing into Kara.

She morphed into a black imp with bloodred eyes.

"Black is *so* not my color," the Kara imp said. She turned the magic diamond white and twinkled into a small purple pixie with huge sparkling lavender eyes.

"Okay, okay, try this one." Behind the net, Tweek had projected a new line of symbols. " 'Rathroo migwump.' "

"Fix my shoe," Ozzie called out.

Ozzie's left foot expanded into a huge red shoe "Gah! This is ridiculous! What kind of magic is this?"

"Oops, wrong dictionary. That's pixie magic."

Again, the knight hurled his vile green magic at Kara. The blazing star fought back with a stream of shining white light. The dual forces of magic crashed into one another—slamming back and forth in a magical tug of war. No matter how hard each battled, neither Kara nor the dark knight could hold the advantage over the other. They were at an impasse.

Dreamer and Lyra stood on either side of Kara, guarding her, helping to keep her magic focused.

"You cannot hold out forever," the knight hissed as the blazing star morphed into a massively ugly ogre.

"You're right," Kara's gruesome ogre voice bellowed like thunder. "There is *no* way I'm missing the school dance next week!" The blazing ogre forced a huge wave of magic back at the knight.

"What is this?!" the knight shouted, as a pink halter top now adorned his upper body, matching the bunny slippers on his feet.

"Ozzie, hurry up!" Adriane called out impatiently.

"Okay, try this one," Tweek said, stopping the scrolling symbols at a page of incantations. " 'Ngop maj beembo!' "

"Open the freezer!" Ozzie yelled. A pile of ice cubes dropped on his head.

"Close, but no twig," Tweek fretted. "Focus the magic with your jewel!"

Ozzie concentrated on his stone.

"Bimidee bootilee aoool!" Tweek shouted.

Ozzie held up his jewel. "Release the booods!"

"No, *aoool!*"

"Binds!" The ferret stone blazed with light. "Oh, yeah!" Ozzie quickly spread the golden magic over the net. The green grid that had trapped the unicorns melted away and vanished.

*"Fuzzy did it!"* Ralfie hooted.

"Way to go, Fuzzy," Adriane said.

The ferret quickly shone the light over his feet and face, removing the giant shoe and beard.

"Quickly now." Emily and Adriane herded the group into a semicircle behind Kara, Lyra, and Dreamer. "Just like we practiced."

*"How? We don't even have our magic anymore!"* Dante cried.

*"And Kara's a—!"* Calliope looked at the magical duel. *"What is she?"*

"That was low!" The blazing star's voice bubbled from a mass of slimy yellow tentacles. Still holding the evil knight at bay, her jewel blazed and she became a magnificent fairy princess with shining silver wings. "Much better. Wings never go out of style."

But Emily saw that Kara was starting to lose the tug-of-war. The blond girl couldn't keep this up much longer.

Under the power of the knight's jewel, the blazing star twisted into a goblin with knobbly green feet, then snapped into a whiskery rabbit like brimbee. Finally, she morphed into a scaly, lizardlike skultum, the creature from whom she'd absorbed her shapeshifting powers in the first place.

The Kara skultum snarled, lizard eyes flashing in panic. "I can't change back! Help!"

"Release the magic in the jewel!" The knight jerked his staff backward, extracting a flash of glowing magic from Kara's gem. The magic warped, expanding into the shape of a skultum. Scaly snakeskin shimmered along its reptilian body.

Kara morphed back to her regular self, but her eyes were wide with fear. She held up her jewel—but nothing happened. She couldn't shapeshift!

"This is not unicorn magic!" The knight roared.

The blazing star stared in shock. The knight had taken her shapeshifting magic. The unicorn magic wasn't in her gem after all.

Kara quickly regained her composure. "You really didn't think I'd hide the unicorn magic in here, did you? Oh, like, that is *so* obvious."

Swirling his staff in the air, the knight hurled a trio of magical whirlwinds at the mages.

Adriane, Kara, and Emily all fired their jewels at once. Each mage struck a tornado, forcing the whirlwinds against the rocks. Magic sparked as the rock towers began to quiver and melt.

*"BAWeeeMOWAYYYee!"*

A loud, sour note blared across the desert.

Spruce held his horn up and blasted another one.

The other unicorns honked a few feeble notes.

*"It's not working!"* Violet cried desperately

The knight thrust his staff forward, sending the whirlwinds spinning furiously surrounding the mages and unicorns.

"Hey, why don't you pick on someone your own size!" Tweek's voice rang out loud and clear across the desert.

The Experimental Fairimental stood right behind the dark knight, peering out from the base of a rock tower. "Hey, metal head" The E.F. rattled his twigs at the startled knight. "Perhaps you should try fighting a real Fairimental."

The dark knight glowered. "I will have your power, Fairimental!"

"Stick and stones may break my twigs . . ."

Emily's heart raced, fearing for Tweek. But she knew he was buying her enough time. She turned to the unicorns. "We may not be able to work our magic alone, but we can do this together."

"You cannot defeat me!" the knight shouted at the E.F.

"Well, you're right. I give up."

Where Tweek stood, the air suddenly filled with flying twigs, tiny pebbles, and dusty brown patches of dirt. The valiant E.F. had exploded, scattering over the dry desert floor.

The dark knight laughed.

"Oh no!" Emily cried. "Tweek!"

The knight turned his pulsing red eye-slits toward the mages and unicorns. There was nothing to stop him.

# Chapter 14

The dark knight raised his staff, hurling the whirlwinds at the mages.

"Fire together!" Adriane called to Emily and Kara.

Bolts of blue, gold, and white entwined and smashed into the cyclones. The whirlwinds slowed, but kept spinning.

*"We don't need our horns to make magic,"* Riannan called out. The brave unicorn closed her eyes tight and concentrated. A sound, tiny, but sure, came out: *"Poot."*

*"What was that?"* Dante asked, shocked.

*Her horn sparked! I saw it, too. How did she do that?*

"Wonderful! That's the spirit, Riannan," Emily encouraged. "Everyone, hurry!"

Thirty young unicorns concentrated now, but all they could manage were tentative poots and hoots.

"Just sing from your heart," Emily instructed.

174

The horns began to pulse, then squeak and squonk.

"That's it," Adriane called out. Dreamer stood by her side, helping to focus the magic.

The cacophony of honks and tootles blended together, building into a wave of sound.

The knight's jewel flared unevenly as the wobbling whirlwinds began flinging magic everywhere.

Was it working? Suddenly, from high above, a single note hung in the air, strong, confident, and unwavering.

It was Riannan. The unicorn held her horn high. A rainbow of lights shimmered up and down her crystal horn as a surprisingly sweet melody flowed as beautiful as a sunrise.

*"Way to go, Riannan!"* Ralfie's awed voice came from the middle of the group.

Another note rang out, sweetening the sound of Riannan's melody with a delightful harmony.

Pollo's horn began to glimmer, faintly at first, then shone pure silver.

All at once a flurry of silvery notes soared over the circle, ringing against the wild winds. More notes flowed, blending in perfect rhythm, melody, and harmony. Even the tall rocks vibrated with a pulsing beat.

"Get your dance on!" Kara called out.

Moving to the beat, the unicorns danced,

shuffled, and grooved to their glorious music. Magic glittered up and down the unicorns' horns as lustrous vivid colors returned to their coats. A dazzling bright flash surrounded Riannan. Her coat gleamed like a treasure chest of shining gold and sparkling diamonds.

"Impossible!" the dark knight roared. "They have no magic to make music!"

*"We have music by heart!"* Riannan sang out, smiling at Emily.

> *"When rhythm, melody, and harmony meet*
> *It's music by heart*
> *The magic complete."*

As the music engulfed her, Emily felt something sweet and familiar. Something she thought she'd lost. Her own healing magic was stirring to life, bright and pure as when she'd first discovered it. Emily sang, healing magic blazing in her gem— stronger than ever.

In a soaring chorus, the unicorns focused magic with the steady pulse of their horns. As the music reached a crescendo, swirls of rainbows cascaded over the circle. The whirlwinds burst apart as the unicorn magic touched them.

"How did they get the magic back?" The dark knight's cry echoed across the desert. "Ak—!"

Something was standing on the knight's head. A pile of twigs and scrub brush leaped from his helmet and landed on the tip of his staff.

"Tweek!" Emily shouted.

The knight frantically tried to shake the E.F. loose. But Tweek held on, prying the jewel free of the staff.

The knight lurched forward, grasping.

"I'm open! Pitch it here!" A "berret," big beaver tail flapping, scurried across the sands.

Tweek threw the gem, sending it flying across the circle. Ozzie swatted it with his wide tail, batting it right through the rainbow of unicorn magic. At the top of the rainbow, the crystal's green glow faded, replaced by brilliant white light.

Adriane leaped into the air, golden wolf fire blazing from her gem. This time, she didn't stumble. Her balance was perfect. Dreamer matched her movements exactly, warrior and mistwolf fighting side by side. Adriane fired her magic straight at the knight.

Flung back by the impact, the knight smashed into a rock tower.

Emily raised her hands high, conducting the unicorn choir. Gold, blue, and diamond-white mage magic mixed with the rainbow magic of the unicorns. Together, mages and unicorns turned the magic on the dark knight.

Surrounded in rainbow magic, the dark knight writhed. A high-pitched scream echoed inside his helmet. But it was not the grating voice of the knight. It came from someone else.

The knight crashed to the ground—his black armor screeched as he sprawled into a motionless heap.

The last strains of lyrical melody echoed over the desert as the unicorns and mages drew their magic back to horns and gems.

"Bravo!" Tweek called, walking from behind a rock pillar.

"Tweek!" Emily exclaimed. "We thought you'd exploded!"

"Naturally," he answered. "That was all part of our plan."

Ozzie strolled up behind him, giving the E.F. a high twig.

"I must say we pulled that off quite well," Tweek told the ferret.

"What'd you guys do?" Adriane asked.

"I made a dummy Tweek," Ozzie explained. "And I used my jewel to make it seem like the fakemental was talking."

The mages were impressed.

"*YaY! FuzzY!*" The unicorns all cheered.

Ralfie bent and scooped the ferret onto his back, bouncing Fuzzy high in the air.

"*GaG!* Can't you just give me a medal?" the ferret screamed as he somersaulted.

Tweek walked over to the fallen knight.

"*Is it dead?*" Electra asked.

"Quite. Without its jewel, there was nothing to sustain it." Tweek explained.

"Let's see who our mystery guest is." Adriane and Dreamer knelt by the lifeless suit of armor. The warrior carefully raised the faceplate.

"Ahhhh!" the group screamed, all peering into the empty space where a head should have been.

Emily couldn't believe her eyes. "It's empty!"

"It's a golem," Tweek cried.

"Say what?" Kara asked.

"An inanimate object given life and controlled by magic," the E.F. explained.

"Like a puppet." Adriane said.

"Yes," Tweek agreed.

"So someone else was operating it?" Kara asked. "How?"

"With that!" Tweek pointed at the knight's transformed crystal.

It floated in the air now, shining with rainbow prisms.

"Glorious blossom!" Tweek cried. "I'll be promoted to a full mental!"

"What is it?" Emily asked.

"It's a power crystal!" Tweek explained. "One of the nine that were washed away from Avalon."

The unicorns and mages stared at the fantastical gem.

"Wow." Kara walked up to the beautiful power crystal, its rainbow light reflecting in her wide blue eyes. "It's amazing!"

"Everyone in the known web is going to be after this baby, and we've got it!" Tweek said happily, then stopped short.

Suddenly a bolt of lightning split the air. The flash glimmered into a giant circle of light. Behind the mist-shrouded opening, lines of stars arced across infinite strands of web. Two shadowy figures loomed at the portal, ready to emerge.

"Look out!" Adriane shouted, ringing the group in a shield of gleaming wolf light. "I think someone's already found it."

# Chapter 15

*"Listen to the sound*
*I'll always be around*
*You and me*
*We'll always be*
*Friends forever."*

Music drifted from the swirling portal, a beautiful song of friendship.

Emily knew that music—she would never forget it. Just as she hadn't forgotten the elegant creature now coming through the portal, traveling between worlds. A sleek white unicorn stepped onto the desert sand, her horn twinkling with magic.

"Lorelei!" Emily cried, running to embrace her friend. "I can't believe it's really you!" The healer buried her face in Lorelei's silky soft mane.

*"I've missed you so much, Emily."* The unicorn lowered her beautiful head over the healer's shoulder, her silvery voice chimed in Emily's mind.

The young unicorns rushed forward, horns gleaming, crowding around the mages and the new unicorn. *"Ooo, a unicorn! She's so pretty! How did you find us? Did you come from Dalriada? Did you bring apples?"*

"By the great tree!" rattled another voice from the portal.

Silhouetted against the swirling doorway stood a creature that looked like Tweek, made of branches, thick leaves, and bits of earth.

"Master Gwigg!" Tweek cartwheeled over to the Earth Fairimental. "Thank goodness! Look! We found one of the power crystals!"

"Well done, Tweek," Gwigg's rough voice rustled. "It will be kept safe until the others are secured."

Lorelei turned her sparkling eyes to the herd of baby unicorns. *"Your horns are tuned already!"*

The unicorns' horns glowed as they proudly displayed their brightly colored coats.

*"We couldn't have done it without Emily,"* Riannan said, her golden hide shimmering.

"Lorelei must bring the new class to the Unicorn Academy right away," the Earth Fairimental rumbled. "She's one of the best teachers the U.A. has ever had."

"How cool," Emily said.

"How are things on Aldenmor, Gwigg?" Adriane asked. "We haven't heard from Zach and the mistwolves in weeks."

"Thanks to you three mages, Aldenmor is healing nicely." The Fairimental's voice rattled like pebbles. "The Garden is blooming, and your friends say they miss you all the time."

Adriane smiled widely.

"Dreamer is looking very good indeed," Gwigg added.

*"Warrior wolf!"* the mistwolf barked, rustling Gwigg's twigs.

Adriane hugged the black wolf. "Emily's magic helped me heal Dreamer."

Emily held her sparkling rainbow gem next to her friend's wolf stone. The two magic jewels flashed with gold and blue light, warrior and healer, forever linked.

"Sharing the magic has made each of you stronger," Gwigg rustled, and then turned to Ozzie. "Sir Ozymandius, you've changed, as well."

"Yes, I'm tuning my jewel." The ferret proudly held up his ferret stone.

"No, I mean that." Gwigg pointed a branch at Ozzie's new giant beaver tail.

"*Gah!* Can you fix it?"

Gwigg approached the "berret." "I can give you two choices. You may get your original tail back and remain a ferret."

"Or?" Ozzie asked, hopefully.

Gwigg paused, tendrils of magic glowing around him. "Or you can become a beaver."

"*GAH!*" The ferret's eyes bugged out. "I'm already gaining weight! I'll take my cute fuzzy tail, thank you very much!"

A glowing swirl of mossy green magic sparkled from the branch that served as Gwigg's hand and surrounded Ozzie's rear.

"What's going on back there?" the alarmed ferret yelled, whirling around to try and see his behind.

"A very proper ferret tail," Tweek informed him.

Kara clutched her unicorn jewel worriedly. "What about my magic? Is it all gone?"

The mass of shrubbery shook as Gwigg regarded the blond girl. "There is great magic inside you, blazing star. But you must be patient. Tuning it is a lifelong process. With practice, and the help of your friends, you may be able to master the fairy magic inside of you."

Kara didn't look convinced.

"*Where were you?*" Pollo asked Lorelei.

"*We almost got eaten!*" Violet added.

"*With the web emergency, all the unicorns are busy at their sectors so we sent the centaurs to bring you to* the academy," Lorelei explained. *"In case you were attacked, the protection amulet had a fail safe built in to take you to the mages. Once the power crystal of Avalon stabilized the portals in this area, we were able to jump through and track your magic."*

*"How did you know we still had our magic?"* Dante asked Emily.

"The knight couldn't find it because you didn't believe you had it anymore. But the magic was always inside you." The healer smiled at Lorelei. "You just had to believe in yourselves."

*"The magic is especially strong with you, Prince Pollo,"* Lorelei said.

Pollo's forelock poked straight up. "Prince?" On his forehead, a star-shaped blaze shimmered beneath his crystal horn.

*Pollo! He's the prince! Way to go, Pollo!*

*"O' me twig!"* Pollo cried.

Riannan held her head high. "Congratulations, Pollo." Looking at her brother's mark, her dark eyes flashed with disappointment. "You'll make a great prince."

*"And you will make a great princess, Riannan,"* Lorelei said.

Everyone stared at Riannan's forehead.

Pollo's eyes opened wide. *"Riannan, you've got the royal mark, too!"*

"I do?" Riannan exclaimed.

The unicorns gathered around the pair, hooting and honking in surprise.

"Inconceivable!" Tweek cried, twigs dropping to the sand. "I've never heard of a prince *and* a princess!"

"This is a very good sign, indeed," Gwigg rumbled. "Two unicorn leaders will keep the magic twice as strong on the web."

Emily hugged Riannan. "You're going to make a wonderful princess, I just know it."

*"I'll always try my best,"* the princess promised.

"I'm so proud of all of you," Emily told the unicorns.

Tweek's quartz whirled in his twigs. "Well, let's get back to Aldenmor."

"You can't, Tweek," Gwigg said. "You were designed to stay on earth.

The little E.F. shuddered.

"Gwigg, can Tweek come back with us to Ravenswood?" Emily asked.

"You'd have the whole preserve as your home," Adriane added, smiling.

"A little Ravenswood moss would really bring out your quartz," Kara said.

"The mages will face their most difficult challenges in the days to come, Tweek," Gwigg rumbled.

"Well, I—" Tweek twiddled his twigs.

"Someone my own size for a change." Ozzie wiggled his tail. "Join the team, Twighead."

Tweek nodded. "Very well."

Ozzie threw a paw around the E.F.'s shoulders. "Great! What do you eat, anyway?"

"Eat?" Tweek asked. "Why, nothing."

"Perfect." The ferret beamed. "That's more for me!"

Gwigg rustled as he approached the mages. "The unicorns will do all they can to stabilize flowing magic. But we need you to find all the missing power crystals."

*"The web is in great danger until all nine crystals are returned to Avalon."* Lorelei said.

"Do you know where they are?" Emily asked.

"We have reason to believe that one is in the Fairy Realms," the Fairimental said. "They will be attracted to great magical power."

The power crystal and it floated into one of Gwigg's twigs.

"This one ended up in the fairy Otherworlds. A group of fairy creatures used it to control the golem—the dark knight who tried to kidnap the unicorns. They will try to find the others."

The mages exchanged worried glances.

"There is much to do." Gwigg whirled toward the portal. "Stand ready, mages!"

"I'm going to miss you guys." Emily moved between the unicorns, hugging each one.

*"You'll always be our favorite teacher."* Violet nuzzled Emily with her lavender nose.

*"Come see us for our graduation concert!"* Spruce bleated.

Kara sniffled, arranging Calliope's pale green forelock. "Remember, check your mane and tail after every class and you'll look perfect all day long."

*"One day we will ride the web together!"* Calliope exclaimed proudly.

"You know it!" Kara broke out crying.

"Oh no, Kara, now you're going to make *me* cry," Emily hugged Riannan and Pollo.

*Ahhhh! Bweeeee! SnnIFFle!*

Adriane hugged as many unicorns as she could grab while Dreamer and Lyra nuzzled the others.

Ralfie and Dante shuffled over to Ozzie.

*"We're going to miss you most of all,"* Ralfie said.

The baby unicorns swarmed around Ozzie, nudging him with their brightly colored muzzles.

"All right, all right, now get going," the ferret said, waving his paws toward the portal. "Beat it, you pests."

*Bye, Fuzzy. We love you!*

Lorelei herded the baby unicorns toward the portal. One by one, they jumped through. Lorelei looked back at Emily before following them in. *"Until we meet again, Emily."*

Gwigg whirled in after the unicorns. "The magic is with you, now and forever."

The mages waved until the last of the group vanished. The portal swirled closed and winked out.

Emily spotted Ozzie standing to the side. The ferret's back was turned, heaving in deep breaths.

"Ozzie," she said, gently petting his back. "Are you crying?"

"No way!" The ferret sniffled.

"We're all going to miss them," Emily said, lifting the sobbing ferret into her arms and hugging him tightly.

    &#10050;   &#10050;   &#10050;

Emily patted Domino's neck as she and the twelve other riders executed their final moves in the Happy Trails horse show. Lining up in the center of the riding arena, the riders tapped their ponies' necks. In one fluid movement, all the brightly splotched ponies dipped their heads to the ground in a deep bow.

Sierra rode Apache to the front of the group and he reared on his hind legs, whinnying happily.

"Good job, Domino!" Emily petted the black and white pony's sleek neck.

Domino nickered, pleased with her performance.

Applause and cheers broke out from the crowd in wooden bleachers set up outside the arena. Emily smiled as she saw her dad and stepmom waving to her and cheering. David's arm was around Dreamer, ruffling the wolf's fur. The mistwolf howled his approval, white star on his chest gleaming in the sun. Ozzie sat next to Veronica, happily munching a corn dog.

It was still weird to see her dad with Veronica. Emily had been so afraid that her dad's new wife would take him away from her, but now she knew nothing was further from the truth. Like her magic, the bond she shared with her dad was something that would last forever. Nothing in the world could ever change that.

"Whoo! How about we go for another ride?" Adriane said, scratching her pony, Taco, behind his ear. He was nearly all white, with a few black spots and a flowing black and white tail.

"My last day is going to be spent buried in mud to get all this dirt out from under my nails," Kara advised her friends. She smoothed her golden and white pony's blond mane and adjusted her cowboy hat.

The show over, the riders followed Sierra outside the corral.

"You guys did great!" Sierra told them, taking the reins as the mages dismounted. "I'm so glad we could spend some time together!"

"Thanks again for helping," Emily smiled. "We couldn't have gotten the unicorns home safely without you."

Sierra shook her head. "Don't forget. You guys better keep me filled in on everything going on at Ravenswood!"

Kara looked intently at Sierra's turquoise necklace. It almost seemed to be glowing. "Your jewel is looking more *magical* all the time!"

Sierra glanced at her gem, then whispered. "Ever since the unicorns came, I've been feeling much more in tune with my jewel."

The three mages traded glances, eyebrows raised.

"Promise to e-mail us and keep us up to date on your jewel," Emily said.

"And any other magically interesting news," Adriane added.

"I will," Sierra promised, leading the horses back into the barn. "I'll see you guys at the farewell dinner tonight." The brown-haired teen paused, smiling. "Unless a herd of dragons shows up."

"Don't worry, dragons travel alone," Adriane said.

"Well, the big ones do," Kara argued. "But

the smaller ones like the dragonflies travel in packs."

"True," Adriane agreed. "Then there's the wyverns, they mate for life."

Sierra's brown eyes widened in astonishment.

"We'll be there, Sierra." Emily promised.

The mages walked over to David, Veronica, and Dreamer.

"That was wonderful, girls!" David praised them, leaping down and hugging Emily.

"Emily, you were terrific," Veronica said, an overstuffed ferret lying facedown over her shoulder.

Emily pushed her red curls from her eyes and smiled shyly at her stepmom. "Thanks."

"Hey, Veronica's got a great idea," David said enthusiastically. "A trip to the Living Desert Zoo State Park! How 'bout it?"

"David," Veronica stopped him. "Only if the girls want to go . . ." she looked expectantly at Emily.

"We'd love to," Emily said.

Veronica's dark eyes sparkled. "They have all kinds of rare desert plants and animals," she explained excitedly.

"Snakes and spiders!" David added with a wink.

"Cool!" Emily said.

"Rad!" Adriane's eyes shone.

"Ewww!" Kara frowned.

David put his arm around Emily's shoulders. "You're so lucky, Emily, to have such good friends."

"Yeah, I know," Emily agreed, relaxing into his embrace. "Daddy, I'm really happy for you."

"Thank you, sweetheart."

Emily smiled. Funny, she thought. Life was like an unending circle of discovery. Questions were answered only to have new ones appear. Mysteries were revealed only to bring new challenges.

How were they supposed to return nine power crystals to Avalon when the Fairimentals didn't even know where eight of them were? How could three Level One mages, well, four with Ozzie, master their magic enough to save the magic of Avalon itself?

Looking at her friends, her family, there was one thing she knew for sure. The magic blazed inside of her stronger than ever. And, like her warrior best friend, she would always fight for what she believed in.

"You know, the Living Desert Zoo has a whole collection of unique species," Veronica said, patting Ozzie's back as he lay over her shoulder.

"*UrrrrP!*"

David nodded. "I bet you'll find animals unlike anything you girls have seen before."

Emily, Kara and Adriane exchanged looks, their magic gems sparkling brightly in the warm desert sun.

Emily smiled at her dad and stepmom. "You might be surprised."

# Epilogue

The Dark Sorceress stood before the fairy creatures gathered in the chamber of black ice. She met the group's malevolent stares with her own icy glare.

"I told you they were clever," she said, her voice echoing along the glistening walls.

"Too clever for you, obviously," one of the fairy creatures accused. A finely wrought cloak covered her face, but inside the dark hood the pixilated eyes of an insect flickered gold and green.

"Your plans are notorious for not succeeding," another creature hissed, oily wings draped behind its wide back. "The power crystal is gone."

Trembling with rage, the Dark Sorceress dug her silver talons into the pale flesh of her palms. Much as she hated it, she needed these creatures. None of them alone had the power to escape the Otherworlds. "The power crystal is right where we want it," she explained in a steady voice.

"How so?" the foul winged creature demanded.

"It is being held in the heart of the Fairimental's magic!"

"Exactly," the sorceress smiled, vampire teeth gleaming. "Can you think of a safer place?"

It had been a bold move, going after the young unicorns. A pity the golem had not captured them. But something much more important had been accomplished.

The cowled creature stood. A swarm of shadowy spiders rippled over her strangely bulky cloak. "We must act now, while the web is in chaos. Once we possess all nine power crystals, we will control the magic of Avalon itself."

Black wings fluttering like a giant cicada, the second creature sneered. "And what about the mages chosen to stand for the Fairimentals? They have constantly proven their ability to be . . . shall we say, lucky."

"Beginner's luck runs out." The sorceress averted her eyes from the foul thing. "I will deal with the three mages," The Dark Sorceress's vow rang across the black ice with deadly certainty.

"No," the cloaked figure corrected, her voice skittering like spiders' feet on ice. "*We* will deal with them. Against all of us, they do not stand a chance."

# AVALON
## QUEST FOR MAGIC

BOOK 2

# All's Fairy in Love & War

by Rachel Roberts

# Chapter 1

"**O**w!"

Kara dropped her script for the school play and shook her fingers hard. Ordinarily the thirteen-year-old wasn't clumsy, but in her haste to "rise and outshine" this morning, she'd grabbed for the safety pin without looking to see that it was closed. It wasn't.

Unsurprisingly, Kara had nabbed the starring role in her school production of Shakespeare's *A Midsummer Night's Dream*. She'd play the Fairy Queen Titania, with typical grace and style—*and* a killer costume. This pink and poufy dress, to be exact.

She whipped around in front of her full-length mirror.

*Whack!* The costume's wide silk wings flapped open, smacking the back of her head. Okay, scratch the grace and style.

"They're still crooked!" she whined.

*"Stand still, I'm not finished."* The reproach came

to her telepathically, in a familiar purring voice. It was from the exquisite leopard-like cat at her side, whose whiskery mouth was clamped down on six safety pins.

"That doesn't look right, Lyra," Kara complained to her feline friend, looking over her shoulder at her reflection.

*"I think I know a few things about wings,"* the cat replied, emerald green eyes twinkling. She wasn't kidding: She was a magical animal, a winged cat Kara had bonded with.

*Ding!* Kara's pink laptop, perched precariously on the edge of her canopy bed, signaled an incoming IM.

She sighed dramatically. What would her friends do without her? With one wing attached, the other half-pinned and dragging on the carpet, she grabbed the hem of her dress and strode over to her bed.

The IM-er was Molly, aka goodgollymolly:

goodgollymolly:  k, u sure this green base will come off? ☹

With one hand, she tapped back a message to Molly, who was working on her makeup for her role as one of the fairies in the play.

kstar:  just apply a light coat, u'r a fairy, not the hulk!

Kara had started back toward the mirror when the pink phone on her desk began to ring. Without thinking, she hit the speaker.

"So what's the story on the cast party?" Heather was already in full-whine mode. "And these sleeves are too puffy."

"Hello? They're cap sleeves. They're supposed to be puffy," Kara reminded her friend.

Tiffany cut through the convo, reading her lines dramatically: " 'Those be rubies, fairy favors; in those freckles live their savors.' How's that?"

"No one will notice with that incredible costume," Kara assured her, inspecting her own dress. She adjusted the scoop neck on the bodice, checking that the crystal beading was threaded perfectly down the front.

Lyra nimbly nosed the wide wings in place.

*La-la-la-la-la-la.* Her cell phone, half-buried in her pillows, sang out. Now what?

A split second before hitting "Talk," she glanced at the Caller ID, and frowned.

"Hi, it's me," Emily said, her voice betraying a trace of anxiety. "How's the play going?"

"Fine," Kara answered. She knew she sounded curt, but Emily didn't seem to notice.

"I just called to remind you we're meeting with

Adriane at Ravenswood this weekend," Emily said, "We need something really exciting to announce the new tourist season."

Ravenswood was an animal sanctuary that she, Emily, and Adriane were in charge of. A year ago, Kara would have scoffed at such a lame idea—but a year ago, she didn't know she was a mage. And she could never share that secret with Heather, Tiffany, and Molly.

"Hey, Princess Rapunzel!" Suddenly, another voice, impatient, broke in. "How are we going to keep feeding the animals without the council's support?" It was Adriane, already channeling her inner Warrior. So early in the morning! Kara refused to respond.

"And we're swamped at Ravenswood with e-mails," Emily added. "Not to mention the mage mission of retrieving the missing power crystals."

Not trying very hard to hide her exasperation, Kara told them, "Yeah, yeah. The show's tomorrow, so you'll have to live without me until then."

"Kara, we need you!" Everyone wailed and dinged at once from the phones and the computer.

"Take a chill pill. It's under control," Kara said. "Fairies, pick me up in thirty minutes." She hung up the landlines.

"Good luck with the show," Emily said.

"Thanks. Later." Kara hit the "End Call" button, tossing the cell into the pile of stuffed animals that lined her window seat. Then she stomped back to the mirror. Why did those two girls always make her feel so . . . so angry! There was more to life than using magic, even if it *was* for the cause of Ravenswood and the . . . she turned to see Lyra staring at her with her big green cat eyes.

Kara flushed. "It's not about you."

*"You don't have to apologize for how you feel,"* the cat said, stretching on the wide rug and licking the fur on her left front leg.

"Stop being so . . . understanding!"

Her whole morning routine was being disrupted! She adjusted the sparkling tiara and brushed her long golden hair.

Adriane and Emily took to magic like ducks to water. Kara's magic only frustrated her. Sure, Kara was totally into the excitement, the thrill of using magic. But the kind of excitement she had managed to stir up was the kind that could kill a person. And who needed that kind of stress? Not me, thought Kara. All this worrying about how to use her magic was enough to bring on a stress attack— or worse, a bad complexion.

And after all she'd been through, she still couldn't understand her blazing star powers. She'd accidentally absorbed shapeshifting magic, only the ability didn't come with instructions. She had finally gotten it under control only to lose it again.

And now she was right back where she had

started. One incredibly powerful magic jewel and no idea what to do with it.

It was time to face facts: She was never going to master the magic of the unicorn jewel. It was high time to get back to what was real. In just three short weeks Kara had managed to work on all kinds of projects, including putting herself in the middle of the school play, part of Shakespeare Day at Stonehill Middle School.

But now she was beginning to feel totally swamped—being pulled from all directions. Between the mage quest, Ravenswood, the school play, and her friends, it seemed she had no time to spare.

Chill, she told herself. I'll figure this out, and *without* magic!

She looked at Lyra and reprimanded herself. Without magic, she never would have met her best friend. She thought about how many lives were at stake. After all, she, Emily, and Adriane weren't the only ones in danger. The whole reason they had gotten involved in this mess was to help the animals— Phel, Ozzie, Stormbringer, and countless others from Aldenmor and beyond. And now Storm was gone. Who knew what had happened to Phel. And the web was totally flooie. And they were the ones, no—*she* was the one—who had released all that magic from Avalon. Not Emily, not Adriane, not Ozzie, not the Fairimentals. She, *moi!* How could she be the only one to have released that much power?

Kara was overwhelmed just thinking about it. What if she was never meant to use magic? What if it was all some horrible mistake? What if she never found out what being a blazing star really meant? The thoughts made her sick to her stomach. She wanted to tell Emily and Adriane how scared she was, but she couldn't. People depended on her to be a certain way. Calm, cool, and in control. It was as though they expected her to be as flawless on the inside as she was on the outside. And who was she to let them down? Sure, the pressure to be perfect was hard to bear. But the thought of disappointing people was even harder.

If you have a test, you prepare, she thought as she slipped into the outfit's matching sparkly slippers. But how do you prepare for a fight to save the entire web of magic? Or creatures that could eat you alive and still have room for your friends?

She flopped down on the bed, yanking up her white leggings under the skirt. Then she stood in front of the mirror. "Perfect!" Kara was pleased with the full effect of the glorious costume. The pearly white wings looked especially real, sparkling like a magical butterfly.

A sudden static charge sparkled through the room. The lights dimmed, went black, and came back on.

That's odd. . . . It's not the season for a brown-out, Kara thought.

Then she noticed something *really* odd, a bright light outlining her closet door. Even with the door closed, she could see the light shimmering and swirling from inside.

Kara looked to Lyra questioningly. The cat was crouched, ready to spring, hair bristling along her neck.

Kara cocked her head. She heard sniffing and whispering—someone was in her closet!

"Eeek!" Kara leaped onto her bed.

"Where are we?" a squeaky voice asked.

"I don't know," a second voice answered gruffly.

"Well, look at the map," the high-pitched voice whispered.

"It's not on the map!"

"Lemme see that thing!"

The closet door slowly creaked open, sending bright light spiraling around Kara's room.

A long nose poked through the crack in the door, sniffing. "I smell magic!" the squeaky-voiced creature said, whiskers twitching.

"Get out there and take a look!" the other said.

"No way. *You* go!"

"No, you!"

The door burst open. A large rat and a pointy-eared goblin-like creature rolled onto the rug, tussling.

"Hey!" Kara leaped to the floor, Lyra growling at her side.

"Ahhhh!" The startled creatures jumped back, scrambling into a case of books and knocking over a shelf of fashion magazines.

"We can explain everything!" the squeaky-voiced creature said, shaking with fear. It looked like a big dog-sized rat, long nose and whiskers quivering.

"Sparky, it's her!" The other eyed Kara and her glittering outfit carefully. He looked like a boy, except he had green skin and pointy ears. He wore a leather aviator cap with goggles, black vest with lots of pockets, and red pants tucked into knee-high boots. A thick belt full of brightly colored vials wrapped around his waist.

"We're rich!" the rat thing squealed. "Oop—"

Lyra stepped in front of Kara, growling.

"Spare us, Princess." The rat quivered, eyeing the ferocious-looking cat.

"Who are you?" Kara demanded.

The strange boy bowed. "Princess, I am the great hobgoblin explorer, Musso the Magnificent, and this is my assistant mookrat magic sniffer, Sparky."

"Assistant?" The mookrat shifted beady black eyes.

"Quiet, you still get thirty percent."

"Hey!" the mookrat snarled, wiggling his long nose. "You said I could get twenty-five!"

"Fine, have it your way." He turned back to Kara. "My *associate* and I have been surfing the magic web for days. We have braved the treacherous wild magic in nothing but a bubble on this most excellent adventure to find you."

"Is that a portal in my closet?!" Kara asked, looking at the unbelievable swirling light hanging in the middle of her Capri pants. Through its center, Kara saw spirals of stars stretching across the infinite lines of the magic web.

"It's a porta-portal," Sparky said.

"What my hairy friend here is saying is that this portal is moving."

"I sniffed our way here," Sparky announced, nose wagging proudly.

"Yes, so if you are ready, Princess, we must be off before it clos-ak—" Musso reached for Kara, but was blocked by a mouthful of Lyra's razor teeth.

"What are you talking about?" Kara asked Musso.

"We were hired to find you so you can save the magic web."

Sparky looked at Musso. "How's she gonna do that?"

Musso poked Sparky on the snout. "She's the blazing star, you nosepod!"

"Ooo, blazing star!"

"I'm not going anywhere!" Kara said adamantly. "So go back wherever you came from."

"But there's major trouble," Musso cried. "Everyone needs you!"

"Take a number," Kara said, holding up her jewel. The gem suddenly erupted with diamond-bright light.

"AK!" Musso and Sparky dove out of the way as the portal pulsed wildly, drawing in the magic of the unicorn jewel.

Kara was jerked forward, her necklace biting into the back of her neck. "Ahh, Lyra! It's pulling my jewel in!"

Lyra sprang in front of Kara, pushing the girl back.

Musso and Sparky leaped, pulling Kara forward.

"Hurry, it's closing!" Musso yelled, looking anxiously as the bright portal spun in on itself.

With a fierce growl, Lyra swiped at the two intruders. They scrambled apart, trying to avoid the sharp claws.

Kara went flying forward, jewel first, into the portal. "Lyra!" she screamed.

Lyra raced into the closet and leaped, diving through the dwindling hole. The portal closed and vanished, leaving a perplexed Musso and Sparky stranded in Kara's bedroom.

# Chapter 2

**K**ara fell like Alice down the rabbit hole, tumbling and landing in a heap.

"Lyra!" she called frantically, struggling to untangle herself from her voluminous skirt, spitting blond hair from her face.

*"I am here."* The cat was behind her, emerald eyes warily surveying the immediate area.

Kara followed Lyra's gaze. Golden brown trees with wide trunks soared overhead, twisting sunlight into shafts of shimmering shadows. She'd fallen into a glade in the woods. A clump of purple heather had cushioned her fall. Jasmine, peach blossoms, and clover filled her senses.

Something flew by Kara's face, accompanied by a flourish of tinkling bells.

"Hey!" Kara stammered, readjusting the straps on her fairy wings.

Luminous wide eyes looked at Kara. They were tiny figures, about the size of butterflies. Translucent wings of intricate beauty pulsed with light and formed swirling patterns in the air.

"*Fairy wraiths,*" Lyra explained as they merrily whirled around her. "*We must be in the Fairy Realms.*"

Kara stood and smoothed out the long dress, checking for stains.

"Great! No sign of a portal for weeks, and one opens in my closet!"

Catching a glint out of the corner of her eye, Kara spun around. Furry heads peeked out from behind rocks. Something that looked like a small bear with glimmering purple fur sat staring at Kara with big golden eyes. Birds of deep greens, reds, and purples fluttered above her head, chirping excitedly.

"Shoo!" Kara tried to swipe them away. "Let's just find that portal and jump back through," she said to Lyra.

"*That's what I've been looking for. There's no sign of a portal anywhere around here,*" Lyra responded.

"Then how did we get here?"

A troop of brave squirrel-like creatures with orange tufted ears had moved toward Kara's feet. Their bushy tails swept the forest floor as they investigated the girl.

Kara looked down to see the front of her dress glowing with a brilliant hue. She fished the unicorn jewel from inside her bodice. The gem was ablaze with light.

"I'm a magical lighthouse!" Kara quickly willed her jewel to calm down.

"Scritch!!!" An adamant orange squirrel thingy demanded.

Kara sighed. Fine. "One scritch." She reached out—but the animal squealed in horror.

In a mad rush, *all* the creatures bolted, leaving Kara and Lyra alone.

"What? I took a shower." Suddenly she gasped. "Oh great, will you look at this!" Mud had stained the glittering hem of her dress where the squirrels had been.

"Ssshorrrible."

"Take it easy, Lyra," Kara said, brushing the mud away. "The dry cleaner can get it out."

*"That wasn't me,"* the cat answered, crouching low, green eyes searching the woods.

Something moved among the trees. Hints of light sparkled from yellow eyes.

"What else am I attracting?" Kara asked, suddenly aware of how vulnerable they were in the open forest.

*"Stay behind me,"* the cat ordered, hackles raised.

There was something in the shadows. It was as if the trees themselves had spawned horrible misshapen creatures. Their bodies were thick wood, standing on bowed legs. Thorns sprouted from thin arms ending in long, sharp fingers. Wide, flat faces rimed with thorns displayed mouths full of long, splintered teeth. They did not look friendly.

"What you dooin' in woods, witch?" one of them snarled.

"Um, we're lost. If you could show us the nearest portal we'll be on our way in a jif—"

Scratching and hissing voices scraped the air as the creatures closed their ring tighter.

"—fy."

Lyra snarled, teeth bared.

The creatures stopped short. "We take witch's magicsss!"

Shaking with fear, Kara pointed her unicorn jewel at the beasts. "You stay away from us!"

The gem crackled with energy as light shot straight up, twisting into a diamond beam. Kara winced as her magic dissolved into fragments, shooting in all directions at once. She'd managed to slow the advance of the tree monsters, but she had not stopped them. Kara would eventually tire, or worse, have to find the ladies room.

Lyra carefully eyed the creatures on the left side. *When I say so, run.*

"No! I'm not leaving you," Kara declared.

"Comes closer, crispie critter. Looks tasty." Sharp fingers beckoned as the creatures taunted the cat.

Kara looked around desperately. She had to hold her magic together. Lyra wasn't going to win this fight on her own, and without Kara's magic, they were helpless.

"AieOOO!"

A bloodcurdling scream tore through the forest.

Something black flew across the glade, extending a deadly looking sword and swiping it over the creatures' heads. It yelled again, savage and loud.

The tree creatures grumbled angrily but melted back into the shadows of the woods . . . leaving Kara and Lyra alone with this new menace.

The figure let go of a thick vine, landing with a thud on its rump.

Kara's jaw dropped. It was a boy. Well, it looked like a boy. He was covered in black. What she thought had been wings was really a sleek, black cape.

The boy sprang to his feet and bowed deeply. "Good day, milady."

"Who are you?" Kara demanded.

"I am the Forest Prince." The boy stood. "And I am at your service."

"Great, then you can kindly lead me to the nearest portal," Kara responded. She could play this game.

"When you failed to show at the ring, I thought you could be in trouble," he said cheerily. "And by the looks of those wrags, I would say my arrival was quite timely."

Sheathing his sword, the stranger approached Kara. He was dressed completely in black, from boots, pants, and shirt to gloves. A black bandanna around his head concealed even the color of his hair. He looked young, maybe a few years older than Kara, but with a black mask covering his features, it was hard to tell. All Kara could see was a pair of pale green eyes.

Lyra moved in front of Kara, daring the boy to so much as breathe.

"Whoa, nice kitty." The boy raised his arms and took a step back. "The woods are full of magic trackers. Allow me to escort you."

"Okaaay." Whoever this guy was, Kara needed to steer him toward a reality check. "Thanks," she said brightly. "Leave me your e-mail and I'll get back to ya."

He sprang toward her, generating a warning growl from Lyra. "Everyone's waiting for you."

"Exactly! Molly, and Heather, and Tiffany. I've got a play to rehearse for—"

"We must hurry." The boy's voice took on a new tone of urgency as he reached to grab her arm.

"Wait a minute. I'm not going anywhere with you!" Kara declared, hands on her hips. "What's going on here? Where am I? And why are you all dressed like Zorro?"

The boy looked puzzled. "You are in the Fairy Queen's enchanted woods."

When Kara didn't budge, the stranger pressed on. "The Five Kingdoms have gathered to meet you. Any time lost will only goad them toward the path of war."

"I hate to disappoint you, but I'm not staying," Kara answered. "Where's the portal that brought me here?"

The mysterious stranger started canvassing the nearby bright purple bushes, waving his sword this way and that. "No portals connect to the Fairy Realms, Princess."

"Then how did I get here?"

With a *clink*, the sword hit something.

"You arrived here through this."

Kara walked closer and saw the outline of a rectangle set into the ground. It was large, thin, completely flat, with no frame. The gray surface seemed to absorb everything around it, making it virtually invisible. Kara ran her hand over the front, sending ripples fanning out along the surface. Deep silver gleamed beneath, revealing Kara's image like a reflective pool.

"A mirror?" Kara asked.

"We only use mirrors here" the boy explained.

"Then how did those two knuckleheads get in my closet?"

"Ah. The two adventurers Master Tangoo hired to bring you here," Zorro guessed.

"I was kidnapped!" Kara protested.

"The mirror was connected to the portal. Very dangerous way to travel to the Fairy Realms. But you're here." The boy smiled, warm and unthreatening.

"Listen, Forest Gump," Kara said. "How do I go back?"

"Are you a mirror master?"

"No!"

"Then you can't. Only a mirror master can open a traveling mirror to the web."

"Well, stand back, Zorro. I have my own traveling accessories," Kara said. She closed her eyes, fighting the fear creeping along her spine. "Dragonflies! Attention all minis. Front and center!"

Instantly, the air began to bubble. Bright lights erupted like popcorn.

*POP! pop! POP! pop! POP!*

Five mini dragons dove around Kara, squealing and whirling with excitement. Kara couldn't control all her magic, but at least she could count on the dragonflies. Red Fiona, purple Barney, orange Blaze, and blue Fred all buzzed happily. Yellow Goldie landed and nuzzled Kara's neck. "Kaaraa!"

"I'm glad to see you, too," she cooed, stroking the mini's head. Goldie's golden jewel eyes swirled in pleasure.

The stranger in black gaped at her. "Fairy dragons! Surely you are a princess of magic."

"Yeah, just call me Snow White," Kara quipped. She turned to the dragonflies. "I need you guys to make a portal home, pronto."

The d'flies had helped the mages before by

creating portals for them to jump through—surely they could make one now.

The minis put their heads together, squeaking uncertainly. After a few seconds they locked wing-tips, spinning into a circle. The air between their wings stretched and warped, spitting flashes of jagged light.

"What's wrong, bad reception?" Kara asked.

The dragonflies stopped spinning and faced Kara.

"Nokee dokeee," Barney said sadly.

"Flooieeeee," Blaze added. The other four d'flies nodded in agreement.

*"It's too risky for you to use their portal to travel across the web,"* Lyra interpreted.

Kara couldn't believe it. "How am I supposed to get home?"

"If I may make a suggestion, Princess Snow White," the stranger in black offered, "Tangoo is a very powerful mirror master. He would be able to get you back home."

"How do I find this Tang-dude?" Kara eyed the maze of giant trees stretching in all directions.

"He's at the Fairy Palace. I'll take you."

Kara narrowed her eyes suspiciously. "Why should I trust you if you won't even show your face?"

"Those tree creatures will be back," the boy in black said. "And there are others. Ever since the web went wild, creatures of all sorts have shown up hunting for magic."

Kara sighed. "Okay, but I need to do something first. Don't look!" she warned.

The boy spun around, his back to Kara. "Your wish is my command."

Kara quickly huddled the five minis close together and whispered. "Can you make a d'fly portal phone? *Please* tell me you can at least find Emily and Adriane." The brightly colored dragonflies scrunched their jeweled eyes, working through the challenge, then nodded eagerly. Locking wingtips again, they whirled in a circle.

"No peeking!" she called to the boy, shielding the small window.

Blaze and Fred peeped, signaling a connection had been made. A pulsing light formed in the center of the d'flies' wing circle. Kara held her jewel tight and leaned in close, trying to see what the minis had found.

She looked at a pocked, white surface, indented with rings and rivulets. It moved back and forth, swaying to a beat.

"What is that?" Kara asked, shifting back.

"Deedee!" Fred squeaked.

The craggy image moved, revealing a seat—right in the middle of the school auditorium. Adriane sat forward, her long dark hair spilling over the seat. She slid a pair of headphones to her neck and looked into the portal. Kara had been looking at the bottom of Adriane's sneaker.

"Fred?" Adriane whispered. "Is that you?"

"Is meemee, Deedee," Fred chirped quietly. "KeeKee heer."

"All right, all right, enough with the small talk." Kara pushed her face to the little window. "Hey."

"Kara?" Adriane gasped. "Where are you?

"I'm in the Fairy Realms."

"What!?" Adriane cried, then quickly contained her voice to a whisper. "How did you find a portal?"

"It found me. One opened in my closet, and I fell into it," Kara explained hurriedly.

"Are you okay?"

"Yeah, yeah, fine. Lyra's here with me. No time to explain right now."

"Everyone's expecting you here in like a half hour!" Adriane exclaimed. "Can you get back?"

"Not yet. This is the best the d'flies can do. And Heather, Molly, and Tiffany will be at my house any minute. You have to get over there and cover for me until I can find a way home," Kara said. "Oh, and there's a mookrat and a hobgoblin in my closet. Keep them away from my shoes!"

"Huh?"

The window shifted left as the mini dragons tried to hold it together.

"Wait a minute, who's that?" Adriane could see the boy in black standing patiently to the side.

Kara didn't quite know how to answer. "He's a little light on the shining armor, but he's taking me to some dude to see about getting out of here."

Adriane thought for a second. "Can the d'flies open phone portals to one another if they separate?"

Fiona nodded her little head. "Eezee, keekee."

"Okay, I get your drift." Kara eyed the dragonflies. "We can all keep in contact through d'fly cell phones. Fiona, you go and stay with Emily. Fred, go with Adriane. And Blaze and Barney, go to my room and keep an eye on those two chuckleheads. Goldie stays with me."

"Sounds good," Adriane approved. "And be careful."

Kara nodded. "Okay, d'flies, let's move out."

The window winked out in a flurry of rainbow bubbles, taking four of the five dragonflies with it. Goldie remained, sitting on Kara's shoulder, preening her golden wings.

"Can I turn around now?" the boy in black asked.

"Okay," Kara anwered. "Let's go."

"Right this way, Princess Snow White." Adjusting the silver sword at his side, he started into the woods, Kara and Lyra following close behind. "May I call you Snow?"

"No."

The boy eyed her warily.

"But you *can* call me Kara."

There was no trail, but the stranger strode confidently along a twisting course. The fairy creatures of the forests soon began converging again, following at a distance, scuffling and giggling.

"I've never seen anyone attract so many creatures," the Forest Prince said, walking alongside Kara.

"Back off, bub!" Goldie squeaked harshly.

The boy stepped back. "You have some very loyal protectors."

*"And don't you forget it!"* Lyra snarled.

Kara gave Goldie a scritch between the mini's wings, the d'fly's favorite scritching spot.

"So, I take it you're from around here?" Kara ventured, hoping to find out something about her mysterious new friend.

He nodded. "I'm familiar with all of the Five Kingdoms in the Fairy Realms."

"Huh?"

"The five major races that live here: Goblin, Troll, Dwarf, Elf, and Fairy," the boy replied, pulling aside a thorny branch hanging in the path. "You should have arrived in the Fairy Ring." He gestured for Kara to walk ahead.

"The what?"

The Forest Prince pointed a black-gloved hand. "There."

Kara squinted through the tree trunks. Stepping

around the giant trees, she stood at the edge of the forest. "Oh . . . my . . . ," she gasped.

Before them stretched an organic city, made entirely of flora. At one end, an enormous palace seemed to grow from the gardens themselves. Deep golden trees formed elegant shining towers, and thick, blooming vines intertwined to make lush green walls. Countless bright flowers adorned the palace, framing arched windows and encircling the high towers. Other structures lay sprawled among the grounds.

"Follow this path through the main gardens," the Forest Prince instructed. "You'll find the Fairy Ring on the far side. Good luck." The stranger in black bowed and began backing into the woods.

"Aren't you coming with me?" Kara asked.

"I can't." He edged farther back into the woods, his masked face hidden in the shadows. "Be seeing you, Princess."

He melted into the darkness and vanished.

"Not if I see you first!" Kara called.

*"He did help us."* Lyra moved onto a pathway lined by silvery green weeping willows.

"Uh-huh," Goldie concurred.

"Well, if *he'd* been lost in an enchanted mall, I totally would've helped *him.*"

Smoothing her hair, Kara walked forward, Lyra following. She wished she had a comb. A little lip gloss wouldn't hurt, either.

Kara followed a winding path through the gardens. She turned a corner and before her stood a huge, round amphitheater made of purple wisteria vines. Four archways wrapped in bright red and yellow flowers served as entrances and exits to the open-air structure.

Angry voices echoed inside. Kara toyed with her unicorn jewel nervously. The Forest Prince had said she was expected, so she assumed she could get help. But Kara had learned it was dangerous to assume anything when magic was involved.

"I guess we'll just have to announce ourselves," Kara said, walking into the Fairy Ring.

Suddenly Kara stopped in her tracks. A huge gathering of creatures was crowded within. Enormous trolls, green goblins, delicate fairies, squat dwarves, and nimble elves were crammed into the Fairy Ring. Several were standing in the center of the ring, shouting at the top of their lungs.

"I grow weary of waiting!" an angry troll yelled, pacing on huge, knobby feet and waving a giant calloused fist in the air.

"You talk about saving the Fairy Realms, yet each day it grows worse," accused a stout dwarf.

"We demand to know where she is!" an enraged goblin jumped and shouted.

"And so I shall tell you!" a clear voice rang out. The argument instantly ceased. Kara could barely see a tall figure in long robes adorned with strange symbols. Long green hair tied back, his gaunt face sported a goatee, hawkish nose, and deep black eyes that bored straight into Kara. "The answer we have been waiting for is here."

# Chapter 3

**K**ara stood at the arched entrance to the Fairy Ring, shocked and speechless. The only thing anchoring her to reality was Lyra's reassuring presence by her side and Goldie's nervous twittering at her shoulder.

Inside the Fairy Ring, five pairs of thrones grew from the gleaming wood of the structure. The rulers from each of the Five Kingdoms, Elf, Goblin, Fairy, Troll, and Dwarf, occupied the royal pedestals. Circling them, crowds of creatures sat upon tiered toadstool seats, crammed all the way to the top.

A regal woman adorned with a glittering jeweled crown and richly embroidered robes glided gracefully toward Kara. She was a tall, delicate fairy, with flowing hair the color of honey. Sparkling wings of swirling rainbow patterns fluttered at her back. Her rich violet gown accented her almost purple eyes.

She must be a queen, Kara realized.

"Welcome, Princess Kara," the Fairy Queen said, smiling brilliantly.

"Look, she's got a fairy dragon!" A wood nymph stood in the bleachers, pointing a long, green finger.

Goldie waved excitedly. One glittering wing of Kara's costume, already loosened in the forest, ripped off and clattered to the floor.

The mini looked back over Kara's shoulder. "Oops."

The crowd stared at Kara in mute horror. Eyes of all shapes, sizes, and colors widened in disbelief.

"Uh-oh." Kara suddenly got it. These creatures had thought her wings were real!

The Troll King rose from his seat, drawing his bushy eyebrows together in a ferocious scowl. His massive body looked like it was carved from a mountain, with thick gray skin, dark brown hair, and moss green eyes. He wore thick leather armor.

In a voice that sounded like grinding rocks, he laughed. His outburst set off a round of guffaws from the entire troll contingent, all massive brutes.

"Do you mock us?" the Troll King bellowed. "You think this human girl is going to save the Fairy Realms?"

"I would not joke in such dire times, King Ragnar," the Fairy Queen answered respectfully, keeping her eyes on Kara. "This is no ordinary girl."

"She most certainly is not." The tall, wizened, green-skinned goblin walked in front of the queen. Looking down his hawk-like nose, he scrutinized

Kara with sharp, black eyes. He smiled and called to the audience, "This is the blazing star."

Gasps of disbelief ran through the crowd.

"You are quite right, Tangoo," the queen said proudly.

Everyone looked at Kara expectantly. She had no idea what to do.

"I am Queen Selinda," the fairy said softly. "Step forward."

Kara did as she was asked. Gulping, she managed to squeak, "Hi, what's up?"

"Selinda, this is an outrage!" the Goblin Queen shouted. She stood from her throne and walked into the Ring, green cheeks flushed purple with anger, eyes gleaming. A meek-looking Goblin Prince followed behind her. Slicking back black spiky hair with green highlights, the prince placed his other bejeweled hand on the Goblin Queen's shoulder, trying to calm her down.

"Mother, this is the girl chosen by the Fairimentals."

The stout Goblin Queen pushed between her sorcerer and the Fairy Queen to look Kara over. "Where is her mentor?"

Lyra stepped forward with a snarl, making the four back off.

"I would refrain from any more outbursts if I were you, Raelda," Selinda advised, smiling at the big cat.

Flustered, Raelda stepped back.

"My luminous ladies." Tangoo bowed to both queens. "I will guide the girl through the whole thing."

"What's going on here?" Kara asked. "What thing?"

Queen Selinda turned her violet eyes back to Kara and smiled. "I am sorry you were brought here so abruptly. You were supposed to arrive through the mirror here in the Fairy Ring." Selinda pointed to a large mirror set by her throne. Unlike the camouflaged gray glass mirror in the forest, this one was bright silver, elegantly framed by intricate golden flowers.

"Well, I fell out in the middle of the forest," Kara said, irritated.

"Connecting mirrors to portals is not a precise magic," Tangoo explained.

"I would've been blazing stardust if the Forest Prince hadn't rescued me," Kara huffed.

The Fairy Ring suddenly erupted in chaos, everyone shouting and yelling at once.

"She's working with that bandit!"

"What deceit is this?"

"Arrest her at once!"

Kara winced. Goldie squeaked. Lyra stood steady.

"I was attacked by tree wrags," Kara said meekly.

"Wrags in the queen's woods," an elf yelled. "I told you the situation is dire!"

"She is in league with that thief of magic," the Dwarf King spat, leaping up on short, squat legs. He was only as tall as a pixie, but four times more massive, with a long, braided beard on his aged face.

"This boy saved my life," Kara explained. The mystery guy *had* saved her, but Kara had known there wasn't something quite right about him. No one who was being completely truthful needed to hide behind a mask.

"Temperance, Rolok," the Elf King interjected, speaking evenly but firmly to the Dwarf King. The short, kindly elf smiled warmly at Kara, but spoke to the crowds. "The blazing star is a friend to the elves, as are the other two mages, the healer and the warrior."

They knew about Emily and Adriane? Kara thought wildly. What else did they know? And what did they want?

"Let us give the young mage a chance."

"Fine, but she must find the power crystal now," the Goblin King growled. "Or we proceed with our plans to seal off the Fairy Realms from the rest of the worlds!"

"You cannot do that, King Voraxx!" the Fairy Queen entreated. The crescent-shaped jewel on her crown glittered as she looked at the other rulers. "If you seal off the Fairy Realms, the magic web will surely be destroyed and all worlds with it!"

Kara gulped. "*All* worlds, as in Aldenmor, and *Earth?*"

"Sacrifices must be made. We can reconstruct the web," Voraxx insisted stubbornly.

"You don't know if that will work," the Elf King argued.

"We must save ourselves while there is still time!" the Troll Queen shouted in agreement with the Goblin King.

"It is our sworn duty to use Avalon's magic to enrich *all* worlds," the Fairy King interjected.

"The magic runs wild," the Troll King growled.

"Precisely why we need the power crystal to stabilize the Five Kingdoms," Queen Selinda said, keeping her voice calm. "The Fairy Realms depend on magic more than any other place."

"I have authorized Tangoo's plan to bring the blazing star here," Raelda spoke, looking sharply at Selinda. "Let us see if the sorcerer is as smart as he looks."

Selinda's lips twitched in a smile.

"However," Raelda continued. "If she fails, we will do what we must to save ourselves and our lands."

Fairy King Oriel stood and moved to the center of the ring, his sky blue robes rippling around his lithe form. "Anyone who tries to seal off the Fairy Realms will have to deal with me first."

"And the elves," said the Elf Queen firmly, her

distrust of goblins reflected in her brown eyes. "The blazing star proved her courage by sending the magic of Avalon to save Aldenmor. We stand with the fairies!."

The Goblin Queen countered, "If this so-called blazing star had not released the magic of Avalon, we wouldn't *be* in this mess!"

"I didn't know what would happen!" Kara protested.

The Fairy King glowered at Queen Raelda. He spoke in a threatening whisper. "The Dark Sorceress was aided directly by *your* people. I wonder how high up the chain of command that went?"

Realda gasped in shock.

"That is enough!" Selinda commanded. "The mages have already found one of the power crystals."

All eyes focused back on Kara.

She stammered, "My friends and I gave it to the Fairimentals for safekeeping. We're supposed to find the other eight."

The crowd muttered. Some even began laughing again.

The Fairy Queen raised her voice. "Magic attracts magic, and who is more magical than a blazing star?" She looked at the other rulers. "Surely you will give her a chance before we resort to war."

"Why can't you find the power crystal yourself?" Kara asked quietly.

"We've tried," the queen explained. "But without the magic of Avalon, we grow weaker every day. You are the blazing star."

"Show us some magic, blazing star," a nymph called out.

"Er . . . magic?" Kara asked nervously. "I've got dress rehearsal at school in, like, fifteen minutes."

"Let the blazing star prove herself!" the Troll King rumbled.

"Agreed!" the Dwarf King added.

The doubting Goblin Queen stood back and crossed her arms.

Arguing with these fairy creatures wasn't getting Kara home any sooner. Besides, if what they said was true, there might not be a home . . . an earth . . . to go home to. "Lyra, what should I do?" she whispered.

*"Stand close to me and we will focus your magic."*

Goldie hugged Kara's neck. "I help."

"All right." If she could pull off a tiny bit of flashy blazing star power to dazzle her hosts, maybe they'd help her. She held up the unicorn jewel dangling from her silver necklace. It sparked with power.

Awed by the gem, the crowd fell silent.

*"Picture in your mind what you want to accomplish,"* Lyra advised.

Closing her eyes in concentration, she imagined a beautiful rainbow arcing from her jewel. She reached for Lyra. "Okay, here goes."

*ZzzaPPP!*

A beam of light shot from the jewel straight above the ring. Fireworks of rainbow sparkles exploded in the air, making everyone duck.

Kara struggled to control her jewel.

Lyra and Goldie tried to help with their own magic, but theirs was like a sprinkle of raindrops on a forest fire.

*They want magic, I'll show them magic!* Everything seemed to fall away as the white-hot center of Kara's magic flared to life. Power rushed through the very fabric of her being. Diamond fire spun around her body, engulfing her in dazzling spirals. She was a tower of blazing light.

Somewhere through a curtain of bright fire, she saw people running away, horrified by the outburst of such immense power.

Suddenly panic tore through her. Everything she feared about her magic bubbled to the surface and erupted over. She could not hold it—could not control the power.

Screaming, Kara staggered backward, stumbling against Lyra. A jagged bolt blasted from her jewel, sending the crowd scattering.

Pixies dove to the ground. Dwarves rolled head over boots onto outraged fairies, while trolls caught startled hobgoblins flying through the air.

Kara's magic slammed into the bleachers, slicing

through three layers of seats. Uprooted toadstools sent smoldering spotted caps bowling over a group of boggles.

Trying to keep away from the crowd, she spun. The magic smacked into the large mirror, splitting into rainbow shards, and ricocheting everywhere.

A scream of anguish came from behind her. She whipped around to see Lyra bombarded by rainbow fire, turning green, red, orange, purple, and finally blazing silver.

*"Kara!"*

"Lyra!" Kara shrieked, her stomach burning with panic. Desperately wrenching her magic back, she slammed the fire downward, razing deep slashes across the center of the ring.

"Stop!" Kara screamed. The unicorn jewel suddenly dimmed.

Kara wobbled unsteadily. Lyra! What had she done? Instead of warm orange and black fur, the cat had been transformed into shining silver. Mouth half-opened in a roar, tail held high, Lyra was a frozen, lifeless statue.

"Extraordinary," the Dwarf Queen declared, looking closely at the frozen cat.

"Wow, look at that!"

"She's good to go!"

The crowd broke into excited cries.

Kara burst into tears.

"The girl has obvious power," the Fairy King bellowed, examining the smoking trenches that now scared the ring. "Raw, but impressive."

"Calm, child," Queen Selinda said. "Now turn your friend back."

"I . . . I don't know what I did!" Kara wailed, a distressed Goldie crying on her shoulder.

"Quicksilver," Raelda concluded, examining the frozen cat.

Kara watched in horror as a drop of glimmering silver melted from Lyra's tail and landed in a small puddle on the ground. "What's happening to her?"

"She is melting," Raelda explained unsympathetically.

Kara looked at the crowd through blurred tears. "How do I turn her back?"

The Goblin Prince knelt, studying the Lyra statue. "Tangoo, what say you?"

Kara looked at the young boy: tall, lanky, and—green.

"Hmmm." Tangoo looked over the frozen cat. "I haven't seen this kind of spell in years, Prince Lorren."

"How long do we have?" Selinda asked.

"A day, maybe more," the sorcerer replied casually. "Once the cat melts completely there is no way to counter the spell. But," he added emphatically, "a very powerful gem like the power crystal would cure her for sure."

Kara gulped. This couldn't be happening. But one look at Lyra, melting into the scorched earth, and she knew it really was.

"I suggest we proceed immediately, my lady," Tangoo stepped forward, adjusting his long robes.

Kara's stomach lurched. If he expected her to use magic again, she had no idea what would happen. But she *had* to find the power crystal now!

"The elemental fairy horse is ready and waiting," Tangoo said excitedly. "All she has to do is ride it."

"With such a powerful steed, she will become an even stronger magic magnet," the Elf Queen mused. "The power crystal will surely be drawn to her."

"I can do that," Kara said immediately, so relieved, she almost laughed. This was her big magic thing? Lyra would be cured in no time.

"An excellent idea," the Fairy King approved. "We are all anxious to finally see the horse you have created."

Tangoo smiled smugly. "You will not be disappointed."

"I rode a unicorn across the magic web," Kara boasted, holding out her jewel but quickly pulling it back as the crowd gasped. Giving the kings and queens her best winning smile, she faced the Ring. "I'm an excellent rider. Of course I can ride some cute little fairy pony."

The Fairy Queen addressed the other monarchs.

"We will give Princess Kara twenty-four hours to find the power crystal."

"Agreed. But if the girl fails," the Goblin Queen said, her glimmering green eyes glaring harshly, "we will meet on the battlefield."

The trolls and dwarves rumbled in agreement, but the elegantly dressed Goblin Prince looked queasy, his green eyes wide with fear.

"It will not come to that," the Fairy Queen said confidently. "The blazing star will not fail."

"She has one day!" the Dwarf King said. "Our armies will be ready."

Kara's head was pounding. If she hadn't turned Lyra into a melting statue, she could've walked away from all this and figured out how to get home by herself. She could regroup with Emily and Adriane and they'd work out a plan, like usual. But now she had no choice. She had to save Lyra.

# Chapter 4

**"I**t's about time!" Ozzie, the golden brown ferret, had been nervously pacing Kara's front lawn, waiting for Emily and Adriane to show up.

"What's the scoop?" Adriane asked as they quickly made their way up the walkway to the Davies's large tudor home.

"Kara's parents left," Ozzie reported, adjusting the leather collar that secured his golden ferret stone. "Her brother is still inside. Rasha, Ronif, and Balzathar report no activity from the Ravenswood portal."

"So this portal is isolated to Kara's closet," Emily mused.

"She does have a knack for attracting magic," Ozzie continued.

"Any sign of other strange visitors?" Adriane asked, hoping they wouldn't be surprised by other portal-openings.

"Not so far. Dreamer's been canvassing the

grounds." Ozzie waved a paw at the large black wolf pup emerging from the trees.

Dreamer, a mistwolf and natural magic tracker, trotted to Adriane's side, his rich ebony coat shining in the sun. On his chest, a star of snowy white matched the white bands on his paws.

Adriane ran her hand over her pack mate's smooth fur. "What'd you sniff out?"

Scrunching his long nose, the mistwolf's voice echoed in the others' minds. *"Something smells terrible!"*

"Gah!" Ozzie sniffed under his arm. "My shipment of ferret shampoo is behind schedule!"

Emily gave the ferret a stern look.

Adriane hid a smile and nodded at the others. "Let's go." She rang the large brass doorbell.

Almost instantly, the double doors swung open. "Hark, what wind through yonder doorway breaks?" Kyle, Kara's older brother, was doing equal opportunity damage to a chocolate Pop-Tart and Shakespeare. He grinned at them. "Forsooth, it's the odd squad."

"Charming as always, Kyle," Adriane quipped.

"Hey, boy, how you dooin'?" Kyle ruffled Dreamer's head. "What are you feeding him—he's huge!"

"Pooot toots!!" Fred and Fiona squeaked inside Emily's backpack as she struggled to hold it in place.

"Say, you finished with that?" Ozzie asked, eyeing the half-eaten Pop-Tart in Kyle's hand.

"What?" Kyle was confused: Who just said that?

"I said is Kara finished . . . getting ready?" Emily covered up, pushing Ozzie behind her and pointing to his magical ferret stone. He was supposed to use his jewel to speak telepathically when around others.

"The princess is upstairs," Kyle said, wiping sugar sprinkles and wolf saliva from his shirt. "Hey, guess who's here?"

"Who?" Emily asked, anxiously peering beyond Kyle.

"Joey. You've *got* to see his costume!" Kyle walked back toward the kitchen.

"Joey?" Adriane said incredulously. "I just left him backstage. He was setting up the lights—"

"Oh, so that's why you were hanging out in the auditorium," Emily teased, walking into the foyer.

Adriane's cheeks flushed bright red as she followed. "Not! Joey asked me to help him, that's all."

*"It's in there."* Dreamer pointed his nose toward the kitchen.

Adriane raised her wrist to check her amber wolfstone. The gem was not pulsing. "I don't sense anything dangerous."

"Just be careful." Emily checked her own rainbow jewel. Although hers reacted to animals in distress, it, too, would warn her of impending danger. "These are the first creatures to cross over in months," she continued anxiously. "No telling what kind of magic they have."

The mages entered the kitchen and stifled gasps of shock. A strange-looking boy—really strange— was at the breakfast table, greedily pouring a bowl of cereal into his mouth. Dressed in a weird pirate costume, which included aviator goggles and tan knee-high boots, no one would guess he was human. Which, of course . . . he wasn't.

Two dragonfly heads popped out of Emily's backpack. "Oooo, Froot Loops!"

The costumed creature turned big gray eyes to the group and, "SplOOOF!" spit out the cereal in shock. The bowl crashed to the floor as he leaped to his feet, reaching into his wide utility belt for several colored vials.

"Goblin!" Ozzie yelled, then quickly slapped his paws over his mouth and telepathically added, *"It's a goblin!"*

Adriane instantly swung into a fighting stance, crossing her arms in front of her face. Dreamer crouched to strike, teeth bared, a deep growl rumbling in his throat.

"Mistwolf!" the creature screamed, edging backward and knocking into Kyle.

"Freeze, goblin!" Adriane hissed, her jewel pulsing with restrained fire.

"I'm not a goblin!" The creature raised his hands, eyeing the glowing jewel with fear. "I'm a *hobgoblin!*"

Kyle howled with laughter. "Shakespeare is way cool!" he said, slapping the startled hobgoblin's shoulder.

Emily gently pushed Adriane's arms down. "So, Joey," she said carefully, sending calming magic to Dreamer. "Nice of you to . . . drop in."

"I came for the princess! She is—"

"Yes," Emily cut him off. "We all want to find the princess."

The hobgoblin's eyes narrowed suspiciously. "The reward is already claimed."

"Dude, you're way too into this play," Kyle chortled.

"My name is not Dude," the hobgoblin said, still eyeing the mages warily. "My name is Musso."

HONK! Honk! HONK!

A series of brisk beeps sounded from the driveway, followed by the ringing doorbell.

"There's Kara's ride," Kyle said, jumping to answer the door. "What's taking her so long?"

The minute Kyle walked away, Adriane demanded, "Listen you, whoever you are! Where is our friend?"

"The princess is in the Queen's Fairy Ring," the hobgoblin blurted.

"No she's not, she's in some forest!" Adriane countered.

"Uh-oh." Musso scratched a pointy ear. "The porta-portal must have misfired."

"Who else is with you?" Emily asked.

"Sparky—he's a magic tracker. We are great adventurers. Perhaps you've heard of us?" Musso puffed out his chest. "We rode the web to get the princess."

"You mean kidnap her!" Adriane snapped.

"Yeah!" Ozzie added.

"PhhooooL!" the dragonflies chimed in from inside the backpack.

"How do we get her back?" Emily asked the hobgoblin.

"The portal is moving," he squawked. "I can't tell when it will open again."

"Hark, what reeky, clay-brained, dewberry arrives?" Kyle called from the foyer.

"Stay here!" Adriane warned the hobgoblin.

" 'Course, my calculations could be off—the web is totally flooie," Musso explained. "I have to find the nearest portal!"

The mages raced through the foyer just as Kyle opened the door, bowing deeply. Sparkling fairy wings, silky outfits, and expertly applied glittery makeup twinkled in the morning sunlight.

"I do believe in fairies. I do beliv—"

"Zip it, Kyle," Heather said, stepping past him. "Where's Kara—"

"What are *you* guys doing here?" Tiffany asked. Her pale green brow furrowed as she looked at Emily, Adriane, the golden ferret, and the large black wolf pup.

"Uh, just here to check on Kara," Emily explained.

"Shake a wing, girls," Molly said impatiently, heading for the stairs. "My mom's already late for work."

"Kara's sick," Emily said quickly. "You *really* don't want to go up there."

"She is?" Heather said.

"She is?" Adriane echoed, then caught herself. "Oh, totally."

"She's got a stomach ache," Emily blurted—

Just as Adriane blurted, "Really bad pimple. On her stomach."

"We talked to her, like, fifteen minutes ago, and she was fine." Tiffany swept past Kyle, her pale yellow wing smacking him in the face.

"We'll tell her you were here," Adriane promised, blocking the stairs.

"Jeez, you guys are weirder than normal," Heather said as she and Tiffany and Molly edged past Adriane and trotted upstairs toward Kara's room. "We'll tell her ourselves."

Emily and Adriane ran after them, Dreamer following close.

"Look, it's probably just a little stage fright,"

Tiffany said, her hand already on the door to Kara's room. "She asked us to pick her up."

The mages winced as she flung the door open.

Kara's room was empty.

"K, you in here?" Tiffany asked, scanning the cluttered mess.

"*Zzzrrrrp.*" A sleepy grunt came from a lump under Kara's fluffy pink and white quilt.

Adriane pushed past the trio and dashed inside, pulling the covers down tight as the lump began squirming.

"Hey girl, what's wrong?" Molly asked.

"*FooaaaRTT!*"

"Bad taco," Adriane yelled as she struggled with the lump.

"Oh Kara, you sound awful!" Tiffany exclaimed.

"You poor thing!" Heather added.

Emily gulped as she saw Barney and Blaze sitting frozen in a pile of Kara's stuffed animals.

"She got sick, like, so totally fast," Tiffany said worriedly.

HONK! HONK! HONK! HONK! HONK!

"Come on, my mom's waiting!" Molly waved a painted green hand.

"Kara, you just rest up," Tiffany said.

"*BlaaaaPHH!*"

"See, she's feeling better already," Adriane said, smiling.

"We'll check on you later," Heather called out.

"She'll probably be taking a long nap," Emily said, "so just leave her a message."

"Bye!" Emily, Adriane, and the d'flies chorused, cheerful smiles plastered on their faces.

As soon as Heather, Tiffany, and Molly closed the door behind them, Adriane yanked the quilt back. A long, whiskered nose popped out, attached to a big, fuzzy head.

"What are you trying to do, smother me?" the mookrat demanded, whiskers twitching. His beady eyes widened as he saw three magic jewels trained on him.

"Ahhh!" He dove back under the covers.

"Come out of there," Emily said. "We're not going to hurt you."

"Much," Adriane added.

The mookrat stuck his nose out again and took in the group. "Sparky's the name," he said, quivering voice muffled by the quilt. "Magic's my game."

"We just heard the news," said a new voice from Kara's window. A little figure made of twigs and moss was perched atop a beautiful white owl.

"Just in time, Tweek," Emily exclaimed, walking over to the little Earth Fairimental. "Hi, Ariel," she greeted the magical snow owl.

The owl ruffled her feathers, displaying shimmering streaks of gold, lavender, and turquoise. *That is not Kara,* the owl observed, liquid eyes looking accusingly at Sparky.

"It's the mookrat who kidnapped Kara!" Ozzie informed her, glowering.

"We were hired to find her," Sparky protested, pointing his nose toward Kara's closet. "We followed the portal into that chamber."

Tweek leaped from the owl and dashed into the closet. Lifting a sparkling turquoise jewel from a chain about his neck, he started scanning Kara's shoes. "Hmmm, magical residue."

"Stay here with Barney and Blaze!" Adriane ordered the EF and Ariel. "If this mookrat moves a whisker, you call us."

"We have to get that hobgoblin," Emily said.

*"There's one,"* Ariel said, perched on the windowsill.

"What?"

The group rushed to the window. In the driveway, Kyle was climbing into Molly's mom's minivan. Musso clambered in behind him, hands poised by his utility belt full of strange vials. He slid the door closed just as the minivan pulled out of the driveway.

"Oh no!" Emily groaned. "Kyle's taking a hobgoblin to school!"

❧   ❧   ❧

Kara followed Queen Selinda, King Oriel, and Tangoo along a path surrounded by bright wildflowers. The path wound through the gardens, leading to the fairy stable.

The Fairy Queen led Kara to a beautiful stall made of glossy green ivy and daisies. Inside, a pale green horse with bright flowers in her lustrous mane stuck her head over the half-door and nuzzled the queen's face lovingly.

"This is Gaia, an Earth Elemental Horse," the Fairy Queen said, laughing as the mare turned curious azure eyes to Kara.

*"Welcome, blazing star."*

Kara smiled and petted Gaia. The animal's strong magic was warm and pure. She instantly felt a little better. Everyone had acted like this was going to be such a big deal, but she could totally ride this nice horse. Lyra was going to be saved even sooner than she'd hoped.

"Should I just ride her now?" Kara asked.

Selinda shook her head. "Gaia is my horse. Elemental horses only bond with one rider."

"Oh." Kara was a little disappointed, but there were probably pretty horses just like Gaia in the other stalls.

King Oriel reached into a stall of gleaming crystal to pet a powerfully built silvery blue horse. "This is Frost, a Water Elemental Horse. We've been bonded since I was a child."

*"The blazing star will make a strong rider."* Frost's sapphire eyes regarded her thoughtfully.

Kara smiled, then frowned. Frost was bonded to

the Fairy King. She wasn't going to be riding him, either. Where was *her* elemental horse?

*Boom!*

A huge blast shook the corridor, followed immediately by loud cries and snorting from somewhere outside the stables.

Queen Selinda walked straight toward the commotion, leaving the stables through the rear doorway.

Kara followed. Out back, a dark and ominous stall stood isolated from the others. Kara couldn't tell exactly what the structure was made of, but it looked like thick gleaming black glass. It was completely enclosed except for a small window set in the front door.

Tall fairies standing guard yelped as a jet of fire erupted from the open window.

Goldie quivered and grabbed a talon full of Kara's hair to hide behind.

Whatever was in there was angry. Best to keep away from that one, she thought.

The door buckled as something slammed into it from inside. An eye, wide with terror, appeared in the small window. Kara felt a jagged bolt of fire rip through her body, as if her blood were boiling. She gasped, feeling her magic swirling inside, climbing to a fever pitch—it felt like it was going to explode!

Then in an instant it vanished. The window was empty.

"What's in there?" Kara asked breathlessly. "A manticore?"

Tangoo grinned proudly. "This, Princess Kara, is *your* horse!"

# Chapter 5

The Stonehill Middle School auditorium buzzed with activity. Backstage, it was jammed with costumed students preparing for dress rehearsal. It wasn't going to be easy for Emily and Adriane to find their runaway hobgoblin.

"Our fairies are here," Adriane noted dryly, pointing to center stage.

Molly, Heather, and Tiffany were putting finishing touches on the Fairy Ring set. It was decorated with bright silk flowers and papier-mâché toadstools, with a backdrop of painted forest trees.

"Whatsup?" Joey—the real Joey—approached, carrying a box of lightbulbs. He smiled broadly at Adriane. "Good call on the bulbs—the ones I was using were way too low wattage."

"Cool," the warrior answered, still scanning the auditorium.

"What foul news!" someone cried in a loud, grating voice. "Our Fairy Queen hath fallen ill! We cannot read this scene without Queen Titania!"

Incoming: Rae Windor, student director of the

play. She glared at the mages, irritation blazing in her steely eyes.

"Alack, poor Kara," Emily called out.

Rae grasped her frizzy brown hair and scowled at Joey. "Whither wander you? You're playing Puck and you're onstage in five minutes! Get ready!"

Joey shrugged. "I gotta change. See you guys later." He hurried off stage right—just as Musso emerged from stage left with Kyle.

The hobgoblin's eyes widened as he took in the scenery. "A Fairy Ring!"

"Hark! Shall I compare thee to a brick outhouse?" Kyle quoted from his Make Your Own Shakespeare Insults book.

Rae glowered. "That is so not hilarious."

"Sure it is. Right, Joey?" Kyle asked the hobgoblin.

Rae's eyes widened. "Forsooth! That's the fastest costume change I've ever seen. You'll make a perfect Puck."

A fairy rushed across the stage. "Have you the heard news about the Fairy Queen?"

"Everyone's heard," a girl dressed in a toga chimed in dramatically. "She is deathly ill."

"The queen is sick?" cried the hobgoblin. "This is terrible news! Not with the fairy wars brewing!"

Adriane and Emily needed to run interference. Fast. They hurried over. "Joey, could we speak to you for a minute, alone?" Adriane asked.

Kyle stepped back, grinning. "Don't let me get in the way of true love, Romeo. Break a leg."

"Break your own leg!" Musso grumbled angrily.

Rae grabbed Musso. "Joey, stand in for the Fairy Queen in this scene."

Musso flailed as Rae dragged him onstage "But it's illegal to impersonate royalty! I'll be turned into a flobbin!"

Emily and Adriane tried to snatch Musso back, but Rae raised her hand imperiously. "Only actors onstage! Places, everyone." She clapped, herding Molly, Tiffany, and Heather. "Mustardseed, Peaseblossom, Cobweb, into position."

"Where's Nick Bottom?" Rae looked around as she pushed Musso to center stage.

"Ready, milady." Marcus, a friend of Kyle's, was playing the role of Nick Bottom, the character in the play who turns into a donkey after a spell is cast on him. He stopped next to the mages. "I heard Kara has some rare disease!"

"Oh, great," Adriane said, and rolled her eyes.

"What Fairy Ring is this?" Musso gaped as he stepped onto the fake flowerbed. "Where's the magic mirror?"

"Stick to the script!" Rae yelled. She gestured to another boy standing offstage. "King Oberon, front and center! Okay, now this is your big scene, where you cast a love spell on Queen Titania. And when Nick Bottom comes out, he'd better be wearing his donkey costume. Got it? And . . . action!"

Adam, a cute eighth grader dressed in the flowing robes of a fairy king, adjusted his golden crown and stepped onstage.

Musso yelped, diving face first while grabbing the boy's legs. "O great Fairy King," the hobgoblin groveled. "I have traveled the web and found the Fairy Princess."

"Hey man, take it easy, Joey!" Adam hopped up and down, trying to shake Musso loose.

Rae got frantic. "People! Stop adlibbing!" She shoved Musso facedown into the bed of silk flowers. "Stay there and don't move!"

Musso lay in the flowerbeds, eyes darting left and right. "The Fairy Ring has been infiltrated," he mumbled.

Adam cleared his throat and read his lines in a loud, clear voice.

" 'What thou seest when thou dost wake,
Do it for thy true love take . . . ' "

Musso dug frantically in his utility belt. "I must protect the Fairy Ring!"

" 'Pard, or boar with bristled hair,
In thy eye that shall appear. . . . ' " Adam recited.

Musso held out a small, round vial. It glowed briefly.

"What's he doing?" Adriane asked, startled as her wolf stone pulsed, signaling danger.

"He's using some kind of magic!" Emily exclaimed.

"The fairies will reward me generously for dealing with spies!" Musso cried out.

" 'When thou wak'st, it is thy dear.

Wake when some vile thing is near.' "

Musso lobbed the glowing green orb at Adam. "I'll show you a vile thing!"

Racing over from the wings, Adriane and Emily swung their wrists up. Glimmering gold and blue light streamed toward the stage, shielding the unsuspecting Adam from whatever Musso's spell was about to do.

With a *twink*, the green spell ricocheted off the mages' shield and flew offstage.

"Very cool lighting, Joey." Adam gave him props. "Really rad."

"That was close," Emily said, letting out a breath as the shield faded.

*PooF!*

A flash of green light erupted offstage.

"Uh-oh." Adriane grimaced.

"Okay, Nick Bottom, you're on!" Rae ordered.

"HEE-HAW!"

A loud donkey bray echoed throughout the auditorium, making everyone jump. Marcus stumbled onstage, tugging at the ears on his donkey-head costume.

"Excellent!" Rae said. "Best interpretation of a jackass I've seen since Kyle Davies. And . . . action!"

"HeeHawww!" Marcus tried to read a line, stumbled across the set, tripped over Musso, and flew backstage next to Adriane and Emily.

"Marcus, are you okay?" Adriane asked.

"Never better, why?" He scratched his ears and continued to read his lines. " 'I see their knavery.' "

Adriane tried to pull off his mask. It wouldn't budge.

" 'This is to make an ass of me, to fright me, if they could.' HeeHaWW!" brown fur covered Marcus's shoulders and arms.

"Musso's spell!" Emily's hand flew to her mouth as she watched Marcus's tail swish behind him.

"It turned Marcus into a real donkey!" Adriane cried.

❧    ❧    ❧

Kara watched anxiously as the black glass cage was pushed into the riding arena on huge rollers. Rocky walls several stories high circled the stadium. The arena bleachers were filling fast with the kings and queens of the Fairy Realms, and all their entourages.

"Everyone will be perfectly safe when the shield goes up," Oriel reassured Kara.

Safe from a horse? She bit her lip. "What kind of horse is this?"

"He is a fire stallion," Tangoo replied proudly. "One of a kind, forged from the very heart of elemental fire magic."

"Do not worry, Princess," Queen Selinda murmured. "The stallion cannot get out."

"Neither can I," observed Kara.

"I have faith in you," the queen said as she gracefully headed toward her seat.

As the guards placed the glimmering cage and its angry occupant into the center of the arena, Kara thought about the Firemental that had once paid her a visit in the Ravenswood Library. Composed of free-flowing elemental magic, the creature was dangerous and unstable, but it had helped her. How she wished she were back in the warmth of that room now, safe with her friends.

She looked to the brave little dragonfly on her shoulder. "Goldie, I want you to leave—"

"Stay with Kaaraa!" the dragonfly protested, gripping Kara's shoulder.

"Thank you," Kara said softly, petting the mini's head. She was grateful for all the magical help she could get. In fact . . . "Goldie, can you call Fiona?" Kara asked. She held her jewel tightly. "I need to talk to Emily, and fast!"

"Okieee-dokieee." Goldie positioned close to Kara's ear, softly squeaking a series of beeps. "Kaaraa for emeee," the mini whispered.

Kara heard an answering peep.

"Hello?" Kara said tentatively.

"Kara?" Emily's voice floated near Kara's ear, surprised and relieved.

The blazing star jumped. "Emily, it's me!" Kara whispered into Goldie's yellow belly.

"Are you okay?" Emily asked.

Kara fought back tears. "No! I turned Lyra into a quicksilver statue, and she's melting!"

"Oh no!" The healer's voice echoed with concern.

"I don't have much time. I have to bond with an elemental horse to save Lyra," Kara explained hurriedly. "What should I do?"

"Deep breath, Kara," Emily urged her friend. "Magical animals love you. You've already bonded with Lyra, the dragonflies—not to mention half the unicorn population."

The fire horse snorted and kicked wildly inside his cage. Kara gasped for air. "That's different."

"No, it's not," Emily continued, calm but firm. "Trust is everything. Open yourself. Feel what the horse is feeling."

Kara let out a long breath. "Okay."

"Kara, we'll get you home! Don't panic—"

"Good luck, Princess, you'll need it!" the guards yelled, fleeing the arena.

Sparkling beams crisscrossed the air, forming a

glittering dome that enclosed the arena. It was some kind of force field trapping the horse inside. And Kara with it.

"Emily!" Kara cried urgently, but the connection to her friend was lost.

With a violent flash, the front of the black cage fell away.

"Ahhh!" Goldie dove behind Kara, who staggered as intense heat blasted from the open stall. Something seared through her, piercing her mind, burning away any resistance she could offer. Then a wave of power broke over her, pulling her down as if she were caught in a riptide.

A blur of bright orange surged from the stall and flew across the sand. Choking, her eyes watering, Kara squinted through clouds of dust and smoke.

Beyond the shield, the crowd surged to its feet, awed by the sight of the powerful creature.

He was huge—almost twenty hands high. Blazing plumes of flame swirled from his body. He snorted, and smoke billowed from flared nostrils. Hooves of molten lava pawed the sand; strong legs nervously danced. His crackling mane and tail thrashed fire. Kara struggled for breath. She had seen many magical creatures, but the thing standing before her was beyond her wildest dreams.

The horse was made entirely of fire.

The stallion's wild eyes, smoldering like golden coals, turned—and caught Kara in an iron grip of power. She stumbled forward as diamond fire erupted from her jewel, running up her arms and swirling around her body.

Kara hadn't meant to retaliate, but her magic tore across the sand and slammed into the stallion. Rearing in defiance, fire exploded from his body. Searing heat practically singed Kara's hair as the creature towered above her and Goldie.

"I'm sorry," she cried to the stallion. "I can't stop it!"

A second bolt from Kara exploded like fireworks, sending the stallion staggering back.

With all her might, Kara willed her jewel to stop.

"Nice horsie," she croaked, clinging to Emily's advice. Open yourself. Kara stepped forward.

The horse reared back.

*"Stay away from me!"* the stallion's voice roared through Kara's mind.

She felt the sheer force of the horse's rage surging through her own body. The stallion raced around the perimeter in a blur of reds and orange.

This is good, she told herself, trying to calm her mounting terror. Any breakthrough is good.

Grasping her unicorn jewel tight, she thought of Lyra. Kara always felt so protected, so safe, when her friend was near. Gathering her courage, she advanced toward the horse.

He snorted and backed away, stirring trails of scorched earth.

"I know you don't trust anyone," Kara said soothingly, willing the stallion to feel the friendship she was offering. She pleaded with all her heart. "But my friend is hurt, and if I don't ride you, she is going to die."

The horse held steady; he did not back away this time.

Encouraged, she took a step closer.

"*I am fire!*" the horse thundered.

The unicorn jewel flared white-hot in her hands as a whirlwind of feelings bore into her like a drill. Hopelessness, fury, confusion, pain, and overwhelming sadness.

"*I run alone!*"

Trails of fire streaming from his mane, hooves, and tail, the horse charged straight toward her.

The crowd broke out in pandemonium, yelling in fear for the girl.

Before Kara could think, the stallion was on her. She screamed, and diamond fire erupted from the unicorn jewel, slamming into the horse with the force of a cannon. The horse fell headfirst, sending dust and debris flying as it dug a smoking trench into the ground.

"I'm sorry!" the blazing star cried, tears streaming down her dirt-streaked face as the horse staggered to his feet.

Somewhere through the buzzing in her ears, she heard the crowd panicking.

"That's enough!"

"Get her out of there!"

"She'll be killed!"

Guards were running toward them, long spears with sparkling blue tips held high.

"No!" Kara screamed. "Leave him alone!" She reeled, half-blinded as the magic swelled inside her. She struggled to separate her feelings from the stallion's, but he bore down harder, overwhelming her. Kara's heart threatened to break apart as the horse's despair filled her being. She *was* the stallion, trapped, desperate, and alone.

More than anything, she wanted to be free.

Kara's eyes locked onto the stallion's. The truth hit her.

The stallion couldn't control his immense power—just as she could not control hers.

The unicorn jewel erupted, blasting diamond fire into the shield in an explosion of blinding colors.

"Stop! Please!" she cried out. But the magic kept flowing, stronger and stronger, as if there were no end to the ocean of power within her. Kara swooned, terrified. Without Emily and Adriane at her side, she was losing herself.

The shield exploded in splinters of light, disintegrating as horrified onlookers scrambled from the bleachers.

The fire stallion leaped to freedom, fiery muscles

careening over the fleeing crowd in a single bound. Like a flash of lightning, the horse vanished.

The last thing Kara realized before she blacked out was that she was lying on the ground, Goldie circling overhead frantically calling out her name.

# Chapter 6

**K**ara was floating. Long, golden hair swirled around her head as she bobbed gently upon a sea of night. Stars winked faintly, falling in and out of focus.

"Still trying to play with your magic," a familiar voice chided.

The stars pulsed and formed a shifting kaleidoscope. Though fragmented, Kara could make out three figures. They were all draped in long dark cloaks, cowls covering their heads.

One was large, an unnatural bulk shifting beneath the robes; one was tall and lithe, her long, silver hair streaked with jagged lighting. The third—Kara gasped, repulsed by the image of a large cockroach. Oily wings jittered. Antennae twitched.

"How did you find me?" Kara croaked as she tried to crawl away. A shiver ran down her spine.

"My dear girl." The voice was calming, engulfing, drawing her in. "You so underestimate your power. It is like a beacon. No one else could possibly have that signature."

*Kara reached for the shifting rainbow lights, but it was like trying to grasp smoke.*

*"There's so much more to magic than talking to cute animals, isn't there?"*

*Kara flashed on Lyra, melting away. Her fault. She didn't deserve magic.*

*"So many willing to risk everything for a taste of your power," the Dark Sorceress said softly. "Everyone uses the blazing star."*

*Kara could almost feel the cold breath in her ear.*

*"Until there is nothing left."*

*Soon Lyra would be nothing. Kara struggled to move.*

*"Don't you worry your pretty little head. We're going to help you."*

*Above her, the light blossomed, forming an exquisite flower. Kara struggled to reach its spreading petals—*

*"Just as you will help us."*

—and opened her eyes, disoriented. Her heart pounded as she struggled to unwind herself from her voluminous costume. Where was she? She was safe at home, dreaming, in her own comfy bed! Relieved, she smiled and rolled onto her back. And looked up startled. Twined tree branches, golden and shimmering like sunlight, lined the ceiling. This wasn't her room at all.

Urgent whispers broke through her jumbled thoughts. Someone was in here with her.

"What if it's a sleep spell?" a chirpy voice asked worriedly.

"Oh no! That could last a hundred years!" another voice, this one high-pitched, exclaimed.

"That's absurd! She's not enchanted," a third voice added.

"I think she's up!"

"Someone go look."

"No way. I'm not messing with that fairy dragon."

Kara lifted her head from a lavender-scented silken pillow and looked around. Her eyes found Goldie patrolling the foot of the big bed, marching back and forth.

"Goldie," Kara rasped.

Startled, the d'fly squeaked and leaped. "Kaaraa!" Goldie dove, clasping her wings around Kara's neck in a tight embrace.

"I'm so happy to see you," Kara said, hugging her little friend tight.

Kara noticed the walls and floor were made of the same interwoven trees as the ceiling. Here and there lush bluebells and foxgloves peeked between the golden bark, brightening the room with rainbow-hued petals. Thick rugs in vibrant colors covered the floor.

"Goldie, what's happened?" Kara asked. "What am I doing here?"

"I told you it wasn't a sleep spell," a voice whispered.

"Who's there?" Kara demanded, instinctively grabbing her unicorn jewel. She swung her feet to the floor and carefully stood up, surveying the room. But no one else was there.

She walked to the open double windows. Outside, the moon was rising, casting a silver sheen over the magnificent fairy gardens. She must have been out for hours. She remembered now. She was stuck in the Fairy Realms, and had failed to bond with the fire stallion. The Fairy Realms would go to war, possibly destroy each other—and the worlds she loved—and Lyra would melt into nothing.

"Look at that jewel!"

Kara went rigid. The voices were louder now, closer.

A large oak vanity table carved from an entire tree grew straight up from the floor. A chair sat before it, facing an oval mirror ringed with purple heather. Kara caught her reflection and grimaced. The girl staring back at her was a mess! She was covered in dust and grime. Her hair was matted in a tangle of knots. Her Fairy Queen costume was ripped and filthy.

"Stop squirting me, Whiffle!"

"Oh, I can't stand it!" another voice whispered loudly. "I'm delirious with excitement."

Kara rubbed her eyes. The voices seemed to be coming from the top of the vanity table. Was she still dreaming?

An odd assortment of accessories lined the top

of the vanity below the mirror: a jade green brush, a silver comb with long handle, a gold clamshell mirror, and a quivering white powder puff.

"For a second there I thought *they* were talking," she muttered to Goldie, shaking her head at the ridiculous idea.

Goldie nodded. "Uh honk!"

Or not.

Suddenly the big white powder puff launched itself from the vanity top and flew at Kara's face in a sparkly white cloud.

"Ahhhh!" Kara ducked. The powder puff collided in midair with Goldie.

"Eeeeee!" the mini screamed, furiously flapping sparkly powder-coated wings as she and the powder puff plummeted downward. Goldie landed on the puffball, releasing a lushly scented cloud. Kara watched in amazement as the powder puff wriggled like an excited puppy.

"Bad Puffdoggie!" a voice scolded.

Now who said that?

Kara gaped in disbelief. The silver comb walked across the dresser on two legs formed by its long handle! Glowering at the shaggy powder puff, the comb cleared its throat and took a deep bow. "A thousand apologies, Princess, and allow me to say I am shocked by this most unseemly behavior."

"Whoa, what are you?" Kara blurted.

"We are designed to serve the Fairy Princess," the silver comb said proudly. "My name is Angelo."

"What if that's not she?" the clamshell mirror wailed, and snapped shut.

"Of course it's she, Mirabelle!" the green brush shouted at the mirror, exasperated.

"Well, yeah, I guess I am, that is . . . ," the blazing star stammered, twirling the diamond-bright unicorn jewel between her fingers. "My name is Kara, and this is Goldie."

"We've been waiting a hundred and twenty-five years to serve a Fairy Princess! I'm so happy I could cry!" Mirrabelle started bawling.

An atomizer spray bottle shaped like a skunk shuffled along the table. "I am Whiffle, and I shall make you smell divine." The glass skunk squirted an amazingly lush perfume from his nose.

The brush pushed the atomizer away, hopping up and down on her handle "Can't you see the princess needs immediate attention!"

"Skirmish, calm down," the silver comb said, sighing. "That's why we're here."

Kara self-consciously ran fingers through her tangled tresses. "It's been, like, hours since I even brushed my hair."

The accessories gasped in horror.

"Tell me about it," she said.

"This is no way to welcome our new princess!" Angelo scolded the others, trying to move them back in an orderly line. "Forgive them for not following protocol, Princess Kara, but Queen Selinda ordered us into service on such short notice."

Puffdoggie hopped up and down excitedly, sending sparkling powder flying.

Oh, this is great, Kara thought. Locked away in a tree house with a bunch of enchanted toiletries! Could things get any stranger?

THWAP! BoNnk!

Without warning, a scraggly, bespectacled flying creature zoomed through the open window, smacked into the far wall, and landed in a crumpled heap on the floor.

"Ow."

"Oh!" Kara rushed over and knelt by the creature. "Are you all right?"

It looked vaguely like an owl, with a combination of dark gray fur and moss green feathers. Long, floppy ears drooped forward, half-covering luminous yellow eyes.

Goldie immediately stepped between it and Kara.

The bird straightened his small glasses. Dazed yellow eyes wobbled and then focused sharply on the dragonfly. "You are the Fairy Princess Kara?" he demanded querulously.

Goldie pointed at Kara.

"Oh." The bird reached into a leather shoulder pouch and withdrew a rolled-up piece of black parchment tied with a dark purple ribbon. "I had to try three windows before I found this one!" the creature huffed, struggling to his feet and handing Kara the scroll.

"Thank you, um . . . ," Kara began. "Who are you?"

"Alwyn, Secret Fairy Air Delivery, Second Division," the creature supplied, then continued his complaints. "Royal deliveries are most difficult. You never know what kind of fairy guards are out there!"

"Would you like something to drink?" Kara gestured to a table on the opposite side of the room, piled high with brightly colored fruits and a large bowl of sparkling purple liquid.

"Don't mind of I do," Alwyn grumbled, heaving himself into the air. He landed with a giant splash in the middle of the punch bowl and sighed happily. "Ooo, that feels good."

The enchanted accessories gathered around as Kara slipped the ribbon off the parchment and carefully unrolled it. Glowing purple and silver calligraphy shimmered from the black paper:

**MIDNIGHT MASQUERADE RAVE**
**TONIGHT @ THE FAIRY ISLE—BY INVITATION ONLY**

"A party!" Skirmish shrieked, falling off the table in her excitement.

"That's no ordinary party, it's a fairy rave!" Whiffle cried eagerly.

"Yaaaay!!" The accessories all jumped up and down.

"Who sent this?" Kara asked the strange bird.

"Turn it over," Alwyn answered, floating on his back and gargling

Kara flipped the invitation over. On the back was a handwritten note: *If you want to help Lyra, meet me at the rave. The Forest Prince.*

The Forest Prince. He'd saved her life, but everyone at the Fairy Ring had called him a thief. Could she trust him? And a secret midnight rave didn't sound exactly aboveboard. Still, if he could tell her how to help Lyra . . .

Alwyn hauled himself out of the bowl and leaped to the windowsill. "Back to work—I still have many more invitations to deliver. Your ride will pick you up at eleven-thirty sharp." With that, the bird fell out the window and dropped like a stone. "Ahhh, wet wing, wet wing!"

"Wait!" Kara cried, running to the window as the gray and green creature careened crookedly across the fairy gardens. She turned, stomped back, and flopped facedown on the bed.

"Are you going?" Mirabelle asked excitedly, her small round mirror flashing.

"Look at me," Kara cried into the pillow. "How can I possibly go to a party?"

Angelo and Skirmish leaped onto the bed and began inspecting the princess up and down.

"Hmmm, yes, this is a challenge," Angelo concluded, and snapped to attention. "Puffdoggie, prepare the princess's bath at once!"

The powder puff bounced into an adjoining room. Kara heard water filling a tub.

"I can't wear this," Kara groaned, "and I don't have anything else." She flopped backward on the bed. Her beautiful dress was ruined.

"If you will please follow me, Princess." Angelo jumped off the bed and walked to a golden door in the left corner of the room.

"A Fairy Princess closet?" Kara could totally go for that. There were bound to be dozens of gorgeous gowns in there.

She flounced over and flung the door open excitedly.

"It's empty!" she wailed, looking inside the vacant, white-walled closet.

"Well, of course it is!" Skirmish said. "Step inside and tell it what you want!"

"No way!" Kara walked inside, Goldie chirping excitedly on her shoulder.

The closet expanded, instantly surrounding them with gleaming walls. The rest of her bedroom disappeared, leaving only she, Goldie, and the enchanted accessories in a bright white void.

Kara cleared her throat and said, "I want a costume."

In a burst of twinkles, a black and white cow costume appeared and rotated slowly in midair.

"Hee heee," Goldie chuckled.

"Not *that* kind of costume!" Kara said.

Mirabelle snapped open and closed. "The princess needs beautiful dresses!"

The cow costume disappeared, and dozens of glittering ballgowns of various designs and colors twirled before her wide eyes. This was more like it.

"No, no, no! Be gone!" Skirmish commanded.

The rows of dresses vanished, and Kara frowned, dismayed.

"She needs something different, something that will make her really stand out in a crowd!" the brush continued.

Another burst of twinkles morphed into an outrageous orange sequined suit with a pair of stilts.

Kara and Goldie looked at each other and shook their heads dismissively.

Angelo clapped his feet. "Something in a more classic style!"

A drab dress of dark blue with a high collar and straight skirt rotated in the air.

"Much better," the comb said happily. "Elegant and understated."

"And boring," Kara commented. It was time she took things into her own hands, now that she saw how this worked. Standing in the center of the closet, she called out, "I need a ballgown in violet silk, with an embroidered bodice, long sleeves, and a dropped A-line skirt."

A richly colored dress materialized and spun in the air. It looked exactly as Kara had envisioned it.

"Marvelous!" Skirmish cried.

"Inspired!" Angelo exclaimed.

Puffdoggy barked in agreement.

"Wait!" Tapping fingers to her lips, Kara considered. "It needs something else." She put her fashion sense into overdrive. "Emerald, sapphire, and yellow topaz beading along the bodice."

"Ooooo." The accessories swooned at the swirling patterns of glittering gems.

The color theme gave Kara another idea. "Peacock feathers along the back of the neck and embroidered on the cuffs, and a violet satin mask with peacock feathers to match."

Kara's alterations magically appeared, until the most amazing dress she'd ever seen twirled gracefully before her eyes.

"She is a genius!" Whiffle cried. "An auteur!"

"I *so* have to get one of these closets at home," Kara exclaimed, overawed.

"Shoes!" Goldie squeaked.

"How could I forget the best part?" Kara gratefully hugged the mini. "With matching purse!"

By the time she was through, she had a pair

of purple satin slippers with two-inch-high square heels, each glittering with a jeweled peacock feather.

"Amazing!" Mirabelle whispered. "Your fashion magic is unequaled in the Fairy Realms."

"And on Earth." Kara bowed.

"Come, we must bustle!" Angelo clapped his feet. "Princess, in there!" Angelo pointed his comb-teeth to the steam-filled bathroom and the large golden tub in its center. "The rest of you"—he pointed to the others—"let's get busy!"

The accessories quivered with excitement as they prepared Kara's magical makeover.

Once totally scrubbed and squeaky clean, Kara sat in a fluffy pink robe at the vanity, munching on sweet fruits and flaky pastries. Skirmish dove into her hair with a wild cry and twirled among her tresses, creating gorgeous looping curls on the right side of her head. Angelo combed the left side straight until it gleamed like a sheet of gold. Comb and brush glared angrily at each other when they saw what the other had done, and started tussling.

Mirabelle flapped open, and iridescent sparkling eyeshadow soared out, dusting Kara's lids. The eyeshadow's opalescent shine highlighted her blue eyes perfectly.

"And now for the dress." Kara disappeared behind a vine-covered dressing screen in the corner of the room and emerged a moment later. She reached up to the curls piled high atop her head.

"No!" Skirmish cried. "I've been fighting tangles all my life, and I know what's what. Don't touch anything!"

Kara smiled, tugging free a lock at her temple. It spiraled down, gently framing her face.

"Except that!" Skirmish was beside herself. "You are a diva, my lady!"

"One final touch." Whiffle spritzed a pink mist. A wonderful scent of jasmine enveloped Kara, with a hint of citrus to balance the sweetness.

"It's incredible, Whiffle!" Kara exclaimed.

"I know," the crystal atomizer sniffed. "I call it 'Morning Pew.' "

Carefully arranging the peacock mask, Kara surveyed the final effect. The rich colors of her dress set off her gleaming blond hair and sparkling blue eyes.

"Hey, where's Goldie?"

The closet door swung open, and Goldie appeared, decked out in a glittering silver and gold lamé tuxedo, complete with a feather mask.

"Perfect!" Kara squealed, clapping her hands.

Unable to control themselves, the accessories burst into a rousing cheer as Kara and Goldie pirouetted in front of the mirror.

"Da bomb!" Skirmish and Angelo cried happily— for once in absolute agreement.

Something darker than the night alighted just outside the window. Large as a horse with shimmering black wings, a giant bat creature turned bright green eyes to Kara.

"Princess, your ride is here," Angelo announced.

Kara nodded. She was ready to go.

# Chapter 7

Kara gripped the leather saddle as the large bat creature sliced through thin clouds into silvery night sky. Below were lush forests, and every so often, mysterious glades hidden in star shadow. Dark mountains ringed the distance, hugged by billowing clouds, deep and thick barriers at the edge of the world.

With a slight rumble, the bat ducked its head and swooped low, gliding over a huge lake that gleamed like liquid moonlight. In the distance, a mist-shrouded island rose from the luminous waters. Ablaze with lights, the isle twinkled like a floating jewel.

The bat glided onto smooth silver stones near the lakeshore, setting down neatly between a giant Pegasus and a flying carpet. Music echoed across the still waters.

"Thanks." Kara patted her steed's leathery neck as she slid to the ground and straightened her dress. She looked up in awe. Hordes of costumed creatures were entering through a crystal archway. She had no idea what kinds of creatures hid beneath the elaborate disguises and sparkling masks; it was probably just as well.

Relax, Kara told herself. Parties were her natural environment. If anyone knew how to handle a tricky social situation, it was her.

"Let's get this party started," she told Goldie and walked briskly through the arch—and straight into the wildest party she had ever seen! Music thundered, pounding across the open glade. Floating fairy lanterns strobed deep colors across a mass of costumed fairy creatures rocking out on the dance floor. The place was jammed!

"Goldie, see if you can spot mystery guy," Kara said, searching high and low among the costumed throngs.

The d'fly took off just as dozens of small winged fairies glided over Kara, dusting her with twinkles of lights. Goldie twirled in the air, spinning and tumbling happily.

"GaK!"

A large, clawed hand grabbed the d'fly in a huge scaly fist. Goldie burst into sparkles and vanished.

"What do you think you're doing?!" Kara's temper flared red hot, her jewel pulsing dangerously inside her dress.

"I caught a fairy dragon," a massive lizard creature chuckled, revealing a long set of sharp teeth.

"That's *my* fairy dragon!"

"Fe, fi, fo, fum. I smell magic, gonna get me some." The giant creature advanced menacingly, making Kara cringe. Its thick neck and torso were covered in black leather studded with chrome buckles and spikes.

"I smell something worse." Another lizard monster loomed over her, blocking any escape. "A *human* with magic!"

A golden bubble popped behind Kara. Goldie walked up her shoulder, straightened her tux and stuck out her tongue.

"Who invited you here?" the first creature sneered, fanged smile shining wickedly.

"I did." The Forest Prince materialized from the crowd, smiling. His silver sword glittered dangerously in its sheath.

The creatures snarled, but stepped back.

The masked boy bowed. "My lady, would you do me the honor of a dance?"

"Totally," Kara breathed, grabbing his outstretched hand.

He led her onto the crowded dance floor, where disguised creatures of all shapes and sizes whirled, spinning and dancing among the flashing lights.

"Friends of yours?" Kara asked.

"Bulwoggles," the Forest Prince said, moving to the thudding beat.

"I thought fairies were all cute and sparkly." Kara stood checking out the crowd.

"They're not fairy. They're creatures that feed on darker magic, like werebeasts or demons."

"What do they want?" Kara asked.

"What do you think?" he nodded at the silver necklace around Kara's neck. "Ever since the web went wild, more and more creatures have come here searching for magic. They're the bad guys, not me."

"Everyone seems to think you steal magic too." Kara glared.

"A lot of stuff gets blamed on me. That's okay, as long as I can help those who need magic most."

"So, sometimes bad is good, huh," Kara commented.

Goldie was frolicking in milky moonbeams, sommersaulting with a small flying bear-like creature wearing a tutu and a pirate hat.

"Goldie's made a new friend," Kara said, watching the pair chattering up a storm.

"That's Spinnel, an evolved form of fairy dragon," the boy explained.

Kara regarded the strange assortment of creatures. It felt like they were all eyeing her, checking her out. It gave her the creeps. "Your note said I could help Lyra," she said adamantly. "Where is she?"

"In the goblin castle," he said spinning away. "But I really brought you here to convince you to go after the fire stallion."

"Ride it yourself," Kara said, annoyed. Had he

lured her here just for her magic? No way was Kara Davies putting up with that! She bolted.

"This is a rough crowd, don't go wander— Princess?" The Forest Prince stopped in mid turn, looking around. "Wait." He ran to her side, grabbing hold of her arm. "It's the only way to help Lyra."

Kara stopped short, cheeks flushed with anger, acutely aware of his fingers on her arm.

"She's at the goblin castle being treated by Tangoo," he said quickly, removing his hand. "But I don't trust him."

"Why should I trust you?" Kara asked suspiciously.

Green eyes shone from behind the black mask as he stared deep into Kara's eyes. "You are the blazing star. You defeated the Dark Sorceress."

Kara went rigid.

"But now she's working with two dark fairy creatures. One is an elemental magic master, the Spider Witch, the other is . . . something else."

Fear inched along Kara's spine. How much did he know about her real connection to the Dark Sorceress?

"I think they're working to escape the Otherworlds," he told her.

"And you know this how?"

"I work with the fairy underground, a secret group organized to fight them. According to our information, something big is going down. Mirrors have been popping up all over the place, strange creatures roam the lands, and magic is in very short supply." He looked around and continued. "The Spider Witch had one of the power crystals, but foolishly used it to try and capture a herd of young unicorns."

"My friends and I stopped them," Kara said.

"Yes, you did." The boy's eyes twinkled in admiration. "Now they seek another one, here in the Fairy Realms. You have to find it first."

"The only thing *I* want," Kara said hotly, "is to help Lyra!"

The Forest Prince continued as if Kara hadn't spoken. "Rumor has it, the Spider Witch is going to attempt to reweave the web. Starting with the Fairy Realms."

"Is that even possible?" Kara couldn't picture it.

"The power crystals control the magic of Avalon itself. I'm not willing to take that risk, are you?"

Kara gulped. She had failed to ride the fire stallion. How was she supposed to find the crystal all by herself, with only Goldie to help her?

"We have to keep moving," the boy said, scanning a suspicious group that was pushing through the crowds. Kara recognized the yellow slitted eyes of bulwoggles as they locked on hers.

"We must leave before the stroke of midnight," he said worriedly, trying to find the exit.

"What happens at midnight, you turn into a pumpkin?" she quipped, then gulped. The bulwoggles were making their way right toward them. "What now, mystery man?"

The largest bulwoggle pushed masked dancers aside and stomped toward her. But before it had taken two steps, a red and green striped bunny-like creature with dragon wings flew in graceful figure eights around the lizard. Glimmering circles on the creature's body shimmered like a collection of magic gems.

"Out of my way, Elfan," the bulwoggle snarled.

"Let's Bulwoogie!" Elfan grabbed the bulwoggle and started dancing away.

Suddenly loud chimes echoed across the glade.

"We're too late!" the boy's voice held an edge of desperation.

"Fairies, trolls, and hobnobblers!" A voice broke over the speaker system. "Amaze your friends, shock your date, it's time to take off your masks and reveal your true identities!"

"I see," Kara smiled wickedly. "What's your rush?"

"On my count . . ." The DJ continued.

Giggles of excitement ran through the rave as the crowd eagerly prepared to take off their masks.

". . . one, two, go!"

Masks flew high in the air as dwarves, sprites, gnomes, and dozens of other fairy creatures revealed their own grinning faces.

"It's not much of a surprise anymore," Kara said, taking off her elaborate peacock mask, blinking ice blue eyes at the boy.

The Forest Prince gasped. "Only a fool would not be stunned each time he beheld your beauty."

Kara blushed. "Stop stalling. Your turn," she ordered.

He leaned in close and smiled.

Kara reached up and untied the black silk mask. His green eyes twinkled as she pulled it away.

"Hey!" she exclaimed.

He was wearing another black mask, exactly the same, underneath it.

Kara looked to Goldie, widening her blue eyes. The d'fly immediately understood Kara's thoughts and casually flew by the Forest Prince's shoulder. With one swift flap of her wing, Goldie snagged the second mask and ripped it off.

"You!" Kara gasped.

"You!" the bulwoggle sneered, towering over Kara.

"You!" Goldie squealed to the flying bunny.

"Hello," the bunny smiled.

The boy snatched the mask and turned away, quickly tying it around his face again.

It was the Goblin Prince, Lorren! But the handsome boy looked nothing like the primly dressed goblin she'd seen earlier that day in the Fairy Ring. 'Cept they both were green.

"What is going on?" Kara began, wondering what game Lorren was trying to play.

The bulwoggle chuckled, eyes flashing eagerly as it reached for Kara. The others appeared behind her, separating her from Lorren.

"Unhand that princess!" Lorren grabbed the bulwoggle and spun it around.

Razor teeth flashed as the creature roared, taking a swipe at the boy with a massive fist.

Lorren easily dodged the blow. He turned, giving the creature a kick in the rear, sending it flying. But the others were on him, locking his arms behind his back. The first bulwoggle towered over the boy, ready to rip his head off.

"Let him go!" Kara commanded.

Lorren and the bulwoggles stopped.

The blazing star stood, arm raised. In her hand, the diamond-white unicorn jewel pulsed with power.

Lorren groaned. "Oh great."

The bulwoggles' eyes flashed with hunger.

Kara held her gem with trembling fingers. Uh oh, maybe this wasn't such a good idea, she thought, surveying the mass of magic starved creatures around her.

"It's only a girl," the bulwoggle taunted.

Kara felt the hot rush of power flowing through her as the jewel erupted with blazing white magic. The bulwoggle howled as its angry companions dove out of the way.

"Kaaraaa!" Goldie's claws dug into her shoulder.

The d'fly's voice snapped Kara back to reality. She had to get control of her magic before she lost herself completely in the swirling brilliance of her own power. Screaming with the effort, she wrenched the magic back.

The crowd of costumed creatures stared at her in shocked silence.

A cluster of fairies zipped above her head, forming a bright blue spotlight. Her jewel pulsed, draping her in shards of sparkling diamond magic.

"She's got a jewel!"

"Magic!"

"It's the blazing star!" squeaked a pixie, hopping so excitedly her pickle costume fell off.

Costumed creatures shoved and pushed each other, everyone trying to nose in and get a good look at Kara and her magic. The Forest Prince began ushering her to the door. A riot was about to break out.

"Take a picture!" Kara cried, holding up the sparking gem. "It'll last longer."

Jagged lighting split the skies over the isle as clouds swirled. A gust of wind howled through the rave. Discarded masks skittered across the floor and fairy lanterns bobbed in midair.

Something flew from the clouds, spinning like a whirlpool. It glided down, skimming over the heads of the crowd. Partygoers yelled and cheered. The swirling light came to a stop and landed right in front of Kara, expanding as it spun in rainbow spirals. This was no light show. It was a portal.

"Kara!" Emily's voice echoed through the portal. "Can you hear me?"

"Emily!"

"Jump through," Emily screamed.

The portal followed Kara as she turned and moved away.

"Not without Lyra!" Kara yelled, backing away from the snarling bulwoggles.

"This might be your only chance," the healer's voice echoed desperately. "Tweek doesn't know if it will open again!"

"Give me the magic!" the bulwoggle leader roared, his crazed eyes locked on Kara's jewel.

"Stay away from me!" Kara shrieked.

"What?!" Emily asked, startled.

"Not you, the bulwoggle!"

"Bulwoggle?!" Ozzie screamed from the other side of the portal.

The bulwoggle lunged, huge muscled arms outstretched.

"Stay back," Lorren yelled. Sword in his hand, he took on all three bulwoggles, trying to keep them from Kara.

Something rattled in Kara's purse.

"I gotta go. I have a situation."

The bag burst open and Mirabelle flew out. "I

couldn't stay away, let me reflect your radiant beauty—*arkq!*"

A giant clawed hand swiped at the clamshell mirror sending her spinning as Puffdoggie sprang out. It hit the bulwoggle in the nose with an explosion of twinkly puff powder.

"AhhHHH ChOOOO!"

Mirabelle, Puffdoggie, and Goldie tumbled head over heels as the bulwoggle staggered backwards.

"Oh no!" Kara watched in horror—as the vicious lizard creature fell into the swirling portal and vanished.

Kara waved her arms, trying to swat the portal away from the dance floor. The portal veered crazily on its axis and dove sharply into the screaming crowd. Three more creatures were sucked in before she could send it airborne again.

"We have to get out of here before the entire rave falls through!" Lorren yelled.

"Whooo! This rocks, dude!" A dwarf whirled skyward and vanished into the portal.

"Let's get out of here!" Lorren yelled.

Stuffing Mirabelle and Puffdoggie in her purse, Kara grabbed Goldie and ran after the prince. The portal followed, zipping overhead.

Troves of trolls dove out of the way, overturning the food stands

Together, princess, prince, and dragonfly charged through the mists and out of the archway, skidding down to the water's edge.

Hordes of enraged creatures poured from the archways, chasing them.

"You sure know how to show a girl a good time," Kara commented.

"Thank you." Lorren let out a piercing whistle.

With a whoosh of giant wings, the goblin bat swooped out of the night. The crowd ducked and rolled to avoid the huge wings. A clipped bulwoggle went flying face first into the muddy bank. Lorren took a running leap, grabbed hold of the saddle and hauled himself up.

Lorren reached out his hand. "Shall we escape?"

Kara hesitated. Her new friend was not only an outlaw, but also a goblin. But bandit or not, she had to trust someone.

Grabbing Lorren's hand, she swung into the saddle behind him. In a flash, the bat was airborne, the Fairy Isle shrinking far below. The portal followed, zipping into the sky, trailing after them.

"Emily!" Kara squashed Goldie to her ear. "Come in, Emily!"

But all she heard was screaming, crashing, and the sounds of her room being completely trashed.

# Chapter 8

The spinning portal shimmered and glowed like a small sun in Kara's closet. Everyone had stepped away, huddled in the center of the room except—

"The portal's opened!"

Musso and Sparky barreled for the bright circle.

"Incoming corporeal particles transporting across the astral planes!" Tweek announced, focusing his jewel like a magnifying glass at the edges of the swirling hole.

"What?" Musso asked, running by the little twig figure.

"Something is coming thr—*aaArgghk!*"

A mass of scaly muscles crashed through the portal, sending Musso and Sparky flying back into the bedroom.

Roaring with fury, the bulwoggle destroyed a row of Kara's summer dresses with one deadly sweep of its claws.

"A bulwoggle!" Musso cried, crawling onto the

windowsill, fumbling with his utility belt to free a few spells. "Mercenaries! The war has started!"

Tearing a pile of pink sweaters off its head, the lizard creature stomped into the bedroom. "What place is this?" it bellowed.

"Go back!" Adriane yelled, as she and Dreamer stepped in front of their friends. "You don't belong here!"

Yellow slitted eyes moved from the snarling black mistwolf to the golden magic sparking from the warrior's wolf stone.

"I will take that magic!" it bellowed, eyes shining wide.

Adriane spun and kicked the closet door closed. Twisted hangers shot from the closet as the beast smashed the door back open, crushing Tweek into a mass of moss and twigs.

Ozzie dove under the bed as Spinnel suddenly barreled out of the portal, smacking into the back of the bulwoggle's head.

Trying to pry the bear creature loose, the bulwoggle rampaged across Kara's room, wreaking havoc.

Dreamer leaped, locking teeth into the monster's leather armor, spinning around the room in a wide circle. He crashed into Musso, sending the hobgoblin's fistful of spells flying. Magic splattered against the shelves, covering two stuffed bears, a hippo, and a moose. The stuffed animals twirled to the ground in a fluffy tangle of limbs just as a flailing dwarf flew from the portal and crashed through the canopy of Kara's bed.

"Whoa, dude! Is this the VIP room?" the dwarf hung upside down as the ripped material caught his feet.

"I will swallow your magic, and you with it!" the bulwoggle roared.

"Eat this!" Adriane yelled, Dreamer at her side, Fred and Fiona on one shoulder, Barney and Blaze on the other, lending their magic to her intense golden fire.

"Beeeeat it!" the d'flies chorused.

Golden wolf fire slammed the beast right in its armored chest. The bulwoggle tottered and fell across the bed, bringing the canopy down with it. The bedspring collapsed, and the bed crashed to the floor.

"Hey, keep it down up there!" Mrs. Davies's annoyed voice floated up the stairs.

A screaming bunny with dragon wings hurtled from the portal and bowled Ozzie into Kara's stereo, sending CDs flying.

"Sorry!" Emily answered Mrs. Davies, her stone glowing bright blue as she grabbed Ozzie out of the way of Elfan. "Just helping Kara rehearse!"

A red, yellow, and blue fox dressed like Robin

Hood in green tights and cape stepped from the closet and bowed. "Cotax, fairy underground. May I be of some assistance?"

"What is this, a convention?" Ozzie exclaimed, sliding across the floor on loose CD cases.

"Roll it up in the quilt!" Adriane commanded.

The mages, Ozzie, the d'flies, Dreamer, Spinnel, Elfan, Cotax, and Kara's stuffed animals all jumped on the roiling lump entangled in the large quilt.

"Your friend has caused quite a scene at the rave." Cotax smiled, holding down the monster's thrashing tail.

"Leave it to Kara to find a party," Adriane commented as she and the others lugged the rolled-up creature back toward the closet.

"Give me that magic!" The bulwoggle mumbled, now wrapped like a mummy in Kara's quilt.

"The portal's shrinking!" Tweek yelled, sticking his flattened twiggy head dangerously close to the flashing circle.

Together, the group heaved the screaming quilt into the closet.

The bulwoggle fell into the portal, Kara's blouses and sweaters tangled on flailing scaly limbs.

"Hurry!" Emily shouted, herding the fairy creatures toward Kara's closet.

Elfan, Cotax, and Spinnel dove through, the dwarf charging behind.

"Thanks for the party, dudes."

Sparky ran at top speed, Musso right on his heels.

But just as the dwarf disappeared, the portal shuddered and vanished.

"Gaahdooooff!" Sparky and Musso hurtled through the suddenly empty space and smashed nose first into the back of Kara's closet.

"I see stars . . . ," Musso said dreamily, sliding down the wall into a heap.

"Tha webbbb ith bootifull," Sparky slurred, and collapsed nose first to the floor.

"Tweek, is it going to open again?" Adriane asked anxiously.

Everyone gathered around the little Fairimental as he raised his turquoise gemstone and scanned the closet. After a tense moment of silence, he smiled broadly.

"No problem," the EF said, riffling through holographic numerals. "It should open again in about three years!"

❧   ❧   ❧

Lorren's gloved hand gently clasped Kara's as she slid from the bat's saddle into the fairy palace bedroom window.

"Thanks for a great time!" She tossed her bag onto the dresser.

"Hmph!" Goldie snorted, then flew into the room, shaking off her costume.

"Hey, it could have been worse. We could still be

raining fairy creatures all over the kingdoms," Lorren quipped.

"And my Capris with them!" Kara turned her eyes down. "I'm sorry. I didn't know that portal would follow me."

"Hey, I'm sorry, too," Lorren said, then paused. "If I'd known the rave was going to be so dangerous, I never would have asked you there."

"At least it wasn't boring," she answered, smiling, but then frowned as she looked up into his masked face. "Prince Lorren, or whatever I should call you."

He touched the edge of his mask absently. "The Fairy Realms are in real trouble. I can't work with the underground if everyone knows who I am," he explained, then smiled. "Besides, my parents would lock me in the dungeon if they knew what I was doing."

"Maybe your parents would like the Forest Prince," Kara suggested.

"Were yours thrilled when you told them you were a mage?" he countered.

"Well, I, um, I see your point," Kara stammered. None of the mages had told anyone—who'd believe them?

Lorren nodded. "Ironic, isn't it? I have to hide who I am so I can be myself. You should understand my secret better than anybody, blazing star."

Kara gazed into his pale green eyes with new understanding.

"Look, I have no right to ask you, but if you still want to go after the fire stallion, I can take you to Tangoo," he said, gathering the bat's reins.

"But you said you didn't trust him."

"It was his idea to combine the blazing star with a firemental horse to attract the power crystal. If anyone knows how to find the fire stallion, it'll be he." He looked at her, waiting.

Kara wondered if she should trust Lorren. It was all so confusing. But if he'd wanted to hurt her, he could have left her to the bulwoggles. Instead, he'd risked himself to save her. And if he had secret-identity issues, well, so did she.

The boy turned away, bowed his head, and raised the reins, about to fly off.

"Lorren," Kara called out as the bat moved away from her window.

"Yes, Princess?" He turned, his face a silhouette rimmed in starlight.

"See you tomorrow."

Kara watched him glide over the gardens until the darkness swallowed him.

"He's cute!" Skirmish broke the silence, clattering across the vanity table.

Kara's purse wiggled and fell open. Mirabelle flopped open on the dresser. "What a party!"

Puffdoggie burst out barking, sprinkling powder over Angelo.

"This is completely against regulations!" the comb cried to the stowaways. "You really rattle my teeth!"

"They were a big help," Kara called as she walked from the bathroom, wrapping the fluffy robe around her.

"Well?" Whiffle asked Kara, huffing a cloud of lilac. "Details, we need details."

Kara flopped onto the bed, exhausted. "Bulwoggles, flying bunnies, riots, random portals, secret identities—everything a girl could want."

"Ooo!" Skirmish shouted, leaping up to brush out Kara's hair. "How were the snacks?"

"Shhh, Skirmish, can't you see she's tired?" Mirabelle scolded.

Kara sunk into the big pillow. Tomorrow she would visit the Goblin Castle and Tangoo. But what if Lorren was wrong? What if the sorcerer couldn't help? Lyra would melt into nothing, all because Kara couldn't control her magic. Then she'd be trapped and alone in the Fairy Realms, in the middle of a war that could destroy everything she loved. Even if by some remote chance she found the fire stallion, how could she bond with it? Her magic sure didn't work last time. And how could she possibly find the power crystal? What if the Dark Sorceress got her hands on it first! Hot tears stung her eyes. Why was all this resting on her shoulders? If only she'd never had magic in the first place, this never would have happened.

Goldie nuzzled into Kara's neck.

"Goldie, can you call Fiona?" Kara asked, petting the d'fly's soft, golden hide.

The mini settled next to Kara's ear and sent a series of squeaks to Fiona.

"Kara?" Emily's voice asked.

"Hi," Kara sniffled. "Anyone miss me?"

"Everyone. How are you?" Emily asked.

"I dunno," Kara answered quietly. "How's my room?"

"Well, Blaze and Barney are redecorating, but everything's quiet, finally. Ozzie took Musso and Sparky to Ravenswood for the night—"

"I messed up so bad," Kara cried, words suddenly pouring out. "If I lose Lyra, I don't know what I'll do. I'm not strong like Adriane. And the fire stallion hated me. I don't know what to do!"

"Kara," Emily said gently. "You can't change what happened. There's so much we don't know about our magic."

"Yeah, but your magic *works*. I don't know what mine is supposed to do, except make a giant disaster out of everything. I wish I didn't have it at all!" Kara started sobbing.

The enchanted accessories clambered onto the bed, trying to calm the princess, brushing and spritzing everywhere.

"Your magic is part of you now, Kara," Emily said. "Wishing you didn't have it is like wishing you weren't yourself. We all know there's only one Kara, and that's the way we like it."

Kara hiccupped a bit of laughter. "Guess I'm stuck with me no matter what."

A strange beeping noise blared from Goldie.

"Hold on, call waiting," Kara said. She poked Goldie's belly, making the d'fly giggle.

"Kara, are you there?" Adriane's voice asked worriedly.

"Hey."

"How you doing?"

"Better, thanks, I'm on the other line with Emily," Kara said. "Let me see if we can do a conference call."

Goldie gurgled, and Kara heard the other two mages talking through their dragonfly phones.

"I'm glad you called, Adriane," Kara said.

"Where did all those creatures come from?" the warrior asked.

"Long story short, I went to a fairy rave with the masked mystery guy," Kara said. "The portal followed me. "And guess what else?" Kara rolled onto her stomach, propping herself on her elbows, knees bent, feet in the air.

"What?" Emily asked.

"He's really the Goblin Prince Lorren in disguise!"

"No way!" Emily and Adriane chorused.

"Totally."

Emily giggled. "You're dating a goblin!"

"Somebody get Mrs. Davies a Valium," Adriane said.

"And get this, Lorren is totally cute!" Kara exclaimed, then felt herself blushing. "I mean, he's like, different from other goblins we've seen."

"No warts?" Adriane asked.

"No." Kara paused, feeling a sudden smile spread over her face. "He's just like a real boy."

"So what if he happens to be green," Adriane added.

"Yeah, so, anyway," Kara continued seriously. "I have to find the power crystal to save Lyra."

"And you need the fire stallion to get the crystal?" Emily asked.

"Yeah, Lorren thinks this goblin sorcerer can help me find the horse. Supposedly the combination of our magic will draw the power crystal to me."

"Magic attracts magic," Emily concluded.

"What if I can't . . ." Kara's words faded.

"Listen to me, Kara," Adriane said firmly. "You're not going to lose Lyra. Okay?"

Kara sniffled again. "Okay."

"We'll cover for you tomorrow at the play," Emily reminded Kara.

"I totally forgot! Someone is bound to notice me missing."

"We'll figure it out," Emily assured her. "Get some rest. Fiona and Fred are here if you need us."

"Okay, guys. Thanks."

Kara lifted Goldie from her ear, breaking the connection. She hugged the d'fly close, clinging to the words of her friends and the strength of their magic.

# Chapter 9

Kara stood in the bright morning sunlight, Goldie on her shoulder, taking in the expansive Fairy Gardens. Elaborate pathways wound through, fountains, gazebos, and floating fairy bridges. But here and there delicate flowers were fading, their once vibrant colors washed and pale, leaving a feeling of emptiness throughout the gardens.

The golden sun felt too hot, and Kara removed her dark blue jacket trimmed with white fleece, tucking it under her arm. She'd chosen a very fashionable riding outfit from the closet this morning, complete with tan suede riding pants tucked into knee-high leather boots and a white silk blouse. Her long blond hair was pulled back into a ponytail, her unicorn jewel blazing on its necklace against her tan skin.

Goldie squeaked and pointed.

In the distance Kara saw what looked like a rainbow cloud sweeping over the gardens. It was dragonflies, dozens of them in every conceivable color, leaving sparkling trails like miniature crop dusters.

Goldie squeaked and pointed.

"That's an amazing fairy dragon you have."

Kara turned to see Queen Selinda approach, regal in a flowing golden gown. She gave Kara a smile. "I've never seen one bond with anyone. They are usually so independent."

"Goldie's special," Kara said, scritching between the mini's ears.

"As is her bonded." Selinda smiled.

"What's happening here?'" Kara asked as they walked under a purple and white willow whose branches drooped with withering leaves.

Selinda sighed. "Not even the fairy dragons can keep the gardens alive. The heart of the magic is fading."

"But if magic is flowing wild everywhere else, why is it fading here?" Kara asked.

"That is precisely why. Avalon's magic should flow here first, then to the web, and then to all other worlds. But now that's not happening."

Kara looked at the gardens. "Then this is all my fault, too."

"Aldenmor would have perished if you had not released the magic of Avalon," the queen explained. "You did what was needed."

"I messed up, as usual." Kara's eyes were brimming with tears. "Look what I did to Lyra."

Selinda wiped slender fingers across Kara's face, drying her tears. "We don't really know what happened, do we?"

"I . . ." Kara replayed the moment in her mind. She'd been using her jewel and something had gone wrong. Her magic had reflected off a mirror and hit Lyra. "So maybe that wasn't my fault?" Kara asked, mulling over the possibility. Could the mirror have altered her magic?

"I don't know, Kara. But I do know that humans who bond with magical animals make the most formidable magic users."

"I didn't do so well with that horse," Kara reminded the queen.

"It's a Firemental," Selinda said, as if that explained everything. "A very bold plan from Tangoo. Some might even say desperate."

Looking out over the grand gardens, she continued. "Magic is our most precious resource, part of a delicate ecosystem connecting us to the web and all other worlds. Each of the kingdoms and all the different fairies and fairy creatures that live here help to make magic stronger."

"Even the goblins?" Kara asked, trying to imagine the hot-tempered Goblin Queen spreading magic for the good of the worlds.

Selinda's fine features tensed. "The goblins and fairies have had their differences, but they have been terribly manipulated by the Dark Sorceress. I know Raelda wants the best for her kingdom, and I would like to think we could become friends. But if we have to go to war to save the Fairy Realms, we will."

Kara thought of Lorren. Was she his friend or his enemy? Whose side was *she* on, anyway?

Seeing Kara's troubled expression, the queen fell silent for a moment as they walked toward the Fairy Ring.

"I heard there was quite a party last night on the Fairy Isle." The queen raised an eyebrow, a twinkle in her eye.

Kara gave the queen a quick glance. "I, um . . ."

"Angelo filled me in." The queen smiled.

Kara frowned. Ooh, that big mouth comb!

"Fairy raves are very much a part of us," Selinda explained. "Music, dancing, and creative expression are what we live for. Although in these times, raves can be dangerous."

Kara glanced at the queen. "I'm sorry I snuck out."

"Evidently you had good company."

"He's not what he seems," Kara said quickly.

"Now that's your fairy blood speaking," Selinda chuckled softly. "Many things are not what they seem in the Fairy Realms."

"Wait, how can I be part fairy? Does that mean my family is, too?"

Selinda shook her head. "Fairy blood skips human generations but is particularly strong in you. You are directly descended from Queen Lucinda, the greatest of all Fairy Queens." `

"Tell me about her," Kara asked.

"She was a great leader, a blazing star. She truly believed in the goodness and magic of all living things."

"What happened to her?"

"She had a sister."

Kara stiffened. The Dark Sorceress.

They walked into the empty Fairy Ring, heading through archways of yellow and red flowers swaying gently in the breeze.

Selinda smiled, her violet eyes searching Kara's troubled expression.

"I wish I had all the answers for you, Kara. In a few hours, this ring will be filled again with the kings and queens from the other kingdoms and we must decide the future of the Fairy Realms. And perhaps the future of the web itself."

Kara looked in Selinda's eyes. They were full of compassion.

"You do not have to stay here against your will.." The queen paused. "You have a legacy of great goodness, and also of darkness. But your path is your own."

Kara steeled herself. There was only one path for her right now. "Queen Selinda, I'm going to save Lyra."

"Then you must go to the goblins."Queen Selinda waved her hand to the grand mirror by her throne. ""You *are* the one we've been waiting for. Be strong and proud of who you are."

"Thank you. I will." Kara stepped to the mirror and held up her jewel. It blazed with the mighty power of the unicorns. The image swirled, spreading like circles in a stream. Kara put her hand up and slipped it through the glass. Before she could change her mind, she stepped through and vanished.

❧　　❧　　❧

On the other side of the mirror, Kara found herself in a bustling courtyard in the center of a huge castle. Towering walls surrounded her. She looked over the ramparts and gasped. The enormous castle was built of gleaming gray stone, perched on a cliff overlooking amazing waterfalls that plunged straight down into clouds of white foam. In the distance the landscape was covered with thick forests, deep blue lakes, and gray boulders that lay on surging green hills like sleeping giants.

"Good morning, Princess." Lorren ran to greet her, his voice slightly high and nasal. "Welcome to Castle Garthwyn!" he said proudly, smoothing his deep blue tunic. Sweeping his velvet cap from his head, he bowed deeply. Spiky black hair with green highlights stuck out over pointy ears.

Lorren the Goblin Prince was nothing like Lorren the Forest Prince. A gleam in his green eyes was Kara's only hint of the dashing outlaw in black she had come to know. But which was the real Lorren?

"Lorren!" a loud voice echoed throughout the courtyard.

He tensed, turning toward his mother, Queen Raelda, who charged down the castle's steps, looking angry as a thundercloud.

"Is this any way to welcome the princess!" the stout green woman demanded. "Princess Kara, we are honored to have you here." Raelda curtsied formally, making Kara uneasy.

"The honor is mine, your highness," Kara returned with a bow, not knowing what else to do.

"So, you have decided to continue on your quest." Raelda guided Kara up the grand stone steps leading to the castle's enormous wooden doors. Crystal torches lit the cavernous entryway.

"Yes, ma'am."

"Good, good, you have guts. I like guts."

Goblins paused in their duties to nod respectfully to their queen, some even smiling shyly at the blazing star. Kara smiled back, amazed. She didn't feel anything but curiosity from the Goblin folk here.

"Terrible business with that horse," Raelda fretted.

"Frankly we had our doubts Tangoo could pull this off. Firementals are so unpredictable."

"Queen Raelda, thank you for helping Lyra," Kara said to the queen. "She means more to me than anything. I'm very grateful to you."

Raelda's eyes softened. "I am familiar with familiars." She eyed Goldie, raising an eyebrow as the fairy dragon grinned. "The fact that you are here, ready to keep trying, shows me what you are truly made of, Princess."

She stopped and looked Kara directly in the eye. "But make no mistake. I will do what I must to save my kingdom." Then she turned and walked away. "Good luck. May the magic be with you."

"This way, Princess." Lorren led Kara to an elevator door on the right end of the entry hall. "Impressive, you did good," he said, smiling.

"You think?"

"You're still here." Lorren whisked Kara into the elevator and pulled the winch. Gears turned noisily as the car rose.

"How is Lyra?" Kara asked.

"I won't lie to you," Lorren said slowly, as the elevator rose up the tower. "You had better prepare yourself."

Kara swallowed the lump in her throat.

The elevator opened before a large bronze door.

"Welcome to the goblin laboratory, Princess," he said, flinging the door wide.

Kara stared in amazement at the incredible round room. A domed ceiling flooded light through several skylights. Shelves built into the stone walls held countless vials and bottles of colored liquids. Metal instruments, scales, and mysterious twisted objects were scattered about next to smoking cauldrons. Along one section of rounded wall, sunlight reflected off dozens of immense magic mirrors at least fifteen feet high, dazzling Kara's eyes.

Something clattered among a pile of crystals and lenses. "Lorren!" a girl's voice said. "You've got to see this!"

Blinking away the mirror's light, Kara saw a young goblin girl rising from the far side of a wooden table. Her skin was light green, and she wore a long smock covered in splotches of colors. She lifted a pair of protective goggles back onto hair black as midnight, pulled into a tight bun. She had been working on a strange hand mirror whose silver frame was adorned with two metal antennae. "Oh." She stopped when she saw Kara. Her green skin blushed purple.

"Princess Kara, this is Tasha, Tangoo's assistant," Lorren said.

Goldie squeaked, insulted.

"And Goldie, the wonder dragon," he added.

Tasha bent into a low, clumsy bow and stammered, "An honor, your magnificent, wonder highness."

"Please, just call me Kara," she said, and smiled. The goblin girl seemed about her age, Kara noticed. "It's nice to meet you."

Tasha stood, self-consciously wiping the smudges from her smock.

"Look at all these spells Tasha made all by herself," Lorren proclaimed, proudly pointing to a rack of shelves neatly stacked with labeled vials. "What are you working on now, a love spell?" he teased.

Tasha flushed purple again. "I finished those in my first year of training."

"Ah, those things never work, anyway," Lorren said, and laughed.

"How would you know?" Tasha asked slyly.

"Funny. Where's Tangoo?" Lorren surveyed the cluttered laboratory.

"He's checking the mirrors for the princess's ride," the goblin girl said, and looked to Kara. "I'm so sorry about your friend. I've been keeping her as cool as possible." Tasha gestured to an enormous tank sunken into the floor. It was filled with a pool of shimmering quicksilver, with a strange lump in the middle. Kara gasped. The lump was Lyra's head and broad shoulders! The cat's blurred features were a melted mockery of her once beautiful face.

"Lyra," she sobbed, kneeling by the tank. She didn't need a sorcerer to tell her that Lyra's time was running out fast.

"Yes, it certainly is a shame," a cool voice echoed across the room.

The trio whirled around, startled to find Tangoo standing right behind them.

"Master Tangoo!" Tasha cried.

"Tangoo, Princess Kara is here!" Lorren pointed.

"I can see that, Prince Lorren." The sorcerer smiled thinly, looking down his hawk nose at Kara. "Princess, you did not fare so well with the Firemental horse."

That's an understatement, thought Kara.

"But, I am happy to say, you look ready to ride now," he continued.

"If I get the crystal, can it save Lyra?" Kara asked anxiously.

"The crystal of Avalon certainly has the power to bring the cat back," Tangoo assured her.

"If her unicorn jewel enchanted the cat in the first place, why can't the princess undo the spell herself?" Lorren asked suspiciously.

Yeah, why hadn't she thought of that? Kara asked herself.

Tangoo's sharp eyes darkened. "Well, my obstinate yet positive young prince, if the princess were a magic master, that *might* be possible, otherwise"—he waved his long fingers—"Good-bye kitty." The old sorcerer smiled thinly.

Lorren's brow furrowed.

Kara's heart sank as she fought to stay strong. "How can I find the stallion?"

"It will not be easy," the sorcerer warned. "Firementals are most difficult to harness. That spell took months to conjure. But it cannot hold. The creature will dissolve back to fire."

"Oh no! How long have we got?" Kara asked, frightened.

"The horse may have already reverted to fire." He tapped his goatee with a slender, green finger. "However, if you were to find the Blue Rose, that would give the Firemental enough magic to stay in its stallion form, long enough for you to ride the mirrors."

"The Blue Rose! An ancient talisman that holds powerful elemental magic!" Tasha cried, reciting her schooling perfectly.

"Quite right, my eager-eared apprentice," Tangoo smiled.

Tasha beamed.

"The Blue Rose is a myth!" Lorren said dismissively. "Everyone knows that."

"I beg to differ, my inexperienced but pigheaded prince," Tangoo countered. "I know where it is hidden."

"Where?" all three asked.

"In the lair of the Spider Witch."

Kara frowned. That didn't sound good at all.

"Oh, don't worry, Princess," Tasha reassured her.

"The Spider Witch is locked away in the fairy prisons known as the Otherworlds."

"The Blue Rose fuels elemental magic," Tangoo continued. "If you were to get the rose, the horse would come to you. It is the only way for it to survive."

"How do you know all this?" Lorren asked.

The sorcerer arched an eyebrow. Kara caught a spark of anger in his eyes, but it dimmed quickly. "My plucky but pimply prince, I was an expert in elemental magic long before you were a little goblet."

"But you'll have to be careful!" Tasha told Kara, her pointy ears twitching. "The Blue Rose is entwined on the same vine with an identical rose, which is extremely deadly to elemental magic."

"How do I tell them apart?" Kara asked.

"The Fairy Rhyme—every young sorcerer learns it in Spellology 101." Tasha cleared her throat and chanted, "The roses are blue, but only one can be true. The flower with the power is the bloom with the fume. The bud that's a dud seems a rose to the nose. Get it?"

"Got it," Kara affirmed.

"Good."

Tangoo smiled. "I have located a mirror in the Spider Witch's castle."

"Are you sure about this?" Lorren asked. "The Spider Witch might have left traps."

"These are dangerous times," the sorcerer replied.

"I'm going with her," Lorren declared.

"Prince Lorren." Tangoo's thin lips stretched into a frown as he studied the prince and the sword strapped to his side. "I thought you hated mirror jumping."

"I . . . uh . . . I'll live."

"Yes, astral plane jumping can turn one's stomach." Tangoo tapped his goatee thoughtfully. "I think I have something that will make the jump a bit less disorienting."

"Okay, let's do it." Kara nodded.

"Tasha," Tangoo said, handing her a slip of parchment, "prepare a mirror with these coordinates."

"Yes, Master Tangoo." Tasha walked up to a sleek gray mirror. She adjusted nearly invisible knobs and buttons along its edges.

Like a little hawk, Goldie watched the tall sorcerer reach a long-fingered hand up to a row of vials.

"Thanks, Tasha," Lorren said.

Tasha blushed. "All ready."

"See you on the other side," Lorren said to Kara.

Tangoo walked to Lorren. "I think you'll really *love* this spell, Prince Lorren," the sorcerer chuckled.

Twinkly magic flew from the sorcerer's outstretched hands.

Goldie squawked and leaped, intercepting the spell meant for Lorren. A bright flash surrounded Goldie, knocking the d'fly off balance and sending the mini plummeting through the mirror.

"Goldie!" Kara screamed, flashing on Lyra's horrible enchantment.

She reached out to grab the mini and fell head over heels into the mirror's murky blackness.

# Chapter 10

"**T**his is never going to work." Adriane stood backstage in the school auditorium, looking uncertainly at Emily.

A blond wig adorned with a sparkling tiara covered Adriane's black hair. Her usual jeans and pullover had been replaced by a pink dress that poofed out in a mass of shining taffeta.

Emily tried to keep a straight face as she straightened the tiara. "You look like Tinkerbell."

"Pinkerbell," Ozzie corrected, polishing his ferret stone with the hem of Adriane's dress.

"She owes me big time for this!" Adriane groused, stomping her black hiking boots to straighten the dress.

"All you have to do is read this part." Emily pointed to the Fairy Queen Titania's lines. "Ozzie's magic will do the rest."

"Blah." Fred leaned over Adriane's puffy pink shoulder, head drooped.

"I agree," Adriane said, then noticed that Fred's

usually bright blue eyes were dulled and listless. "Hey, what's wrong, Fred?"

"Tummeee, Adriee," the blue mini complained.

Fiona's, Barney's, and Blaze's little heads lolled out of Emily's backpack.

"Aw, you guys eat something that upset your tummies?" Emily gently ran her rainbow gem over the dragonflies.

Four little heads nodded.

"Bad spell," Musso pronounced, looking into Fiona's half-closed eyes.

"What?" Emily said.

"They absorbed a bad spell. I ate an ice-cream spell once. It was so sweet, I passed out."

"What did you do now, Musso?" Adriane demanded.

"It wasn't me," Musso protested.

Fiona flapped her ruby wings. "Goldeee."

"Goldie sent the spell?" Emily placed her ear to Fiona's belly. It rumbled like a backfiring car.

"Forsooth, it's time for the costume check!" Rae hollered from center stage, clapping her hands. Student actors scurried onstage and lined up, straightening togas, wings and crowns.

Adriane shot a significant look to Ozzie. "Show-time."

Ozzie nodded and concentrated on his glowing golden ferret stone.

"Testing, one, two, pink shoe—" Adriane spoke—in Kara's voice!

Ozzie smiled. "Not bad! A ventriloquist mage."

Kyle ambled by, wearing a green-feathered Robin Hood hat and clutching his Shakespearean insult book. His eyes fell on Adriane and widened. "Thou reeky, plume-plucked pignut of a sister! I didn't see you leave for school this morning!"

"Be gone, flap-mouthed varlot!" Adriane bellowed, her voice a deep bass tone.

"Gah!" Ozzie sputtered. "Needs some minor magical modulation." He shook the stone and scrunched his whiskers in concentration.

"All hail the drama queen." Kyle strolled onstage, narrowly avoiding Rae. The director charged into the Fairy Ring set, tugging on a chartreuse velvet gown, her Shakespeare Day costume.

Backstage, Fiona's red hide flashed as Blaze's orange body started blinking brightly.

"I'll keep an eye on the d'flies," Emily reassured Adriane.

"Here goes." The warrior grimaced and stepped onstage, nearly running into Heather, Molly, and Tiffany as they scurried by, making some last-minute adjustments to their sparkling makeup and glittering costumes.

"K, why didn't you pick up your phone last night?" Tiffany demanded. "We were totally worried about you."

The warrior's voice came out squeaky and high pitched. "I, like, needed my beauty rest." Adriane sent an irritated look to Ozzie.

"I *love* your color contacts!" Molly grinned, looking into Adriane's dark eyes.

"If you ask me, everyone is acting weird," Heather exclaimed.

"HeeHawhello, ladies!" Marcus shuffled by, combing his donkey ears.

Rae marched back onstage, critically eyeing her actors' costumes. Her steely eyes bugged out when she saw Adriane. "Our Fairy Queen hath returned, and in a new dress!"

"Yeah, K, why'd you ditch the old costume?" Tiffany asked.

"It, like, totally wasn't pink enough," Adriane hissed in a voice like Darth Vader. She glared daggers offstage. "Excuse me," she peeped like a chipmunk, and stomped toward the ferret.

"Gak!" In the shadows offstage, Ozzie smacked his ferret stone furiously. "Er, Emily, I could use some help here."

But Emily's attention was on Barney, who suddenly shuddered in her arms.

"Fred, are you all right?" Adriane forgot the flabbergasted ferret as she held Fred.

The blue dragonfly belched like a trombone, barfing magic all over Adriane and covering her with sprinkly twinkles.

"Scooz meme." Fred dove into Emily's backpack, feeling better.

The warrior's eyes went hazy as she tottered and knocked into Marcus.

"Heew, you're all blue!"

Blue light surrounded the warrior in a shimmering halo as she gazed at the dreamy donkey.

"People, people, what is going on now?" Rae cried, marching over to look at Adriane's glowing head.

"BLaaaPHHHf." Fiona suddenly tumbled in the air and hurled, sending azure twinkles smacking into Rae's frizzy head. Rae careened backwards and fell onto Kyle.

"People, some professionalism, please!" Rae's eyes glazed over as she tried to disentangle herself from the sandy-haired boy. "Ooo, baby!" She stared at Kyle, a giddy smile suddenly plastered on her face.

"Whoa!" Kyle jumped to his feet and stumbled away from Rae.

"Come back, thou dreamiest of hunks!" the director cried. "Let me pledge my eternal love!"

"Kara, what is with you?!" The fairies shuttled over.

"BLrrrAAAFFF!" Barney and Blaze both tossed up the magic spell.

Molly, Tiffany, and Heather shrieked as clouds of twinkly bits covered them in a dazzling shower of popping lights.

"The dragons picked up a love bug." Musso observed Heather, Tiffany, and Molly, their eyes glazed over in ecstasy. "Those fairies will fall in love with the first—oop."

The three girls were advancing straight toward Musso, their shining eyes locked on him.

"Those are the cutest ears I ever saw! He's so *totally* cute. I saw him first. No way!"

"Ak!"

"Oh, no." Emily frantically stuffed the d'flies in her backpack before anyone saw them. She tried to catch Adriane's eye, but the warrior was completely ignoring her. Adriane's total attention was riveted on a very confused donkey. Marcus shuffled across stage, Adriane draped over him like a cloak.

"Don't ever leave me, my hairy Romeo."

The four minis peeked out from Emily's backpack as students started filing into the auditorium for the performance.

"Help!" Kyle yelled, Rae chasing him.

"Help!" Musso ran the other way, three fairies bounding and leaping after him.

"Heehawwwelp!" Marcus ran into the auditorium, plowing through crowds of students. Adriane hurdled over the seats, hot on his tail. She landed on the donkey's back, wrestling Marcus to the ground.

Students started whistling and hollering. "Shakespeare rocks!"

Ozzie walked to Emily, proudly looking at his ferret stone. "Things are going well, don't you think?"

❧   ❧   ❧

Lorren and Kara stepped out of the mirror and into a sticky mass of . . . something.

"Goldie?" Kara called, as she wiped at the silky strands covering her face.

"Icky!" The d'fly popped in front of Kara, pulling long, tacky strings off the blazing star.

"Are you okay?" Kara's heart pounded.

"Uh honk." Goldie flew up and fluttered happily onto Kara's shoulder.

Kara hugged her friend so tightly, the d'fly squeaked.

Then she looked around. She stood on a platform in a dark, narrow chamber. Dull lights emanated from yellowish crystals embedded in the walls. The high ceiling faded from view overhead, rising into darkness. Behind her was the mirror, a dull gray piece of glass ornately framed in carved metal. It stood on silver clawed feet. Everything was draped in shiny webbing.

"What is this stuff?" Kara asked, unsure if she really wanted to hear the answer.

"Phhhllaf!" Lorren spit out a mouthful. "Spiderwebs!" The boy appeared from the adjoining corridor.

"Eww!" Kara brushed at herself frantically, assisted by Goldie.

"Come on, let's get in and out of here as fast as possible."

She followed him through rusted metal doors that creaked with age.

Something skittered overhead in the darkness.

"Are you sure this place is empty?" Kara asked nervously.

"No," Lorren muttered, clearing a path with his sword to reveal a long corridor.

"Even if we find this rose, how do we find the stallion?"

"Don't know."

"How do you know where you're going?" Kara held Goldie close, eyes darting up, down, left, and right. She could hear the sound of tiny feet moving against stone. It seemed to be coming from everywhere at once.

"In here!" Lorren called.

She ran to catch up. In the gloomy dimness, Kara made out a large room of dark stone. Weak sunlight filtered in through tiny window slits in the sloping ceiling, illuminating thousands of twisting spiderwebs throughout the room. Cauldrons, dusty vials, cracking leather books, and mysterious metal structures were all draped by milky webs.

"It's the Spider Witch's lab," Lorren exclaimed, cautiously stepping deeper into the abandoned laboratory. "I heard she got really messed up using dark magic."

"What do you mean?" Kara asked, her breath quickening.

"She's like half fairy, half spider," Lorren continued. "Really creepy. Some wizard finally trapped the witch and her insect warrior and sent them to the Otherworlds. But that was way before I was even born."

Kara shuddered, thinking of twisted magic and dark dreams. "Let's just hurry."

"The flower won't be in plain sight." He pointed to the unicorn gem clutched in her hand. "Track it with your jewel."

Steeling herself, Kara edged forward, swiping webs aside with her hands. She held up her jewel, releasing a bright light.

A flash of pixilated insect eyes gleamed as a large bug buzzed into the light, dodging between the sticky webs.

"Gross!" Kara exclaimed, waving her jewel and bouncing light everywhere. "I hate bugs!"

"Probably just a few leftovers from the old tenants." Lorren noted.

Kara peered at a shelf strewn with broken glass and dried liquid. Signs hung below, written in strange slashes and markings. She squinted at the wavering writing. "What's this say?"

"Extremely dangerous spells. Don't look."

Kara jumped back involuntarily, then caught

herself. "Oh, that was so funny!" She edged around a wicked-looking machine with rusted metal spikes.

"I don't like this," Lorren said uneasily.

"This place could so use an interior decorator," Kara agreed, ducking under another web as she approached an iron table in the center of the room. "And a few tons of bleach."

"No, I mean, how did Tangoo know the elemental rose is here?" he asked, walking up to the opposite side of the cluttered table.

"Your secret club has inside information," Kara pointed out. "A powerful sorcerer like Tangoo must have ways of finding things out, too."

"He's a wily old goblin. I don't trust him," the prince stated.

"You keep saying that, but he's been trying to help me ever since I got here. He wants to help all of us!" Kara gingerly picked up an old book of spells.

"He works with quicksilver all the time to make the travel mirrors. He should know how to cure Lyra," the prince insisted. "I think Tangoo wants the crystal to do something else."

Exasperated, Kara slammed the rotting spellbook shut. "It seems to me if there's one person who really wants the power crystal, it's you!" she accused. "You found me first in the Queen's Forest, you were in the Fairy Ring, and when I let the fire stallion go, you took me to the rave to convince me to find it. It seems like you're willing to do anything to find that crystal!"

He looked at her steadily. "I believe Tangoo's plan could work. And I believe that if anyone could attract the crystal, it's you. You're the key to saving the Fairy Realms!" Lorren insisted. "You know me, I would never betray you."

"Know you?" Kara echoed, walking away from the table and casting a beam of unicorn light on another section of the room. "You and your Batman act? I have more reason to trust Tangoo than to trust you. He's not hiding behind—"

Kara broke off in mid-sentence. Her unicorn jewel had suddenly sparked bright white as she walked by an iron door. She winced, terrified that her jewel would explode with uncontrolled magic, but it held steady.

The boy rushed to her side. "Help me push this open."

They shoved the door inward and cautiously peered inside.

"Nothing here but plain stone," Lorren observed, walking into the empty room.

"No, look!" Kara pointed at a dark red mark on a block of stone near the floor. Kneeling down, she shuddered as a spiderweb brushed the back of her neck. Deeply carved into the stone was a small red spider. But what did it mean? On a hunch, she reached out and pushed the carving. Nothing happened.

"What now, Scooby Doo?" she muttered, standing up.

"Shh, wait!" Lorren leaned closer to the wall.

A faint noise, like a latch clicking, sounded deep inside the stone. Without warning, an entire section of wall sank soundlessly into the floor and vanished. Behind it was a huge chamber. Unlike the laboratory, there were no spiderwebs in the pristine space. The high walls were lined with ornately decorative tapestries.

Kara held up her jewel, scanning the room. Bright diamond light fell over an altar of gleaming black marble against the far wall. And floating above it were two delicate roses entwined at the stems. They were both dark as midnight and gleamed with pale blue light.

"The roses!" Kara breathed, her face haloed in white by her shining unicorn jewel.

The fragile flowers seemed made of crystal, but their deep blue petals were alive with swirling elemental magic. Like the fire stallion, the flowers were creations of pure natural energy, bound together in an exquisite form.

Gulping a shuddering breath, she anxiously walked toward the altar.

"Careful," Lorren warned in a hushed voice. "There might be traps!"

But nothing happened as she approached the black marble and stood inches away from the impossibly beautiful flowers. The unicorn jewel illuminated the magical roses like a spotlight.

"Which one?" Lorren worried. "They both look the same."

"The bud with the dud is a rose to the nose, no . . ." Kara muttered, trying to remember the rhyme Tasha had told her. "The rose with the nose—why didn't I write it down! Let's just take both and figure it out later."

"No, it's too dangerous."

Kara closed her eyes in concentration and willed herself to remember Tasha's rhyme. "The flower with power is a nose rose . . ."

"The flower power is blue, but only one dud can be true," the prince said.

"No, no," Kara exclaimed.

"Great, now you made me forget it!" Lorren fretted.

"Oh, like you even remembered it to begin with." She stood on tiptoes and leaned in close to the flowers, sniffing. The first smelled awful, like rotting eggs. Coughing, she took a deep breath and smelled the second. A beautiful aroma of roses and lilacs wafted from the sparkling petals.

Smiling confidently, she reached out for the

stinky flower. Her jewel flashed as her hand closed around the smooth stem.

"The bloom with the fume is the flower with the power!" she cried triumphantly, pulling the rose free. Then she looked around at the room. Something wasn't right.

Goldie's jeweled eyes looked everywhere.

The sudden noise of claws skittering against stone surrounded them.

"What is that?" Kara asked, holding her gem tighter.

"Let's get out of here before—" Lorren stopped, looking behind her, eyes dark with terror.

The massive stones around the room were sliding apart.

Clutching the crystal flower, Kara spun around— and screamed. A hideous mass of spiders surged from behind the wall, a voracious black wave that came straight toward her. She backed up, but more grotesque insects advanced behind her in a seething dark carpet. The ceiling shuddered and cracked, raining a swarm of writhing bugs.

"Eewwee!" Goldie swiped at the falling insects with her wings, batting them away from Kara.

"Ahhh!"

Thousands of black legs, putrid green abdomens, and oily wings glinted in the ghostly light as waves upon waves of gruesome bugs and spiders gushed from the walls.

Kara's gem exploded in light, spinning her back against the altar. She swung the jewel wildly, magic fire scorching an entire wall of bugs.

"Kara!" Lorren screamed.

The floor jolted beneath her, nearly sending her sprawling. The entire floor was sinking, drawing her down into a pit of squirming insects.

"Help!"

Suddenly, Lorren gripped her hand, pulling her onto the altar next to him. She scrambled up and stood watching as a sea of bugs rose below them. Centipedes, beetles, and spiders crawled out of the dank pit, clamoring for a foothold.

"I hate bugs!" Kara wildly swung the unicorn jewel, sending piles of bugs scattering.

Lorren slashed the top edge of the nearest tapestry, ripping an end free from the wall. "Hang on!"

He put his arm around Kara's waist and grabbed the loose end of the tapestry.

"Jump!"

Clinging to Lorren, Kara leaped as high as she could, and swung out over the teeming chamber. Shielding the rose with her curled body, she landed roughly on the stone floor and tumbled through the door.

"Run!" Lorren cried.

With Goldie hanging on, Kara scrambled to her feet and fled, yanking crawling beetles off her legs.

High-pitched shrieking scratched from thousands of tiny fanged mouths as the vicious swarm followed.

Running through the nearest cobweb-covered door, Kara and Lorren raced down the murky hallway and stopped short. The entrance to the mirror room was blocked with thousands of insects.

"How are we going to get to the mirror?!" Kara cried, panicked.

"We can't go back in there!" Lorren swerved to the right, leading Kara up a short flight of uneven stairs. She stumbled, but kept pace with Lorren, putting distance between them and the rustling black mass of slithering bugs.

Kara and Lorren dashed through a dilapidated set of huge doorways and skidded to a stop.

Before them lay an octagonal courtyard. At the far end an immense gleaming spiderweb stretched from the floor all the way to the highest turret.

Kara quickly made her way across the stone yard. Light reflected crazily off the silken strands, forming shadows as deep as a cave. Three shimmering black mirrors were imbedded in the sickly pearl-like threads. There were other things imbedded as well, large cocoons tightly wrapped, stuck to various points on the web. She didn't want to even think about whose snacks those were.

"Which mirror?" Kara cried, glancing nervously over her shoulder.

"I don't know!" Lorren exclaimed.

The bugs surged through the doors, hungry for their escaped prey.

"The rose!" Lorren exclaimed, reaching out for the shining crystal. "Give it to me!"

"What are you doing?" Kara whipped the precious elemental magic from his grasping hand.

"The spiders are protecting it. You'll be safe if I take it!"

Kara's stomach lurched. This was her only chance to save Lyra, and he was trying to take it from her. Then it hit her: He'd been using her all along, just like everyone else. All they wanted was her magic, her blazing star powers to save their world. Well, what about her world? Her world was Lyra!

"No one takes advantage of Kara Davies. You'll just have to find your own power crystal, Prince whoever you are." Kara jammed the rose into her pocket and ran toward the mirrors.

"Wait!" Lorren shouted desperately.

She pulled Mirabelle out and flipped the clamshell open.

"Princess." Mirabelle beamed. "How may I assist you in your radiance? Might I suggest some lip gloss—"

Kara held Mirabelle up, showing her the three gleaming mirrors. "Which one?"

"Well, the right one is nice, but it reflects several deep layers of astral planes."

"Then that one?" She swung the little mirror to the left.

"Excellent craftsmanship. But the shimmer seems off. Could be fatal to molecular reconstruction."

On the web above them, a dark shape shifted. Eight enormous hairy legs moved in horrifying syncopation as a gargantuan black spider rose from the web's center.

Goldie, Kara, and Mirabelle shrieked.

"Mirabelle! Which one?!"

"Ooo, I don't know, just jump!" the compact squealed.

Kara took one last glance at Lorren's horrified face and aimed herself toward the center mirror.

"See you on the other side, Prince Butthead."

She barreled into the center mirror.

"No, not that one!" Mirabelle screamed.

Kara plummeted through twisting, blinding space, clinging to Goldie. Dazzling lights streamed past her eyes spiraling to infinity. Suddenly she slowed, as if she were falling through water, then stopped. She found herself standing on an impossibly bright glowing plane of light.

Kara looked up at the tall, shimmering figure that stood before her.

"I've been waiting for you, blazing star," the Dark Sorceress said, smiling.

# Chapter 11

"**S**tay away from me!" Kara yelled, recoiling from the Dark Sorceress. Had the mirror taken her to the Otherworlds?

"I'm not who you think I am," the tall woman said, her voice soft.

Kara shuddered, clutching her jewel protectively. Was this another trick? Suddenly Goldie flew to the woman's shoulder.

"No!" Kara cried.

"Hello, little one." The woman laughed. Silver hair draped her shoulders, falling over a shimmering dress. Goldie sat, calmly preening herself. "You are a very clever little dragon, aren't you?"

Goldie nodded.

The woman's warm eyes locked with Kara's.

Like the Dark Sorceress, she had deep green eyes and flowing silver hair. But the eyes were not cold reptilian slits, and her hair had no jagged lightning streaks. The Dark Sorceress's deeply etched features were set in cruel, mocking lines. This woman's face was soft and friendly. And fluttering behind, so delicate that Kara had not seen them before, were iridescent wings.

"Who are you?" Kara asked tremulously.

"I am Lucinda." Waves of radiant magic glowed around her as she moved closer.

"As in Queen Lucinda?" Kara asked, astonished.

"Yes," the woman smiled warmly.

"What is this place?" Kara looked around for the mirror that had brought her here, but a mist-like sparkling rain obscured visibility in every direction.

"You are inside the mirror, on the astral planes of fairy magic," Lucinda explained, her voice pure and sweet. Then her warm smile faded. "We must hurry—I can only shield you for a few minutes. They will sense you here."

"Who?"

"The Dark Sorceress and her allies."

"Is she really your sister?" Kara asked.

"We have grown apart."

"How can she be human, then?"

"The part of her that *was* human is long gone."

Kara stiffened, remembering the terrifying nightmares that reached for her. "They're trying to steal my magic."

"You are the blazing star," Lucinda said simply.

Kara hung her head.

Lucinda's bright eyes reflected the shimmering

of Kara's unicorn jewel. "The jewel that adorns your neck was once mine," she told the girl. "It has been waiting for the right match."

"You have the wrong girl."

"You are the spark, waiting to ignite a fire."

"Everyone is telling me what to do, but I don't even know who I am," Kara cried, feeling vulnerable and lost.

Lucinda's rosy lips curved in a gentle smile. All at once, glowing planes of light appeared, wavering and rippling, taking on dreamy, hazy images . . . scenes from Kara's memories. They began playing like movies before her eyes. She watched, transfixed.

*Five years old—ignoring her mother's instructions, she swept from the beach into the ocean, terrified as the strong undertow pulled her down.*

This is surreal, Kara thought, as the next one came.

*Age eight—riding her favorite gelding, Sugarpie, in competition. The moment she had dreamed of, so sure she would come in first because she was always the best. She had come in third and had thrown a tantrum.*

*Age ten—Kara singing karaoke to Britney Spears and making a total spectacle of herself. Heather, Tiffany, and Molly were rolling and laughing so hard, they spit up their popcorn. She was always the most popular, always the center of attention.*

Kara watched the memories continue to play

before her eyes. She was surprised that her emotions had grown stronger with time, how this video-diary shaped who she was and set the stage for what would come next.

Two girls she hadn't even known before, had nothing in common with, and who couldn't possibly know what she was all about. But they had something Kara didn't. Something beyond anything Kara had ever dreamed possible.

—*Clumsy Emily walking a whole pack of dogs and getting herself completely entangled in the leashes. Tiffany and Heather were so mean to her, and Kara didn't do anything about it. . . . Kara was not proud of her first encounter with the healer.*

—*Dark-haired, tough Adriane, in Kara's face because Kara had promised not to tell anyone about the "purple bear," Phel, but that's exactly what she had done. Kara grimaced, knowing how she had jeopardized the lives of all the animals and the secret of Ravenswood.*

—*Kara placed her trembling hands on Emily's healing jewel and Adriane's wolf stone. Magic fire flooded through her senses. She didn't understand it, but knew she wanted it more than anything.*

—*Kara reached for the horn of the unicorn, stealing it from the Ravenswood Library. She didn't care what happened as long as she got the magic.*

All Kara had wanted was her own jewel. How selfish that seemed now.

They had accepted her in spite of who she was:

spoiled, vain, and inconsiderate. But Kara had changed. She saw that now, as crystal clear as a mirror.

The images disappeared, and Lucinda stood before her. "What we leave behind makes us who we are."

"But what's wrong with me?" Kara cried. "Why can't I use my magic?"

"Because, Kara. The magic is not for you."

There it was. Panic twisted Kara's stomach. It had all been a mistake. The magic had never been meant for her.

"Kara, the gift of a blazing star is to make *others* shine more brightly. Not yourself."

Kara took a deep breath, trying to think it through. She had always been strongest with Adriane and Emily by her side, giving her magic to them.

"This is your time," Lucinda said softly. "You are a teenager, Kara, when the magic first comes alive. It is already being crafted, shaped like a fine sculpture. You can feel it, can't you?"

Kara nodded helplessly. Even now, she could feel the magic blazing inside of her. If she let it go, she feared she would blow apart, vanish like a dream.

"It's too strong," Kara cried. "I don't know how to use it."

"So many love you, and will help."

"Like Lyra." Kara lowered her eyes.

"Kara, there is something else."

Kara turned wide blue eyes to Lucinda.

"You have some idea of what the Dark Sorceress is capable of."

Kara nodded grimly.

"She covets your magic. Even though trapped, she reaches out through dreams." Lucinda's eyes flashed. "But make no mistake, she will strike again and she will strike hard."

Kara felt shivers down her back. "What could happen?" she whispered.

"Are you sure you want to see?"

Kara steeled herself. "Yes."

Lucinda waved her hand, summoning an unfamiliar set of images.

—*A beautiful teenager, seventeen years old, golden blond hair trimmed neatly below her shoulders, stood at the entrance to the Ravenswood Preserve, cold blue eyes looking through a chain-link construction fence. Bulldozers cut through the still morning air, and trees toppled over as the destruction of the preserve began.*

Shock, grief, and guilt consumed Kara. Why hadn't she stopped this from happening?

—*The Dark Sorceress sat upon her throne, ready to command the vast armies at her feet. All she had to do was give the order, and worlds would be hers. The power of the magic was inescapable, growing, seducing, and infecting every part of her being.*

Kara looked closer at the animal eyes of the sorceress and gasped. They were ice blue—Kara's eyes.

—*Queen Kara lazily touched her unicorn jewel, then fingered two bracelets upon her wrist. Each held a different gem—the rainbow jewel and the wolf stone.*

"That can't be what will happen!" Kara cried as the horrible images faded.

"That is up to you," Lucinda said.

"I won't use my magic!"

Kara would never risk all those terrible things.

"You cannot hide from your life just because there's a chance you might get hurt." Lucinda smiled gently. "The future is shaped by your choices. It is what makes you so powerful."

Kara nodded.

"You must chose to become the blazing star!" Lucinda's luminous form began to waver like a reflection in rippling water—

"Wait!" Kara cried

—But Kara was already moving, falling. She stepped out of the mirror blindly, wincing as bright light seared her eyes.

A sharp cry pierced the air—something was in agony.

Goldie was searching for the source.

"Where, Goldie?"

Goldie took off, Kara running behind.

They crested a grassy hill and skidded to a stop. Rocky outcroppings, brush, and tall reeds lined a river as it coiled like a snake through higher banks. In the distance, the mountains kept rising, blanketing the horizon with sparkling crystal peaks.

Another cry. Kara's heart twisted. Her jewel surged, compelling her to move forward. She ran, boots crunching through tough cattails.

Scrambling over jagged rocks, Kara followed the pull of her gem and rounded a bend. At the base of a rocky hill was a large hollow, protected by a jutting overhang. Goldie fluttered above, squeaking and screeching. The entire hollow glowed pale reddish orange, reflecting flames. The fire stallion flashed and fluttered, taking then losing shape.

Without thinking, Kara rushed forward, her heart pounding.

The stallion was down, entangled in wet grass and reeds. His fiery body sizzled and flickered as he lashed out with a flaming hoof, struggling to get to his feet. Redhot waves surged up, licking greedily at Goldie as if they would devour the small dragon.

"No!" Kara cried, dashing into the shallow waters. Desperation hit her like a fist. She could feel the horse's need pulling at her magic, drawing her closer.

The horse looked nothing like the awesome stallion she had seen less than a day ago in the arena. Spots on his flaming coat were dark, dissipating like dying coals.

Fire flared in swirls and loops, bursting into the

shape of a horse before melting back into pure flames. The horse was desperately trying to hold his form together.

"Please, let me help you," Kara implored. Sparks flew from her unicorn jewel as she stepped closer. She clamped down her magic and focused on the horse's ferocious need.

"Easy," she said. "I can help you."

The horse snorted smoke, fire streaking up and down his back, sending snaking tendrils into the sky. The spell that held him together was gone.

Kara moved closer, realizing that her unicorn jewel was protecting her from the intense heat. She reached into her jacket and pulled out the shining Blue Rose. The stallion's wide eyes locked on the swirling blue magic. Gasping, he struggled forward.

Kara felt her magic surge from her jewel, but she held it steady. Something had changed. Kara had reached another level of control.

The glimmering azure magic of the rose grew more intense. Closing her eyes in concentration, Kara reached out to the stallion. His wildly unstable magic trembled across her senses, pulling, grasping at her.

Magic fire burned through Kara, struggling for release. But she wasn't afraid. She opened her heart to the stallion—and let her magic go.

This time there was no crazy, unfocused explosion—just the Blue Rose blooming in her hand, its shimmering petals spreading and brightening. The rose slowly lost its form and changed into a ball of elemental magic. Spreading her hands, Kara washed the magic over the stallion.

Instantly a blast of heat surged from his body. Trails of raging fire pulled back and tightened into solid form. In one powerful movement, the stallion was on his feet, his strong muscles pulsing with whorls of brilliant fire. The reeds and swamp grass melted away in a hiss of smoke.

Stamping fiery hoofs, the huge stallion ran up the bank and stopped. He turned his golden eyes to Kara.

*"Who are you?"* the horse asked, bright flames trailing from his mane and tail.

"I'm Kara." She smiled.

The horse snorted, accepting her name.

"And you?"

The stallion reared, fire raging from his body. He stamped the ground, spilling flames across the damp grass.

Kara climbed up the bank and stood near the stallion. "What's wrong?"

*"I have no name,"* the stallion cried, eyes flashing in pain and sadness.

Kara moved closer.

The stallion lowered his blazing orange head. She stretched out her hand wonderingly. As her fingers touched the stallion's glowing cheek, rays of brilliant magic flashed from her jewel, sending her long hair flowing back from her face and ruffling the stallion's fiery forelock. This was not the uncontrolled storm of magic fire she had come to fear. This was soft and gentle, full of love and kindness. The horse stepped back, but Kara moved forward, protected by her jewel, until her hand tamed the wild fire of his mane.

"You're so beautiful," she spoke softly, running her hand over his neck, settling the flames. "Like a star shining on my heart. I will call you Starfire."

The stallion stood straighter.

*"Starfire. It is a good name,"* he said proudly.

The horse whinnied and snorted, prancing and dancing.

Kara laughed joyfully as Goldie tumbled happily above her head. The blazing star reached out impulsively and hugged the stallion's great neck. She felt the magic fire drumming through his form, a fierceness barely contained, as wild and intense as her own.

Starfire lowered his head over Kara's shoulder. She closed her eyes. They stood together on the bank listening to the river flowing gently past.

"What is it?" Kara pressed her face against Starfire's cheek, sensing his great need.

*"I am fire,"* he said sadly, and Kara understood.

She saw the images from his mind. Tangoo had created the horse from Firemental magic, then locked him in a cage. Like the Blue Rose, the stallion was just a shell to hold magic; nothing more than a tool to be used to get the power crystal.

"We are both being used," Kara said.

*"We will run away!"* Starfire snorted.

"I can't do that. My friends need me."

*"I don't understand."* The stallion's voice was resigned.

Kara gazed at her new friend. He had been formed from fire. How could he choose anything when he had no one to help him, to love him?

"Do you remember anything else?" she asked.

The horse whinnied sadly. *"I have no past."*

Kara stepped back and stared into Starfire's brilliant golden eyes. "Then I'll give you mine."

Starfire returned her stare curiously.

Holding the unicorn jewel tightly, Kara closed her eyes and let the memories flood through her. Everything Lucinda had shown to her and more, she now gave to Starfire, freely, unconditionally, opening her heart and sharing the very essence of herself with the stallion. All the joy, pain, love, and loneliness of growing up. Images of her family, her friends, everything that meant something to her and, finally, Lyra.

The unicorn jewel streamed with dazzling light and entwined with the stallion's glowing red flames. Starfire's eyes opened in wonder.

Kara moved to his side. She grasped his mane

and leaped onto his back. Settling in, she felt as comfortable as if they had ridden together every day of their lives.

Suddenly Kara laughed aloud, stretching her arms wide, reveling in the strength of their combined magic. She had given Starfire a reason to live and the freedom to chose his own future. And, in return, he had freed her, too. Freed her to do what she must.

Sensing his bonded's need, Starfire reared. *"We must ride."*

# Chapter 12

The rulers of the Five Kingdoms all sat in their respective thrones, waiting. The air bristled with energy, filling the ring with a sense of urgency that made the gathered crowds even more anxious.

Selinda rose and walked to the center of the ring. "I was hoping Tangoo's plan would work."

Queen Raelda joined her. "The blazing star was a worthy choice, but not even she can change the inevitable."

As if on cue, lightning split the skies overhead, leaving jagged streaks of purple and red.

"What say you, Tangoo?" Selinda spoke as the gaunt sorcerer approached. He looked haggard, as if he hadn't slept in weeks.

"We must have patience, my ladies." Tangoo's eyes darted up as another bolt tore a blaze of green through the sky.

"We are out of both patience and time," Raelda said brusquely, her face set in grim lines. "The Fairy Realms must be completely sealed off."

The Fairy Queen's intense violet eyes met Raelda's. "You know we cannot allow that. The web as we know it would be destroyed."

Raelda's gaze hardened. "So be it."

"Surely there must be another way," Selinda implored the Goblin Queen and her sorcerer.

Tangoo looked at the Fairy Queen. "Only Avalon's magic can save us."

Selinda raised her hand, drawing all eyes toward her. She took a deep breath and called out: "Before the die is cast and war is upon us, I ask our brothers and sisters of the Five Kingdoms: Is there anyone here who will ride for the fairies?"

Her challenge echoed over the Fairy Ring. It was met with silence.

Selinda took a breath and called out again. "Who will ride for the fairies?"

Suddenly, a thunderous roar shook the ground as a jagged bolt of lightning shot across the Fairy Ring. The crowd shrieked as fire blazed where the bolt had struck.

Then the firelight dimmed, and an awed silence washed over the crowds.

Kara sat proudly upon the fire stallion's back. The blazing star called out, her voice strong and confident, "We will ride for the fairies!"

Pandemonium broke out as the kings and queens all rose at once. Selinda, Raelda, and Tangoo rushed to the stallion's side.

"You see, I told you!" Tangoo's eyes were dancing with delight.

"Well done, Princess Kara," Selinda said, smiling radiantly.

As Tangoo drew closer, the stallion stamped and snorted, his fire leaping and licking the air. Kara ran her hand over the mighty horse's neck, instantly calming the flames.

Raelda's eyes were wide in amazement. "Indeed, Princess. You have shown tremendous resolve."

"Yes, yes." Tangoo rubbed his hands together anxiously. "That is precisely why this plan will work."

"What do you require of us?" Kara asked.

Tangoo rushed to the mirror by Selinda's throne, his long, patterned robes billowing out behind him.

"The princess and the fire stallion will jump through a series of four mirrors," he explained. "Each mirror leads to a place of extremely strong elemental magic. You must gather enough magic to forge four talismans, one each of water, air, earth, and fire."

"So the magic will take form like the Blue Rose," Kara said. She felt Starfire tense.

"Precisely, Princess." Tangoo pulled a shimmering silver pack from beside the mirror and handed it to her. "Place the talismans in here. The combination of the four should be enough to attract the power crystal."

Kara nodded, slinging the pack over her shoulders.

"A fifth mirror will return you here, to the Fairy Ring." Tangoo's black eyes seemed to bore into her. "I have every confidence that events will unfold *exactly* as I have planned."

Over the chatter of the excited crowd, Raelda said, "I am sure I speak for everyone here, Princess Kara, when I wish you success. May your magic keep you safe."

"Thank you." Kara nodded her head respectfully, then scanned the ring for Lorren. But the boy wasn't there. She felt a sudden pang of guilt. She hoped he had made it safely back from the Spider Witch's lair. At least there was one thing she knew for sure. She patted the fire stallion, this creature forged from magic, now risking his life for her. The blazing star and the Firemental stallion, their destinies intertwined, riding for Lyra, for the Fairy Realms, the magic web, and Avalon itself.

Kara looked to Goldie and smiled gratefully. Without Goldie, Kara would never have made it this far.

Kara thought of Lyra and everyone else depending on her. She would not let her friends down. It was time to become the blazing star.

Starfire reared, sending licks of fire streaking into the air. Kara held up her jewel, surrounding them with diamond-white magic. "We are ready," she called out.

The crowd surged to its feet, their cheers ringing into the skies.

Starfire leaped through the first mirror. Kara's long hair streamed behind her as they vanished into the rippling glass. The ride of the blazing star had begun.

❧　❧　❧

Kara and Starfire landed hard, the horse's fiery hooves melting tracks across a wide, icy ledge. They were in the foothills of a glistening mountain range. Before them a mammoth mountain of glittering ice towered into the sky.

*"Ice mountains of the Troll Kingdom,"* Starfire snorted nervously as his molten hooves melted through the ledge supporting him. Plumes of steam rose from the ground as they started to sink.

"We'll have to move fast," Kara said, realizing the mountains were made entirely of ice.

"Kaaraa," Goldie squeaked, and pointed.

Kara looked up to the remote peak of the mountain. A bright spark winked in the sun.

"The mirror!" Kara cried. She held up her jewel, flashing beams of light into the sky. "Everyone ready?" she asked, leaning forward, letting the stallion's fiery mane envelop her.

*"Ready!"* Starfire stamped his hooves, eager to run.

"Let's ride!" Kara shouted

"Yippee!" Goldie squealed as Starfire shot like a bolt.

The stallion galloped to the base of the mountain, his heat leaving watery trails in the ice.

Kara focused on her magic, and on Lyra. Starfire's immense power blazed into her, steadying her, filling her with a new confidence she had never felt before. Streams of diamond sparkles burst from her jewel, trailing behind like a comet. Firemental stallion, blazing star, and dragonfly streaked up the mountain.

With a mighty leap, the stallion hurled into the air. They landed on a small outcropping about halfway up.

Starfire stamped his legs, the melting ice sizzling at his hooves. This only made him sink deeper.

*"Water fights fire,"* Starfire said worriedly.

"Let's see if I can make you some leggings." Kara swung her unicorn jewel, sending the bright magic flowing over the horse's legs, protecting him from the corrosive ice. Starfire now shone fire red with bright diamond legs.

"Pretty," Goldie said.

*"Thank you."* Starfire admired his new look.

"No, there," the dragonfly pointed.

Crystalline sparkles mixed with the diamond magic whirling in the air before them, glowing pale blue.

*"Elemental water magic,"* Starfire said.

"All righty, then." Kara fired a blast from her unicorn jewel, encasing the whirls, molding them into a mass of shiny blue light. "One talisman, hold the pickles," Kara said, thrilled with the new control over her magic.

She focused as the shards caved in on themselves, forming two lumps, elongating and stretching into—

"Oooo, bunny shoes!" Goldie pointed at the newly formed, long-eared purple shoes.

The shoes shuddered and fell to the ground. Ears flapping, they took off, running up the mountain face and disappearing out of sight.

"Lets hop to it!" Kara yelled, whipping her magic around them. Starfire bounded up the mountain, jumping from ledge to ledge, narrowly avoiding the cascading ice that rained down the frozen mountain.

"Hey, remember the time I threw my bunny slippers in the pool?" Kara laughed.

*"I thought they were quite comfortable,"* Starfire said, focusing on Kara's memory.

Finally there were no more ledges in sight for Starfire to jump on to. Only the hissing river of the melting mountain, an avalanche of jagged ice floes rushing by.

Starfire turned in circles, snorting.

This was her first challenge. She was not about to fail. There had to be another way to get to the top of the mountain.

Looking at the melting ice, Kara suddenly

smiled. "When life gives you an iceberg, make some ice cream."

Kara pointed at the sheer mountain face behind them. Understanding her perfectly, Starfire wheeled around and faced the solid ice wall. Focusing their combined powers, Kara sent red, white, and Goldie magic boring into the mountainside. Kara bent low as the stallion dove into the mountain, melting a tunnel through the solid ice.

They punched through the other side, higher up than they'd been before. In a blur of movement, the purple bunny shoes scampered by on a thin, frosty path that coiled up the pointed pinnacle of the mountaintop. Starfire charged after them, careening around the path as it wound tighter and tighter.

"Now this is real power shopping," Kara yelled.

With all her strength and concentration, she scooped up the fleeing shoes with her magic. Goldie held open the silver bag as Kara tossed them inside.

"And I thought it was hard to find shoes at Neiman's."

Starfire rocketed around the last curve. The magic mirror was set into the mountain's peak.

Encouraged by her awesome new abilities, she grabbed Goldie and hugged Starfire's neck. "Let's see what's behind door number two." Kara held on tight as Starfire dove through the glistening mirror—

—pHOnk!

A strange honking noise reverberated as Kara and Starfire landed.

Starfire stood on a fluffy cloud floating high above a dense, leafy forest. Kara's stomach lurched as she looked down at the trees far below. Clinging to Starfire's neck, she closed her eyes, convinced they would sink through the billowing clouds.

*"Air supports fire,"* the stallion reassured her. *"We will not fall."*

Kara looked around. What were they supposed to do here? A gust of wind moved them gently drifting between a collection of other puffy white clouds.

"There's nowhere else to go but another cloud," Kara mused, twirling her jewel in her fingers.

*"We must leap!"* Starfire bunched his fiery muscles and leaped onto the nearest cloud.

GONG!

As he landed, a deep ringing filled the air. "Hey! Musical clouds!" Kara looked at the other clouds, all of different sizes. "Jump to the next one."

The stallion soared over empty sky and onto a smaller cloud.

A high-pitched note chimed through the air, harmonizing with the other clouds.

Something about those three notes sounded familiar to Kara, part of a melody she couldn't quite place. . . .

"Try the others."

Starfire leaped to each of the clouds, until they had heard eight different musical notes.

What would Adriane and Emily do? They were good with music.

"I know. Maybe we can arrange them together!"

Starfire's coat blazed as he sent his elemental magic into the winds around them, summoning air. The clouds moved closer, puffing squeaks, gongs, dings, and rings.

"Okay, we'll have to hit the different clouds at the same time to make the song sound right," Kara fretted. "Starfire can do it. Goldie can play, too, but I'll fall right through."

*Your new shoes are made of water magic,"* Starfire pointed out.

"Clouds and water work together!" Kara exclaimed. "Huddle."

Goldie flew close to Kara's face as she leaned over Starfire's neck. "Feel the music. I'll tell you the right order, and jump when I say so!"

Goldie carefully opened the silver bag. The purple shoes hopped into Kara's hands. She slid off Starfire's back, closing her eyes as she slipped into the bunny shoes and touched the cloud. Taking a deep breath, she let go of the stallion—and stood atop the cloud.

"At least I don't have to sing," Kara muttered.

Goldie flew about the clouds excitedly.

"Okay Starfire, you first!" Kara raised her arms, pointing to a puffy cloud.

Starfire jumped and landed with a powerful *Bong!*

"Goldie, now you," she said, pointing to the small cloud.

Goldie bounced up and down, releasing a flurry of notes.

Kara jumped, adding her musical harmony.

Conducting the cloud symphony, Kara sang along as she, Starfire, and Goldie created the chorus of her favorite Be*Tween song.

"I'm—on a—su-per-nat-ural—high!"

As the last note filled the air, the clouds swirled with glittering white magic. Starfire was on Kara's cloud in an instant, and she scrambled onto his back. The clouds continued to swirl in on themselves, gathering together to form an elemental air talisman. It was a pearly U-shaped frame, with eight golden strings.

"A harp." Kara smiled.

"No bunnies?" Goldie frowned.

A lone cloud drifted nearby, a shimmering mirror shinning in its center.

"Go!" she ordered.

A ripple of light flashed through the stallion as his fire sprang wildly out of shape. Kara felt it; for a split second he had lost his magic. Starfire leaped as Kara snatched the talisman in midair. She had completed two challenges, but Kara knew something was terribly wrong.

# Chapter 13

Overwhelming darkness swallowed Kara, Starfire, and Goldie as they tumbled, free-falling out of the mirror until they finally landed.

Kara eased herself down from Starfire and gripped the horse's fiery flank to steady herself from pitching forward. The floor tilted steeply, making a screeching sound like rusted metal. "Where are we?" she asked,

*"Dwarf mines,"* Starfire said, tottering precariously backward as Kara peered over the edge.

They had landed in some sort of mining car. Beneath the car, jewel light bounced off steel tracks that dropped into complete blackness. Kara gingerly took a half-step forward, and confirmed her fear—they were precariously perched on the tip of a terrifying drop.

"Nobody move!" Kara ordered.

Everyone froze as the car teetered forward and back.

"Affg. . . ." Goldie slapped her feet to her mouth.

"Goldie!" Kara hissed.

"Ahhh. . . ." The d'fly's cheeks puffed out.

Kara put her finger under Goldie's nose and the mini relaxed.

"Whew." They all breathed a sigh of relief.

"AH-CHOOOIE!"

The car lurched forward and plunged straight down into the black, dropping like a runaway roller coaster.

"Ahh!"

"Ahhhhhhhh!"

*"Neighhhhh!"*

Kara's stomach rolled over as the car plummeted through blinding gloom. She clung to Starfire. Goldie clung to her neck.

The car swung wildly around a bend, then dropped again, whisking them farther down.

"Where's the breaks?" Kara screamed, grabbing the edge of the car, her knuckles white.

The car veered up and around sharp corners, swinging Kara and crew back and forth, finally lurching to a sudden stop at the cavern floor.

"Watch that first step." Kara staggered to her feet and clambered out.

Starfire leaped out and sniffed the air.

The trio gazed in awe at an immense underground grotto. Pools of silvery liquid cast steely shadows upon the high walls soaring above them.

Some pools lay still, but sudden violent currents churned others, swirling the smooth surfaces.

"*Quicksilver,*" Starfire warned. "*It's very volatile.*"

"Quicksilver?" Kara flashed on Lyra, melting in the goblin laboratory. Looking at her own distorted reflection in a silver pool, her throat ached.

The quicksilver sizzled and popped, exploding in a frothing mass of bubbling liquid. Kara backed away and ran her hands over Starfire's flaming hide. She could sense the horse's fatigue. "How are you doing?"

"*I am still here,*" the horse snorted.

Kara glanced at the silver pack, glowing on her back. "We have two talismans. Let's use one to increase your magic."

"*No,*" Starfire said sternly. "*We need them to attract the power crystal.*"

Kara bit her lip. She steeled herself and surveyed the area. "Where to?"

Goldie sprang into the air, pointing like a little retriever.

On the far side of the cavern, a corridor disappeared into darkness.

"*Let's go,*" the stallion said. Kara was already swinging up onto his back.

Starfire carefully threaded his way through the bubbling quicksilver and trotted into the dark corridor. Feeling her jewel pulse, Kara slowly released a tendril of magic, watching it snake forth.

"I can feel it pulling at my magic!" Kara's voice echoed down the dark passage. Starfire snorted anxiously. *"There is strong elemental earth magic ahead."*

The unicorn gem illuminated shimmering walls leading deep into the mines. Rounding a bend, the corridor split in two directions.

"It's a giant maze!" Kara realized.

The wall behind them trembled. With a roar like thunder, a section of it detached and shot toward them.

"Look out!" Kara screamed.

Starfire jumped just before the slab of rock slammed against the opposite side. Doubling back was no longer an option.

Suddenly a section of maze in front of them shuddered and disappeared as if the earth had swallowed it whole, opening up an entirely different section.

Goldie fluttered overhead, trying to survey the maze from above. But the little dragon was getting confused as walls opened and closed, hiding the correct direction to the maze's center.

Before they knew it, they had lost all sense of direction.

*"This is worse than the time you couldn't find the pretzel kiosk at the galleria,"* Starfire said, picking up one of Kara's memories.

They stopped as one corridor forked out on either side of them.

There must be a way to navigate this moving maze, Kara thought. Her unicorn jewel could light up sections of the corridors, but they'd have to waste time exploring every dead end if they relied on light. Kara considered the other tools at hand. The bunny shoes wouldn't do much here, but what about the harp?

Reaching into the pack, Kara removed the instrument and plucked a few notes. The chorus of "Supernatural High" reverberated in the passage to her right, dramatically amplified. But the passage to her left seemed to swallow the music, leaving only a faint echoing.

"The passage to the right is a dead end," Kara announced. "The sound bounces right off a wall and makes it louder."

*"But to the left is a long tunnel, making the music echo,"* Starfire concluded.

The stallion stepped into the left tunnel. A long passage stretched before them, and they advanced quickly until they came to another fork in the shifting maze. Kara strummed the harp. Following the echoes, they made swift progress, but the corridors were moving more rapidly as they traveled deeper into the mountain.

"We're getting close." Power snaked through Kara's senses, a tingling presence along her skin.

Rounding a curving wall, they found themselves suddenly standing at the edge of a giant quicksilver pool. Floating above it was a pulsing silver heart. The glistening heart turned slowly, reflecting twinkles of light around the dark walls.

*"The Heart of the Mountain,"* Starfire said quietly. *"The heart is a strong vessel for distributing magic."*

Goldie flapped, pointing to the bright mirror on the other side. Behind them the sound of sliding stone closed in.

"Okay, Starfire, let's do it."

The stallion backed up a few steps, then took a running leap. Soaring over the pool, Kara reached out and grasped the gleaming heart as they plunged through the mirror—

—Crisp air lifted her hair and sent flames licking from Starfire. A dark and foreboding forest surrounded them, deep woods where the sunlight could not penetrate and all was cloaked in shadow.

A bolt of jagged lightning seared across the sky.

Kara's pack now contained three talismans of elemental magic, symbolizing water, air, and earth—which meant this new one had to be fire. But in a forest?

She felt a tremor run through Starfire as howls erupted from the forest.

*"Something comes."* Starfire shifted, ready to run.

Kara's jewel burned hot against her chest. Something itched along her arms, a darkness clawing at her, turning her stomach.

*"We will outrun them."* With his fiery legs still protected by Kara's diamond magic, the stallion took off at a gallop. Twigs and leaves flew as his hooves pounded the earth.

Kara bent low, intent on one thing: finding the fire talisman. Holding her jewel high, magic streamed behind them.

Everything was a mass of shadows and mist as the woodlands flew past. Kara leaned forward, Goldie clutched close. She watched the timber begin to thicken steadily around them as they charged through leaf-strewn gullies, leaping over deep hollows and log-jammed ravines.

Suddenly, Kara was jolted forward, nearly knocked off, as Starfire reared and spun. Flashes of black fur and snarling teeth were all Kara saw as the horse erupted in flames. Something huge had lunged into their path, sideswiping the stallion. The ridge-backed beast stood upright like a man, with a long, spiked tail keeping it balanced. Massive claws on long fingers flailed as it sprang forward on powerful legs. Kara's jewel blasted diamond light, throwing the beast back as Starfire charged forward.

Three more of the things leaped from behind trees, trying to bring down the stallion.

"Are you okay?" Kara cried, watching fire trail behind them in long tendrils.

*"Yes, hang on,"* Starfire cried, dodging between two beasts.

Before them lay a twisting path of glowing purple trees arcing through the forest.

"They must be markers," Kara exclaimed. "Follow them!"

Starfire galloped onto a wide path laid out like a bright racecourse. As he passed each purple tree, their trunks and branches flashed and glimmered back to green, illuminating the whole forest with an eerie emerald glow.

They were far from safe—more and more creatures were joining the race, closing in from all sides. There were packs of scaly lizards and dozens of snarling wolf-like creatures, all charging after them.

Two lizards blocked the stallion's path, heedless of Starfire's flaming hide. But the stallion leaped high, trailing fire over their howling fury.

Starfire staggered as he hit the ground, stumbling, unable to stop Kara from pitching forward. She watched in horror as Starfire lost all form, erupting into pure flame, then sprang instantly back to his horse shape. Fear ripped through her. Starfire was fading fast.

"Hang on, Starfire!" she cried. She could feel his magic depleting as if it were her own. The spell that Tangoo had used to create him had an expiration date: It was never designed to last. Now, whatever magic he had left, he was giving to Kara in a last desperate race to save the Fairy Relams.

Starfire plunged through towering oaks and elms that surged from of the ground like massive spears. And still the creatures came after them.

Kara saw the line of purple trees end a short distance ahead, seeming to lead into a wide clearing. "We're almost there!" she shouted.

They shot through the last line of trees like a blazing comet, streaking full force onto the field.

Behind them they heard the rush of mighty winds as the forest gave up its magic. Brilliant orange-yellow flashes surged from the trees forming a whirling ball of elemental energy. It launched into the field, drawn to the fire stallion and rider. Kara pulled Starfire in a tight circle as the glittering energy formed a golden stone, sparkling with the magic of sun fire.

"There it is!" Kara cried, urging the horse forward. Reaching out with her hands, she sent her magic to ensnare the last talisman. The golden sunstone gushed light as she jammed it into the bag with the other talismans. The bag billowed, the elemental magic binding together in a storm of dazzling power. Streaming magic, the stallion raced forward.

"Where's the mirror?" Kara cried to Starfire and Goldie, wind whipping her hair into her eyes. She scanned the area. Deep woods lay to the right, left, and behind her. Ahead lay a vast, open plain with rolling hills. Then something sparkled over the next hill, reflecting sunlight. "There!"

Despite the intense power surrounding the trio, Starfire was slowing down. Fearfully, Kara glanced behind them. The pack of beasts had broken from the woods and was gaining on them.

"Starfire, take the magic!" she screamed, pushing the bag of talismans against his fiery hide. "Use it for yourself!"

The horse ignored her. Head lowered, he pushed faster, shimmering in and out of shape.

Kara felt it before she saw it. The air above her rented, splitting open with a jagged tear. An incredible glittering jewel of blues and greens skimmed behind her just out of reach, gliding on the air streams of elemental magic.

The power crystal! The talismans had done what they were supposed to: attracted the power crystal of Avalon.

Behind them, the horde of beasts closed in, howling and roaring, driven mad with the desire for magic.

Starfire raced up an incline and skidded to an abrupt stop, fire spilling across the damp ground.

Kara's heart sank.

It wasn't a mirror she had seen reflecting the light.

Before them stretched an immense lake with deep blue waters as smooth as glass.

No way could the horse leap over it. It would be death for the fire stallion to jump into it. Kara swung Starfire around, but it was too late.

The creatures were fanning out on all sides, surrounding them, edging closer and closer.

The power crystal bobbed gently, floating on the mass of elemental magic behind her. She desperately tried to pull the crystal to her, but every second that went by, she felt the stallion fading away and, with it, her own magic.

Suddenly she heard the *thwack-thwack* of flapping wings overhead. A giant bat dove into the charging beasts. Glittering sword flashing, the masked rider shouted and screamed, fighting the monsters and pushing them back.

"Lorren!"

Kara jumped off Starfire, hit the ground, and slipped, the world spinning dizzyingly around her. She was so weak. But she grabbed the silver pack of talismans and struggled forward, each step a Herculean effort. Screaming, Kara reached out, desperately trying to pull the power crystal toward her.

Suddenly, another bat and masked rider swooped from the skies. A second Forest Prince? What was going on here?

"Princess, throw it to me," the first boy yelled,

struggling to block the magic-starved beasts from advancing.

Goldie fluttered wildly about Kara's head, blocking the second masked rider's grasping hands.

She blinked in disbelief. One of them was the real Lorren. The other, an imposter. She hesitated, not knowing which Lorren to trust.

"Princess, I'm the real me!" the first boy yelled as the beasts pushed past him, advancing on Kara. "Can't you see what he's trying to do?"

Goldie shot in front of Kara protectively.

"Hey, look! Magic!" the first masked rider yelled to the creatures. Pulling out a small, clam-shaped object, he flipped it open.

"Princess! You're so pale," the object exclaimed. "Do you need some blush?"

It was Mirabelle! Kara searched her pockets frantically. She must have dropped the small compact when she escaped from the Spider Witch's lair.

Ahhh!" The mirror screamed shut as the horde of beasts turned and grabbed for the enchanted object. Lorren took off, the mass of creatures giving chase.

"Lorren!" That had to be Lorren. But then who was the other—

The second rider angled his bat and swatted Goldie away. With a black-gloved hand, he reached out and wrested the bag of elemental talismans from Kara. She was too weak to resist.

The power crystal swerved away from Kara and flew to the rider.

"What I'm *trying* to do is remove that pimply pimpernel of a prince from ever irritating me again," the masked rider cackled, but it was not Lorren's voice.

"Tangoo!" Kara exclaimed.

"Oh come now, don't act so surprised. You think I could stand one more day listening to that constant bickering? Fairies complaining, goblins fighting, trolls bellowing, elves whining, do this Tangoo, do that, Tangoo, save us, Tangoo, blah, blah, blah!" he groused. "I'm amazed I didn't turn myself into quicksilver!"

Fear tore through Kara as realization struck home.

The sorcerer's black eyes shone behind the dark mask. "The time has come for a new order in the Fairy Realms, and the construction of a new web. Avalon is finished. You made sure of that yourself when you released all the magic."

"Lyra, what about Lyra?" Kara sobbed.

"Ah, yes. I know how strong the bond is between mages and their animals. How could you resist getting the crystal for me?" He laughed. "My quicksilver spells work much too well. Say bye-bye to your wretched kitty."

It wasn't Kara's magic that hurt Lyra! This was all set up, carefully orchestrated by Tangoo. Now he was going to steal the power crystal and blame the whole thing on the Forest Prince. She had been wrong about Lorren from the start.

"Nice job collecting the magic, Princess, but I have a much better use for it." Tangoo held up the bag of talismans in one hand and turned the power crystal toward the lake. Light flashed from the crystal, spilling over the waters. The surface glimmered with intense blue, then rippled to gray as the entire lake transformed into solid quicksilver.

"The lake is the last mirror!" Kara realized.

*"Kara,"* Starfire was on his knees, breathing hard, fire streaming from his form. He struggled to stay whole, but Kara felt his Firemental magic breaking away. There wasn't much time left until he dissolved into pure elemental energy.

"He needs the talismans!" Kara screamed to Tangoo.

"The Firemental has served his purpose beyond all my expectations," Tangoo said, smiling evilly. "In fact, so have you, Princess."

Kara felt the magic drain from her. She fell to the stallion's side, hugging him fiercely as if she could keep his life from slipping away.

"Please," Kara pleaded. "He needs the elemental magic!"

"And I just happen to have an extra-special talisman, just for him." Tangoo reached into his pocket and held up a sparkling dark blue flower.

"No!" Kara screamed, realizing what it was. The second Blue Rose.

But it was too late. Tangoo threw the deadly magic at the stallion. The talisman exploded into Starfire. Sparkling black energy raced over his body, eating away the last of the elemental spell.

Starfire's eyes locked with Kara.

*"Remember me,"* he said. The horse erupted into a final ball of flame and vanished.

Kara was hurled backward. She tumbled down the incline, sliding out across the slippery surface of the lake mirror.

"Time to say bye-bye, Princess," the goblin sorcerer sneered.

Helpless and too weak to stop it, Kara's unicorn jewel exploded with the last of her power. She was enveloped in blazing light as a crackling beam shot from the lake and sizzled through the air. All of her magic was wrested from her, reflected into a blazing beacon reaching high in the sky.

The sky, already weakened by constant lighting, crackled and ripped, revealing a swirling mass of electric purple. Her breath caught in a silent scream. She was looking into the Otherworlds.

Kara felt the mirror drop away below her as she fell through—and landed with blinding lights shining in her face and the thunder of applause in her ears.

Kara blinked the light from her eyes, expecting to see fairies and elves and trolls in the Fairy Ring.

Instead, she saw her math teacher, her brother, and the entire student body of Stonehill Middle School on their feet, clapping.

The mirror had dropped her center stage, right in the middle of the school play.

# Chapter 14

Kara stood frozen in shock, the last of her radiant magic drifting away like dying embers of a fire. Her jewel lay cold and lifeless against her heaving chest. Starfire was gone, and soon the Fairy Realms would follow. And Lyra. All because of her.?

Eyes stinging with tears, she looked offstage, desperately searching for Emily.

" 'I will sing!' Hee honk!" A tall boy was standing next to her, wearing an amazingly realistic donkey costume. Even his long hairy ears were twitching. " 'That they shall hear I am not afraid'."

She then remembered the play, *A Midsummer Night's Dream*. Marcus was reading the character of Nick Bottom, who gets turned into a donkey. He didn't even notice she had just crashed the play.

A tall girl with long blond hair wearing a bright pink fairy princess costume hung on the donkey's arm—was that Adriane?

" 'I pray thee gentle mortal, sing again,' "

Adriane read dramatically from the donkey's book. " 'Mine ear is much enamour'd of thy note.' "

Kara gasped at hearing her own voice coming from the warrior's mouth.

"Gah!"

Offstage, Ozzie was hopping up and down, waving his gleaming ferret stone. He was trying to contain Barney, Fred, Blaze, and Fiona inside Emily's backpack as they chattered with Goldie.

Thank goodness Goldie was okay.

Emily stood next to them, face scrunched in concentration, her rainbow jewel pulsing. But Kara couldn't hear what the healer was trying to say.

Finally Emily just blurted out, "Kara!? Can't you hear me?"

"It's gone!" Kara wailed. "It's all gone."

Tiffany, Heather, and Molly, their eyes twinkling under the spell of love, tackled Musso, sliding across the stage in a heap. Heather plopped French fries down the hobgoblin's mouth. "Here you go, my dashing, handsome, lovebug!"

"Splaff!" Fries flew out of Musso's mouth as the hobgoblin met Kara's gaze. "Princess!" He scrambled to his feet, looking everywhere. "There must be a portal here somewhere!"

The three fairies chased after him as Kyle suddenly sprinted across the stage.

" 'Be gone, thou fawning, dizzy-eyed giglet,' " he screamed.

Hot on his heels, Rae charged after him. "Come hither, thou cutiest patootiest!"

They plowed through the Fairy Ring, running circles around the actors.

Had the entire world gone nuts? Kara felt a nudging at her side. "Here," the donkey whispered, shoving a book into her hands and pointing to lines.

She stared at the book—it was the scene where her character, Queen Titania, falls in love with the Nick Bottom donkey.

"Wow—two Fairy Queens!" Someone in the audience exclaimed, as others cheered.

Startled, Kara blurted out her line, " 'What angel wakes me from my flow'ry bed—' " and burst into tears.

"She's good."

*ZzzappPP!*

A beam of golden wolf magic collided with Kara.

"Ahhh!" Kara staggered back.

The audience, riveted now, clapped at the innovative special effects.

Adriane grabbed the donkey, gem blazing. "Nobody sweet-talks my jackass!"

Someone wearing a papier-mâché wall costume suddenly ran onstage, pushed past the three leaping fairies and hopping hobgoblin, and stood between the two queens. A rainbow gem glowed from the wall's wrist, protruding from the costume's side.

"Emily!" Kara cried. "Everything's gone wrong! My magic is all gone, I lost Starfire, and Lyra's almost melted, the goblin sorcerer betrayed everyone, he's opening the Otherworlds, Lorren is being chased by monsters, the Fairy Realms are falling apart—"

"What page is that?" the donkey asked, scratching his head.

"I have to go back!" Kara exclaimed, holding up her jewel.

"Put down the jewel and step away from the donkey!" Adriane yelled, storming around the wall.

"What is with her?!" Kara asked.

"They're all under love spells." Emily explained. "Courtesy of the d'flies."

Kara gulped. So that was what Goldie had intercepted in Tangoo's lab!

Musso barged over. "Where's the portal?"

Heather, Tiffany, and Molly scrambled after the hobgoblin.

Adriane raised her glowing wolf stone.

Everyone onstage was crowding around Kara.

"I have to go back!" she cried. "Starfire!"

*WHOOSH!*

A fireball hurtled over the astonished audience and landed onstage.

The flames shimmered and took shape.

Kara's breath caught in her throat.

Strong and proud, the magnificent fire stallion stood before her.

"Starfire!" Kara flung her arms around his neck, sobbing in disbelief.

Magic surged through her, filling her jewel with fire and her heart with joy.

The stallion looked down, and Kara followed his gaze. Set into his powerful flaming chest was a gleaming power crystal, pulsing with magic.

"You got it!" Kara exclaimed.

*"Our magic attracted a second crystal,"* the stallion explained.

"Two crystals!" She turned to Emily and gasped. "We got two crystals!"

"That is one amazing costume," the drama teacher approved. "It looks like it's really on fire!"

"It's those Ravenswood girls with their wild animals!" Kara's math teacher yelled disapprovingly.

"What kind of stunt is this?" the vice principal demanded.

Kara stammered.

Emily swept off the wall costume and smiled broadly to the audience. "We'd like to take this opportunity to announce the blazing-hot new tourist season at the Ravenswood Wildlife Preserve!" she cried out. "Everyone is invited to come on over and meet the animals! You won't believe your eyes!"

Emily took a bow as the audience cheered the impressive publicity stunt.

Kara leaped onto the stallion's back, her heart soaring as the magic rushed through her, fueled by the love of her bonded horse.

"Kara, give me a boost," Emily said. "Let's break these spells."

Aided by Starfire's strength, the blazing star reached out and grasped Emily's hand. Instead of flashy magic fire, Kara sent soft tendrils into Emily's jewel.

The healer smiled, impressed by Kara's elegant control. Her rainbow gem glowed bright blue, sending a spark of magic to the wolf stone on Adriane's wrist.

The warrior blinked and shook her head, staring incredulously at the fire stallion. "Kara? What's going on? Are you all right?"

"Yes!" she answered. And she was!

"Ewwww!" Heather shook her red hair and squealed, pulling herself away from Musso. "Where did you come from, Mars?!"

Molly and Tiffany took one look at the hobgoblin and ran offstage, screaming.

"Back to normal," Emily said, smiling.

Marcus shook his now human head as if he were waking from a dream. Scratchy donkey hair floated in the air around him. " 'And yet, to say the truth, reason and love keep little company together nowadays,' " he kept reading, oblivious of any change.

"I'm going back," Kara said to Emily and Adriane.

"We're coming with you!" Emily said adamantly.

"I'm the only one who can ride Starfire," Kara said. "But I won't be going alone."

Goldie popped onto Starfire's neck, in front of Kara, little fist raised.

"Let's ride!" she squeaked.

The horse kicked up onto his rear legs with a dramatic flare and charged up the center aisle, rocketing past the hooting and clapping students and out the main double doors. The standing ovation reverberated throughout the auditorium as cooling trails of flames vanished into thin air.

❧   ❧   ❧

Fueled by the pure magic of Avalon, the Firemental stallion returned to the Fairy Realms. Landing on the shore of the mirror lake, Kara, Goldie, and Starfire instantly felt the change, as if the air itself had mutated. The sky above flashed and whirled in seething coils of purple and glowing green. A fairy quake tore through the forests, twisting trees into dark and horrible shapes. The Fairy Realms were unraveling, for the darkness of the Otherworlds had already spread into the lake mirror, seeping into the lands.

Tangoo stood in the center of the mirror, the original power crystal in his raised hands, amplifying the towering beam of magic between the mirror and the Otherworlds.

"Princess!"

Kara turned to see Lorren running toward her, breathing hard.

"Lorren!" she shouted, relieved.

"Tangoo betrayed us all."

"I know," she hesitated.

"Listen to me," he said, looking into her eyes. "Tangoo is spreading the magic of the Otherworlds through the network of mirrors he set up."

Kara flashed on all the mirrors she had seen since arriving here. They had been placed in the most magical parts of the Five Kingdoms. No wonder the realms were falling apart so fast.

"You have to reverse the power!" he implored.

"I . . . how?" Even with Starfire, the power crystal, and her unicorn jewel, the task seemed immense, beyond her abilities.

"You are the blazing star, Kara," he said. "You are connected to the magic of Avalon itself."

"Oh, for crying out loud!" Tangoo's voice fell over them. "Give it up already, Princess. I'm sure my mistresses will be merciful if you join us."

"Stay away, Tangoo," Lorren cried. "You've done enough."

"Oh, but my plan is just beginning." He searched the forests for the hordes of creatures.

"Looking for your crew?" Lorren flashed a grin.

"Where are they?" Tangoo bellowed.

"They ran into a some "fairy" bad trouble." The boy let out a whistle.

Dozens of armed creatures emerged from the woods and ran forward to join the Forest Prince. Elfan, Spinnel, and Cotax were in the lead.

Kara recognized the creatures from the rave. They were Lorren's friends.

Tangoo focused on Kara, his black eyes glinting with rage. "No matter, Princess, the Otherworlds will replace the Fairy Realms," the sorcerer snarled. As if in response, the skies ripped open, sending beams of purple into the lake mirror.

Kara steeled herself, Starfire strong beside her, Goldie on her shoulder. Closing her eyes, she focused her unicorn jewel into Starfire's power crystal. Red-gold magic flared from his chest. She directed it toward the lake, trying to disrupt Tangoo's connection to the Otherworlds.

But Tangoo was not about to be foiled. He sent her magic slamming back at them. Flames skyrocketed from the stallion. Kara stumbled, reeling from the force of his attack.

"Twinkle twinkle, blazing star . . . how I wonder when you'll *die*!" the sorcerer snickered.

A jagged firebolt screamed across the sky and plunged into the forest. Foul plumes of purples and greens billowed in the distance.

"You can feel it, can't you?" he cried, eyes feverishly raised to the sky. "Dark magic seeps into the very core of the Fairy Realms, spreading like wildfire. Nothing can stop this, not even the blazing star."

The combination of the talismans, a power crystal, and the magic of the Otherworlds made Tangoo's power immense.

The earth rumbled beneath Kara's feet as waves of spiraling light surged from the mirror lake, forcing dark magic into the lands. She could feel the very fabric of the Fairy Realms ripping apart.

Lorren braced her, his hands on her shoulders. "Don't be afraid to be who you are," he said, his green eyes locked to hers. "Use your magic, Kara."

Her magic. The magic of the blazing star. Lucinda had told her the magic was strongest when it was used to help, to make others shine brightly.

"I can't do this alone." Kara's stomach twisted with panic. She needed her friends. But her jewel couldn't reach Emily and Adriane across worlds.

"I help!" Goldie flapped to Kara's shoulder, determination gleaming in her jeweled eyes.

"Goldie!" Kara exclaimed, remembering that the mini had bounced a love spell to the other d'flies. But she needed a lot more magic than a love spell.

"Can you connect me to Adriane and Emily's magic?"

Goldie leaped into the air, face scrunched in concentration.

Kara held on to Starfire's mane as another fairy quake warped through the forest behind them.

Then Goldie flashed, her wings shimmering, strong and vibrant, eyes glowing radiantly. "Let's rock!"

Kara held up her jewel and drew diamond light as Starfire flamed red fire. She wove their magic into a brilliant band and sent it shooting into the dragonfly.

"HooWeee!" The d'fly was engulfed in a flash of magic and blinked out.

Kara bit her lip, carefully adjusting the magical flow. Goldie had never transferred so much power before. Was her little friend up to it?

At first she didn't think anything was happening.

In her mind, Kara suddenly saw four bright flashes of magic. Goldie was linking with Fred, Fiona, Barney, and Blaze. Kara embraced the magic of each dragonfly, joining them to her and Starfire, until she had a view of all four of them, wingtips touching, twirling in a circle.

"Go Kaaraa!" Their happy voices squeaked.

Kara practically shouted with joy as the dragonflies' magic mixed with Starfire's and Goldie's. She had the weird sense of being two places at once.

Her body was in the Fairy Realms on the lakeshore, but her mind was on Earth, where she could see the now empty stage of the school auditorium.

Kara suddenly felt another boost of magic, kind and loving. She reached for it, connecting to the familiar blue magic of Emily's healing stone. The red-haired girl stood in the center of the dragonfly ring, eyes closed, jewel pulsing.

"Kara," Emily said warmly.

A jolt of wolf fire shot through Kara, strong and determined. Kara grasped the magic of the wolf stone as Adriane joined the circle, hands clasped in Emily's.

"I was hoping for a warrior, not a Fairy Queen," Kara said to her costumed friend.

"You can put a wolf in pink clothing, but she's still a wolf," Adriane replied with a grin.

"I can't do this without you," Kara cried.

"We are with you," they responded.

But an important piece was still missing.

Strong, fuzzy magic suddenly filled the gap as Ozzie stepped into the ring. His ferret stone glowed with power as he gave his magic freely.

Reaching out, she took Ozzie's gift.

"We love you, Kara," the ferret simply said.

And she was flying, gliding on glowing streams of magic, threading her way to Ravenswood. She flew through the thick woods, rich with greens. Beside her ran a black mistwolf, strong and proud.

Dreamer looked into Kara's eyes. *"I will always run with you, blazing star!"*

Kara felt the mistwolf's magic join her growing network as she soared high into the sky. Over the open fields, she found Tweek, riding atop the beautiful snow-white owl, Ariel.

"We are with you," the little Earth Fairimental yelled.

"As are we!" Voices echoed into the skies.

Below, the animals from Ravenswood stood together in the field, their voices joined in support. She welcomed them all to the expanding network, their magic thrilling her senses, filling her with new strength. She wrapped the magic of her friends around her.

There was no stopping her now.

As if summoned by her thoughts, the glimmering Ravenswood portal spiraled open in the field below, beckoning her on.

Kara shot through the portal and reached out for Aldenmor. She soared over the wondrous lands, now strong and vibrant, healed by the magic of her friends.

The howl of the mistwolves filled her with joy as the wolfsong washed through her senses. The pack, hundreds strong, thundered over a hill, lending their fierce strength to Kara. Bolstered by their power, the blazing star flew faster over the magical world, soaring above the glittering blue oceans.

Merpeople and seadragons cheered as Kara wove them into her ever-growing tapestry of magic and life.

She swept over the the old desert lair of the Dark Sorceress, now covered over with brilliant gardens. A sandy-haired boy stood beside a huge red dragon, sending Kara their magic through a bright red dragon stone. She felt Adriane's golden magic surge with happiness at the sight of her two friends, Zach and the Drake.

Whirling figures of earth, air, and water converged.

"The magic is with you now and forever!" Gwigg, the Earth Fairimental, called out.

Kara gasped as the incredible power of the Fairimentals joined her web of friends. She reached to Starfire, his fire taming her, keeping her in control.

Blazing with light, Kara soared across the lands as the magic of Aldenmor itself—the trees, the mountains, every living thing, big and small—sent its magic to her.

Kara could barely contain the building forces as she flung herself across the glittering magic web. Careening along arcs of stars, she reached for the most powerful of magical animals. Dazzling flashes popped along the looping strands. Crystal horns in all colors of the rainbow flooded Kara with power as the unicorns' mighty hooves thundered across the web. Thirty smaller horns chorused in perfect harmony as the Unicorn Academy happily added their song.

The rush of power made Kara laugh aloud. It thrilled through every part of her being. Everyone was giving his or her unique magic to Kara, each link connecting to everything else.

She was ready!

Kara soared into the Fairy Realms and swept through the Fairy Ring. The kings and queens quickly gathered the crowds into the center of the ring. Clasping hands, they all joined together to aid the blazing star.

Kara sped through the Fairy Realms like lightning, releasing her network's vast well of magic through the mountains—forests—lakes—rivers—into the very fabric of the land.

She vaguely sensed her physical body enveloped in a tempest of power. Something was tugging insistently at her mind. She suddenly realized Emily and Adriane were trying desperately to pull her back.

There was too much magic flooding through her. She was blazing out of control, too fast. Even Starfire could not pull her back now.

*"Everyone uses the blazing star."*

Through the dazzling brilliance, a presence was worming its way into Kara's mind, calling to her, drawing her in. Desperate, she grabbed for it and felt another magic, dark and compelling.

Anger welled inside Kara. Everyone was after

her power, using her for their own ends. The kings and queens were no different from the packs of magic-starved creatures, or even Lorren. None of them cared what happened to her as long as her magic was theirs to use.

*"The magic is yours. It is time for you to use it!"*

The magical network flickered, its brilliant light taking on darker hues. Kara felt the magic of the Otherworlds working through her, infecting each level of her network.

The white-hot center of her magic blazed as the seductive force engulfed her. She felt the need and thirst and hunger for more magic. It would never be enough. She could twist the magic of all those linked to her however she wanted, reweave worlds any way her heart desired. And no one could stop her.

No! Kara screamed, reaching for someone to help her.

She felt herself drowning, spiraling into the darkness, burning out like a blazing sunset.

*"Kara."*

Lost among the seething patterns of magic, she wondered where that voice was coming from.

*"Kara! Hang on to me."* Someone was supporting her with calm, strong magic.

Kara had a fleeting image of orange-spotted fur, sparking emerald eyes.

With a jolt, Kara came back to herself, trembling.

"Lyra?" she whispered. She reached for her friend. Lyra had never left her. The cat was always there, looking out for her. Watching over her.

Kara reached for the silver Heart of the Mountain, easily wresting its power from Tangoo's grasp. She sent the full force of her network through the quicksilver heart and focused on Lyra. She felt her friend's magic blaze to life, warm and loving.

Holding tight to Lyra, Kara let her friend's love wash over her, spreading back down the network.

One by one, she gently let the network go, breaking the hold of the dark forces.

Kara opened her eyes and stared at the mirror lake.

Starfire and Goldie were right by her side. Lorren stood nearby, watching her carefully.

Suddenly the boy leaped in the air and whooped. "You did it!"

Kara looked around. The lands were stable. No fairy quakes, no jagged lightning in the skies above. She had saved the Fairy Realms. No, she realized. Her friends had saved it through her.

A scream turned her attention back to the lake. Tangoo stood on the mirror, shaking with fear.

Kara had reversed the flow of magic. The mirror was now sending strong magic from the Fairy Realms, closing the Otherworlds.

She faced Tangoo, her heart filled with rage.

Tangoo held the power crystal in his hand. "If

you join us, the power will be yours," he said, flustered. "You can rule as you were meant to!"

Kara's ice blue eyes burned into the sorcerer. "Don't put it in your Day Planner."

She held up her unicorn jewel and fired.

Brilliant magic seared through the air. Tangoo swung the crystal to deflect the blast as Kara's fury smashed into him. Kara was jolted as the pure magic of Avalon touched the very soul of her being. She tried to pull her own magic back, but it bored into the power crystal with the full wrath of the blazing star. The jewel splintered and cracked, shattering into dust.

Screaming, Tangoo was caught in the mirror's powerful beam and sent hurtling up through the rift and into the Otherworlds.

The sky swirled in on itself, whirling with purples and greens. Great winds screeched over the rippling quicksilver. With a final burst of light, the rift closed. The lake shimmered and transformed back to shining crystal waters.

Kara stared at the blue sky, frozen. She had destroyed a power crystal, a crucial part of Avalon's magic. At the final moment, she had lost control of her magic after all.

Lorren stared at her, open mouthed. "You had it! You could have taken the crystal."

Kara hung her head. He was right. Tangoo was

helpless. She could have easily taken the power crystal.

*"You still have another."*

"Starfire!" she cried as the stallion's form rippled and wavered.

With a jolt of panic, Kara realized the stallion had let go of the second power crystal.

"No, you don't have to do this!" she cried.

*"It is my choice,"* Starfire said gently. *"Avalon's magic beckons to me, I belong there now. I am with you, blazing star, now and forever."*

In a flash of Firemental magic, Starfire's stallion form dissolved and vanished.

Kara looked down, feeling the power crystal heavy in her hands.

"What happened to Starfire?" Lorren asked.

"He's free," Kara murmured. Her heart ached, but she did not feel the unbearable loss that she had expected. The stallion was still with her, a warm spark in the heart of her magic. He would give her strength and temper her fire forever, whether he was physically by her side or not.

She looked at Lorren and deposited the crystal into his hands. "This is what you wanted, isn't it?"

"A second crystal!" Lorren looked at her, amazed. "How did you do it, Princess?"

"I didn't. My friends did," she told him.

From out of the golden glow of the setting sun,

shimmering wings glittered. A large leopard-like cat, lustrous spotted coat bright and healthy, emerald eyes twinkling, flew across the lake.

Kara ran to the shore, tears streaming down her face.

The cat landed next to her.

Flinging her arms around Lyra's neck, Kara cried happily. "You're okay!"

*"I'm glad to see you are in one piece, too,"* Lyra purred. *"Your magic reversed the quicksilver spell in time."*

Kara drew back, looking at her friend. "You saved me." She shivered with the memory of the dark magic pulling her under.

*"I am always with you."*

Kara hugged the cat, burying her face in silky orange fur.

Lyra eyed the power crystal clutched in Lorren's hand. *"I hope I didn't miss much."*

Kara smiled, suddenly exhausted. "Just the usual."

*"That bad?"* the cat asked, alarmed.

Kara sniffled, then laughed as Goldie landed on Lyra's head. She grabbed the mini and hugged her friends. "Let's go home."

# Chapter 15

"This will never do!" Raelda yelled, sharp green eyes flashing.

"It is the only way!" Selinda shouted back.

"I fear you are wrong!" Raelda matched her peer's obstinate tone.

The stout Goblin Queen and the tall Fairy Queen faced off, staring defiantly at each other, faces flushed with anger.

"Ladies, ladies." Kara swept into the room, alarmed. "Your guests are waiting!"

"Ah, Princess Kara." Selinda stood back, arms crossed. "Would you please tell my stubborn neighbor that *my* choice is correct—"

"Kara, my dear," Raelda broke in, hands on hips. "Tell the most gracious Fairy Queen what is best for *my* ballroom." She waved her hands, indicating the vast room in Castle Garthwyn, which was lined by huge, bare windows.

Kara studied the two rolls of fabric covering a long

table. Selinda had chosen a flowery yellow damask. Raelda's selection was a deep blue velvet brocade.

"Curtains are *totally* crucial in any decorating scheme," Kara said, tapping her fingers to her chin. She scrutinized the completely opposite fabric selections, and then took in the sun-drenched ballroom. Rich oak paneling covered the high walls, and tiles of deep muted gold, like falling leaves, spanned the wide floor. "What this room needs is color . . ."

Selinda nodded smugly.

"But also regal elegance."

Raelda nodded back at Selinda.

"How about this?" Kara selected a roll of beautiful lavender sateen, accented with streaks of royal blues and deep violets.

"Not bad," Raelda mused, holding up the fabric.

"Royal yet colorful," Selinda agreed.

The two queens smiled at each other.

Lorren hurried into the ballroom, buttoning his black jacket and slicking back his dark hair.

"Whoa, this time we're gonna have a real war!"

"King Rolok?" Raelda asked.

"Everyone." Lorren smiled at Kara. "They've all been arguing ever since they got here."

Raelda led Kara out to the ballroom's grand balcony overlooking the grotto. "Come, we must settle this matter of your mentor."

"We've been doing fine by ourselves," Kara said.

"Tsk, tsk!" Raelda wagged her finger. "My dear, it is simply not proper for young mages to not have a mentor."

"Your power surprised even me," Selinda said seriously.

"She did everything you asked of her," Lorren muttered. "And more."

Raelda whispered loudly to Kara. "I've introduced him to every Goblin girl in the kingdom."

Kara glanced at the queen.

"But I think he has eyes for someone special," Raelda winked.

"Mother!" Lorren's cheeks flushed green.

"Oh, hush!" She slipped Kara's arm into his as they walked down the wide staircase. "Now escort the princess to the party!"

If not for the hundreds of frolicking guests and lively music, Garthwyn Grotto would have seemed a sanctuary hidden deep within the heart of the forest. Sparkling waterfalls tumbled down huge quartz rocks, filling a series of stone pools with crystal blue waters. Lush ferns grew near the glittering mist of waterfalls, and giant redwoods ringed the grotto like silent sentinels.

Guests from the Five Kingdoms were chatting, eating, laughing, and swimming, enjoying the spectacular afternoon.

All eyes turned to the princess of magic and the

Goblin Prince as they descended the gleaming marble staircase that led into the grotto.

Kara felt like Cinderella at the ball.

Kara and Lorren strolled near the food stands that lined the grotto's edge. Amazing pastries, strange-looking pizzas with green cheese, and bowls of purple chips and flower-shaped chocolates sat on tables jampacked with endless varieties of snacks. A thick, yet delicious-smelling steam billowed from one table. The bright banner draped high above the grill proclaimed: MUSSO AND SPARKY'S MAGICALLY TASTY CHEESE!

Kara coughed, waving away a cloud of smoke, and smiled at the two fairy creatures working furiously over the hot grill. "I see you're on to your next daring mission."

"We're out of the adventuring game," Musso declared, smearing a gob of barbecue sauce on his white apron. His aviator cap had been replaced with a tall, puffy chef's hat. "With the Fairy Realms at peace, everyone's gonna want to rave."

"And our barbecued cheese sticks are going to be the life of any party!" Sparky added, waving a skewer dripping with cheese in the air.

"Not bad," Lorren said, sampling a cheesy bit.

Kara searched the crowd. With the Ravenswood portal now opened, all her friends had been invited to the celebration. She found them standing near a glittering waterfall, and waved.

Kara had given Emily and Adriane a complete

tour of the Fairy Palace before the party, including the magic closet. Emily looked beautiful with her hair piled into a mass of flame red ringlets and wearing a sky blue sundress and heeled beige sandals. Her healing jewel glowed with bright rainbow sparkles. Adriane stood next to her, gleaming dark hair pulled back in a simple ponytail. A wraparound white silk shirt set off her sparkling black eyes, with stylish jeans and matching jacket completing the outfit. Her golden wolf stone shone proudly upon her black and turquoise band.

Kara herself had chosen cream-colored linen drawstring Capris with small flowers embroidered on the hems, a matching pink tank top, and strappy off-white sandals. Her hair fell down her back in a cascade of gentle golden curls.

Dreamer dashed onto the sprawling lawns beyond the grotto, playing with a group of excited young pixies. Goldie zoomed around with Fiona, Fred, Blaze, and Barney sampling the snacks.

Kara walked toward her friends, Lorren at her side. "Emily, Adriane, this is Prince Lorren."

Healer and warrior grinned at the cute goblin.

Lorren bowed deeply. "Never has there been a day when such lovely ladies have graced Castle Garthwyn. Your beauty outshines your jewels."

Emily mouthed to Kara, *He's adorable!*

Kara blushed, then elbowed Lorren playfully. "Watch it Prince, your Zorro is leaking."

"No more disguises for me—I've hung up my cape," Lorren said. "My Zorro days are over."

"Aw, and we were looking forward to seeing the dashing mystery guy in action." Adriane grinned.

"A friend taught me not to hide who I really am." He smiled at Kara. "I'll be able to do more good as the Goblin Prince than I ever could have as the Forest Prince."

"Honored guests, your attention, please." Queen Raelda's voice rose above the clamor, commanding everyone's attention. A beaming young Goblin girl in green velvet robes stood beside her.

Raelda continued, "With the recent departure of our sorcerer, it is my pleasure to present the new Goblin court sorceress, the lady Tasha!"

As the guests clapped, Tasha ran to the mages. "Do you believe this?" she asked, giggling.

"You deserve it," Lorren told his friend, giving her a hug.

"Congratulations," Kara said with a warm smile.

"Now we must settle the matter of our princess," Dwarf King Rolok called out. "She must have a proper mentor."

The Dwarf King stood among a group of trolls, goblins, elves, dwarves, and fairies. In the center, shampooed, fluffed, and wearing a bright Hawaiian shirt, was Ozzie, trying to balance a plate piled high with waffles.

"Princess," Troll King Ragnar said. "You have

shown us brilliant power by saving our lands. But frankly, we could have given the Fairimentals not one power crystal, but two! Power such as yours, as well as the others', can be corrupted."

A chill ran down Kara's spine.

"We insist the mages accept a mentor from the dwarves!" King Rolok demanded. "After all, we are the hardest-working race in the Fairy Realms."

"Oh, I suppose you think fairies are just cute little woodfolk who spend their lives prancing about in the moonlight?" Fairy King Oriel demanded. "Well, we don't. We work!"

Brownies, spriggens, and sirens floating in pool chairs and sipping tall glasses of lemonade waved.

"Princess Kara, who would you chose to be your mentor?" Troll Queen Grethal asked.

"Hey, what about me!" Ozzie demanded. "The Fairimentals sent me to find the mages in the first place!"

"Sir Ozymandias, with all due respect, you are not trained in the magic and natural sciences," Dwarf King Rolok said dismissively.

"GaK! These are teenage girls, they don't come with instructions!" Ozzie sputtered.

"The mages need a fairy mentor," the Fairy King continued. "There's conjuring, spells, and spellsinging; black magic, white magic, wizard magic; witches' brews, horrible curses—"

"And what about focusing the magic?" the

Goblin King joined in. "There's magic mirrors, crystal balls, power jewels, talismans—"

"Gentlemen, ladies," Raelda called out. "Please, this is a party, not a debate."

"Tell us, young mage," King Rolok commanded, "what do you know about magic?"

Everyone stopped arguing as a hush fell over the entire party. All eyes turned to Kara.

"I know what I feel." Kara's hand went to her heart. "I know magic always starts here. And here, with my friends." She nodded, indicating Emily, Adriane, Ozzie, Dreamer, Goldie, and Lyra.

The healer and the warrior stepped forward and handed Kara the silver pack she'd gotten back from Tangoo. Even though Kara's magic had made the elemental talismans, they had never belonged to her. She understood that true power was not in using the talismans for herself, but in recognizing where they would do the most good.

Confidently, she stepped forward to address the kings and queens.

"King Ragnar and Queen Grethal," she said, turning to the massive trolls. "This gift is for you, so you may always feel the magic of laughter."

She handed the perplexed Troll King the shining purple bunny shoes. He broke out in a wide, toothy grin as he held up the elemental water magic.

The crowd cheered.

"King Landiwren and Queen Elara, this is for

you." She handed the Elf Queen the glowing pearly air elemental harp. "So you may always have the magic of music to inspire you."

The Elf Queen held the harp high in her graceful hand, setting off another round of applause.

"King Rolok and Queen Praxia." Kara took the Heart of the Mountain from the bag. All eyes went wide, appreciating the beauty of the glowing quicksilver heart. "For you, so you may always know the magic of love and kindness."

The dwarves cheered.

"And for you, Queen Raelda and King Voraxx," she said as she smiled at the goblins and placed the sparkling yellow sunstone in the queen's green hand, "so your wisdom and grace may shine over us all."

Raelda took the gift and hugged Kara tightly. "Thank you, Princess."

Finally, Kara turned to the fairy rulers. "Queen Selinda and King Oriel, I have a gift for you, too." Kara took the final talisman out of the bag and handed it to the queen.

Selinda gasped at the dazzling fire-red rose, exquisitely constructed from pure elemental magic. Its glowing light sparkled brightly in her violet eyes. "Child, where did you get this?"

"I made it." Kara paused. "Well, Tasha and Goldie helped me. It contains each of the four elements, working together to make strong magic."

Kara and Selinda hugged warmly.

"I shall treasure this always."

The crowd cheered.

Queen Selinda addressed the royalty, and all the creatures gathered. "I think the princess has shown us that, in spite of our differences, we are unified by a common cause: our love for our lands and respect for all living things. Is that not true magic?"

The crowd cheered in agreement, whistling and applauding enthusiastically.

"But what about a mentor?" King Rolok pressed.

Selinda smiled at Kara, Emily, and Adriane, then answered. "We will give the mages full access to *all* of our resources. We shall pledge to help them however we can, together."

Selinda smiled and reached for a silver carrying case. "Now, I have something for you, Princess." The case shook and rattled persistently. "They insisted."

The case popped open, releasing clouds of powder and perfume.

"We were born to beautify!" Skirmish cried joyfully, hugging Whiffle and squeezing another cloud of perfume from the atomizer's nose.

Puffdoggie leaped out, wriggling and barking, running circles around Kara's feet.

Mirabelle snapped open and closed excitedly. "We cannot bear to be parted from you again, Princess!"

"I will fluff! I will spritz!" Whiffle cried.

"Will you calm down!" Angelo yelled, pushing everyone in line.

Kara lit up—now it was her turn to cheer.

Emily and Adriane eyed the amazing accessories curiously, looked at each other, and shrugged.

Lorren walked to Kara. "You truly know how to work a crowd."

"I'm really a party mage." Kara giggled, then said seriously, "Lorren, I want you to know I didn't mean to destroy that other power crystal." She turned away. "At the last minute, I just lost it."

"After what Tangoo did, who could blame you? No one here, certainly." He looked into her eyes. "Kara, you never intended to destroy the crystal. It was an accident."

Kara wasn't convinced.

"You saved the Fairy Realms." Lorren clasped his hands over hers. "And together we'll find a way to save Avalon!"

"Okay." She smiled.

He bowed. "Now my friends are all insisting on dancing with the mages. So please help me or I may have to fight them off."

"Wait right here," she told Lorren, then dashed over to her friends.

Taking in the scene, Adriane quipped, "How are they ever going to keep Cinderella down on the farm?"

"That's your job," Kara responded, throwing her arms around Emily and Adriane's shoulders. "Whatever happens, I'm counting on all of you and . . ."

They looked at Kara.

"I love you all very much."

Lyra, Dreamer, Ozzie, Emily, Adriane, and Kara stood together, Goldie whirling overhead. Clasping hands to paws, the mages and their magical animal friends smiled at one another.

"Now let's dance!" Kara commanded.

Cotax spun Adriane on the dance floor as Emily whipped Ozzie into a ferret-stomping frenzy. Lorren and Tasha moved and shimmied, laughing as all the guests whirled around the floor in celebration, their joyous laughter filling the air.

Kara looked on and smiled. She raised her unicorn jewel and gazed into its light. Diamond white and red fire entwined and sparkled. Her magic had changed, and she with it. Starfire's magic had mixed with her own, strengthening and tempering her power. She was no longer trapped by her magic. She didn't fear it. Come what may, she was now free to choose *how* she would use it. She might make mistakes—correction, she probably would make mistakes—but there was no going back. The past shaped who she was. But the kind of person she would grow to be, well, that was all in her hands, like the magic running through her jewel. Her friends loved her. She knew that as sure as the bright sun shining over the wondrous Fairy Realms. But it wasn't about how much love she could gather in her life; it was how much she was willing to give back. That was the magic of the blazing star.

# Epilogue

The gigantic black spider thrummed down its web, dragging cocooned bodies past the three black mirrors embedded in the silken strands. Long, spiked legs paused as it hissed at a cloaked figure that stood below.

"Yes, my pet, I missed you, too." The Spider Witch laughed, pixilated eyes roving gleefully around the octagonal courtyard of her lair.

The Dark Sorceress stood a few steps back, watching uneasily as her ally stroked the spider's massive head.

Appendages wriggling, the spider's huge fangs slipped from its mouth, sinking into a carcass as it began to feed.

The Dark Sorceress turned away, shuddering as the spider clicked and slurped. There were some things not even she could stomach.

The witch's insect warrior, standing across the courtyard, smiled wickedly at the sorceress's disgust.

The Dark Sorceress cursed herself for showing such weakness. But this was a small price to pay for freedom. She had to admit the Spider Witch's plan had worked perfectly. The three of them had slipped undetected from the Otherworlds during Tangoo's use—albeit short lived—of the power crystal. It had been enough. They were free, and their enemies were none the wiser.

The Fairimentals now had two crystals in their possession, and soon it would be time for the Dark Sorceress's own plan to begin. She needed only one more crystal in place to begin turning the Fairimental she had chosen to serve her.

The rustle of legs broke her thoughts as the Spider Witch approached.

"Poor thing hasn't had fresh meat for a long time."

The two swept into the castle's dimly lit main chamber, where the witch had already begun work on a new tapestry. Hundreds of spiders hung from the stone ceiling, releasing silken strands of webbing that stretched down to the floor.

"How do you like it so far?" the Spider Witch asked, multifaceted eyes glistening yellow-green within the folds of her hood.

"It has its merits," the Dark Sorceress replied, looking at the patterns already forming on the exquisite strands: trees, rivers, a map of a forested region.

"The blazing star outdid herself," the Spider Witch hissed.

The Dark Sorceress smiled, vampire teeth catching the light. "Your sorcerer made her angry."

"Angry enough to destroy a power crystal. Did you know she had such power?"

"Yes."

"And you still think you can bring her around?"

"Yes."

"I am not so certain, unless, of course . . ." Her words trailed off as she ran her pale, blue-veined fingers along the webbing. In the center, a large, gothic manor house was forming: Ravenswood Manor.

The Dark Sorceress raised an eyebrow.

"The mages must be taught a lesson. It is time for them to learn the meaning of revenge."

# Ghost Wolf

# THE WORLD OF AVALON

❧ ❧ ❧ ❧ ❧ ❧ ❧ ❧ ❧ ❧

*The Mages:*

Emily — The healer, wears the rainbow jewel

Adriane — The warrior, wears the wolf stone

Kara — The blazing star, wears the unicorn jewel

Ozzie — An elf trapped in the body of a ferret, wears the ferret stone

Three teenagers and a ferret whose lives crisscross at the intersection of magic and friendship. Together they fight the dark powers bent on controlling the home of all magic, a mystical place called Avalon.

*Magical Animal Friends:*

Lyra — Winged leopard cat bonded to Kara

Dreamer — Mistwolf bonded to Adriane

Stormbringer — Mistwolf bonded to Adriane

Ariel — Magical owl

Starfire — Elemental fire stallion bonded to Kara

Dragonflies — Mini dragons, Goldie, Blaze, Barney, Fiona, and Fred

The Drake — Dragon bonded to Zach and Adriane

❧ ❧ ❧ ❧ ❧ ❧ ❧ ❧ ❧ ❧

❧ ❧ ❧ ❧ ❧ ❧ ❧ ❧ ❧ ❧

*Aldenmor:*

| | |
|---|---|
| Fairimentals | Protectors of the magic of Aldenmor, take form in different elements |
| Tweek | Experimental earth Fairimental sent to mentor the mages |
| Zach | A teenage boy raised by mistwolves, wears the dragon stone |

*Home Base:*
The Ravenswood Animal Preserve

*The Dark Mages:*

| | |
|---|---|
| The Spider Witch | Elemental magic master |
| The Dark Sorceress | Half human, half animal magic user |

*The Quest:*
Return nine missing power crystals to Avalon. Without these crystals, the magical secrets of Avalon will be lost forever.

❧ ❧ ❧ ❧ ❧ ❧ ❧ ❧ ❧ ❧

# Chapter 1

The full moon rose, illuminating the forests of Ravenswood with a cold silver glow. Adriane Charday stood surrounded by the mass of great trees. She could not stop the memories, vivid with pain and terror, from flashing through her mind. The dreams of her first pack mate were always the same: Stormbringer sacrificing herself to save the other mistwolves, and Adriane powerless to help her.

The musky scent of fear filled her senses, a palpable trail on the soft breeze. She swung around, knowing that a doe and her yearling fawn were hiding in the brush behind her.

Somewhere in the distance a wolf howled—a high, keening note that quickly descended in pitch. Instinctively, Adriane raised her face to the moon and howled. Another joined in, and then a chorus echoing through the trees. Mistwolves!

But something was wrong.

The pack was lost, separated from its home. Adriane stood for a moment, listening. She knew what it was like to be lost and alone.

The golden wolf stone burned upon her wrist.

A mournful, sliding yowl thrummed through her. Adriane recognized the call instantly. The mistwolves were in danger. She had to help!

Her black eyes gleamed as she charged through the undergrowth, wildly dodging low-hanging oak branches and leaping over fallen logs. She felt her lips draw back in a snarl.

Suddenly, the forests around her started rippling and distorting. Earthy browns and greens shifted into bizarre blues and reds. Majestic trees took on jagged shapes as their colors wavered into ghostly purple hues. Even the familiar forest scents of pine and loam were lost in this unnatural wood.

Panic ripped through her. What was happening?

Adriane plunged ahead, ignoring the sharp brambles, as the forests lurched around her, warping into brilliant pinks and ambers. Terrified, she cried out for help, but only a ragged howl tore from her throat.

The familiar scent of her first pack mate filled her sharply enhanced senses, making her heart pound.

Then her wolf senses were picking up something else, as if the forest itself were calling to her, calming her magic.

Something flashed in the distance. Her vision, sharpened with wolf's eyes, locked onto a tower of bright light glowing in the depths of the trees. She ran toward it.

Adriane barreled headlong into an open glade,

drawn by feelings that she could not name. She looked up at the massive stone tower, its pinnacle pointing like a thin finger to the sky.

The Rocking Stone. She was in the magic glade of Ravenswood. Willow trees bordering the lake glowed within the stone's light, their golden bark pulsing with power.

A song, rising and falling like a mother's lullaby, drifted across the glade. Adriane closed her eyes, feeling the magic with her wolf senses, letting the melody soothe her.

*"I have been waiting for you, warrior."*

Adriane swung around, jewel light slashing across her eyes like fire. "Who's there?"

A willow tree near the lakeshore moved, rippling the radiant waters of the lake.

Adriane approached cautiously and saw her— what appeared to be a tree was a figure, a fairy creature. Adriane knew instinctively that this was the source of the glade's magic, the heart of Ravenswood. The extraordinary figure raised her head, grassy hair flowing down her back in long curling strands of green and brown. Sinuous branches unfurled into long arms stretching wide to embrace the glade and the surrounding forests. Moonlight danced across bright flowers dotting her gown of velvety moss. Slender legs twisted down into strong roots.

The forest creature turned her head expectantly, luminous eyes shifting from greens to blues to browns, reflecting all the colors of the forest. Spotting Adriane, a smile as bright as sunlight spread across her beautiful features. *"I have watched you with great joy, young warrior."*

The voice flowed through Adriane, filling her with the sweetness of life.

"Who—what are you?"

*"I am Orenda, a sylph bonded to these forests,"* the figure said stiffly, as if the effort to speak were painful.

Bonded to the forests? Adriane and her friends, Emily and Kara, certainly knew about bonding with magical animals. It was essential to using their magical abilities. But this was something entirely different.

Adriane looked closer. Silken threads snaked through the willow's branches, forming a net that cut like wire. Green oozed from split bark, dripping like blood.

The sylph's face twisted in agony as the webbing tightened.

Adriane gasped, her heart twisted by the sylph's pain. "What's happening to you?"

*"I am sick."*

A profound sadness swept through Adriane.

*"I cannot protect my forest,"* the wondrous creature said, her voice like a soft breeze. *"It is now up to you."*

Suddenly, webbing surged from the shadows, ensnaring Orenda's willowy arms. The sylph jerked forward, grassy hair crackling. An immense cocoon was forming around her.

Adriane swooned as dizzying waves of dark magic attacked the forest sylph. Gleaming strands closed tight, crushing the sylph's graceful limbs with sickening cracks.

Adriane desperately summoned her magic, her wolf stone casting a blaze of light across the glade. "Tell me what to do!"

Orenda's voice was urgent. *"The ones that are lost must be found."*

"Who is lost?"

*"The mistwolves,"* the sylph whispered, the song of life all but crushed from her breath.

Mistwolves? The mistwolves were on Aldenmor. "I don't understand."

A vicious snarl rumbled from the woods.

Adriane swung into a fighting stance as wolf eyes materialized in the gloom, glittering malevolently.

"Storm?" she called out in a panic.

The ghostly figure crept from the trees, circling the warrior. The mistwolf was massive. It didn't look real. Cold blue light shimmered through its translucent body. One eye glowed blue, the other green. Silver teeth bared, lips pulled back, the creature snarled the death grin of a hunting wolf.

*"You do not belong with the wolves,"* it challenged. *"A wolf protects the pack."*

"Who are you?" Adriane tensed, torn between fleeing and fighting.

*"I am the pack leader,"* the wolf snarled.

"This is *my* home," Adriane said, her wolf stone blazing in warning. "You are the intruder."

The wolf circled, smelling its victim's fear.

"I don't want to hurt you." Adriane raised her jewel, sparks of light edging along her arm.

*"It is your nature, human. You will always hurt the mistwolves."*

Jaws snapping, the pack leader rushed in without warning, his shoulder ramming Adriane's left side. Savage magic hit her like an electric shock. The wolf stone exploded in golden light.

"No!" The air rushed from Adriane's chest as the massive wolf pinned her to the ground. She tried to move, but her legs and arms were held motionless. Struggling, she rolled over and fell, landing hard.

Suddenly her eyes flew open, though she hadn't realized they were closed. Something black as night loomed over her, a snarling shadow barely visible in the darkness. Screaming, she rolled away, desperately trying to free her wolf stone and defend herself.

The wolf's wild emerald eyes locked onto her panicked gaze as she wrenched her wrist free, wolf stone sparking dangerously.

"Dreamer?" Adriane breathed.

Her pack mate's jet-black fur gleamed, the snowy star upon his chest reflecting the gold of her magic.

The mistwolf nosed twisted blankets away from her arms and legs, snapping at the air, his hackles raised.

"Dreamer!" Adriane's hands flew to protect her face. "It's okay. It's me," she reassured her pack mate, taking in the familiar scene of her own room. It had only been a dream.

The dreamcatchers over her bed caught the moonlight, casting shadows like spiderwebs.

*"Pack mate."* Dreamer's voice sounded faintly in her mind, as if he were having trouble communicating.

"Easy." Adriane knelt and grabbed the wolf gently by the ears and stared at him, nose to nose. "Shhh. It's okay."

She held her friend close, feeling his heart pounding against her own.

She felt the wolf trying to speak, his thoughts brushing at the edge of her mind.

"What's wrong?" Adriane asked, concentrating on the jagged connection.

Dreamer stood back, his tail between his legs, ears flattened. No longer snarling, he tilted his head to one side, embarrassed and uncertain.

A cold fear rushed through her. Something was wrong with his magic.

Snarling in frustration, the wolf sent a flurry of jumbled images crashing into her mind.

*The forests of Ravenswood twisting and warping—*

*dark creatures hunting in the pale starlight—her grand-*
*mother, motionless, slumped over the kitchen table—the*
*sickly gleam of a terrifying spiderweb—*

"Dreamer!" Adriane gasped, reeling from the impact of the horrible images. "Is there something wrong with Gran?"

Dreamer raised his nose and barked, confirming her fear. Adriane leaped to her feet and raced out of her bedroom, Dreamer on her heels. Fear was thick in her throat as she sped down the stairs and skidded into the kitchen.

"Gran!" she cried.

Just as in Dreamer's vision, her grandmother sat at the round wooden table, slumped over a cup of tea.

The old woman looked up slowly as Adriane rushed to her side, her face pale and drawn. "Little Bird . . ."

"Gran, are you all right?" Adriane asked.

Gran smiled weakly and gestured to the chair opposite hers. Silver and turquoise bracelets clanked on her thin wrists. Adriane turned and saw hot cocoa steaming in her favorite blue mug, as if Gran had expected her.

Dreamer lay down near the table, head resting on his paws.

Sitting down, Adriane closed her hands tightly around the warm drink and studied her grandmother. Nakoda Charday had always been so vital and full of life, it was impossible to mark her with age. But now, deep lines ran from her eyes, creasing her weathered, dark skin like patches of worn leather. Her black eyes were sunken and glassy. Adriane breathed deeper. She had never seen Gran look so—old.

Gran drew her long white braid over her shoulder. Her tired eyes sharpened and focused on Adriane. "The forest spirit is dying."

"The forest spirit?" Adriane echoed. First Dreamer had shown her images from her nightmare, and now it seemed Gran knew about the sylph.

Gran nodded. "I know you feel it, too, Little Bird. The forest called to you."

Adriane fought to appear calm, but her heart was racing. It had been over a year since her parents had first brought her to Ravenswood, but the memory was still fresh. The forest had called to her then as well. It had given her something wonderful. She watched her grandmother study the gem upon Adriane's wrist. The golden wolf stone pulsed with light.

"Do you know why I insisted your mother bring you here?" Gran asked.

Adriane shrugged, her long black hair falling over her face. "She and Dad were busy touring with their art."

Gran shook her head. "Your mother never had the gift. But you do."

"The forest spirit was just a dream," Adriane insisted. "Wasn't it?"

"Just because it was a dream doesn't mean it's not real," Gran said, a shadow of a smile deepening the wrinkles around her eyes and mouth. Her long, slender fingers reached out and covered Adriane's precious stone of magic. "I was right to bring you here."

Startled, Adriane regarded the jewel on her black and turquoise wristband. She had found the wolf stone in the forests of Ravenswood not long after she had come to live here. Was it all supposed to happen this way? Had she been destined to meet Storm? And then to lose her?

Gritting her teeth against the tears that always threatened when she thought about Storm, she looked down at her hands. And froze. Black dirt streaked her fingers and nails. Her blue T-shirt and sweatpants were covered with grass stains and mud.

Frantically, she pushed up the right leg of her pants. Streaks of dried blood marked her ankle— where she had run through the brambles in her dream. Or what she thought had been a dream.

"The wolves . . . they call to me, Gran," she told her grandmother quietly, head bowed. "Sometimes . . . I dream about running with them and never coming back."

Gran nodded, her grip tightening on Adriane's wrist.

"It seems Little Bird has found her true name," Gran said. "Little Wolf."

# Chapter 2

The golden brown ferret's voice echoed though the Ravenswood Manor library as Adriane walked in.

*"Listen, my friends, to this wondrous tale,"* Ozzie read dramatically, arms waving, nose twitching:

> *"Of a hero whose courage would not fail.*
> *"When all seemed lost and our fate tragic,*
> *"Along came a princess of strong heart and magic.*
> *"With her jewel of power and fiery steed,*
> *"She saved the Fairy Realms in its hour of need.*
> *"She came from afar, she didn't come in a car,*
> *"This was the ride of the blazing star!"*

"Hooo." Ariel, a magical snow owl, nodded her feathery head, blinking her giant sky blue eyes. She was perched on the library ladder admiring Kara's dazzling unicorn jewel. Sun streamed through the huge bay windows, sending sparkles of white, pink, and red dancing across the high-domed ceiling of the grand library.

*"Not bad,"* Lyra, a leopard-like cat, said, washing her shoulder with long licks.

"What is that, Ozzie?" Emily asked, walking over to the computer console. The workstation was set behind a secret panel in the library wall. Ozzie had officially become the computer expert mage, ordering supplies for the preserve online, as well as handling all the e-mail.

"E-mail from the Fairy Realms," Ozzie reported, his golden ferret stone shining on his leather collar. "Lyrics for 'The Ballad of the Blazing Star.' "

"Looks like you made quite an impression, as usual." The red-haired healer smiled at Kara, then turned to Adriane. "Hey, Adriane. What do you think of the blazing ballad?"

With a grunt, Adriane plopped on the couch, propping her boots on the long oak table.

"Are you okay?" Emily asked.

"Just a little tired."

Gran still wasn't feeling any better, and Dreamer had been agitated all morning. Adriane had been up early, checking the glade. In the light of day, everything seemed normal. No sign of the magical tree sylph. But she knew something was wrong. Seeing all her friends busy in the sunlit library made her hesitant to say anything—especially when she wasn't even sure what to think herself.

Adriane brushed her hair away from her face and concentrated on calling Dreamer. The mistwolf, a natural magic tracker, was canvassing the rest of the preserve. He would sniff out anything dangerous.

Holding her wolf stone, she called with her mind, *"Dreamer, where are you?"*

Jagged sparks flashed through Adriane's mind.

"I've never seen anything like it!" Tweek exclaimed, perching next to Ariel. Tweek was a small, magical being composed of earth elements. He had been assigned by the Fairimentals to mentor the mages, an Experimental Fairimental. With Kara's help, Tweek had augmented his leafy stick-figure body with flowers and vines.

"It's incredible, isn't it?" Kara's blue eyes sparkled as she twirled the glittering red, white, and pink gem attached to its silver chain.

"I must say, this is the most impressive jewel I've ever seen," Tweek proclaimed, his twiggy body rattling with excitement. "Of course, I've only been around for six weeks."

"What does it mean, Tweek?" Emily asked.

"It means you are now a Level Two blazing star," Tweek told Kara excitedly, his quartz eyes glistening.

"Yeah, and it totally matches every outfit I own!" The blazing star held the jewel next to her sporty pink running pants, jean jacket, and denim hat embroidered with the Ravenswood logo.

*"That's an accomplishment,"* Lyra observed, green eyes twinkling.

"It usually takes years to advance to Level Two.

You did it in two days." Tweek's quartz eyes rattled. "You're breaking all the rules!"

"Not the first time," Kara quipped.

"You mean our jewels can change more than once?" Emily asked, studying her rainbow healing gem encased on its silver band.

"Yes, every time you move up a rank, your jewel evolves to match your magic," the E. F. explained.

Kara twirled her unicorn jewel. "Mine changed after I bonded with Starfire."

Adriane sat forward, absently rubbing her wolf stone.

The jewel had been rough and unpolished when she first found it in the portal field. But as she and Stormbringer became pack mates, it had quickly transformed into a paw-shaped wolf stone.

"Level One mages use jewels to focus the magic," Tweek explained, looking at Kara. "Bonding with magical animals is essential, protecting you from losing yourself in the magic. But Kara has also bonded with an elemental creature, Starfire. A firemental, no less—inconceivable!"

*"And she saved my tail in the nick of time."* Lyra rubbed against Kara's side.

"You're welcome," Kara purred.

Adriane felt a pang of sadness watching Kara and Lyra, a Level Two mage and her loving, bonded animal, together forever.

"Level Two mages find their own unique elemental magic based on one of the four elements: water, air, fire, and earth," Tweek continued. "To reach Level Two, a mage must bond with a powerful creature of the same element like Kara did. It's called a paladin."

"What's the difference between a magical animal and a paladin?" Emily asked.

"Magical animals work side by side with you, and are friends that grow with you through all stages of magic," the E. F. answered. "The tie is extremely deep and unbreakable."

Adriane's wolf stone flared. Emily turned concerned hazel eyes to the warrior, sensing her friend's grief.

"A paladin like Kara's fire stallion is a creature made of pure elemental magic," Tweek continued. "Starfire is inextricably linked to Kara and her jewel. Only she can summon him."

"Really?" Kara asked excitedly, waving her sparkling jewel wildly in the air. "Starfire! Heeere, Starfire!"

"No, no." Tweek shook his twigs. "A paladin only comes when you are in great need. It is a protector of immeasurable power."

"Oh." Kara dropped her jewel, frowning.

"Well, Kara," Emily said. "You were the last to find your jewel, but now you're first."

"Exactly where I should be," Kara said, radiating a dazzling smile.

Adriane crossed her arms and sat back, glowering.

Kara, the blazing overachiever. Things always went her way. Adriane had found her jewel first. She had bonded with Storm first. She had worked on her magic for a full year, and now it seemed she was only going backward.

Adriane abruptly stood and started pacing, her shadow casting strange shapes across the inlaid wooden floor. "Could it ever go the opposite way?"

"What do you mean?" Tweek asked.

"Could the jewels ever get *out* of tune?" Adriane held up her wrist, emphasizing her point with a flash from her wolf stone. "Could we lose our magic?"

"Well, technically your magic is always changing. But as you grow more powerful, the greater the chance it could be corrupted. That's why you have your animal friends. To keep you balanced and grounded."

"I lost my bonded animal," Adriane said flatly.

"I lost my magic, and Starfire helped me get it back," Kara said.

"Adriane and I switched magic powers," Emily said.

"We still have some of each other's magic," the warrior added.

Tweek scratched his mossy head. "Frankly, you mages are entering uncharted areas. With the magic flowing wild from Avalon, extraordinary things are happening. That's precisely why the Fairimentals designed me to stay on Earth."

"Incoming." Ozzie turned back to the computer as it *dinged*. "Kara, your e-mail from the city council."

"Perfect. Print it." Kara grabbed her pink Palm-Pilot and started checking her to-do lists. "Tour bus arrives in twenty minutes, people!"

Today was the opening day of the new tourist season. Kara had convinced her dad, the mayor of Stonehill, to add Ravenswood as a stop for a bus touring company. This was a major break for Ravenswood and the girls. As part of their arrangement with the town council, the girls needed to generate income to keep the preserve open.

In the year since the girls had managed the preserve, with the help of Gran and Emily's mom, Dr. Carolyn Fletcher, the animals had flourished. There were more deer than ever, peacocks, all kinds of wild birds, foxes, rabbits, and even a few bears.

That didn't include the special guests who'd decided to stay after the mages healed their home world, Aldenmor. The magical animals helped the mages care for the preserve and monitor for any signs of unusual magical activity.

With a soft hum, a color print slid from the printer.

"Tah-dah!" Kara grabbed the brochure and read it excitedly. " 'Ghosts, witches, monsters! See for yourself if the legends of Ravenswood are real. The Ravenswood Experience—see it, feel it, touch it!' Pretty cool, huh?"

"Hooyaaa!" Ariel cheered.

"We should be focusing on the animals," Adriane said, annoyed.

"It's just a little spin. Besides, it was the only way I could cement the tour deal."

"Maybe it should say, 'You'll be smitten. Not bitten,' " Adriane grumbled.

"Look, the animals are here," Kara pointed out. " 'Lyra the leopard, Dreamer the wolf, and—Ozzie the wonder ferret?' "

Ozzie brushed his cowlick back. "It's all good."

He suddenly jumped, ferret stone flashing, whiskers vibrating. "The tour bus just pulled through the front gates!" he announced.

"Wait." Kara held Lyra's face, moving it left, then right, carefully smoothing the spotted fur. "Perfect." She kissed Lyra's head and stood. "Time to make some magic."

"Into the great unknown," Adriane sighed, following the group out the door.

❧   ❧   ❧

"Ravenswood Manor was built in seventeen fifty-three," Kara said as she led the group of tourists through the immense foyer of the amazing Gothic manor house.

The group consisted of about twenty ladies and a few camera-laden hubbies who had booked the tour as part of a day trip from Atlantic City. Emily and

Adriane were at the rear of the group, ushering the stragglers along.

"Everything in the manor has animal themes," Kara continued, "some more fanciful than others."

The group passed an ornate mahogany table with carvings of unicorns, centaurs, and dragons, which ended in big, clawed feet.

Several women lagged behind, observing every detail.

"Take your time," Kara said, then touched her unicorn jewel, sending a telepathic message to Adriane and Emily. *"Move 'em along!"*

"These paintings are just wonderful," a woman cooed, admiring the many pieces depicting the history of Ravenswood and the animals that had made their home there.

"Ravenswood has always been an animal sanctuary," Emily piped up from the back. "Through the years, different caretakers have kept it in excellent condition, as you can see."

"This is the most recent caretaker, Henry Gardener," Kara said, pointing to a large painting of a handsome man proudly showing off a pair of white tigers.

"Where exactly is Mr. Gardener?" a man asked, snapping photos of the painting.

"He's—" Kara faltered.

"On vacation," Adriane said quickly.

"We heard he mysteriously disappeared," the man persisted.

"Murdered in the cellar with an ax, he was," his wife chimed in.

"Which is the most haunted room?" a woman in all black asked.

"That would be . . . um . . . this room." Kara pointed to the wide living room with the massive marble fireplace and green velvet and mahogany couches.

"This is a unique part of Stonehill's history," a *Stonehill Gazette* reporter said, directing her photographer to snap photos of portraits hung about the formal room. "Legends have it there have always been ghosts and monsters in these woods."

"This place sure looks like it could be haunted," opined a pale, blue-haired woman.

"Who knows what happens when the darkness of night falls and the full moon rises?" the blazing ham said dramatically.

*"This is stupid!"* Adriane complained to Emily.

Emily shrugged. *"Everyone seems to be enjoying themselves."*

"What about the ghosts?" asked a visitor.

"Okay, I'll tell you a really scary secret," Kara said, warming to her subject as the group crowded around her. "One time, we hosted this big rock star, Johnny Conrad . . ."

"Yes?"

"And I sang a song that died a horrible death."

Adriane snorted.

*"What's going on in there?"* Ozzie complained to the mages through his ferret stone. *"We're all waiting."*

"You've seen some of our regular guests," Emily said, leading the group through the hallway and toward the rear exit of the manor. "Deer, peacocks, hawks—even parrots. And now it's time to meet our special animals."

Kara flung open the tall double doors to the grand marble patio. Beyond were the water gardens and rose gardens sprawled majestically across the great lawn. Tables on the patio were laden with ice cream, chips, sodas, and cookies.

"Meet Lyra," Kara called out. "A rare leopard breed from, uh . . . France!"

Right on cue, Lyra leaped over a hedge bordering the patio and came to a stop a few feet away from the group. Her sleek orange-spotted fur shimmered in the sun.

"Wow, a real leopard!" someone shouted.

Cameras starting clicking as Kara walked up to Lyra and put out her hand.

Lyra roared, raising a few gasps from the group.

Kara petted the cat, smiling brilliantly.

The group clapped, then gasped as Ozzie sprang from the water gardens and tumbled across the lawns. Lyra leaped to meet Ozzie as he jumped onto her back, juggling pinecones in his furry paws.

"Adorable!" a lady proclaimed, clapping her pink-gloved hands enthusiastically.

Kara laughed. *"Nice touch, guys."*

The acrobatic ferret tossed the cones high in the air one at a time for the dazzling finale.

A piercing howl cut across the lawn, startling everyone. Lyra swung around, sending Ozzie and his cones flying onto the picnic table.

A spike of fear drove through Adriane.

"Is that the wolf?" a lady asked, peering through her horn-rimmed glasses.

"His name is Dreamer, and he's coming right out," Adriane said, looking expectantly to her left, where the pup was supposed to make his entrance from behind a cluster of rosebushes. "I *said*, the wolf is coming right out."

After a long pause, Dreamer slunk from behind a thick violet rosebush. His hackles were on end, and he growled low in his throat.

"Say, he looks meaner than an overfried corn dog," a tourist observed.

Lyra eyed the wolf warily. *"Something is not right with Dreamer."*

With a snarl, Dreamer lunged at the cat. Lyra easily dodged his snapping jaws and stepped back.

Emily and Adriane both ran to the wolf, herding him back from the group.

"Dreamer?" Adriane gasped—her wolf stone was pulsing golden, a warning of danger.

"Easy, Dreamer." Emily's jewel glowed blue as she sent calming magic to the agitated mistwolf. "He's not feeling well," she called back to the tour.

"Are you sure these animals are safe?" one of the ladies demanded.

Adriane tried to respond, but Dreamer jumped between her and the visitors, barking protectively.

The tourists started yelling with alarm.

"Dreamer!" Adriane cried. She wrestled the wolf down, holding his head steady, and looked deep into his green eyes. "What is it? "

Images of gleaming claws, snapping fangs, and spiderwebs barraged her mind as Dreamer thrashed, trying to get away.

"Hooooray!" Ariel zoomed from the skies for her part in the show, cooing happily. Dreamer broke free of Adriane's grasp and lunged at the snow owl.

"Hoo-aahhhh!" Screeching, Ariel careened into the air, narrowly avoiding the mistwolf's teeth and barreling into three tourists.

"Help!" the old lady in horn-rimmed glasses shrieked.

"Yes, help yourselves to cookies and ice cream," Kara shouted as she plucked a pistachio-soaked ferret from a gallon tub. She shot a concerned look to Adriane.

"Dreamer, stop it!" Adriane grabbed the wolf's collar, golden light flashing from her gem.

"This is front-page material," the reporter exclaimed, snapping photos of Dreamer and Adriane.

Adriane looked at Emily desperately. "Take him to Gran—I can't get through to him."

"Dreamer is just a little overexcited about the new season," Emily blurted to the tourists, her jewel shimmering as she pulled him away.

The wolf gave Adriane one last concerned glance before following Emily.

Adriane watched him go, wishing her dark dreams had vanished with the night.

❁   ❁   ❁

The large chamber shimmered with movement as hundreds of spiders slid along silken strands, weaving subtle colors into the giant tapestry. An intricate landscape of woods and gardens formed beneath their skittering feet.

"This will be my greatest creation." The Spider Witch waved long fingers, her bloodred jewel pulsing upon its ornate spiderwebbed ring. "A masterpiece of dark magic."

A tall figure, startling silver hair draped below her shoulders, stepped from the shadows. "It is an impressive decoration," the Dark Sorceress allowed, her green animal eyes narrowed.

The Spider Witch spun around, moving quickly despite the heavy black robes shrouding her bulky body. "The forest sylph will become a most powerful demon when this weaving is complete."

The Dark Sorceress raised an eyebrow. After so many months in the Otherworlds, her own magic remained weak and drained. Yet the Spider Witch had been trapped there for many years. How could she be so powerful? There had to be a source feeding her magic.

"We must do more if we hope to eliminate the warrior," the Dark Sorceress said.

"You presume to give me advice?" the Spider Witch mocked. "Let me remind you that *your* attempts to harness the magic of the unicorns, the dragons, *and* the mistwolves all failed miserably."

The Dark Sorceress gritted her vampire teeth. If not for that silver mistwolf, she would have harnessed the power of all the mistwolves and the magic of Avalon itself.

"You don't know these girls like I do. You have to go for the heart—the animals," the sorceress shot back. "Everything the warrior loves must be stripped away, her spirit broken."

The Spider Witch directed a mass of black spiders to weave the next image on the tapestry: the cottage house next to the manor. The witch's insect eyes flashed yellow from the depths of her hood as she faced the Dark Sorceress.

"Then let it begin."

   ❧   ❧   ❧

"Come again tomorrow!" Kara waved to the tour bus and newspaper van as they sped out of the preserve, leaving the mages and animals standing in a cloud of dust.

"This is a disaster!" she wailed, pushing aside the rainbow-colored balloons bending sadly over the welcome sign.

"All that mint chip!" Ozzie cried.

"Ozzie, let's store the food back in the manor freezer," Emily said.

Suddenly, a fierce howl cut through the air.

"Dreamer?" Adriane called, looking nervously toward the cottage.

Jagged lights pierced her mind as she tried to connect with her pack mate. Images flashed: *dark claws; sharp, snapping teeth; glowing blue and green eyes; her grandmother's horrified face—*

Something was attacking her house—and Gran!

Adriane bolted toward the cottage, half blinded by the terrifying images. Her wolf stone blazed with sharp pulses, its golden magic amplified by her fear.

"Gran?" Bursting through the cottage's open front door, she called out frantically, "Where are you?"

A ferocious snarling came from somewhere inside. Adriane raised her wolf stone, sending bands of gold flooding through the afternoon shadows.

"Adriane?"

Emily, Kara, Lyra, and Ozzie ran through the door.

"What's happening?" Emily asked.

"Something's in here," Adriane said quietly.

Kara and Emily instantly took fighting stances behind the warrior, jewels ready.

"Dreamer?" Adriane called out.

Her only reply was sharp static. But underneath she could feel the hunger, the driving bloodlust of the hunt.

The mages crept into the living room.

"No!" Adriane screamed.

Gran lay motionless on the living room floor, frail arms crossed as if trying to protect herself. And standing over her was Dreamer—teeth bared and feral.

# Chapter 3

"The doctors say a severe shock put Gran in a coma, but her condition is stable," Dr. Carolyn Fletcher, Emily's mom, explained, walking with Adriane, Emily, and Kara across the wide parking lot of Stonehill Hospital. "But Adriane, honey, she's also an elderly woman. It could be a stroke. These things happen."

*"She's under some kind of spell,"* the healer said telepathically to Adriane and Kara.

*"An enchantment,"* Kara added, blue eyes dark with contemplation as she twirled the unicorn jewel between two fingers.

Emily shook her head. *"My healing magic couldn't break it."*

"Where's Dreamer now?" Carolyn asked.

"He's with—" Kara started. They hadn't said anything about Dreamer being with Gran.

"He's at my house," Adriane quickly finished. "He's just a little upset."

"Upset?" Dr. Fletcher raised an eyebrow as she stopped at her green Explorer.

"He's fine now, really," Emily assured her mother.

Carolyn took a deep breath as she beeped open the SUV's door lock. "Now listen to me, girls. You know I support your efforts at the preserve."

The three mages stopped near the rear door and looked at one another.

*"Uh-oh."* Emily winced. *"Here it comes."*

"But it might be time to think about other plans," Carolyn said.

"Mom, can we discuss this at home—" Emily started.

Carolyn held up her hand—which meant, *Zip it, we discuss now.*

The mages climbed into the backseat, Emily and Kara flanking Adriane.

"What happened to your plans for expanding the Pet Palace, Em?" Carolyn asked, sliding into the driver's seat. "Not to mention school and band practice."

"Mom, you don't understand!"

"What? What don't I understand, Emily?" Carolyn asked, turning to her daughter. "The city council received a highly agitated call from your tour group."

"Dreamer didn't attack anyone, Dr. F.," Adriane insisted.

"They claim he did," Carolyn replied, starting the ignition. "There have been clear cases of wild animals turning on their handlers."

"Not Dreamer!" Adriane cried, wolf stone flaring.

As Carolyn pulled out of the parking lot, she glanced at the girls in the rearview mirror. "I know this is a lot to deal with right now," she said gently, "but perhaps it's time to think about placing Dreamer in a secure place."

"Like a zoo, or a circus?" Adriane cried. "No way!"

"Mom! That would be terrible!" Emily objected.

"I don't have to remind you of what we went through last summer," Carolyn continued. "Another wild animal getting loose is the last thing the town council wants to hear."

"It's a preserve—they're *supposed* to be loose," Adriane said.

"They see Dreamer as a potentially dangerous animal," Dr. Fletcher said. "I mean, no one even knows where he came from. If we don't do something, someone else will—and they might not have Dreamer's best interests at heart."

"Dreamer didn't attack anyone," Adriane protested again.

"He just wouldn't, Mom!"

"And I suppose he told you that?" Carolyn asked.

"He can't!" Adriane exclaimed, then caught herself. "Uh, I mean, we just know."

*"You can't talk to him?"* Emily asked.

Adriane tensed. *"Something's wrong with his magic."*

*"Why didn't you tell us?"* Kara locked eyes with Adriane.

*"I dunno . . ."* Noting the uncertain look Emily and

Kara exchanged, she added firmly, *"Dreamer was trying to protect Gran."*

*"From what?"* Kara asked, horrified at the revelation.

"Have any of you been listening to a word I've been saying?" Carolyn demanded.

"What did you say, Mom?"

"Adriane," Carolyn sighed, "what about moving in with Emily and me until Gran gets out of the hospital? You're family; we'd love to have you."

"Totally," Emily agreed.

"Thanks, Doctor F., but . . . ," Adriane began.

"I insist you move in with Emily," Kara said, looking from Adriane to Emily.

"I'd feel better at home."

"How about if Kara and I move in with Adriane?" Emily suggested.

"We have lots of food left over from the party," Kara said.

Dr. Fletcher nodded. "If Kara's parents agree, then it's a deal—at least for the weekend."

Emily and Kara leaned close to Adriane, their three jewels pulsing.

*"Adriane, what is going on?"* Emily asked.

*"Something is on the preserve,"* Adriane said.

*"What is it?"* Kara asked. *"How come you and Dreamer are the only ones sensing it?"*

Carolyn's eyes darted to the rearview mirror. "You know, ever since you girls took over running the preserve, it's as if you've been hiding something, keeping a secret."

"That's so silly," Kara replied. *"Tonight, group meeting. Don't tell anyone!"*

❀   ❀   ❀

"Where's my other Elmo?" Ronif, a duck-like quiffle, wailed.

"RRRR!" Lyra growled. She had two moose slippers on back paws, one pink bunny on her left front, and an Elmo slipper on her right front paw.

*"I'll trade you SpongeBob for the bunny,"* Balthazar, a pegasus, said, nodding to the mismatched set of slippers adorning his hooves.

The cottage's cozy living room was filled to capacity with mages, magical animals, and enough sleeping bags, blankets, and pillows for everyone.

Adriane sat curled on the oversized lounger, gently stroking Dreamer's back. The wolf lay at her feet, chin on his front paws, eyes anxiously darting over the room.

*Whap!*

A pair of red pajamas decorated with robots flew across the room, hitting Adriane in the head.

"Sleepover rule number one: Everyone wears pajamas!" Kara yelled, digging in her bulging suitcase, which she had opened in the middle of the Navajo patterned rug. All the animals swarmed around, picking out matching sleepwear.

"I prefer my sweats," Adriane said, eyeing Kara's pink satin sleeping set.

"Those are for Dreamer."

"Ooo, I'll take these." Emily reached into the suitcase and pulled out a pair of blue chenille socks that matched her moon-and-star-patterned flannel pajamas.

"Lyra, heads up." Kara sent a stuffed cat, monkey, and bear flying out of the overstuffed bag. "Everyone grab a snuggly."

Lyra deftly caught the snugglies and walked around distributing a mouthful to everyone.

Dreamer sat eye to eye with a snow-white rabbit with long, floppy ears.

"Ohhhhhhh," Tweek groaned miserably.

"That's not a very good place for you to rest, you know," Rasha, another quiffle, pointed out.

The twiggy elemental was lying flat in the fireplace.

"Popcorn's ready!" Ozzie tottered into the cottage's living room holding a huge bowl over his head. Maneuvering the maze of snugglies, he avoided tripping over the hem of his oversized plaid pj's.

"Yum!" Rasha stuck her beak in the bowl.

"That's disgusting!" Ozzie complained.

Emily helped Ozzie set the bowl on the long coffee table and grabbed a handful. She flopped on the couch next to the white owl so Ariel could snack, too.

Kara rolled her eyes as the animals crowded

around, grabbing wingfuls and pawfuls of hot popcorn.

Dreamer stayed where he was, head down, watching all the activity with wary liquid-green eyes.

"Time to call this meeting to order," Kara said, satisfied that all the animals had matching pairs of sleepwear. She strode to the center of the comfortable living room to address the group. "As you all know, today's opening tour spectacular was . . . not."

"It sucked," a baby quiffle squawked.

"Who's seen anything weird on the preserve?" Kara asked.

Everyone raised a hand, paw, wing, or flipper.

"I mean today."

All eyes turned to Adriane and Dreamer.

"Hey, this isn't a trial," Emily said, then turned to her friend. "So what's going on?"

"Spill it!" Kara ordered.

"Okay." Adriane scratched Dreamer's silky black ruff and tucked her long hair behind her ears. "Last night I had a really weird dream," she began. "I was running through Ravenswood and wound up in the magic glade, but everything was different."

"Go on," Emily urged gently.

"I was attacked."

"By what?" Kara asked.

Adriane took a deep breath. "A mistwolf."

A unified gasp filled the room.

"Inconceivable!" Tweek declared.

With a snarl, Dreamer thrashed his head back and forth. White fur flew in a frenzy as a rabbit ear went flying across the room. The wolf looked up, holding the remains of his snuggly between clenched jaws.

"You killed it!" Kara was appalled.

With a low whine, the wolf slunk back down, head lowered.

"Adriane, things always appear different in dreams," Emily pointed out.

"It wasn't a dream exactly." Adriane pushed up the leg of her sweats, revealing the ragged scratches. "There's more."

Silence fell across the warmly lit room.

Adriane shuddered with the memory. "In the glade I met a forest sylph called Orenda and then a mistwolf—"

"Rewind," Kara ordered. "What's a sylph?"

"It's an elemental fairy creature." Tweek wobbled across the rug. "Every magical forest has an earth sylph as a protector."

"Why haven't we seen it before?" Ozzie asked.

"You have, just not in its original form. A sylph melds into the forest, spreading magic." Tweek twirled toward Emily. "Didn't you tell me you found your jewels here?"

"I found mine in the lake," Emily explained. "Adriane found hers in the portal field."

"Well, I saw the sylph," the warrior murmured. "She was under attack also."

"By mistwolves?" Kara asked.

"No. Spiders."

Tweek's twigs poked out in astonishment.

"She was trapped in a huge spiderweb. It was awful. She was in terrible pain. And"—Adriane hung her head, trying to control her emotions—"there wasn't anything I could do to help her."

"Well, that doesn't sound good at all. What else?" Kara pressed.

"Nothing. Dreamer woke me, and Gran was sick," Adriane continued, taking a deep breath. "Gran said . . . the forest spirit was dying."

Everyone stared at Adriane and Dreamer.

"Why didn't you tell us?" Kara found her voice first.

"Do you tell me about every dream you have?" Adriane challenged.

"If I thought it was important, I would," Kara replied.

"Adriane, we're your friends," Emily said. "You're supposed to tell us."

Kara raised her arms in the air. "After all the work I did with the council, getting my dad to hook up the tour. Everything is in jeopardy!"

Adriane jumped to her feet, jewel pulsing. "Why is it always about you?"

Kara stepped back, caught off guard.

Dreamer sprang to the warrior's side, a low growl rising in his throat.

If Kara perceived any kind of threat, she didn't show it, dismissing the warrior with a flick of her wrist. "That's not what I meant. Hello! If we lose this tour, the council could shut down the whole place."

"You don't think I know that?" Adriane cried. "This is my home!"

"Well, I can't put a spin on all this bad publicity, no matter how good I am," Kara said.

"Oh, you'll figure something out." Adriane stalked across the rug, turning on Kara. "What Kara wants, Kara gets—right?"

The blazing star flushed, releasing a pulse of bright white from her jewel.

Lyra stepped to Kara's side, hackles raised.

The animals shuffled nervously, feeling the tension rising.

"Just go to Daddy, he'll fix it for you," Adriane taunted.

Emily stepped between her friends, but looked at the warrior. "Adriane, that's not fair."

Kara's face fell. "I'm not like that anymore."

Dreamer growled, teeth flashing in a wolf grin.

"You know, Adriane . . ." Kara faced the warrior. "You and I have been through a lot, and believe it or not, I understand how you feel."

"Kara, there is no way you can understand how I feel!" Adriane felt the room closing in. Her chest was tight, emotions raw. "You think it's so easy! You saved the Fairy Realms, bonded with a paladin, and—" She stopped abruptly.

"And what?" Kara's eyes squinted suspiciously.

"Nothing."

"I know what you were going to say."

"Leave me alone." Adriane whirled away, hair flying.

Kara pressed on. "You were going to say I saved Lyra, weren't you?"

"Get away from me!" Adriane's wolf stone sparked dangerously.

"And *you* couldn't save Storm!"

Adriane's jewel erupted with power.

"Adriane!" Emily shouted.

Kara's unicorn jewel flared bright. The two beams smacked together, diamond light against golden fire.

With a snarl, Dreamer lunged.

"Ahh!" Kara jumped back.

Lyra sprang in front of Kara. *"Calm your wolf down, now!"*

The two animals faced each other, teeth bared.

"That's enough!" Amplified by his ferret stone, Ozzie's voice boomed across the room. The ferret marched between the much larger animals and pushed them apart. "You should be ashamed of yourselves!"

"What's going on?" Emily asked in shock, running her healing jewel over Dreamer. "Adriane, I've never seen you like this."

Adriane fell on the couch. Dreamer moved to her feet, head lowered, tail between his legs.

Emily sat next to her friend. "Losing Storm has been really hard on you," she said gently. "And now with Gran—"

"Stop shrinking me!" Adriane cried, all her emotions bubbling to the surface. "I'm sorry. I don't know what's going on."

Storm had been her first real friend, and now she was gone. The thought of losing someone else she loved filled her with white-hot fear.

"It's okay, Adriane," Ozzie said, placing a paw on Adriane's hand.

"I don't know how, but I saw the forest spirit, and she told me she was sick." Adriane wiped her cheeks and sniffled. "But I was at the glade this morning, and there was nothing there. How did I see her?"

"World walking," the E. F. said, pulling his twigs together. "It means traveling through the astral planes. Mistwolves are the only living creatures who connect to the spirit world, and it's difficult for them."

"What are the astral planes, anyway?" Emily asked. "Are they connected to the magic web?"

"The magic web connects all physical worlds like Earth and Aldenmor," Tweek explained. "The astral planes lie hidden from the web, only intersecting in certain places. There are several layers, including the dream state, and on top of that, the spirit world."

"I've been there before," Kara said excitedly. "Lucinda brought me there."

"I doubt if you could go back by yourself. A human world walker is extremely rare—BlaH!" Tweek shuddered violently.

"What's wrong with you?" Kara asked.

"I'm feeling a bit scattered," Tweek groaned. "When mistwolves die, they join the spirit pack, giving their magic back to the living wolves."

"So it was the spirit pack I saw?" Adriane asked.

"Possibly."

"You miss Storm so much, you dreamed about a mistwolf," Kara said. "Case solved."

"But I *saw* it. It was a ghost. And I think it attacked Gran."

"This is the real world," Emily said, unconvinced. "There are no such things as ghosts."

*"There's one,"* Ariel reported, perched on the windowsill.

The mages and animals scrambled over to the window.

Outside, a twinkling light bobbed gently up and down. With a soft flash, the light was suddenly inside the living room.

"What is that?" Ozzie asked, sparkly bits tickling his whiskers.

A small winged creature spun around Tweek, checking him out. Lights ran around its body, pulsing from delicate wings.

"Looks like Tinkerbell," Emily said.

"It's a fairy wraith," Kara exclaimed, holding out her finger so the tiny fairy creature could land upon it. "They loved me in the Fairy Realms."

But the small fairy was not interested in Kara.

With a tinkling of bells, the wraith zipped to Adriane, flashing brightly.

Adriane heard something familiar. The wraith's bells carried a fragment of Orenda's song, the song of the forest.

Suddenly the wraith zipped back out the window, hovering in the air expectantly.

"A Ravenswood fairy wraith," Tweek gasped. "Follow it!"

"Let's go," Adriane said as the light sped off into the woods.

Dreamer howled in agreement, scrambling anxiously toward the cottage's front door.

"Everyone stay here!" Kara ordered as Balthazar barreled past her. "You'll ruin your slippers!"

"It's headed toward the manor house," Emily pointed out, digging for her jacket in the pile of blankets and pillows.

Adriane slipped into her parka vest and stepped outside into the chilly night. It was unusually cold for spring, making her breath cloud in front of her.

Dreamer ran after the glittering trail of fairy dust winding through the dark woods.

Adriane's heart raced as she followed the wolf

along the cobblestone path that led from her house. This felt eerily like her dream, following a mysterious summons through the shadowy forest.

"Wait up, Tink," Kara called to the fairy wraith, as she, Emily, and Lyra hurried through the trees to the main driveway.

The manor house loomed in the night, dark and imposing. Moonlight glinted off the high turrets and peaked roofs. The wraith streaked up the front steps—and vanished.

The mages hurried up the steps, casting beams of jewel light over the large double doors.

Suddenly, the front door creaked open.

Three girls, a ferret, an owl, a cat, a wolf, and a pile of twigs peered into the dark foyer.

The wraith wavered and zipped down the hallway.

The group slowly moved after it.

"It's in the kitchen," Emily whispered.

The light bounced across shiny polished pots and pans hanging from the ceiling, then off the heavy steel of the double freezer before zipping through a wooden door.

Ozzie, Tweek, and Ariel slowly pushed the door open. In front of them, a circular staircase spiraled down into blackness.

"Tink's leading us to the basement," Adriane exclaimed.

"But why?" Kara wondered. "There's just old stuff down there."

"That's the only kind of stuff in this house," Ozzie commented.

"Let's go!" Kara ordered, then stepped out of Lyra's way. "After you."

Creeping down the stairs, the group followed Lyra and Dreamer through corridors stacked with piles of old furniture, lawn chairs, and broken statues.

The mysterious wraith was bobbing in front of them, softly blinking, as if checking to make sure they were all there. It floated into a dusty room filled with metal racks crowded with cardboard file boxes, old crates, and dusty knickknacks.

Suddenly the light vanished.

"Where did it go?" Ozzie asked.

Jewel light pierced the darkness, crisscrossing the room.

"Spread out, there must be a secret panel or door," Kara instructed.

The mages separated, moving down different corridors.

Adriane's head pounded—she felt disoriented, the dark corridor blurring before her eyes. Dreamer stood close, his muscles tense. Something was definitely down here.

"Emily, you see anything?" the warrior asked anxiously.

"Nope," Emily answered, then called out. "Ozzie?"

"Nope, Tweek?"

"I'm standing right next to you!"

"Gah. Kara?"

"Kara?" Emily called again after a few seconds. But there was no answer.

*"She's gone!"* Lyra growled, padding to the wall, sniffing.

"Kara!" Everyone called out.

"Mmhphfff." Something was making a racket, from *behind* the wall. "Getttmmmmeeeouttt!"

Tweek and Ozzie scrambled up an old dusty chair, climbing onto a ledge above Adriane.

"Kara, is that you?" Ozzie asked, knocking on the wall.

A horrible shriek echoed from the other side.

"It's her," Adriane confirmed, running her hands over the ledge on the wall. She felt a small trigger and pushed.

The wall suddenly slid open, revealing a terrified Kara.

"Good work," Tweek said.

But all Kara could do was point to the startling apparition behind her.

Adriane gasped as she stared into the snarling face of a glowing, silver mistwolf. Stormbringer.

# Chapter 4

Ozzie screamed.

The ghostly figure of Stormbringer stepped forward, silvery outline shimmering.

"Storm?" Adriane whispered, wolf stone flashing. "Is it really you?"

"Pardon me." Tweek casually walked past the girls and right through the glowing ghost. The little elemental stopped in the belly of the wolf.

"Gah!" Ozzie grabbed his ears.

Tweek examined the image with his turquoise gemstone. "It's a cohesive light structure."

"A hologram," Emily realized, lowering her rainbow stone. She stepped forward and passed her hand through the image.

"I knew that," Ozzie said, nonchalantly smoothing his fur back in place.

Disappointment flooded through Adriane. Of course Storm wouldn't be here. Her pack mate was dead.

"See her feet and ears?" Emily pointed to the hologram.

"It's a younger Storm." Adriane looked closer. "About Dreamer's age."

"What is this place?" Kara strode into the large room, Lyra close by her side.

Dozens of candelabras abruptly flared to life, illuminating an immense cluttered room.

A table strewn with papers stood by the far wall. Enclosed glass shelves were crammed full of amulets, charms, and vials.

"Looks like a workroom." Emily was awed.

Lyra sniffed the air. *"No one has been in here for years."*

"You!" Ozzie cried as the wraith materialized in front of his nose, waving her tiny hands.

The wraith dove under a pile of papers on the desk. Rifling and rummaging, she emitted a worried, high-pitched humming.

Ozzie scampered after her, sending papers flying. "Come back here!"

The wraith darted to the other side of the room, diving under Lyra's belly and leaving a trail of blue and violet twinkles.

"Here's the hologram's source." Using his gem like a magnifying glass, Tweek followed a thin beam of light to a crystal, set in a strange metallic device on the table. He lifted the crystal out, causing the wolf to appear and disappear. "This is a data crystal, the same design as my HORARFF."

Tweek was referring to the jewel that hung from his neck, his *Handbook of Rules and Regulations for Fairimentals.*

Adriane stepped over Ozzie. "Could there be any more images stored in it?"

The E. F. reset the crystal. "The image was stuck, but I should be able to—"

Suddenly Storm's hologram flashed, dissolving into another image: the forests of Ravenswood. The picture shifted over to a silver wolf pup playing in the field.

"This may be the only record of the last living mistwolf," a disembodied voice floated from the crystal.

"That voice," Kara exclaimed.

"It's Mr. Gardener!" Adriane gasped, stepping closer. Her wolf stone sparked as she watched Storm, so young and full of promise.

The voice of Gardener continued: "After I lost my wolf, I thought I would never see another again."

"Gardener was bonded to a mistwolf?" Ozzie asked.

"Hoo noo," Ariel cooed.

"This is big," Kara confirmed.

"Shhh!" Adriane whispered.

The images of Storm continued to play.

"I don't know where Stormbringer came from. It's as if she just appeared from the forests. I thought she could help me understand what happened, but she has no recollection of the other mistwolves and will not leave this place. It's as if she's waiting for something."

"Someone," Adriane breathed, wiping tears from her eyes.

"I know Storm is the one who can save the pack. I have betrayed them. I can no longer stay at Ravenswood."

The image abruptly cut off.

Adriane was totally stunned. Mr. Gardener had been right about one thing: Storm *had* saved the mistwolves. But she should have lived to see the pack flourish, should have spent a long life with Adriane, mage and bonded animal exploring their magic together. But Adriane had let her die—

Dreamer was at her side, wet nose nudging her hand as he whined with concern.

No. She still had a mistwolf to save.

"Did you have any idea?" Emily asked Adriane.

Adriane shook her head "Gardener was already gone when I got here."

"Something happened between Gardener and his wolf," Kara said.

Just like something had happened to Storm, Adriane thought. And now Dreamer. When humans bonded with mistwolves, did it always end in disaster? Is that why Tink had brought them here? Could

Storm be trying to reach her now? A ghostly presence from beyond—

*Oooooooo.*

"What was that?" Kara spun around, jewel sparking.

Ozzie lay on a stack of flat objects, Tink scratching his tummy. With a sigh, the ferret slid to the floor. Then he looked up to see everyone staring at him. He jumped to his feet. "What?"

The wraith squealed, happily somersaulting in the air.

"Hey, look at this." Ozzie turned over the wooden board he'd been lying on. "It looks like a secret code."

"It's a Ouija board, Ozzie," Emily said, examining the exquisite board engraved with bright red letters and numbers. There was a sparkling jewel in each of the four corners, mounted atop different painted designs. YES and NO were printed in the bottom corners.

"Everyone's seen those in horror movies," Kara explained. "You use them to contact spirits and ghosts."

"No way," Ozzie scoffed.

"Way," the blazing star nodded. "The spirit channels through someone and moves a wooden pointer over the board, spelling out messages."

"Here's the pointer." Emily held up a beautifully carved triangle with a large clear crystal in the center. She set it on the board.

"Wait! There are some very important rules you

have to follow," Kara warned. She held up her hand and counted off. "One, never go into a haunted house—especially after dark. Two, never, *ever*, go into the basement."

"So far, so good," Emily observed wryly. "We've already broken both."

"Oh," Kara continued in a hushed voice. "If the board spells out 'help me,' it always means there's a monster right behind you."

Ozzie whirled around, then jumped back.

Emily dragged a small chest to the middle of the room and set the board on top.

The mages, Tweek, and Ozzie crammed in, sitting cross-legged on the floor around the board. Lyra, Dreamer, and Ariel looked on.

"Okay, everyone: Paws, hands, and twigs on the pointer," Kara directed.

"Ask it a question," Adriane said.

"Can I buy a vowel?" Ozzie asked, surveying the graphic capital letters.

"Oooh, I know!" Kara exclaimed. She paused and cleared her throat, looking around the room with wide blue eyes. "What kind of quiz is Mrs. Herring giving in homeroom?"

The pointer didn't budge.

"Let's try to use our jewels," Emily suggested.

The mages, Fairimental, and ferret closed their eyes in concentration, breathing deeply. Amber, pink, blue, turquoise, and gold light filled the room.

"Is there a spirit in the house?" Emily asked in a hushed tone.

Instantly, an icy gust of wind extinguished the candles, plunging the room into darkness.

"Is that a yes?" Adriane asked.

*Crrrreeeeeak!* The door slammed shut, making everyone jump.

"Allrighty then," Kara said nervously. "Someone ask something."

"Storm, is that you?" Adriane whispered, peering around the room.

The jewel in the pointer started to glow, casting light across the board.

"Ooo." Ariel's big owl eyes opened wide.

"It's moving!" Kara squealed.

The pointer gently vibrated beneath their fingers, moving to the No.

"Are you Orenda?" Adriane asked, resting her fingers lightly on the pointer.

The pointer started blinking more brightly as it shifted and moved across the board to the YES.

Suddenly the jewel blinked and started shaking.

"Stop shaking, Ozzie!" Adriane scolded.

"I'm not doing anything!" the frightened ferret protested.

Dreamer growled and paced up and down, his emerald eyes alert.

The pointer slid across the board, pausing on a series of letters until it had spelled out:

HELP

"This is bad," Kara said, and looked around the room, waiting for the monster to come crashing in.

"How can we help you?" Emily asked.

The pointer flew in zigzag patterns, spelling out another word:

STORM

Adriane's heart pounded. "How do we help Storm?"

The pointer turned bloodred. A sudden wail pierced the room.

"Tink!" Ozzie cried.

The little fairy stretched thin like a rubber band. Her glowing form winked in and out before vanishing in a puff of gold twinkles.

Adriane tried desperately to focus, but the room was spinning, making her dizzy.

"Whoa." Kara grabbed Lyra as the room suddenly started shaking before coming to an abrupt stop.

"That's not Orenda," Adriane said.

The pointer pulsed red like a heartbeat.

"Then who is it?" Ozzie asked.

"Blah!" Tweek shuddered and twitched.

"Who?"

The pointer flashed as the red light zipped into Tweek, sending his twiggy body whirling.

Tweek screamed, his voice deep and raspy. He rattled, twigs jerking and crunching. Suddenly he snapped back to normal. "Fascinating," he declared.

The E. F. spun in a circle, leaped in the air, and landed in a pile. "Chew on this!" he roared, quartz eyes flashing red, spitting loose twigs everywhere.

"What's happening to you, Tweek?" Emily asked.

"Interesting." Seemingly back to normal, Tweek blinked his quartz eyes. "I've been possessed by unspeakable evil."

Suddenly Tweek's limbs coiled, cracking as red eyes glowed malevolently from his distorted face. "I think . . ." His voice warped into a bone-chilling shriek. "Ravenswood will be destroyed!"

Tweek shuddered violently as he exploded in a flurry of twigs and vanished.

# Chapter 5

Adriane walked briskly between the towering firs at the glade's edge. The morning sun glinted through leaves varnished with an emerald sheen by the night's rain. Bushes and ferns swayed, leaving trails of light dancing across small pools of water.

Reaching out with her wolf senses, the warrior tried to feel the presence of Orenda. "Spirit of Ravenswood, are you there?"

Orenda and Storm were both in trouble—somehow they were both connected.

She felt the sudden sting of awareness, as if she were being watched.

Adriane shivered. For the first time since coming to Ravenswood eighteen months ago, the forests felt cold, distant. Was it only the wind? Or something darker, hiding in the shadows.

A growl interrupted her dark thoughts. Dreamer's nose was in a bush, sniffing at something.

Adriane studied her pack mate. The wolf was tall and graceful; his puppy fat had tightened into rippling muscles. Lustrous jet-black fur marked with white paws and a star upon his chest gleamed like velvet. He was awesome.

She trained her senses on him, trying to connect. Jumbled images raced through her head—*gleaming spiderwebs trapping a monstrous figure with blazing red eyes*—

Adriane gasped. Had the mistwolf really seen the spiderwebs? Maybe she and Dreamer were just out of sync, freaked by her strange dream. Or maybe she *had* been world walking, like Tweek had suggested. And the danger only existed in the spirit world—for now.

Adriane focused harder, forcing a connection. Her jewel flashed and Dreamer stopped abruptly, shaking his head with a yowl of pain.

She drew back immediately. "Sorry."

Dreamer locked his deep green eyes on hers. The wolf stone pulsed, and fear tingled along her arms. His magic was slipping away. She turned, casting magic fire from her wrist. With a quick movement, she swirled the fire into a lasso, an easy exercise she had done hundreds of times. But the golden circle flared and fell apart, dissipating to sparks.

Adriane closed her eyes. What was happening? Was she losing the connection to her magic as well?

Tough it out, she told herself. All her life she had toughed it out.

Growing up, she'd moved around too much to make friends. She had always been the strange new

475

girl. She was used to being alone, and it was easier that way.

Stormbringer had been her first true friend. The wolf had opened a whole new world to Adriane. But it wasn't just the magic that filled her with the sense of belonging she so desperately needed. It was also meeting Emily, Ozzie, Lyra—and even Kara. Without Storm, Adriane might never have met the most important people in her life—friends who loved her.

But now Storm was gone. She had not bonded with Dreamer like she had with Storm, and maybe she never would. When Storm died, a piece of Adriane had died with her, and the hole in her heart could not be filled with another.

A cloud passed over the sun, plunging the shimmering forest into shadows.

Dreamer followed her across the Mist Trail and into the open ground behind the cottage house. Gran had made it a real home for her and Adriane. It was always warm and welcoming, with delicious scents coming from the kitchen where Gran spent hours cooking. The responsibility of looking after the preserve must have been overwhelming, even for a woman of such determination and grit as Gran. Now it was up to Adriane. This was her home. Not only the stone and wood house, but also the hundreds of acres of forest preserve itself. And it could all be lost.

Adriane walked by a line of quiffles and brimbees stretching from her house practically to Wolf Run

Pass. The animals edged away anxiously as if they were scared of Dreamer—or of her.

The wolf kept his head low, following Adriane as she stepped onto the front porch. "What's this, the chow line?"

"Pre-tour inspection," Emily answered from the open kitchen window.

"Dear Fairimentals," Kara sang as she walked out the front door. She carried a bright silver case. "Need help. Tweek has exploded—again. Oh, and I got an A in Math!"

Adriane stared wide-eyed. Had Kara gone nuts?

"Message for the Fairimentals," Kara explained, allowing a hint of worry in her voice. "As soon as I can get through to Goldie, she can take it."

"No luck yet, huh?"

"No." Kara smiled weakly.

Adriane understood Kara's concern. The blazing star had formed a deep attachment to the mini dragon, and vice versa. The dragonflies could usually get through all kinds of magical interference, but if they couldn't even hear Kara . . . the mages would be completely on their own.

"In the meantime . . . ," Kara said, observing the long line of animals. She set the case on the porch's swinging bench. "I want everyone looking their best for today's tour."

Dreamer shifted restlessly, then lay down next to Lyra.

"You first, Dreamer," Kara said, popping open the silver case.

A golden clamshell mirror, jade brush, silver comb, powder puff, and skunk-shaped atomizer tumbled out excitedly.

"Quiet, quiet!" The silver comb clapped his feet. "Let the princess speak."

"Special assignment." Kara pointed to Lyra, Dreamer, and the line of quiffles, jeeran, and brimbees spilling off the front porch.

"Oooo! Mistwolf!" Skirmish, the jade brush, dove under Dreamer's tummy, making him leap to his feet.

"He stinks!" Whiffle scuttled toward Dreamer on crystal feet, puffing clouds of rose-scented perfume.

Dreamer took one sniff and sneezed.

"I'll just groom him myself, thank you very much." Adriane ran her own brush over Dreamer's silky fur before Puffdoggie, the powder puff, could unleash a cloud of sparkly powder.

"Princess Lyra's turn," Kara directed.

"Yay!" The enchanted objects dove into Lyra's orange-spotted fur.

*"My fur needs to be extra shiny!"* The large cat primped and preened with every stroke, brush, and spritz.

"I swear, Lyra, you're becoming more like Kara every day," Emily said as she walked through the sliding-screen door.

*"Thank you."*

Adriane turned away as the blazing star beamed at her bonded cat.

Emily knelt in front of Dreamer. Gently holding his head, she looked into his deep green eyes.

"What is it, Dreamer?" Emily's gem pulsed soft greens and blues. "What's wrong?"

The wolf cocked his head, leaned forward, and licked Emily on the nose.

The healer got to her feet with a sigh. "His magic is blocked."

"It's like he's lost," Adriane said softly, glancing at her gem. The paw-shaped stone lay quietly on her black and turquoise bracelet.

"No." Emily firmly faced the warrior. "Not while he has you."

"I can't help him!" Adriane cried, her voice cracking with emotion. She knelt next to her pack mate, hugging him protectively.

The others waited, staring as she took a deep breath.

"Something is here." Adriane gently stroked the wolf under his chin, turning his liquid green eyes to her own. "It's doing something to Dreamer." She was about to add *and to me.*

"We've searched the whole preserve," Kara said. "No one has seen anything."

"Then it's something we can't see," Emily stated.

"How do we fight something we can't even see?" Kara asked.

"We just haven't figured out how to look," Adriane said, rising to her feet.

*"No bows!"* Lyra growled as the accessories attempted to secure a scented purple ribbon around the cat's neck.

Mirabelle, the clamshell mirror, flapped open, releasing a gob of green liquid that settled over the quiffle's head feathers.

"Cool," Rasha said, admiring Ronif's new coif. "What is it?"

"Duckity doo."

"What about us?"

The animals surged forward onto the porch, crowding the mages.

"One at a time," Emily shouted. "Kara, I think your accessories may be a bit overkill—Kara?"

The blazing star was gazing through the oak trees that arched over Adriane's cobbled walkway.

"Heads up," Kara said, pointing to the circular driveway in front of the manor house. "We've got company." A line of cars was making its way down the main road toward Ravenswood Manor.

Kara consulted her watch. "The tour isn't supposed to be here for two more hours."

Dreamer sprang to his feet, a low growl rumbling in his throat.

"Adriane, take Dreamer to the glade." Emily's face was tight with concern. "Now."

"Pancakes are ready!" Ozzie ran from the kitchen, blobs of whipped cream flying off his fur.

"Let's go!" Balthazar shouted, herding the magical animals off the porch and into the forest behind the cottage.

"Dreamer, come on." Adriane's jewel sparked as she saw the dark SUV screeching to a stop in the circular driveway. It was followed by a patrol car marked with the Stonehill sheriff star.

The wolf hunched low, growling and snapping at the air before taking off for the trees.

"Dreamer!" Adriane yelled.

*"I'll go after him."* Lyra bounded off the porch, vanishing into the forest.

"Is it the good witch or the bad witch?" Kara asked, frowning.

The SUV's door swung open, and a stout gray-haired woman stepped out. Beasley Windor's steely eyes darted everywhere at once as she marched toward the cottage.

"What's *she* doing here?" Ozzie asked.

"She's brought Sheriff Nelson," Emily said nervously, watching the angry city council woman approach with the sheriff.

Kara stepped forward. "I'll handle this."

"Good morning, Mrs. Windor." Kara flashed her diamond bright smile. "Hello, Sheriff Nelson."

"Hi, Kara," the sheriff smiled. "How're you doing?"

"I'm terrific. You get the brownies we sent over?"

"We sure did. Your mom bakes them really swell—"

Windor cut him off with an icy stare.

"Sorry, Kara," Sheriff Nelson whispered. "We're here on business."

"We have all our permits," Kara said. "I made sure they were filed—"

"Do you have a permit for—*this!*" Mrs. Windor shouted, holding up the *Stonehill Gazette*.

Bold letters jumped out on the front page: **"WOLF ATTACK AT RAVENSWOOD PRESERVE!"** Below the headline was a full-color photo of the horrified tourists.

"That was an accident," Kara said calmly. "No one was hurt."

"I'm afraid it's gone beyond that, Kara," the sheriff said.

"These wild animals have terrorized the town long enough," Mrs. Windor snapped. "We've come for the wolf."

"He didn't do anything!" Adriane protested. Her jewel pulsed a warning.

"Adriane." Emily held her friend's arm.

"What do you know about taking care of animals?" Adriane cried, wrestling away from Emily to get in Mrs. Windor's face.

"Enough to realize you have no business running

this preserve," Mrs. Windor responded, staring the warrior in the eye. "And now it's over."

Adriane blinked. For a split second, Mrs. Windor's eyes had flashed red.

Kara pulled Adriane back. "My father gave us full authority to watch over these animals."

"Who do you think authorized the sheriff's visit, Missy?"

The sheriff nodded. "Sorry, Kara. We have our orders."

"I'm calling him right now." Kara whipped out her pink cell phone and hit the speed dial.

"Mrs. Windor," Emily said, trying to remain calm. "We have a tour in an hour—it's very important we have all our animals here."

"The tours are all canceled," the city council woman stated, holding the newspaper. "There will be no tour today, or ever."

"I need to talk to my father right now!" Kara screamed into her phone.

Fear gnawed at Adriane's stomach as a plume of dust rose on the main road. Another vehicle pulled up to the manor.

"You can't do this," Adriane hissed.

Beasley Windor smiled wickedly. "Just watch me."

"My mother will straighten this out," Emily said as Dr. Fletcher's green Explorer pulled to a stop.

The vet stepped out the driver's door, followed by two other people in the back.

"Oh, no." Adriane turned ashen.

"Who are they?" Emily whispered to Adriane as the trio approached.

Adriane stepped back. "My parents."

"Adriane." A tall, athletic man strode past Mrs. Windor to stand in front of Adriane. He wore loose blue jeans and a dark blue blazer over a white T-shirt. Brown eyes shone from a ruggedly handsome face framed by long brown wavy hair.

"What are you doing here?" Adriane asked in disbelief.

He stopped and smiled awkwardly. A slightly built, dark-haired woman approached hesitantly behind him. Her olive skin set off intense black eyes.

"How long did you expect us to wait until you called, Adriane?" her mother asked.

"We just came from the hospital," Adriane's father said in a slight French accent. "Your grandmother's condition is unchanged."

Adriane's mother put her hand on her daughter's cheek, a tiny smile fleeting across her pretty features.

Adriane was surprised to find herself standing a little taller than her mother.

Her dad turned his attention to Mrs. Windor and the sheriff. "I'm Luc Charday, and this is my wife, Willow."

"Beasley Windor, Stonehill city council." Mrs. Windor nodded curtly. "Your daughter and her friends have been keeping dangerous animals on this preserve and jeopardizing the entire town," she accused.

"She doesn't know what she's talking about!" Adriane cried furiously. "Dreamer didn't do anything!"

"Dreamer?" Willow asked, her eyes full of concern.

"It's a wild wolf," Windor broke in.

"He's not wild!" Adriane rounded angrily on the stout woman.

Suddenly a howl echoed from the trees.

Willow's long dark hair fell over her black eyes as she anxiously took in the preserve.

"No!" Adriane shouted. "Stay away!"

But it was no use. Responding to his pack mate's distress, Dreamer lunged from the trees, landing between Adriane and Mrs. Windor. He looked fierce and ready to strike.

Emily dashed to the snarling mistwolf, pulling him back.

"You see that?" Windor scrambled behind the sheriff. "That wolf attacked me!"

Luc eyed the big black wolf. "Adriane, this isn't exactly a golden retriever."

"You don't even know him," Adriane shot back, stepping in front of her pack mate.

"Mom!" Emily pleaded.

"We went over this," Dr. Fletcher said evenly. "The animal needs to be in a safe environment."

"We've come to take you back with us," Willow said quietly to Adriane.

"You just show up out of nowhere and expect me to leave? Ravenswood is my home!"

"Adriane, we want—" Luc began, but stopped short as a large yellow and brown van pulled up behind the sheriff's car. Wire mesh covered the rear windows.

Adriane gasped as she read the logo on the van's side: DEPARTMENT OF FISH AND GAME.

"You can't do this!" Adriane grabbed Dreamer in a fierce hug. "You can't take him away from me!"

Two men in tan uniforms jumped out, carrying nets and rifles.

"Why did you even come here?" Adriane cried. Red-hot fear spiked through her. "I hate you for this!"

Willow cringed.

"Mom!" Emily begged.

"Dad!" Kara wailed into her cell.

"Dreamer, run!" Adriane cried, trying to push the wolf from the porch.

*"Pack mates stand together,"* the mistwolf insisted, hackles raised as he stood his ground.

For a second, Adriane was startled—Dreamer had spoken.

"Adriane," Luc said, pulling her away from the wolf. "We'll figure something out. Just let the sheriff do his job."

"He won't feel a thing." One of the game wardens cocked a tranq gun, leveling it at Dreamer.

She heard Emily yell, *"Kara, no!"* as the blazing star raised her jewel.

*"Turn to mist!"* Adriane screamed, trying to break free of her father's strong grasp. *"Please! They won't hurt me."*

Dreamer pawed the ground, unsure what to do. His eyes fixed on his pack mate as the men closed in. Adriane reached out, trying desperately to help him. She felt his magic at the edges of her mind, but it was ragged and broken. He couldn't turn to mist.

Flashes of Storm's golden eyes played through her mind, flooding pain through her until she could barely breathe. This couldn't be happening to her, not again!

*"Pack mate!"*

With a wild snarl, Dreamer lunged.

"Look out!" the sheriff shouted.

Two loud bangs cracked through the still air.

Dreamer howled as the yellow darts sank deep into his side.

"No!" Adriane broke away from her father and ran toward her pack mate.

The wolf fell into Adriane's arms, struggling as the tranquilizer took hold.

"Stay with me," she pleaded, burying her face in his silky fur.

Dulled emerald eyes focused on her as he tried to stay conscious.

Adriane was suddenly pulled to her feet, torn away from the drugged wolf.

"Adriane, let him go," Luc said.

"How can you let them do this?" Adriane shouted wildly, pushing away from her parents, tears streaming down her face.

The warrior watched helplessly as a heavy net tightened over the wolf.

"Do you have to do that?" Emily shouted angrily. "He's got enough tranq to knock out an animal twice his size!"

"He won't be causing trouble again," Mrs. Windor said, watching with satisfaction.

"We're going to get him back," Emily promised.

"I'll convince my dad," Kara said, running to Adriane's side.

*"Dreamer!"* the warrior called frantically, her wolf stone pulsing bright gold. *"Dreamer, are you all right?"*

But the unconscious mistwolf could not answer.

"No!" A primal cry ripped from Adriane's throat as the officers tossed Dreamer's limp body into the back of the van and shut the doors, blocking him from sight.

For the second time, she had failed her pack mate.

# Chapter 6

The Dark Sorceress descended a staircase deep beneath the lair. The stone closed around her like a crypt. "How long must I be confined to this dank place?" she snarled.

To the sorceress's surprise, the Spider Witch cackled, an ugly screeching sound.

"You would prefer the void of the Otherworlds?"

Crystals embedded in the walls cast dull yellow light, illuminating the Spider Witch's bulky form as they moved along a corridor.

The sorceress shuddered. She hated the nothingness of the Otherworlds, but this was getting intolerable. Now, finally free, the craving for magic made her blood pulse fever hot. How much longer could she watch this witch cast weaving spells and not be able to use magic herself?

The Dark Sorceress's animal eyes focused on dozens of faded tapestries lining the walls. They were all nearly identical to the Ravenswood scene the spiders were now weaving.

"You have tried this before." The sorceress ran her

hands over a frayed image of the imposing manor house. "What makes you think you will succeed this time?"

"The wizard who guarded Ravenswood is gone," the witch snapped. "This time, *I* will control the magic of Ravenswood."

The sorceress frowned as she passed more decaying tapestries. "We need to retrieve the remaining power crystals."

"Precisely." The witch turned insect eyes on the sorceress. "I believe one has landed in the astral planes."

The sorceress stopped short. She had used the elusive planes to focus her dream magic, but it was exhausting and unreliable. What was the witch planning? It would be impossible to enter the astral planes, let alone bring back something solid like a power crystal. "And just how do you propose to get to the astral planes?"

"You know very well there is one creature capable of walking the spirit trail."

Mistwolves!

The sorceress flushed with anger. She had come so close to stealing the magic of the mistwolves. She would have succeeded if not for the warrior and her wolf.

Sensing the sorceress's thoughts, the Spider Witch sneered. "Where you failed, I will succeed." She gathered her robes and swiftly moved through an arched doorway.

The Dark Sorceress followed, brushing stray spiderwebs from her pale cheek. She stepped into a large chamber.

An enormous glowing tapestry stretched from floor to ceiling, radiating power. Silvers, blues, greens, and reds looped and twisted in complicated patterns, like interlocking dreamcatchers amid a dazzling array of stars. It was a map of the magic web.

"How is this possible?" Stunned, the sorceress forced her voice to remain steady. "Even a fairy map contains only a small section of the web—it is impossible to map the entire thing."

"At the core, it is a just a web, a pattern of magic," the witch said smugly. "But you are right: This is not the magic web."

The Dark Sorceress breathed a sigh of relief. The thought of her ally having that kind of power was terrifying.

"It is a new design," the Spider Witch laughed.

The sorceress contained herself. "You would need all nine power crystals to control the magic of Avalon. But the Fairimentals guard two, and the blazing star destroyed a third."

"You would need all nine to maintain the web as it is," the witch replied, indicating four brightly glowing points on the map. "By controlling each of these key places, I can harness enough wild magic to re-weave the web. One that I will control."

The sorceress listened with mounting concern.

"You see this point?" the witch said, running her hands along the tapestry, pausing on a bright pulsing point. "It is this lair."

"Ravenswood is another point," the sorceress surmised. So the Spider Witch already controlled one of four points, and was trying to capture Ravenswood as well.

"The third is on Aldenmor," the witch continued, indicating another glowing light. "But you know that." Insect eyes stared, cold and lifeless.

Aldenmor, the heart of the Fairimentals.

The fourth point pulsed erratically and disappeared, then flared again on the opposite side of the pattern.

"The fourth is most elusive. Its location changes— floating hidden among the swirling strands of the web." The witch shrugged dismissively.

"You still have to find Avalon itself," the Dark Sorceress insisted. "It is the source of all magic."

"Once I re-weave the web, Avalon will be revealed."

The sorceress stood back, the enormity of the witch's master plan sinking in. Twisting the magic of Ravenswood made the warrior weak, while strengthening the demon. The demon would create enough chaos on the astral planes to attract the power crystal where a mistwolf would retrieve it.

It was brilliant.

And horrifying.

There would be no place for the sorceress in the web's new design.

"Yes, this is certainly quite a surprise," the sorceress said softly.

The Spider Witch laughed. "The last surprise of the mages' lives."

❦　　❦　　❦

"This is awful!" Ozzie cried, stumbling over a pile of sneakers as he followed Adriane into her closet.

*You should see Kara's room,"* Lyra said, nosing a loose soccer ball as she followed the ferret.

"No, I mean Adriane can't leave!" the ferret protested. "I was sent here to find three mages."

"And you did." The warrior pulled her long hair into a ponytail. Gently lifting Ariel's foot, she thumbed through several hangers.

"Well, this isn't a temporary position." Ozzie climbed up the chest of drawers to stare at the dark-haired girl.

Adriane stood nose to noses as the ferret, cat, and owl pressed forward in the cramped closet. "I don't have much time."

She grabbed a black vest and slipped by the animals. The wall behind her bed was plastered with posters of rock musicians and snowboarders. Part of another wall had been painted with stars and flying comets. Carved blocks of painted cedar littered a table, folk art sculptures she had started. She hadn't gotten around to finishing her projects—it didn't seem to matter much now.

Ariel took wing, turquoise and aqua sparkles running through her feathers as she landed on the headboard. "Hoono!"

"I'm not leaving just yet." Adriane belted her black jeans and tied her boots tight.

"Then what are you doing?" the ferret demanded, ducking as Lyra stretched her lithe body across the rug.

The warrior regarded the three animals, her gem sparkling with contained fire. "Something is out there, and I'm going to find it."

*"All right. Let's go."* Lyra stood, and her sleek muscles rippled under lustrous orange fur.

"Hookay," Ariel agreed, blue eyes blinking.

"I'm going alone."

"Gah! Does Emily know about this?" Ozzie asked, shuffling back and forth.

"No, and you are not going to say anything!" The determination in Adriane's voice left no room for argument.

The animals exchanged glances.

Ozzie started pacing. "You're going to try that world walking stuff again, aren't you?"

"Listen to me," she said, sighing, the corners of her mouth lifting into a smile. "I love you guys."

She gently smoothed down Ariel's head feather as

Lyra rubbed against the warrior's side. "But you can't come with me. You have to trust me on this one."

The three animals silently stared back.

"If I get into trouble, I'll call you, Ozzie. Okay?"

"All right," Ozzie reluctantly agreed, ferret stone flashing on his collar. "But I don't like it one bit."

Ferret, cat, and owl exchanged a nod.

"Remember," Ozzie added. "I'm just a stone call away."

Adriane hurried down the stairs. She had to move quickly. Kara and Emily were busy with school projects and chores, and her parents had gone back to the hospital to check on Gran. But everyone would return soon enough.

Stepping out the back door, she breathed in the cool evening air. The setting sun wrapped the forest in shimmering golden light. Hurrying into the deepening shadows of the trees, she made her way to the immense Rocking Stone, jutting into the sky like an accusing finger.

She hadn't told Ozzie, Lyra, and Ariel all she intended to do tonight.

Focusing on the warm golden glow of her jewel, she cleared her mind and concentrated. She wasn't completely sure how to go world walking, but she had been on the spirit trail once before. She had run with Storm on the ancient mistwolf stream of consciousness when the spirit pack helped her heal Dreamer. Adriane had been able to reach Storm across any distance—even across time and space itself. Could she reach her first pack mate again?

Before she even entered the glade, Adriane felt the sickness seeping into the fabric of the forest.

She reached with her wolf senses, something that had always come so naturally to her. She focused on the silver mistwolf, seeing through Storm's golden eyes, feeling warm, silver fur covering her body, strong muscles running on lanky legs—

"*Storm.*"

Adriane moved silently across the glade, her jewel pulsing in steady rhythm with her heart. Closing her eyes, she steadied herself. She needed to do this, she *had* to do this, or everything she loved would be lost. Storm needed help, Dreamer had been taken away, and the forest sylph was in trouble. It was all connected, she was sure of it.

The gentle pull of something familiar touched her mind. Adriane grabbed for it, focusing her will through her gem. With a flash, the trees suddenly seemed to come alive, glowing silvery green around the edges.

Adriane pushed harder, grasping for the part of her that was wolf, losing herself in the need to find her pack mate.

She could almost hear the echoing refrains of the lost mistwolves.

She staggered forward as her jewel started shifting

through colors. Was she making all this happen? Fire sprang forth, swirling up her arm and surrounding her in a halo of flickering light.

Throwing back her head, she howled.

An answering growl sliced through the air, getting closer. Adriane could smell the animal. It was hunting her.

Adriane tried to focus on Ravenswood, on Storm, but she was trapped inside a spinning kaleidoscope. Fear tore through her like an electric shock. Without Dreamer to help her or Storm to guide her, she was completely lost in the twisting and shifting magic.

*"Storm!"* she called out with all her strength.

The world spun as the wolf stone exploded in a jarring blaze of light.

She was in the magic glade—inches away from an enormous, gleaming spiderweb. Oily, silver strands hung from the trees. Adriane's heart raced with fear.

She tried to steady herself and calm her sparking gem. "Orenda, where are you?"

The spiderweb throbbed and twisted. Suspended in its center, a cocoon pulsed. The fairy creature trapped inside screamed, her pure magic consumed by the suffocating strands.

"Orenda!" Adriane staggered as she tried to use her magic to help the dying sylph. Time seemed to slow down as the warrior fought to stay on her feet. Her wolf stone was glowing a fierce, deep red. She reached deep inside herself, trying to find her own magic, but it was trapped, just as Orenda was locked in the shimmering prison.

Suddenly a blur of light shot from the shadows. She whirled and saw the glowing outline of the ghost wolf, lips pulled back in a death grin. Blue light exploded, stinging her like burning-hot embers. Warped red light shot from the wolf stone as Adriane rolled, trying to get to her feet. But the ghost wolf was standing over her, lips pulled back in a deadly grin.

*"You should not hunt alone,"* he sneered.

Adriane stared into his shining animal eyes. "Who are you?"

*"I am the pack leader."* He lunged, jaws opened wide. *"Your wolf belongs to me!"*

Out of nowhere, a silver shape smashed the ghost wolf broadside, knocking him away.

Adriane rolled to her feet, jewel pulsing. "Storm-bringer!"

Storm locked her golden eyes onto Adriane. *"You must leave!"*

The two wolves rammed together in battle, ripping and tearing at each other's haunches.

"No!" Adriane cried.

Fierce roars tore across the glade, but she was already being pulled downward. Bright colors flashed past her in swirling arcs as she fell from the spirit world.

She landed hard, jewel pulsing with her fear. Rolling over, she found herself nose to nose with Ozzie.

"Wow!" Ozzie yelled, fuzzy ferret hair standing on end. "What a rush!"

❂ ❂ ❂

Adriane pulled the blanket around her shoulders and clutched the steaming cup of cocoa on the kitchen table. She was completely exhausted—physically, magically, and emotionally. She looked into her mug, uncomfortably aware of Emily, Kara, Ozzie, Ariel, and Lyra all staring at her.

"We told you not to go off on your own!" Kara burst out.

"What if something had happened to you?" Emily added angrily.

Adriane sat quietly, head lowered.

"If Ozzie, Lyra, and Ariel hadn't followed you, we don't know what would have happened!" Kara continued.

"One minute you're in the glade, and the next you just disappeared." Ozzie waved his paws in the air.

"I didn't mean to scare you," Adriane said, rubbing her wolf stone. It was gold again—for now.

"What happened?" Emily asked.

"My jewel started going nuts, and then she just fell out of thin air!" Ozzie exclaimed, leaping up and down.

"Calm down, Ozzie," Emily said. "She's okay."

"She must have locked onto Ozzie's jewel to send me back," Adriane mused.

"Who?" Emily asked.

"Stormbringer."

"Wait," Emily gasped. "You saw Stormbringer?"

"Are you sure you weren't dreaming?" Kara asked.

"No." Adriane looked quickly at her friends. "I've seen her before."

Kara and Emily exchanged a glance.

"Storm helped me heal Dreamer in New Mexico. She sent me the magic of the spirit pack."

"And this time?" Emily asked gently.

"This time I think I actually moved between the real world and the spirit world," Adriane said. "She saved me from the other ghost wolf."

"I knew you were going to try that world walking stuff," Ozzie said, straightening his collar.

Adriane sat forward. "I think that wolf attacked Gran."

Emily pushed away from the table and stood up. "But if this wolf is in the spirit world, how could it attack Gran?"

"Through Dreamer."

"I still can't even reach the d'flies," Kara sighed. "We're cut off from the Fairy Realms and Aldenmor."

"This is all about me," Adriane said quietly.

"Not possible. It's always all about me," Kara quipped.

Emily elbowed the blazing star. "Adriane, anything that affects you affects all of us."

"I've lost Dreamer." Adriane looked at her friends, eyes wide with fear. "I'm going to lose my home, my family—everything."

*"Someone's targeting you,"* Lyra growled.

"Hooo?" Ariel asked.

"Tell us what you saw," Emily said.

"The sylph was caught in a spiderweb. The glade was covered in them."

"I've seen those before," the blazing star said. "In the castle of the Spider Witch."

"But she's in the Otherworlds—" Ozzie broke off. "Uh-oh."

"And the Dark Sorceress is with her," Emily finished.

The mages and animals looked at one another, a stunned silence settling over the table.

"They're free," Adriane said, "and they're trying to destroy Ravenswood."

# Chapter 7

"**H**ey Adriane, wait up!"

Outside the math classroom a lanky, dark-haired boy rushed to catch up with her. "This isn't really your last week of school, is it?" Joey asked, concerned.

"I don't know," Adriane said shyly as they walked out the front doors of the school. "I hope not."

"Me, too," he said with a hopeful smile.

Adriane started to return his smile, then froze. It seemed like half the student body of Stonehill Middle School had been waiting for her. They swarmed around her, abuzz with rumors.

"Everyone says your wolf attacked a bunch of old ladies!" Heather, a friend of Kara's, pushed to the front of the group, followed by Molly and Tiffany.

"That's not what happened," Adriane protested.

"The leopard ate Emily's ferret," Kyle, Kara's older brother, announced.

"Is it true Ravenswood is being shut down?" Marcus asked.

"I don't—" Adriane faltered, trying to make her way through the crowd. All she wanted to do was go home.

"Adriane, are you really leaving?" someone at the back of the group shouted.

"You can't leave!" Heather suddenly exclaimed.

"No way," Molly agreed.

"I mean . . ." Heather flushed. "We've put a lot of work into the preserve, too."

Adriane was stunned. Less than a year ago, these kids had made fun of her—now they were suddenly on her side?

"We heard the council is going to shut Ravenswood down!" a kid called out.

"We have to keep it open!" Molly declared.

"Save Ravenswood!" Joey shouted loudly.

A chant erupted from the crowd as kids cheered and clapped. "Save Ravenswood! Save Ravenswood!"

"No pictures, please," Kara's voice rang out as she pushed through the mob and slipped her arm through the warrior's. "How're you holding up?"

"A little overwhelmed," Adriane admitted.

"No one said being popular was easy." Kara smiled.

"Save the animals!" Emily called out, hurrying over as she stuffed her flute case in her backpack. "Wow, word spreads pretty fast around here."

"Come on, K., what's really going on at Ravenswood?" Tiffany asked Kara.

"Absolutely nothing is going on at Ravenswood," Kara declared. "Everything is perfectly fine."

*"Help!"*

The mages jumped as Ozzie's panicked voice blared in their minds.

*"GAH!"*

*"Ozzie, what's wrong?"* Emily responded to the frantic ferret telepathically.

*"The portal is opening!"* Ozzie screamed.

❧　　❧　　❧

Wind whipped the trees as Adriane raced from the woods into the field, Emily and Kara close behind. A swirling circle hung in the sky. Veiled by a rippling curtain of mist, a giant dreamcatcher flashed inside.

"Keep your wings, paws, and hooves away from the portal!" Ozzie commanded as Lyra herded brimbees, quiffles, and jeeran back from the immense doorway in the sky.

Adriane's wolf stone throbbed with pulsing light as the dreamcatcher stretched and warped.

"Something's trying to break through the dreamcatcher!" Ozzie exclaimed, smoothing his static-charged hair as the mages surrounded him.

Adriane stared at the glowing portal nervously. The dreamcatcher was designed to keep out anything that might hurt Ravenswood. "Everyone, take position!" she ordered.

Emily and Kara stood on either side of the warrior, flanked by Ozzie and Lyra.

Head pounding, Adriane jumped as her wolf stone suddenly flashed. She cracked it like a whip, sending golden sparks flying.

Get a grip, she told herself.

"Try to strengthen the dreamcatcher!" Emily called, sensing the warrior's uncertainty.

Girls and ferret aimed their gleaming jewels. Shimmering streaks of gold, white, blue, amber, red, and pink sizzled over the glowing portal, lighting the sky like fireworks. The curtain ripped open wider, revealing more of the finely woven web.

"That's not the dreamcatcher," Kara said grimly.

"Then what is it?" Emily asked.

"Ewww, it's a spiderweb!" a baby quiffle squealed.

The ground shook as something slammed into the web. A wave of power crashed over Adriane.

"What should we do?" Rasha shouted.

All eyes turned to Adriane.

Fear washed through her. Her friends were counting on her. But how was she supposed to be a warrior without her pack mate?

A terrifying howl echoed from the portal.

"Stay cool," Kara ordered the group of frightened animals. "Whatever it is, we can handle it!"

The howls grew into a wailing chorus, sending tendrils of web whipping loose like torn flags. The spiderweb was unraveling.

Adriane flashed on the savage apparition that had attacked her. This was a pack of them, their collective will bent on reaching Ravenswood. She struggled to focus as raw power surged through the wolf stone. Blinding colors swirled, stabbing her eyes and piercing her mind.

Suddenly the wolf stone erupted.

"Ahhh!" Animals dove as magic fire flew everywhere.

"I can't control it!" Adriane screamed, frantically trying to keep her fire away from the terrified animals.

"Emily!" Kara swung her sparkling red, white, and pink magic toward the warrior. "Help her!"

Adriane felt tingling, cool magic wrap the wolf stone in healing power. She tried to connect with her friends, but all she could feel was the creatures' need to break through. Emily and Kara were using all their magic to help her instead of trying to close the portal. She was going to fail when she was most needed.

Instinctively, Adriane reached for the presence that always kept her strong. But Dreamer wasn't there.

Instead, she felt the touch of another magic, offering her the support she so desperately needed. The powerful presence enveloped her, protected her, filling her with pure and unconditional love. Adriane grasped for it like a lifeline.

The warrior smiled, never wanting to let go of the comforting magic. "Thank you," she whispered.

"It's opening!" Ozzie's scream pierced the swirling winds.

With a final fiery explosion, the glowing spiderweb disintegrated, ripping the portal open in a flash of brilliant red.

Adriane staggered back as mistwolves, teeth bared and snarling, leaped over the mages, landing among the terrified animals.

"Incom-*agk*!" Ozzie yelped.

Something huge and red plummeted from the portal and landed with a booming thud. This creature was definitely not a mistwolf.

*"Mama!"*

Adriane blinked. An enormous red dragon the size of a school bus sat in the middle of the field—with a grinning blond-haired boy astride his back.

"Drake!" She stumbled over to the creature and hugged his broad neck.

*"Mama!"* the dragon shouted, wagging his spiked tail, scattering mistwolves and animals everywhere. He dropped his enormous head, hiding the girl under a puff of steam.

"Thought you could use a friend." The boy slid off the dragon, slipping his flying gloves in his wide black belt.

"Zach!" Her two best friends from Aldenmor had come for her.

"You did say to drop by any—" Zach was cut off as Adriane caught him in a bear hug.

"I missed you, too." Zach returned her hug warmly.

Adriane stepped away shyly, wiping her cheeks. "And my baby boy," Adriane said, rubbing Drake between his eye ridges, making the dragon snort with pleasure. "It was you who grabbed on to me, wasn't it."

"Drake's magic can be pretty intense," Zach said, his bright red dragon stone shining from a brown leather band on his wrist. "He doesn't know his own strength."

*"Wolf sister."* A huge mistwolf approached, fur black as night and golden eyes gleaming.

"Moonshadow." Adriane knelt and hugged the pack leader, nose to nose.

*"I have brought twenty-four of the pack to help protect the forest."*

The mistwolf pack gathered around the mages, welcoming them with a frenzy of wagging tails, grinning faces, and low howls of excitement. The sun gleamed off their lustrous coats of silver, auburn, brown, blue, and diamond white. They were magnificent.

"This is incredible!" Emily breathed.

Adriane felt exhilarated as the magic of the pack filled her. She was being welcomed as an equal. A beautiful gold-and-white wolf nosed her way past Moonshadow.

*"We are sorry for the pain caused by our arrival. There was no other way."*

"We'll live," Adriane smiled.

"*This is Dawnrunner*," Moonshadow growled. "*My mate.*"

"You honor me." The warrior bowed to the magnificent she-wolf.

The wolves lifted their heads and howled as one. The wolfsong rang over the field.

"Get off me, you big lizard!" Ozzie pushed his way out from under Drake's belly, smoothing his singed and ruffled fur.

Drake pressed a giant golden eye close to the ferret's head. "*Hi!*"

"*A Knight of the Circle is a friend to the mistwolves,*" Dawnrunner said.

"Gah!"

"Welcome to Ravenswood." The blazing star smiled at the new arrivals. "And are we glad to see you!"

"*Hello.*" Drake bent his head around Kara and peered down at the curious animals.

"Hey, watch it!" Kara covered her hair. "I just had it highlighted!"

"Drake's perfectly friendly," Zach reassured the quivering quiffles.

"*We will check the forests.*" Dawnrunner nudged the pack leader's side as she led the other wolves into the trees. In an instant they vanished, as if swallowed by the woods.

Moonshadow growled. "*She is concerned.*"

"What's happening to Ravenswood?" Emily asked.

"There is a field of dark magic covering this entire forest," Zach explained. "Drake was the only one strong enough to break through."

"No wonder the d'flies couldn't hear me," Kara exclaimed.

"*I broke the portal!*" Drake announced proudly.

"Good boy." Adriane kissed his big red nose.

"Awww, he's portal trained." Kara smiled.

With a sudden spark, the roiling mesh of webbing magically wove back, sealing the portal shut. In a rush of wind, it vanished.

"We could be here a while," Zach observed.

"There's plenty of room for everyone," Emily stated.

"Where's Dreamer?" Zach asked, sudden concern in his eyes.

Adriane's smile faded. "He's been taken away."

Zach's dragon stone flashed in alarm.

"Something's wrong with his magic," Adriane said.

"*It affects all mistwolves,*" Moonshadow snarled.

"You mean it's not just Dreamer?" Adriane asked. "What happened?"

"*The spirit pack is missing,*" the wolf answered.

"Missing?" Orenda had told Adriane to find missing mistwolves.

"*Our magic comes from the spirit pack,*" the pack leader explained. "*Without them, it will fade until it is lost forever.*"

Adriane stared into the wolf's deep golden eyes, sensing how much had been sacrificed to come here. "That's why Dreamer couldn't turn to mist, why I couldn't talk to him."

*"I have brought the strongest of the pack."* The wolf lowered his head before Adriane. *"In this forest, we will make our stand."*

He was submitting to her leadership.

The warrior knelt and raised his head, looking at the pack leader eye to eye. "We must find the spirit pack."

"There's more," Zach said gravely. "The Dark Sorceress and the Spider Witch have escaped the Otherworlds. This dark magic is their work."

"Tell us something we don't know," Kara quipped.

"She's located another power crystal," Zach said.

"That'll do," Kara conceded.

"Why are they attacking Ravenswood?" Emily asked. "What's the connection?"

"We don't know yet. The Fairimentals tried to warn you, but they couldn't break through—" Zach looked around. "Where is the Experimental Fairimental, Tweek?"

"He exploded two days ago, and we haven't seen him since," Ozzie grumbled.

"Let's go back to my house and we'll tell you all about it," Adriane said.

As Emily and Kara started walking across the

field, Adriane was practically giddy with relief. The situation was bad, but the pack, Drake, and Zach filled her with strength and new hope.

"I see you've been getting the Fred-X deliveries," Adriane said, observing Zach's outfit of black Gap jeans, tan sweater, and down vest.

"Thanks for all the care packages." Zach smiled, pushing his neatly trimmed blond hair away from his eyes. "I'm the best-dressed boy on Aldenmor."

"You're the only boy on Aldenmor," Kara remarked.

Adriane noticed Zach had filled out. The soft features of his face now angled into a strong chin that set off his sparkling blue eyes. Broad shoulders and strong arms framed his tall physique.

"Drake looks good," she observed. "You have really taken care of each other."

He smiled. "You look good, too, Adriane."

Adriane felt heat flare over her cheeks.

"What else did the Fairimentals say?" Emily asked Zach.

"The spirit of Ravenswood is being twisted by strong elemental magic."

"That would be one Spider Witch, thank you very much," Kara said.

"The forest sylph is under attack." Adriane scanned the thick trees, sensing the dark force worming its way through the forest.

"These are magical woods." Moonshadow sniffed the air. "It is no wonder the spirit trail runs through here."

Adriane turned to the pack leader. Is that what she had experienced? The spirit trail?

"When the spirit pack vanished, we lost the spirit trail. No one can find it. Soon our magic will fade completely."

"Moonshadow," Adriane said, passing under the huge oaks bordering the trail to her house. "I have seen the spirit pack."

The wolf stared at Adriane. "You saw ten thousand mistwolves?"

"No. One."

"How?" Zach asked, genuinely impressed.

"I don't really know," she admitted. "Tweek called it world walking."

"You are bonded to the mistwolves," Moonshadow said, as if that explained everything. "What did this mistwolf look like?"

"He was silver and black," Adriane said, shivering with the memory of the fierce creature. "With one blue eye and one green eye. He called himself the pack leader."

"Chain!" Moonshadow barked.

"Who's that?" Emily asked.

"Chain was pack leader before me," Moonshadow said. "When he died, he refused to join the spirit pack with the rest of our ancestors. Instead, he turned rogue."

"But why?" Adriane asked.

A low growl rumbled from the black wolf. *"He was betrayed by his human bonded and left in dishonor."*

"Betrayed?" Adriane was stunned.

"Who was his bonded?" Zach asked.

*"A human wizard called Gardener."*

The mages gasped.

"I don't believe it!" Kara said.

*"I forbade the mistwolves contact with humans because I thought they would all betray us."* The powerful black wolf turned his deep golden eyes on Adriane. *"I was wrong."*

But evidently one did, Adriane thought. How could that be possible? The records they had found in Gardener's secret room seemed to indicate he was totally dedicated to saving the wolves.

*"Chain is a vengeful spirit,"* Moonshadow continued. *"And very dangerous."*

"But I have seen another," Adriane said. "Stormbringer."

The wolf's golden eyes were wide with amazement. *"I knew I was right to come here."*

Storm had died to save the mistwolves, but now the pack was in terrible danger again. They were counting on Adriane. She hadn't even been able to save Dreamer—how could she save the entire mistwolf pack?

"This is where I live," Adriane said to Zach and Moonshadow as they left the trees and headed over the grass behind the cottage.

"Really cool." The boy smiled, taking in the wood and red brick house nestled peacefully in the forest. In the distance, Ravenswood Manor loomed, its Gothic towers dark and imposing.

"What do we do with the big guy?" Kara said, pointing to Drake. The dragon was curiously examining the stone chimney.

"Ozzie, you'll be in charge of our guests," Emily said.

"Great . . ."

Several mistwolves appeared from the bushes, sniffing out the grounds.

"Do *not* eat the quiffles!" the ferret shouted.

"I think I know what's going on," Kara said suddenly.

"What?" Emily asked.

"We've seen this happen before. It could only be—"

"My mom!" Adriane exclaimed.

"Gag! How could she be responsible?" Ozzie asked, wiping dragon slobber off his head.

The warrior urgently tried to push Drake into the shrubbery. "You have to hide!"

"Adriane?"

The warrior turned to see her mother rounding the path from the main driveway. Willow stopped dead in her tracks, dark eyes open wide in surprise.

# Chapter 8

Adriane whirled around, her heart hammering. Emily, Kara, Zach, and Ariel waved at her. Drake and the mistwolves were nowhere in sight. Only a faint mist floated through the trees.

"I could have sworn I saw—" Willow began, then shook her head. "Must have been the sun in my eyes."

"Hi, I'm Kara. This is Emily and Zach," the blazing star said as the sounds of cracking and crunching faded behind them.

"I'm sorry we were not properly introduced," Willow said, and smiled. "I'm Willow Charday."

Emily stepped forward, red curls bouncing. Ariel sat on her shoulder, blinking great big owl eyes. "It's very nice to meet you, Mrs.—"

"Please call me Willow."

"This is Ariel," Emily said. "She lives here with Adriane."

"Hoolow."

"She's beautiful." Then Willow eyed the blond boy warily. "Do you live around here, Zach?"

"I uh, live over on Alden—"

"Allentown," Kara finished quickly. "Part of an interschool program to help the preserve."

"That's quite a ways to come to work here," Willow noted.

"This is a special place." He smiled, glancing at Adriane. "I'd like to visit more often."

Adriane turned beet red. Then her mother's voice brought her back to Earth.

"—supposed to meet us at the hotel right after school," she said.

Adriane frowned. "Um, I had chores and I needed help taking care of things around here."

"Maybe you're taking on more than you can handle," Willow said.

You have no idea, Adriane thought.

"Adriane told us you were in Philadelphia exhibiting Mr. Charday's new sculptures," Emily said cheerily.

"Actually, they're not sculptures," Kara explained. "They're free-form light modules."

"You know your art, Kara." Willow was impressed.

"My mom is on the board of the Hammersmith," Kara beamed. "She showed me the program last night."

Emily and Adriane looked at her in amazement.

"What? It's an art gallery," Kara told them.

"Adriane," Willow said softly. "Can we talk . . . inside?"

Adriane turned and stomped up the porch to the front door. She glanced at Zach, and her jewel flashed. *"Keep Drake away while I talk to my mom."*

"We have to finish up those chores now," Emily said, running into the woods.

"Right. It was nice to see you again." Kara waved as she and Zach raced after the healer.

"Your friends are certainly active."

"You should see them on a good day," Adriane said.

They entered the foyer and Willow stopped, taking in the cozy living room. Flowery drapes fluttered in the gentle breeze, slanting soft light over the family pictures on the mantel.

Willow gazed at the photos, her eyes resting on her wedding portrait. "Seems like only yesterday that I left this place."

Adriane followed her mother into the kitchen.

"I brought you something." Willow carefully took a book out of her bag and handed it to Adriane. "This edition has some really cool artwork."

Adriane ran her fingers over the rich leather and gold embossed title: *Alice in Wonderland*. Her favorite. When she was younger, Adriane had always dreamed of being like Alice and finding her own special wonderland. "Thank you."

Willow opened a cabinet and smiled. "Peppermint tea. Gran always kept it here."

She filled a pot with water and set it on the burner.

"When I first met your father, I knew I wanted to be with him more than anything." Willow smiled wistfully. "You should see his new pieces, Adriane. They're his best ever."

"I'm sure they are."

"You know, he talks about you all the time." Willow started to pull out Gran's usual chair at the table, then paused and sat in the chair next to it. "Adriane, why didn't you call us after Gran's accident?"

The warrior placed the book on the counter. What did her mom expect her to say? Because you'd show up and ruin everything for me. And, by the way, thanks for letting them take Dreamer!

"Have you wondered how we got here so fast?" Willow asked suddenly, fidgeting with the silver rings shining on her slim fingers.

Adriane blinked, surprised. "Didn't the hospital call you?"

Willow locked her dark eyes on Adriane. "Gran told me."

"B-but—" Adriane stammered.

"In a dream. Does that sound strange?"

This was the first time her mom had talked about anything like this.

Willow gestured to Adriane's chair. "Please, Adriane. Sit with me."

The warrior hesitated, then slowly walked over and sat down.

"The truth is, I never felt comfortable at Ravenswood. "

Adriane looked down at her hands, her voice strained. "Then how come you left me here?"

"Gran insisted you be here when you became a teenager. That woman is pure stubborn."

"I'm glad she did."

"You've changed, Adriane. I can see it, so beautiful and strong." Willow's slender fingers brushed the hair from Adriane's face. "You've blossomed here."

Adriane shuffled in her chair but didn't move away.

Willow leaned forward. "But we have to deal with reality. Gran is very sick."

"She'll get better," Adriane vowed. Please, she prayed with all her might, she has to.

"I think you've inherited more than her stubborn streak," Willow said with a fleeting smile. "You're more like her than I ever was."

"You say that like it's a bad thing."

"She is very . . . passionate about Ravenswood." Willow got up and brought the teapot to the table. She poured steaming tea in their cups. "When I was your age, all she talked about was our heritage and how it's linked to nature. She said we could talk to forest spirits. I get scared watching *Casper*." She smiled, waiting for Adriane to say something. "I can see this is making you upset. I'm sorry."

Adriane struggled with her thoughts, trying to explain what she was going through, what was really happening. Instead, she went back to what was familiar: her anger. "I'm upset because you're ruining my life!"

"What do you propose I do, Adriane?" Willow's voice raised in frustration. "You're thirteen years old. You can't live here alone."

"Ravenswood is my home. It's the only one I've ever really had, thanks to you."

Adriane stood and walked to the sink, hair falling over her face.

"That wolf. Is that what we're talking about? You can get lots of pets—"

"Dreamer!" Adriane swung around. "His name is Dreamer, Mother!"

"A wild wolf, Adriane. That's not normal," Willow insisted.

Adriane paced defiantly. "Different cities for a few months, then onto somewhere new. You call that normal?" She fought back tears. "I never knew where we'd be going next. How was I supposed to make friends when I'd be gone in six months?"

"You don't understand," Willow pleaded.

"No. I get it. *You* were never happy here, and now you don't want me to be happy."

"Of course I do, honey. I'm glad you've made friends here. But we need to be a family—"

"We needed to be a family ten years ago." Her anger spent, Adriane slumped back into the chair.

The two Charday women sat quietly, the ticktock of the kitchen wall clock filling in the silence.

"Adriane," Willow finally spoke. "Your father has been offered a grant at the Reisfeld Foundation. It's a very prestigious gallery in Woodstock, New York."

Adriane sat up. "New York?"

"We plan to buy a house and settle there. You could work with your father on your art. And we could visit Manhattan together—wouldn't that be exciting?"

"I don't want to live there!"

Suddenly a huge golden dragon eye covered the kitchen window.

*"Mama?"* Drake's voice rumbled in her head.

*"Drake, I'm okay!"* Adriane's jewel sparked as she tried to calm the dragon.

The dragon eye slowly inched out of sight as Ozzie, Emily, Kara, Lyra, Ariel, and Zach dragged him off by the tail.

"Adriane?" Willow was staring at the wolf stone. "Where did you get that jewel?"

"I, uh . . ." Awkwardly, she covered her bracelet. "It was a gift."

Willow sighed. "You've made some kind of connection to this place, Adriane, and frankly, it scares me to death."

"I . . ." How much did her mother really know about Ravenswood? How could she talk about something that wasn't supposed to be real? "What will happen to the preserve if I leave?"

"That's up to the town council."

"I have to stay here!" Adriane pleaded.

"Why?"

"To find out . . ."

"Find out what, Adriane?"

"Who I am."

A huge dragon eyeball popped in front of the window again, followed by a quick turn of his head, a roar, and a blazing burst of fire.

"What is going on out there?" Willow jumped up and opened the back door.

"Ahhhhh!" Ozzie flew by, tail smoking.

Kara, Emily, and Zach skidded around the corner and barged inside.

"Is everything okay?" Willow asked.

"Couldn't be better—why?" Kara smiled.

Willow turned to her daughter. "Your father and I leave for New York on Saturday. You need to be packed and ready," she said quietly, giving Adriane a quick hug.

"Ow." Ozzie walked inside, rubbing his rear end.

Willow glanced at him quickly, then shook her

head and walked to the front door. "It was nice to see all of you."

The warrior watched her mother close the door.

Adriane stomped to the living room and sat on the couch. "What am I going to do? They're going to make me leave and then turn the preserve over to the council."

"You can't leave!" Kara exclaimed.

"We have to do something!" Ozzie declared.

"And we don't have much time," Emily added.

Adriane glanced at Kara. "Any more bright ideas, Miss Artypants?"

"As a matter of fact, Morticia, yes." Kara signaled to the mistwolves, brimbees, and quiffles that were all pressing their noses to the cottage's windows. "Group huddle!"

The animals piled inside, cramming through the back door and shuffling through the kitchen. Once again, Adriane's house was packed with animals.

"Everyone here?" Kara called out.

A loud *thud* sounded at the front door.

"Who is that?" Emily whispered.

"I thought she left." Adriane nervously opened the door a crack—revealing a big red dragon snout.

*"I help?"* Drake asked, peering inside at the over-crowded living room.

"Of course." She hugged the dragon so hard he started purring like a buzzsaw. "Why don't you just stay right there," she said, bringing a few pillows from the couch to prop up his head.

Drake squeezed his massive head through the front door, settling just outside the living room.

Zach turned to Adriane. "Everyone filled me in while you were talking with your mom."

"We need a plan, but we still don't know exactly what we're up against," Adriane said.

"Maybe we do," Kara mused, looking at the group. "I think a power crystal landed in the astral planes."

"Is that even possible?" Emily asked.

"A crystal ended up in the Otherworlds," Kara pointed out. "It turned the Fairy Realms upside down. It's doing the same thing to the astral planes."

"So why is the witch attacking the Ravenswood sylph?" Adriane asked. "What's the connection?"

"She can't find the crystal," Zach exclaimed. "She's using the forest spirit to attract it."

"Magic attracts magic," Ozzie reminded them.

*"And only a mistwolf could bring the crystal from the spirit world to the real world,"* Moonshadow growled.

"Dreamer is a gifted magic tracker," Adriane said.

*"Gifted enough to walk the spirit world without the spirit trail,"* Dawnrunner said.

"But why Adriane?" Emily asked. "We're all tied to the magic of Ravenswood."

Adriane raised her amber wolf stone.

"They get to you, they get Dreamer," Zach concluded.

"And now he's all alone!" Adriane began pacing.

Kara had her cell in her hand, beeping up a storm.

"Gran got sick because of all this," Adriane realized, anger and fear surging through her. "I'm responsible. Ravenswood is going be destroyed because of me."

"We won't let that happen," Zach said determinedly, dragon stone gleaming.

Moonshadow rose. *The mistwolves stand with Ravenswood!*

Adriane knew what she had to do.

"He's being held at the Amazing Adventure Animal Park," Kara said, clicking off her phone.

"That's almost three hours away!" Emily exclaimed.

Adriane walked over and kissed the Drake's nose. "I'd say more like twenty minutes."

Then she turned and bowed to Moonshadow and Dawnrunner. "I am a warrior, sister of the mistwolves." The wolf stone reflected the determination in her dark eyes. "And I am going to save my pack mate!"

# Chapter 9

His magnificent wings angled back, Drake dove through light cloud cover, soaring over the sprawling animal park. The three mages huddled behind Zach on the dragon's back.

Adriane sat behind Zach, Kara in the rear. In the middle, Emily gazed over the gingko and baobab trees dotting the plains below. "We're over the African Savannah."

"Safari so good. Lyra, what can you see?" Kara called out.

Golden wings shimmering against the night, Lyra dropped from the clouds and came up alongside the dragon. Ozzie rode on her back. *"The guards are approaching the yak corral."*

"Good." Kara squashed the map she had printed from the park's Web site, trying to keep it from blowing away. "There's a jungle garden behind the aviary. Over that way."

With a touch from Zach, the dragon responded instantly, banking left and gliding low over a panicked herd of zebra.

"Doesn't seem natural to have so many animals penned up," the boy observed.

"It's for their own good," Emily responded, sounding surprisingly like her mother. "They're taken care of here, and zoologists do research to learn more about them and how to save them in the wild."

"It's so different here."

"Wait till you see the mall," Kara said excitedly.

Adriane watched the boy and dragon fly together, perfectly in sync. She recognized the low-slung leather saddle and attached saddlebags: They once belonged to a griffin named Winddancer, Zach's former bonded magical animal. Windy had sacrificed himself to save Zach and Adriane. Despite his grief, Zach had opened his heart to Drake. The bond between them now was strong and confident.

Adriane turned her attention to the animal park and tried to focus on connecting with her own bonded, Dreamer. But all she got was the buzzing of hundreds of different wildlife.

"Six o'clock." Kara pointed to a large building spiked with a wire-mesh roof. It was next to the main zoo, where animals lived in wide, spacious pens.

"Take us in, Drake." Zach's dragon stone pulsed bright red as he guided the dragon over a dark canopy of green trees. "Hold on!"

"Wha-aaaaaaaaht?"

Drake dropped, his huge feet cushioning the

landing as they crunched to a jarring stop. They were in the middle of a dense tropical jungle.

"He said hold on," Adriane called over Emily's shoulder as she swung off the dragon.

"Next time, speak up." The blazing star landed daintily on her pink sneakers, trying to gauge just how muddy this rescue mission could get.

The garden enveloped them in the scent of sweet flowers mingled with the soft mist of the mini rain forest. Chirping birds filled the air as the larger predators in the aviary squawked out warnings.

"Next time, call a taxi," the windblown ferret said through chattering teeth. He slid from Lyra's back as the cat landed gracefully.

The group peered from the garden onto the pathway that circled the aviary. On the far side it forked—one path toward Polar Bear Cove, the other to the Elephant Camp.

Kara smoothed the map, illuminating it with a pinpoint of light from her unicorn jewel. "There are administration buildings—here, here, and here."

Emily peered over Kara's shoulder. "Does it say where the hospital or lab is? That would be where they keep new animals."

Adriane turned away from her friends and held up her jewel, sending golden rays into the night like a beacon.

"Turn that off!" Kara cried, pulling the warrior's arm down. "Someone's going to see that!"

The warrior angrily shook off Kara. "I don't need a map to find Dreamer."

"The key word is 'find him without getting our rear ends caught.' "

"That's eight words," Ozzie corrected.

Zach led Drake back into the colorful flora. "Drake, you stay here and hide while we look around, okay?"

Drake snorted, settling his bulk gingerly in a patch of ferns, tail flattening a dozen bushes.

"Lyra, up and at 'em," Kara ordered. "You see anything with two legs, give me a shout."

*"Right."* The cat spread her wings and took off, disappearing into the night sky.

"Let's head to the conservation center," Kara said, heading to the left.

Adriane started walking in the opposite direction.

Ozzie looked from the blazing star to the warrior.

"I'll go with Adriane." Zach shrugged, walking off behind the warrior. "Emily and Ozzie, go with Kara."

"Fine!" Kara called out. "We'll cover more ground if we split up, anyway."

The warrior hurried away, dark eyes flashing. Time was slipping away. She shook her jewel and tried to sense Dreamer, pull him to her. Red heat flared over her wrist, and she gasped.

Zach fell into step beside her. "What's wrong?"

"He's in trouble." Adriane spun to face the boy, fighting to control her emotions. "I can feel it."

"We'll find him." Zach looked at her, blue eyes full of understanding.

Adriane fell silent as they walked quickly past a pile of curious lemurs. Her heart pounded, tears welling in her eyes. "In my dreams, I try to save Storm, try to do things differently. But I wake up, and she's always gone."

"When Windy died, I kept telling myself there was something I could have done," Zach said quietly. "If only I'd known a little more magic, or if I'd been able to fly better . . ."

"You've done such an amazing job with Drake," Adriane said.

"Drake and I share something even more magical than a jewel."

"What's that?"

"You."

Adriane blushed. "Then I'm surprised you can still fly."

"Dreamer is special—even Moonshadow says so," Zach said. "And that wolf would rather eat his foot than say something complimentary."

"I couldn't help Dreamer, either, could I?" Adriane said quietly.

Zach stopped and took her hand in his. He focused on his dragon stone, adding his magic to hers.

The wolf stone suddenly flashed. Adriane's eyes went wide as she caught the sounds of ragged breathing, the cold glint of a steel cage.

"I felt something." Adriane swung her wrist up, trying to hone in on the magic. She sped ahead—and ran smack into Kara.

"Oof!" Kara bounced back into Emily, her unicorn jewel flashing with pinks and reds. "Well?"

Adriane shook her head, jewel fire dying. "I lost him."

"He's here somewhere," Kara stated, polishing her jewel with the sleeve of her black cashmere sweater.

Adriane glared at the blond girl. "I almost found him until you got in the way!"

"Where's Zach?" Ozzie asked, looking around in the dark.

"Great. You lost him, too," Kara said.

"Over here." Zach stood outside of the elephant pen. "These are remarkably intelligent animals."

"Africans," Emily said, walking to the pen. "You can tell from their ears." She pointed to the large, droopy ears fluttering like drapes.

*"Heads up."* Lyra's voice suddenly popped in their minds. *"Two guards heading your way."*

"What do we do?" Ozzie shuffled back and forth.

"Why not just ask *them?*" Kara asked sarcastically, pointing to the elephants.

"Good idea," Emily answered. "Ozzie?"

Ozzie straightened his ferret stone importantly. "Well, I have learned some interesting bytes from Tweek on interspecies communication."

Ferret stone flashing orange, Ozzie hopped up on the wall that separated the park visitors from the pen. "Hey, you!"

The largest elephant turned slowly, dropping a trunk full of hay. Its trunk snaked over and poked Ozzie in the stomach.

"Gah!"

"Try to make contact," Emily directed.

"I just did!" The ferret took a deep breath and concentrated. Soon his stone glowed bright gold as orange magic shimmered around the elephant.

Ozzie held up a paw and waved. "We come in peace!"

Water blasted from the elephant's trunk, dousing the ferret.

"FrruFpm!"

"Send the elephant a visual," Kara suggested.

Ozzie squeezed his eyes shut. His fur stood straight out as his ferret stone blasted a beam at the elephant.

Emily added a touch of her magic to Ozzie's as she faced the 10,000-pound pachyderm. "We're looking for a wolf who was brought here yesterday. Can you help us find our friend?"

The elephant waved his trunk, trumpeting to an

ostrich flock next door. An ostrich ran and stuck his head through the next fence over, screeching loudly to a sleeping zebra.

"They're talking to each other!" the healer exclaimed.

The zebra brayed at the Monkey House. A monkey leaped into a tree, gibbering and pointing excitedly across the path toward the reptile house.

"Oh, no," Ozzie said. "I am *not* talking to a snake!"

"There's a facility behind it," Emily said.

*"Hurry, the guards are coming!"* Lyra shouted, swooping by on her patrol.

"Let's go." Adriane sprinted past the wide Reptile Hut toward a secluded two-story adobe building.

She stopped at the bolted front door. A sign read, AUTHORIZED PERSONNEL ONLY.

"We can't break in there!" Ozzie cried, stomping up behind her.

The warrior whipped golden fire into the air. With a loud *crack,* the magic blasted the door open.

"Well, maybe."

Alarms screeched through the night as floodlights blazed to life, illuminating the mages in fluorescent light.

"Very stealthy, Godzilla," Kara said, looking around nervously as her jewel light bounced off the dark interior.

*"What was that?"* Lyra cried.

"We're rescuing," Kara called back.

*"Can you do it a little more quietly?"*

"This way!" Adriane rushed down the dimly lit corridor, Zach and the others close behind. Growling and hooting echoed through the hallway as the animals inside reacted to the piercing alarms.

Adriane scanned every room, her wolf light ricocheting off the metal walls. "There!" She ran to the end of the corridor, smashing the door open.

The large room was full of instruments and tables. A row of steel cages lined the far wall, filled with parrots, a puma, and a baby monkey. Adriane's heart leaped to her throat as she saw the sheen of black fur in the corner cage.

"Dreamer!" the warrior cried, running to her pack mate.

The wolf lunged, slamming into the bars.

"Adriane!" Zach grabbed the warrior's arm.

She shook off Zach's hand and reached to open the cage.

"Adriane, wait!" Emily shouted, healing gem blazing with blue light.

"We have to get him out!" Adriane screamed as Dreamer crashed into the bars again.

Blazing heat seared into Adriane's mind. Pinpoints of red spread before her eyes. She spun away from her friends. With a blast of fire, the cage burst open.

The mistwolf slammed into her chest, snapping viciously at her throat.

"Dreamer!" Adriane fell backward into an examination table, sending instruments flying. Golden fire exploded from her wrist, wrapping her in a coil of protective magic as she tried to fend off the attack. The room lit up in jewel fire as the mages sent blue, red, pink, and orange magic streaming into the wolf.

The world wavered and drifted away as Adriane hit the cold cement floor. From the corner of her eye she saw the wolf's eyes flash red, a ghostly silver outline shimmering against his jet-black fur.

Zach was on Dreamer's back, trying to tear the thrashing wolf away from the mages.

"That's not Dreamer . . . ," Adriane whispered, not knowing whether anyone had heard her—

A familiar mocking voice echoed in her mind: *"How does it feel to betray your pack mate?"*

And she found herself standing in a vast field. A purple sky arced over feathery grass and flowers of red, blue, and green dancing in the wind.

Chain stood in the field, eyes focused on her with a malicious glare.

Wolf stone sparking, Adriane tried desperately to connect with her pack mate. She sensed Dreamer somewhere, submerged under Chain's control. But as her magic touched the ghostly outline, raw savagery overwhelmed her. Her lips drew back in a snarl.

"Let him go!" she yelled.

*"Humans are all the same. Sooner or later, they will betray everything they love."*

"I won't let you take him!"

*"He's already gone."* The wolf surged forward, then skidded to a stop.

Adriane raised her wolf stone, ready to strike. But it was not the wolf stone that reflected sudden fear in Chain's eyes. It was the silver wolf that stood at Adriane's side, ready to fight for her pack mate.

Breathing in deeply, Adriane wanted to laugh out loud as she filled with strength and confidence. She was whole again, as she hadn't been since—

Before Adriane could react, the two wolves hurled themselves forward head on, jaws open wide. With a vicious snarl, they crashed together. Teeth bared, Storm spun around and lunged for Chain's throat. Blue sparks ripped through the air as the two wolves collided in a blur of teeth and claws. Storm howled as Chain ripped at her haunches. Adriane watched in horror as Storm's ghostly outline shredded, mist trailing from her body.

"Storm!" Adriane staggered as a burst of swirling magic abruptly surrounded her, pulling her away.

"Drake, no!" the warrior screamed, unable to resist the dragon's powerful pull.

"Easy." Emily's face was full of concern as her healing gem bathed the warrior in cooling greens and blues.

The world came into focus.

Adriane was back in the lab. Everyone was yelling at once.

"Are you okay?"

"Can you walk?"

"Easy." Zach helped her to her feet, dragon stone flashing.

"What happened?" She held Zach's arm to steady herself until the room stopped spinning.

"You fell . . . and then you saved Dreamer."

Dreamer stood with his head lowered, tail between his legs, emerald eyes filled with shame.

Adriane grabbed the mistwolf in a fierce hug.

"He's okay, Adriane," Emily said. "You did it."

Sirens whined in the distance, fast approaching.

Kara ran to the window. "We've got company."

Harsh white lights cut through the windows as beams flew everywhere.

"We have to get out of here, *now!*" Ozzie shouted.

The building suddenly shook with a loud *thud* as something huge landed above them.

"Drake's on the roof," Zach said.

"Stairs!" Kara ordered.

The group barreled out the door and down the hall, scrambling up a flight of stairs. Bursting through the emergency exit, they piled onto the flat slate roof. In front of them the huge red dragon crouched low, wings spread, glinting eyes scanning the park. Beams of light swept over the creature as the sound of vehicles surrounded them.

Zach was in the saddle slipping on his flying gloves. He turned to help hoist Dreamer behind him as Adriane, Emily, and Kara climbed aboard.

Ozzie took a flying leap onto Lyra as she dove across the roof, gliding right off the opposite corner.

"Let's go!" Zach yelled.

Drake flapped his wings, sending a downdraft that rustled the trees as he flew high into the sky.

Adriane watched the building below shrink as guards ran inside armed with rifles and flashlights.

She tried to steady her breathing, holding tightly onto Dreamer. Then she realized Emily had been talking to her.

"You look as if you've seen a ghost." Emily bent down, healing stone flashing as she scanned the wolf.

Kara raised her arms in the air. "The team's back together again!"

Dreamer wagged his tail, licking all three mage faces at once.

"Wow, that was something!" Zach said.

"Bet life was pretty boring without us," Kara called out.

"No, but it was a lot less fun." Zach turned around, smiling. "You were great, Adriane—" He frowned when he saw Adriane's face. "What's wrong?"

"I didn't save Dreamer," she said. "Stormbringer did."

"How?" Emily asked.

"I don't know, but I saw her. She's fading fast."

"Which means time is running out for all the mist-wolves," Zach said grimly. "We've got to find the spirit pack."

*"The pack must survive."* Dreamer's eyes shone. *"We must run the spirit trail."*

Adriane bit her lip. Dreamer was right, but where would that path lead her? A deep emptiness dimmed the joy at rescuing her pack mate. For a few seconds, she and Storm had been connected, just like it used to be. The only thing Adriane could feel now was a terrible black hollowness clawing at her insides.

She hugged Dreamer, but her mind echoed with the words of Chain. *"You will betray your pack mate. Humans always do."*

# Chapter 10

In the hunt, the wolf pack worked as a unit, many animals with one purpose. But this was no ordinary hunt. On this afternoon, the pack came together to hunt something not of this world.

Adriane ran her fingers through Dreamer's silky sun-warmed fur. "Are you ready?"

The mistwolf's emerald eyes flashed. *"I am always ready to run with you."*

"Moonshadow . . ."

The wolf looked at Adriane with piercing golden eyes.

"What happened to Chain?"

*"He said he was left by his human to die."* Moonshadow's rich voice echoed in her mind.

"But why? I don't understand how that could have happened."

"We thought Gardener was one of the good guys," Emily added.

*"Not all humans are meant to run with us."* The pack leader turned to Zach. *"I spent many years hating my wolf brother, blaming him for the death of our wolf mother."*

Adriane caught the flare of pain in Zach's eyes.

*"I was wrong. And I believe Chain is wrong as well."* Moonshadow looked at Zach with a wolfish grin. *"And now I have my wolf brother back."*

*"And his bonded,"* Dawnrunner added, lips drawn back in a smile.

Drake hopped from foot to foot, sending tremors across the glade.

Adriane studied the mistwolves who had risked everything for this hunt. The forests had strengthened their fading magic and they had strengthened Dreamer's, but it wouldn't last.

Moonshadow's powerful black body was highlighted by the towering Rocking Stone as he faced the pack.

*"We will send our wolf sister and pack mate to run the spirit trail, as mistwolves have done for thousands of years,"* the pack leader began.

Adriane nodded gratefully.

*"From our Circle of Protection, you will be rooted in this world,"* Dawnrunner explained.

*"But we cannot protect you if you wander from the path,"* Moonshadow warned, growling low.

Dawnrunner brushed against Adriane. The warrior knelt, nose to nose with the wolf. She felt hot breath on her neck as the wolf sniffed her, remembering her scent. *"If you lose your way, follow what is in your heart. That is the true path of a warrior."*

"Thank you," Adriane said, and bowed her head. "We are ready."

The wolves fanned out, encircling Adriane. Emily, Kara, Lyra, Ozzie, Drake, and Zach joined them, leaving Adriane and Dreamer alone in the center.

Dreamer looked at his pack mate, love and determination shining in his emerald eyes. He would be by her side, keeping her safe.

Satisfied, Moonshadow addressed Adriane. *"You will have only a few minutes before we pull you back. Any longer is too dangerous."*

Adriane's pulse pounded. What if she couldn't find Storm? How was she going to hold on long enough to find the spirit pack *and* search for the power crystal?

"I don't know what I'm supposed to do," Adriane admitted.

*"You are one of us,"* Dawnrunner told her. *"Listen."*

Adriane nodded. She *had* to succeed.

Dawnrunner began singing softly, a wandering tune that ebbed and flowed like the voice of the river. Adriane closed her eyes and drifted away, haunted by the melody.

Magic crackled along the circle, vibrating in rhythm with the bittersweet wolf song. Adriane sensed her friends' powers forged into one, a ring of protection around her.

She opened her eyes—and she was no longer in

the glade, no longer in Ravenswood. Adriane and Dreamer stood on a twinkling pathway of stars, curving beyond the horizon. The spirit trail.

Its glittering surface flashed bright white, welcoming the warrior and mistwolf. She could sense the generations of wolves who had run this path before her. But there was a loneliness permeating the magical pathway. She felt she might run forever and never find what she was looking for.

*"We have your scent, warrior,"* Dawnrunner spoke in her mind. The wolf stone blazed with power as she felt the circle of protection surge through her, Moonshadow and Dawnrunner guiding her steps.

"Warrior."

Something was calling to her: powerful magic ahead, drawing her forward like a magnet. She moved faster.

On either side of the path, dark shadows flew through the mist, just out of reach.

"Warrior, this way."

A familiar voice echoed across the eerie, shifting magic.

Adriane stopped in her tracks, Dreamer growling at her side. She looked uncertainly into the deep gray fog. What was that? The spirit pack?

"Hurry!" the voice cried out again.

"Tweek?" Adriane asked, astonished.

"You must hurry!" The E. F.'s voice rose in panic.

"Where are you?" The warrior started to step off into the mist.

*"Stay on the path,"* Moonshadow warned.

"Follow me." The Fairimental's voice was closer now. "It's your only chance to save the pack."

Dreamer growled low in his throat, but Adriane pushed past him. She had to risk it; she could feel the magic beckoning her.

She leaped into the gloom. "Tweek?"

The skies exploded with red lightning as the astral planes twisted to murky black.

"Dreamer!" she screamed.

The wolf leaped after her, grabbing hold of her magic.

Adriane tumbled with dizzying speed, losing all sense of time and space.

She landed hard, her shoulder bashing into a jagged rock.

"Dreamer?" she called out, panic washing over her as she looked around.

She was sitting on a wide black rock, mist coiling around her like snakes. Other rocks poked above the surface of a shimmering ocean—not of water, but of magic. In the distance, something rumbled, rising and falling. Huge waves were breaking over a faraway shore.

*"Pack mate."* Dreamer was behind her, his gleaming white star and paws shining against the dull rock.

She hugged him fiercely. If he hadn't been able to follow her, they could have lost each other.

"Warrior."

A small figure stood in front of her, distorted by a shimmering curtain of mist.

"Tweek?" she asked. "Is that you?"

"Come closer," the E. F. said, his voice sharp and mocking.

Tweek stood before her, red eyes glowing. His mass of ragged sticks and moss stuck out at weird angles. Behind him, shadowy creatures closed in, yellow eyes glittering hungrily.

"Take the mistwolf!" Tweek cackled wildly.

"It's a trap!" Adriane cried.

The creatures lunged. Hideous bat-like demons, their dark, tattered wings carried them across the sparkling sea.

Wolf fire sprung around Adriane and Dreamer in a glowing shield. The beasts shrieked, tearing at her magic with ragged claws. She caught glimpses of bony arms, slitted yellow eyes, and wicked sharp teeth as the bat creatures swarmed, their circle tightening.

Using her magic like a battering ram, she broke through the attackers, sending them scattering.

"Run!" she cried.

Warrior and mistwolf leaped from one rock island to the next. Adriane desperately tried to reach Ravenswood, but she'd severed her connection to the pack when she and Dreamer had left the trail. Now they were lost in the spirit world.

"Dreamer, find the way back!"

"Catch them!" Tweek screamed.

The shrieking creatures charged in a frenzied flapping of wings. Adriane ducked as glittering talons swiped at her from all directions. Golden fire shot from the wolf stone, taking out several demons at once.

Thunder rumbled over the ocean. She looked to the horizon and gasped. A coiling mass of sparkling colors was coming at her, moving across the ocean like a magical tsunami.

Suddenly the creatures dove in, grabbing Dreamer, hoisting him into the air.

Dreamer twisted and growled, trying to break free, but the wolf was outnumbered.

Adriane spun and fired, wolf light exploding from her gem. The demons careened sideways on impact, dropping Dreamer.

"You'll never get out of here!" Tweek yelled.

Adriane leaped and grabbed Tweek, tossing the possessed E. F. to Dreamer. Behind them, she heard wings cutting through the air as the creatures pursued them.

Suddenly an enormous force knocked her feet out from under her. She was pulled down, caught in a riptide as the magic crashed overhead. Strands of blue, green, red, and silver coursed all around her, whipping her through the spirit world with incredible speed. Twisting currents buffeted her back and forth, overwhelming her senses. She was being swept away by wild magic.

She clawed to the surface, relieved to find Dreamer's black head bobbing next to her.

"Dreamer!" she cried as another wave built behind them, surging two stories high. They would be crushed in the roaring magic.

The wolf whined in fear and confusion; wild magic reflected in his wide green eyes. His tracking senses were completely overloaded.

Adriane fired her wolf stone, locking an image in her mind. A surfboard of glowing golden wolf fire formed beneath her. Lying on her stomach, she paddled toward Dreamer. "Hop on!"

Dreamer lunged, Tweek firmly in his jaws, and landed on the front of the board.

The wave crested above their heads and curled, forming a tunnel of swirling ruby, purple, and silver magic.

Placing her right foot forward, Adriane stood, arms out wide, positioning herself for balance. Wolf stone blazing, she surfed through the collapsing wave with lighting speed. She shot out of the imploding tunnel and flew onto another wave of glittering green.

Weaving back and forth, wolf and warrior worked together, trying to sense the pattern of the currents.

Ribbons of brightly colored wild magic swirled, chaotically twisting and smashing together. Crackling bands knotted, forming gleaming riptides that tore through the air in all directions.

"Hang on, Dreamer!"

Adriane pitched right, flying straight up the wave.

Dreamer braced himself as the board shot into the air. At the crest of the wave, Adriane twisted and spun, the board trailing corkscrews of golden fire.

"Are you out of your mind?" Tweek sputtered.

"Put a twig in it!" the warrior shouted.

Struggling to focus, she tried to turn back, but she couldn't fight the immensely powerful current. Her wolf stone flashed in panic. The wild magic could take her anywhere. She'd never find her way home!

Knees bent, she skimmed over the magic swells.

The board flew through the air, narrowly squeezing through two twisting ribbons. Adriane threw her weight to the right, sending the board slicing down the face of another wave.

"Drake. Help me!" She focused with all her will on Drake, hoping the dragon could find them.

Dreamer crouched low, sniffing the flow and eddies of the magic tides.

*"That way!"* He turned his nose toward a sparkle of light in the distance. A brilliant tower of light shot bright homing beacons in all directions.

"Stone sweet stone!"

Adriane aimed the board straight toward the

Rocking Stone. Catching an orange wave, she rock-eted through the astral planes like a golden comet.

"Woohoo!"

Drake's magic wrapped around her like sunlight as she surged forward. Through the swirling white light, she could see a small rounded portal hanging above the Rocking Stone.

Weight centered, knees bent, she went for it.

With a dazzling burst of golden magic, she broke through, soaring high over the glade. Her friends gaped as she flew over their heads.

Staying compact, she leaned back and stomped the landing.

She heard her friends screaming and turned to see why. A wave of demon bats had slipped through, riding the wake of her magic.

Tumbling to the ground, Adriane called out, "Drake, toast them!"

The dragon opened his mouth and roared fero-ciously—but only a harmless puff of rocky road breath came out.

"What happened to your fire?" Zach asked, firing ruby red bolts of magic to ward off the flying beasts.

"*Too much ice cream,*" Drake groaned, looking at Ozzie.

"What? It was all going to melt." The ferret leaped to the side as dozens of the tattered bats descended on the glade.

Moonshadow howled, a piercing cry that disintegrated several bats instantly; others slammed into the Rocking Stone itself.

"Help the mistwolves!" Adriane cried.

The mages stood together and fired. Wolf, dragon, unicorn, ferret, and healing magic entwined into a lariat of power. Amplified through the mage's jewels, the howl of the wolves hit the bats like dynamite. Wings dissolved into ash as their bodies exploded and fell sizzling into the lake.

"RoooooR!" Tweek wriggled in Dreamer's jaws.

"Quite an entrance," Kara said, unicorn jewel blazing diamond bright.

"What's happened to Tweek?" Emily ran forward, taking the twitching, screaming E. F. from the mistwolf's mouth.

"He's under the spell of the Spider Witch," Adriane said to the healer.

"Are you all right?" Zach asked Adriane.

"I'm fine, thanks to you guys," Adriane told them.

"*I found you,*" Drake said, wrapping his giant wings around Adriane.

"Thank you." Adriane hugged his scaly chest, then turned to her friends. "I didn't find Storm."

"What about the power crystal?" Kara asked.

"Wild magic swept me away before I could look for it."

"Take the mistwolf!" Tweek screamed.

"Ahhh!" Ozzie ducked as bolts of red magic shot from Tweek's gem.

"I can't get through to him!" Emily struggled with the Fairimental's flailing twigs.

"He's tweeking out." Raising her unicorn jewel, Kara encased the possessed E. F. in a sphere of white and pink magic.

"Maybe you can help him," Emily said to Adriane. "You're both tuned to earth magic."

Tweek thrashed wildly inside the bubble. "I'll destroy you all!"

The warrior shrugged. "Well, he couldn't get much worse."

Dreamer, Moonshadow, and Dawnrunner took position by the warrior's side; Drake and the rest of the mistwolves behind her.

Steeling herself, Adriane drew on the strength of her friends and focused on Tweek's glowing red HORARFF.

She concentrated on the healing magic Emily had given her as golden fire swirled into the glowing red.

Suddenly she sensed another layer to the magic, made up of the deep green of trees, the velvety brown of bark, the sparkling blue of spring flowers—all the vitality and strength of the forest.

She thought of Orenda, and her wolf stone glowed brighter, gold edged with silver and green. Tweek reached to her, climbing out of the darkness and latching on to Adriane's pure magic.

The E. F. stood before them, quartz eyes whirling with golden magic, HORARFF shining bright turquoise.

"Speak to me, Twighead," Ozzie pleaded.

The little Fairimental looked over his twiggy arms and legs, then stared at the ferret. "Inconceivable!"

"You did it!" Emily cried, as Kara and Zach high-fived the warrior.

Tweek shook his twigs and leaves back to a semblance of his earthly body.

"Tweek, what happened to you?" Emily asked, smoothing a section of moss on his head.

Quartz eyes twinkled, focusing on the mages. "The very magic that holds me together was twisted. Disgusting!"

"Just like the forest spirit," Adriane realized.

"The spirit world is completely flooey! There's wild magic all over the place."

"I noticed." Adriane leaned against Drake's soft neck as she caught her breath. The dragon's large head hung over her shoulder, covering her protectively. "Maybe the spirit pack got swept away on the wild magic, like I did."

*"Possible,"* Moonshadow agreed.

"Tweek, what is the Spider Witch doing?" Emily asked.

"She had me release all those . . . things to try to take Dreamer."

"What were they?" Zach asked.

"Dark creatures that live in the astral planes."

Tweek twirled about. "What concerns me is the fact she could twist Fairimental magic at all!"

"Hold up," Kara said. "What about the forest spirit?"

Tweek looked at his HORARFF. "I'm afraid it's going to transform into something horrible."

"What do we do now?" Zach asked.

Tweek straightened his twigs and marched forward. "We study and decipher mysterious, ancient symbols."

Ozzie rolled his eyes, laughing. "You kill me, Twighead."

"No, look."

Everyone turned around and gasped. The Rocking Stone pulsed with bright white magic, ablaze with glowing symbols.

# Chapter 11

"**W**ow, look at this." Zach walked around the base of the towering Rocking Stone.

Symbols pulsed in sequence like glowing hieroglyphics.

"Good gak!" Tweek studied scrolling bytes of data projected from his HORARFF, trying to find a match.

"The Rocking Stone is an ancient Indian totem. I looked it up on the Web," Emily said. "Legends call it a spirit door."

"I flew through it escaping the astral planes," Adriane said.

"Precisely." Tweek continued scrolling through data. "This stone is a place where the real world and the astral planes intersect. My guess is, this is how the witch has infiltrated the glade with her weaving."

"How do we close it?" Adriane asked.

"You can't," Tweek continued. "But you must have activated these markings when you broke through."

"Good job," Zach told the warrior, smiling.

"Yeah, if I knew what I did, it'd be great."

"It seems to be some kind of message," Tweek concluded.

"From who?" Ozzie asked.

"I don't know," the Experimental Fairimental conceded.

"What's it say?" Ozzie persisted.

"I don't know."

"What's the capital of Arizona?!"

"I don't know."

"Ozzie," Emily said, pulling the agitated ferret back. "Let him work."

Tweek scanned his light over the markings. "I think the message has to do with using elemental magic."

"Hey, look." Kara pointed to a symbol of curling flames glowing orange, red, and yellow on the stone's surface. "There's me, fire."

"Yes," Tweek observed, "and this is water, air, earth, and . . . what the—"

Zach's ruby dragon stone gleamed as he ran it over a strange circular symbol with a lopsided triangle. "What is that?"

"Pizza?" Ozzie guessed, squinting at the stone.

"Step aside." Tweek projected a huge magnifying glass and studied the strange symbol. "Hmmm, I don't know about this one."

"Tweek," Emily said. "Adriane helped fix your magic."

"Thank you," the E. F. mumbled.

Kara looked at the darkening glade. "If Adriane healed you, could we use the same magic to heal Orenda?"

"Theoretically. But I'm just a mass of earthly matter," Tweek said. "The forest sylph is an ancient fairy creature, connected to every tree and plant in this forest."

"We have to try," Adriane said.

"No, no, no!" Tweek protested. "My basic elements are tied to earth, like the forest spirit, so I'm susceptible. But so are Adriane and the mistwolves. Orenda is trapped in a powerful weaving. You'd have to be fully trained in elemental magic to protect yourselves against that spell, let alone reverse it."

*"Mistwolves are not afraid,"* Moonshadow growled.

Dawnrunner stood by her mate, eyes glinting fire. *"Better we try than watch our pups grow without magic."*

Adriane thought of the raging magic pulling at her. The same thing was happening to the mistwolves. When their magic disappeared, they would be plain wolves, pure savage animals. What would happen to her?

Dreamer whined low, feeling the warrior's fear.

"Using elemental magic before you're ready is extremely dangerous. Look what happened to the Spider Witch," Tweek said.

Kara shuddered. "You mean she's, like, a spider?"

Tweek nodded. "The transformation gave her

remarkable powers to weave elemental magic, but she is no longer a fairy creature."

The wind howled through the glade, an eerie sound, almost as if the trees were crying.

Kara turned to the group of mages and animals. "There *is* magic powerful enough to save Ravenswood and the mistwolves."

"The power crystal." Adriane clenched her hand into a fist.

"It worked in the Fairy Realms," Kara concluded.

"Forget it," Tweek barked at Adriane. "You were nearly lost in the astral planes. And you!" His eyes spun colors as he turned to Kara. "What makes you think you can handle that kind of power? You already destroyed one."

"It was an accident," Kara said.

"We don't have a choice!" Adriane cried as thunder suddenly rocked the skies. Storm clouds gathered overhead, a dense mass silhouetting the trees in a seething darkness.

"There's isn't much time left." Kara indicated the drooping, graying branches. "If those demons are any indication of what to expect, we have to try!"

"The Spider Witch is only getting more powerful." Adriane's voice rose, her black eyes sparking as she stood firm beside Dreamer. "I say we strike now, when she's not expecting it. It's the only advantage we've got."

*"I agree with the mages,"* Moonshadow said.

"*We must find the power crystal,*" Dawnrunner added emphatically.

Tweek saw the determination on the faces around him. "I will say this: I have never met mages like you before." His body rattled as a few mounds of moss slipped to the grass. "Of course, I never met *anyone* before you."

Moonshadow snarled at the twiggy figure.

"Oh, all right." Tweek hoisted his twigs into place. "First, you need to know a few rules about Level Two mageing."

"Right," Kara agreed.

"Level Two mages must have"—he held up twiggy fingers and counted off—"a tuned jewel."

"Check," Adriane, Kara, Emily, Ozzie, and Zach said.

"At least one bonded magical animal."

"Check," Adriane, Kara, and Zach echoed.

"*And* an elemental paladin."

"Here," Kara responded, looking at the others.

"It's too risky!" Twigs went flying as Tweek cartwheeled about. "You're all over the map!"

"We need to figure out what elements we are," Zach said, studying the markings.

"Who are you, anyway?" Tweek's quartz eyes rolled in his twigs.

"That's Zach, another mage, and my baby boy, Drake," Adriane said.

"BaaWoW, the Drake is famous among Fairimentals!" Tweek exclaimed, then sighed. "Okay, well, we know Kara is fire."

Adriane swung her wolf stone. Gold and red sparks trailed over the stone's surface. A tree wrapped in ivy crackled with green and deep gold against the granite.

"Earth, naturally," Tweek said.

Emily stepped up, passing her rainbow stone over the glowing symbols. A series of cresting wave markings flashed aquamarine and diamond white.

"Emily is water," Tweek said.

"Lemme see that thing!" Ozzie stomped over, nose to rock, scanning the jewel on his collar. Several bright puffy clouds flashed on the stone, edged in gleaming silver.

"Ozzie's definitely full of hot air," Kara remarked.

"Thank you." Ozzie proudly polished his jewel with his furry arm.

"We need room," Tweek said as he wobbled to the lake in the center of the glade.

The mages followed the E. F. expectantly.

"Everyone stand with your bonded animals," he instructed.

Adriane stood with the mistwolves, Kara with Lyra, and Zach with Drake. Ozzie took a step toward Emily.

"Hey! You're an elf, and a mage, too—sort of," Tweek reminded him. "And neither of you have bonded with an animal."

"Maybe Ozzie bonded with himself," Kara suggested.

"That's ridiculous." Ozzie looked himself over, smoothing his cowlick.

"Not everyone is meant for Level Two," the E. F. advised. "Kara happens to have the perfect combination of magic. She is a blazing star tuned to a unicorn jewel, bonded to Lyra *and* a firemental stallion."

"Perfect," Kara mouthed as she coyly twirled her sparkling jewel.

"Wait," Adriane said. "So if the Spider Witch is an elemental master, then she has a paladin, too?"

"I bet it's that big creepy spider I saw in her lair." Kara shuddered.

"Yes . . . ," Tweek said, eyes popping. "If there was a way to get rid of her paladin, we could weaken her powers—"

"*And* her hold on Ravenswood!" Ozzie finished.

"We don't have time to break into her lair!" Adriane insisted. "We have to heal Orenda now!"

"But there's only one of us who is a Level Two mage," Emily said.

"I can boost the rest of you," Kara suggested. "That's what a blazing star does. Uses magic to help everyone else."

Adriane gave Kara a nod and stepped to a line of trees near the lake's edge. "She's somewhere around here."

"Let's kick it." Kara held up her unicorn jewel, swirling diamond magic around her arms.

"O' me twig," Tweek sputtered.

The blazing star concentrated, morphing her magic into red, pink, and orange flames. With a wave of her hands, she pulled the fire together, letting it mix with the amber glow of the wolf stone.

Amplified by Kara's magic, Adriane whipped golden fire around four of the nearest trees. She immediately felt a jolt. The trees were trying to fight the strangling power of the weaving.

"I can feel the webs!" Adriane tried to pull the dark magic away, but couldn't.

Ozzie focused on his stone. "Air—what does that mean, Tweekster?"

"Could be levitation, wind . . ."

Ozzie looked to Kara. His gem glowed bright amber. Then a burst of wind shot from his stone, throwing the ferret backward. He tumbled head over heels into the lake.

"Very good," Tweek commented.

Emily focused on the lake, trying to pull the flailing ferret back to shore. Her rainbow stone shone blue, green, and purple as she bore down harder. The lake surface rippled slightly.

"Kara, give me a boost," she instructed.

Kara draped the healer in pink and white diamond twinkles. A wave surged across the lake, delivering the soggy ferret onto the bank with a splatter.

Adriane's magic sparked. Waves of fire leaped into the air and vanished, leaving the trees untouched.

"This is so not working." The warrior put her stone down, exhausted and disappointed.

Moonshadow gathered the pack around the warrior. *"Try again."*

Focusing, the warrior reached into the earth, feeling dark magic running through the roots. The weaving sapped at her bright fire, swallowing its power. But deep underneath she felt something, a spark of life. Opening herself to the mistwolves, she snarled and grabbed the earth magic.

Tweek went flying across the glade and smashed into the Rocking Stone, releasing a burst of dirt. "Aggooy."

Adriane felt her magic drain away with the effort.

The E. F. spun to his feet, tumbling his way back to the glade. "Yes, well, although she doesn't have a paladin, the pull of the mistwolves is very strong."

All the animals of Ravenswood had now gathered in the glade to help.

"Teamwork, people!" Kara held up her shining unicorn jewel, sending rings of pale orange fire to encircle the trees.

The others held up their gems, concentrating. Blue, green, red, gold, and amber sparkled along Kara's swirling firemental magic.

"Careful," the blazing star cautioned. "Okay, let's take it out."

The circle of magic spread slowly outward, covering several dozen more trees.

"Easy . . . okay." The blazing star nodded to the warrior.

With the mistwolves supporting her, Adriane reached frantically, trying to stop the poison from spreading. But the circle of fire washed harmlessly across the glade.

Mistwolves growled, snapping at the air in frustration.

"That was . . . something," Tweek said.

The mages exchanged anxious glances, their jewels lowered and lifeless.

"Great, now what?" Kara asked.

"If only I knew how to use the magic better," Zach muttered, frustrated.

"If only we could contact the Fairimentals, or the unicorns," Emily said worriedly.

"We don't have enough time to practice!" Kara threw her hands in the air.

A feeling of despondency and hopelessness hung heavy in the air.

"We suck!" a quiffle squeaked.

"You made it worse," Adriane accused Kara.

"I did not!" Kara faced the warrior.

"Did."

"Not!" Kara said to Adriane. "You're doing it wrong."

"I am not!"

"*I'm* the one here with Level Two magic!" Kara yelled.

"Oh, if you're so perfect"—Adriane got right in Kara's face—"why don't you just save the preserve yourself?"

"Maybe I will!"

"We're doomed!" Rasha cried.

*KAooOOGAH!*

Everyone jumped, startled by a booming blast from the ferret stone.

Ozzie marched to the front of the group, determination shining in his eyes, and began speaking in a loud, clear voice. "Listen up! I may be a ferret but—"

"You're an elf," Tweek corrected him.

"I may be an elf, but—"

"He's an elf?" a startled quiffle asked.

*"You look like a ferret,"* a mistwolf observed.

"GaH!"

"Quiet!" Emily demanded.

"It doesn't matter what we are," Ozzie continued. "The Dark Sorceress and the Spider Witch are back and more dangerous than ever. Wild magic is flooeying all over the place. Our home is in danger—"

A few quiffles and brimbees started crying.

"Gah! The only way we're going to succeed is if we work together." He walked to a quivering quiffle, lifting its beak.

"It doesn't matter that we can't even make a simple magic . . . er, thing."

He turned to a brimbee. "When the Dark Sorceress blew up the whatever-that-was, did we back down?"

"No!" the group answered.

Ozzie challenged the mistwolves. "When the mistwolves were trapped, did Stormbringer let them down?"

"No!" Adriane yelled.

"That's right! So are we going to give up when Ravenswood needs us?"

The resounding "No!" echoed throughout the glade.

"Whatever the Spider Witch has planned, whether it's disgusting webs, incredibly powerful elemental magic, giant fanged spiders—"

"Whoa."

"Whatever comes, it just doesn't matter!" the ferret shouted. "We are going to work together and save Ravenswood!"

"Yay!" everyone cheered wildly.

"It's time!" Tweek screamed.

"Let's go!" Ozzie yelled, frizzled hair sticking straight out.

"No, it's *time!*" Tweek's twigs rattled as he found a match for Zach's mysterious symbol on the Rocking Stone. "Zach is *time,* a fifth element!"

"What does that mean?" the boy asked.

"You are the anchor, the one who keeps all the other elements rooted here in the real world," Tweek explained.

*"Like the circle of protection."* Dreamer understood.

"Exactly," Tweek agreed. "With the dragon, you can hold Adriane steady—well, *steadier,* if she goes back in."

Adriane clasped Zach's hands in hers. "You mean *when* I go back in."

"I won't let you get lost again," Zach vowed.

Adriane smiled and nodded. "Okay, here's the play," she said, addressing the group. "Dreamer and I are going back. We'll find Storm, and together we'll find the spirit pack."

The mistwolves howled in a chorus of agreement.

"The magic of the spirit pack will help attract the power crystal," the warrior declared, turning to the blazing star.

"Yeah, that should do it," Kara concurred.

"Dreamer will bring it back," Zach agreed.

"And we'll use the power crystal to heal the forest sylph," Emily concluded.

A cacophony of cheers meant all the animals were down with the brave plan.

Time was running out. Adriane hoped Ozzie was right and that their determination would be enough. It was all they had.

# Chapter 12

The Dark Sorceress edged aside as spiders skittered into the thick mist.

The giant tapestry crackled as the Spider Witch's bulky robed form moved back and forth, conducting the hundreds of spiders busily weaving the final details.

The time for patience is almost at an end, the sorceress told herself. The source of her ally's power would soon reveal itself, and when it did, the sorceress would strike.

She stepped back as a giant spider descended out of the mist.

The Spider Witch laughed, stroking the spider's spiky head.

"I know what you are thinking," the witch said slowly, her voice low and threatening. "Your elemental transformation was never complete. There is a part of you still human, and that will always be your weakness."

"You have the power here, not me." The sorceress bowed her head in subservience.

"Serve me and I can complete your magic."

The sorceress's animal eyes flashed.

"Or I could feed you to my hungry friend."

Clattering mandibles clicked an eerie staccato as the spider watched the sorceress coldly.

"I would prefer the former," the sorceress conceded.

"Then I think you'll like this final touch."

The spider moved away, golden thread trailing from its swollen abdomen. The witch raised her hand. A ruby gem gleamed powerfully on her finger. With a quick slash, she cut the final strand with a sharp fingernail.

The entire tapestry shifted, rippling like a reflection in a pool. Silken threads quivered as the building magic writhed through the design. A sudden gust of wind surged through the chamber, carrying the crisp scent of ancient forest. High, keening wolf howls leaked from the swirling patterns.

The sorceress's skin prickled—the weaving was coming to life!

The Spider Witch cackled gleefully. "Watch and learn what a magic master can do."

It was as if they stood high above Ravenswood, looking down. The details were amazing, every tree, every blade of grass, the woodland trails, blue streams running into lakes, the intricate details of the sculpture gardens, topiary animals, Ravenswood Manor itself. And in the center—the magic glade, the heart of the forest.

The witch waved her hand, and the glade zoomed forward, magnifying every secret in exquisite detail.

"All is ready."

❦   ❦   ❦

The shining spirit trail stretched before Adriane and Dreamer.

She couldn't hear her friends through the layers of swirling magic but she could feel them. Tweek had been right: Dragon magic was as ancient as time itself, and it was Drake and Zach now keeping her steady. With Dreamer guiding her, she kept on the path.

Wild magic swells rose and fell to the sides, attracted to the wolf stone and mistwolf, brilliant spray breaking upon the trail's edge.

A sudden feeling of loss stopped her. Emptiness, like cold rain, swept over her. She felt alone, all her fears and memories bubbling to the surface. But this time, instead of pulling away, she reached for them, allowing the jagged feelings of isolation and sadness to fill her with frozen dread.

She took a deep breath. "Here," she said calmly. "This is where it happened."

The black mistwolf trotted to her side. *The spirit pack was taken here.*

Adriane stood in the middle of the spirit trail, the future ahead, past behind. She closed her eyes and focused, letting wolf magic flow through her. Blues mixed with swaths of white and green swirled in her head. Her nose filled with the extraordinary scents of wood, loam, and wildflowers. Her heart raced with the devotion and love of her pack mates. She pressed on, trying to see through Storm's eyes, feeling what Storm was feeling—and reached for her lost friend.

The shift was slight, barely perceptible.

Through a warm haze, Adriane saw herself. She was standing on a grassy hill, eyes closed, arms outstretched.

She opened her eyes and looked in wonder. The forests of Ravenswood spread miles in every direction, a vast ocean of greens and browns sparkling under skies of blue and white.

But it was not the shock of being back in Ravenswood that made her gasp. In front of her, not ten feet away, stood a lone mistwolf. Her silver-and-white fur gleamed with magic, golden eyes shining.

"Storm!"

Without thinking, Adriane raced to her friend. The large wolf reared up to place her paws on her pack mate's shoulders in a wolfish embrace.

Adriane had never felt such joy. She howled with pleasure, jumping and leaping, rolling on the ground just as they once had.

Atop the rolling hills, amid the wildflowers and tall, sweet grass, Storm lay beside Adriane, golden eyes glinting with light. Together, they looked out upon the forests they both loved.

"Storm, I can't believe it's really you." Adriane

threw her arms around her friend, burying her face in warm, silvery fur. "I never want to leave here, ever!"

*"I wish that could be, Adriane,"* Stormbringer answered.

"So much has happened, I . . . I . . ." She was about to introduce Storm to Dreamer when she realized the black mistwolf was nowhere to be found.

*"The mistwolves are in terrible danger."*

Suddenly, the silver wolf's form wavered, dissipating to mist, before weaving back.

Adriane scrambled to her feet, panic shooting through her.

"Storm, what's wrong?" Adriane asked nervously.

*"I must return to the spirit world."*

"Aren't we there now?"

*"This is only a dream state."*

Only a dream. But it felt so real, so alive.

*"Will you come with me, warrior? See me as I really am."*

"I know who you really are," Adriane said, bracing herself. "Take me with you."

Storm nodded, closing her golden eyes briefly. Her fur shone like moonlight.

In a swirling wash of greens and browns, the forest melted away.

A sudden rush of sound thundered like the crash of a cannon. Dust filled Adriane's eyes and throat.

The scene before her was one of total chaos, a cacophony of noise and confusion. Huge slabs of rock crashed to the floor. Adriane staggered as the walls of an underground chamber fell around her.

Adriane had been plunged into the middle of her nightmare: Her pack mate was trapped, and she was helpless to do anything about it.

In the center of the chamber, the last of the sorceress's crystals splintered and cracked as it filled with waves of magic from Avalon. The Dark Sorceress had trapped the mistwolves in immense crystals, using the wolves to attract the magic of Avalon. Storm stood, wavering in and out of mist as she helped the last of the mistwolves leap free of the death trap.

Across the vast chamber Adriane heard her friends desperately calling to her. Kara, Emily, and Zach tried to reach her, but instead she ran toward her struggling pack mate. She would never let her down. Golden wolf fire sprang from the wolf stone spiraling toward her friend. The magic locked around the fading mistwolf.

*"Do not let go."*

"Never!" With every fiber of her being, Adriane held on to Storm. The world turned upside down as Adriane was swept through an endless forest, wordless memories of sorrow and passion filling her senses.

Time crashed to a stop.

Adriane stood at the edge of a high cliff. Silver rocks glittered, leading from the ledge to the sprawling drop far below. A stream of mist bridged the chasm, stretching over a river of raging wild magic. Ribbons of brilliant blue, purple, red, and silver thrashed in the narrow gap, surging upward, flowing in a fast river.

*"I knew you would find me."*

Storm's voice echoed in her mind, but the silver wolf was nowhere to be seen.

On the far side of the chasm, Adriane could see the glistening lines of the spirit trail. The end of the misty bridge entwined with the glowing lines, fading away in the distance. A bolt of crackling magic burst from the river below, shredding a section of mist to fragments.

Adriane's wolf stone blazed with danger as pain tore through her, as if a part of her were being ripped to shreds.

She fought to stand strong. "Storm, where are you?"

*"I am here."* Storm's disembodied voice echoed in the wide space.

Adriane looked at the bridge of mist and gasped.

The section of spirit trail stretching over the chasm had been destroyed. Now only Storm's mist united the two sides, keeping the trail whole. Once her mist faded, the entire spirit trail would collapse, and the memories and magic of the mistwolves would vanish into nothingness, lost forever.

"*I cannot hold on much longer,*" the mistwolf said, her voice strained.

"What's happened to you?"

"*I am holding the last of the mistwolves' magic.*"

Adriane looked around desperately. "Where is the rest of the spirit pack?"

"*They are lost. You must find them.*"

"I don't understand," Adriane said. "If the spirit pack was swept away by the wild magic, why weren't you taken with them?"

"*I ran with the spirit pack, but I was never part of them.*"

Adriane was unable to speak. The realization rocked her to the very core of her being.

"*I was swept onto the trail from the Dark Sorceress' lair, but I have remained here in mist form.*"

"But why didn't you tell me?" Adriane asked, tears running down her cheeks. "I could have helped."

"*You did. You have held me in your dreams.*"

Adriane flashed on the dark dreams that had haunted her since she lost Storm—her desperate attempts to hold on to her friend, to keep her from slipping away. "I thought they were nightmares," she whispered, horrified. "I didn't know."

Storm's mist wavered, nearly disintegrating before pulling back together.

Fear tingled up and down Adriane's spine. Storm

had replaced the spirit pack, holding the mistwolves of Aldenmor from losing their magic. And that meant if Adriane could find the missing pack in time, she could bring Storm back with her—alive!

Adriane fought to remain calm. There wasn't much time. She had been given a second chance, and she wasn't going to waste it. But only the magic of Avalon itself could help her.

"I have to find the power crystal."

Suddenly a tremor shook the chasm, and the wild magic exploded. A shock wave surged through the air, sending Adriane tumbling through walls of vibrant color.

"No!"

It was too late.

She felt the magic of her friends take hold and drag her from the spirit world, Storm's mist vanishing before her eyes.

She heard the sounds of yelling as magic flashed everywhere.

"Adriane!"

Zach ran toward her. "Are you all right?

"I . . . don't know." She stood in the glade, watching the scene as if this, too, were a dream.

"We're under attack!" Kara yelled.

Sudden pain lashed through her, making her cry out. She saw Emily and Kara, magic blazing from their jewels. The mistwolves ran about the glade, trying to contain the dark forces that had finally broken through. Trees sagged into the water, their flowing branches weighed down by glistening spiderwebs. And in the center of a clump of willows, suspended by twisted hunks of spiderwebbing, hung the sickly, green cocoon. Blistered with pockmarks, the thing pulsed, tearing wicked cracks up and down. The vile apparition shuddered, ready to unleash the demon inside.

"The webs appeared out of nowhere!" Emily cried, running to Adriane's side as she fired intense volleys of healing magic.

Adriane tried to add her magic to that of her friends, but all she felt was the agony of the forest sylph.

Adriane ignored the intense emotions bombarding her and searched for the one who could help her most.

"Dreamer?" she called out desperately.

But Dreamer was gone.

# Chapter 13

In a flash of bloodred light, heavy webbing exploded over the glade as the cocoon burst open. Adriane felt the world spinning, twisting her stomach in a knot. Wolf stone sparking, she looked around frantically for Orenda, but all that remained was a mass of strands coiling over the trees. Whatever was in the cocoon had disappeared.

The mistwolves leaped through the glade, snarling as they searched for the forest sylph.

The healer rushed toward Adriane, red curls tumbling wildly over her sweat-streaked face.

"Emily," Adriane whispered, dark eyes shining. "She's alive."

"Who?" Kara raced over, Lyra landing beside her.

"Stormbringer."

Emily and Kara gasped.

Adriane turned to Moonshadow and Dawnrunner. "She's been trapped in mist form ever since she saved the mistwolves from the sorceress."

*"Storm is the one holding us to the spirit trail,"* Moonshadow realized, his eyes glinting with feral light.

"I have to go back before it's too late," Adriane said. "Dreamer's still there."

Dawnrunner addressed the pack. *"No one gets left behind."*

The mistwolves howled as everyone gathered behind Adriane.

"We have to stop that sylph!" Tweek rattled atop Ariel's back as the owl landed. "If she takes the magic of Ravenswood to the spirit world, she's going to get the power crystal."

"Where did she go?" Kara nervously asked.

Wind screamed through the forest, tangling the remaining webs draped in the trees.

"That way." The warrior pointed toward broken branches and downed trunks littering the forest floor.

*"I can smell the foul thing,"* Moonshadow confirmed.

The group moved cautiously to the edge of the glade, following the trail of destruction.

"Tweek, where is it?" Adriane asked, eyes narrowed, jewel held high as she swept a beam of magical light over the surrounding trees.

Tweek stretched his twigs out like antennae, pointing to a giant fir. "O' me, me, me—"

"Keep your twigs together, man!" Ozzie shouted.

"TWI—!" Tweek exploded in a burst of mud and sticks.

With a wrenching *crack,* the tree trunk split, spewing red light across the ground. The mutated forest sylph emerged.

"Orenda!" Adriane gasped as the demon's twisted magic slammed into her.

The sylph had been monstrously transformed. Red eyes glowing from its shifting, translucent form, the nightmarish thing floated in the air. Root legs like spider limbs reached out. Crooked needle fingers grew from bent limbs. The sylph's once beautiful features were wracked by livid scars, pulling her mouth into a malicious grin.

Adriane's tears felt like fire on her face.

"Warrior," the demon sneered, expanding its ghostly form. Leaves, branches, and pieces of earth flew toward it like a powerful magnet. "You have nothing left."

The magic of Ravenswood swirled inside the vengeful spirit, pure green and gold warping to red. Adriane's wolf stone erupted in a shower of red sparks.

Zach and Kara fired their jewels, slamming dragon and unicorn magic into the thing.

The demon roared, gathered its thrashing roots, and plunged into another tree. Bolts of energy raced through the trunk as the demon fed on the tree's earth magic.

Adriane doubled over as the screams of the trees burned through the wolf stone.

Golden magic shimmering along their lustrous fur, Dawnrunner and five wolves lunged at the infected tree. Shrieking at the touch of the wolves' pure magic, the demon zipped out, disappearing into the next tree.

Struggling as her gem flickered between red and gold, Adriane fought the demon's pull. Her friends were firing volleys of magic, but without her earth elemental magic, they could not heal Orenda.

The demon shot from the glade into the depths of the forest, devouring everything in its path.

"What do we do?" Kara shouted, unicorn jewel sparking in her hand. "Can we heal Orenda, turn her back?"

"We have to get her in one place long enough to find out," Emily responded.

"We need to set a trap," Adriane said.

"What's the bait?" Zach asked.

"We give it what it wants." Adriane held up her wrist, wolf stone pulsing with light.

"That's crazy!" Kara cried.

"No way!" Emily protested.

Adriane faced her friends. "*I'm* the one attuned to earth magic."

"It's too dangerous," Ozzie exclaimed. "What if that only makes the demon stronger?"

"We have to try." Before the others could talk her out of it, she quickly continued. "We need a distraction."

Zach swung onto Drake's back. "Leave *that* to us."

"Lyra, follow Orenda!" Kara ordered.

The cat gave Ozzie a flick of her head.

"Doh!" The ferret reluctantly climbed aboard. "I really hate flying."

The cat's golden wings shimmered and unfolded as she soared upward, Ozzie hanging on.

"Moonshadow, try to herd it away from the deep forest," Adriane ordered.

The black wolf started barking orders. *"I want four groups led by Dawnrunner, Whitefang, Comet, and Aja."*

*"I will go with Adriane."* Dawnrunner stepped between Moonshadow and the warrior.

Moonshadow stood nose to nose with his mate. A spark flashed between their eyes as the pack leader submitted and padded to the other wolves.

"We'll meet in back of the manor," Adriane continued. "Good luck."

A flaming maple tree shot into the air like a rocket, streaking across the sky as it disintegrated into embers.

"The demon is making its way through Turtle Bog!" Ozzie reported from high atop Lyra.

Moonshadow bounded into the woods. The rest of the wolves raced after him.

Adriane ran her hand over Drake's neck, feeling the dragon's strength. "Be careful," she said to Zach.

"*Let's fly!*" Drake snorted fire. With a beat of enormous wings, dragon and rider took to the skies.

Healer, blazing star, warrior, and mistwolf took off toward the manor.

Drake and Zach sliced through the sky, swooping in as the poisoned sylph burrowed through a line of pine trees.

Howling their battle cry, mistwolves forced the demon across a grassy clearing to the topiary garden on the eastern hills of the preserve.

In a blaze of red dust, Orenda shot down a slope and engulfed a topiary brontosaurus.

The green dinosaur sculpture flashed red—and came to life. It swung a massive tail at the wolves. But Moonshadow bore down from the west, snarling and ripping at the dino's haunches. A blast of dragon fire from the skies smacked into the bronto, forcing the demon to jump into the tyrannosaurus topiary. The huge shrub sculpture shuddered, its neatly shorn leaves crackling and glowing red as it thundered toward the dragon. Zach and Drake rounded on the T rex, encasing it with pure ruby dragon magic. The demon dino dodged aside, sinking glowing red teeth into Drake's tail. The dragon bellowed, tail smoking.

"Drake!" Adriane cried, feeling the dragon's pain.

"Come on, we have to hurry while it's distracted," Kara called, running past the mermaid fountain in the water gardens.

Emily slipped a steadying arm through the warrior's as they followed Kara and Dawnrunner across the great lawns. They came to a stop at the forest's edge.

"Which one?" Emily asked, scanning the magnificent trees bordering the lawn.

Adriane had to choose. She stopped in front of a giant oak. Its immense trunk rose into a mass of branches thick with green leaves.

*"You must ask the tree to help us,"* Dawnrunner urged.

Adriane placed her hands on the tree trunk, the bark rough against her palms. She closed her eyes and concentrated. Magic tingled up and down her arms. She could feel the gnarled roots draw strength from the land. She reached farther, touching another tree, then another. With love and patience, Orenda had woven each tree into an intricate network, nurturing the natural magic of Ravenswood.

"Great tree," Adriane spoke quietly. "Orenda has given so much to make you strong and healthy. Please, help her now."

The tree groaned and creaked. Adriane winced. She thought she heard the entire forest scream with the agony of the demon's attack.

"I'm sorry," Adriane whispered to the oak. "Please help us."

As if acknowledging the warrior's presence, the tree seemed to calm.

Wolf stone shining, Adriane sent earth magic into

the tree. The healer and blazing star added their magic, entwining blues, pinks, and whites into the wolf stone. Adriane directed the flow of power through the trunk, into every root and every branch. The leaves glowed with swirling colors.

"We stand with you," she told the tree as the magic shone into the sky like a beacon.

On the other side of the preserve, the dino-tope turned, attracted by the vibrant magic. With a withering red flash, the demon zipped away from its host. The enormous scorched-leaf sculpture stood suspended for one precarious moment before crashing to the ground, crushing a triceratops topiary.

*"Heads up!"* Lyra soared over the mages.

"It's coming!" Ozzie yelled, arms flailing. "Right toward you!"

The red glow of the demon filtered through the trees like an unnatural sunset.

Eyes blazing, it streaked across the lawn.

Dawnrunner turned to face the oncoming monster.

Kara and Emily took position on either side of the tree, jewels raised.

"Steady." Adriane breathed deeply, struggling to contain the magic roiling inside the tree.

The haggard wolves fanned out in a U shape, Drake zooming overhead, guiding the demon as it headed straight for the huge oak—and Adriane.

With a fierce snarl, Dawnrunner crouched low, magic crackling along her coat.

"Dawnrunner!" Adriane cried.

*"Stand strong, warrior."* The wolf held her ground, sending her magic not to defend herself from the demon—but to protect Adriane.

The demon collided with Dawnrunner in a sickening rush. For a split second, wolf and demon merged, exploding in a blaze of fire. Waves of twisted magic crashed over Adriane as the demon leaped into the glowing tree.

She saw Dawnrunner's limp body sprawled across the ashen ground. Once again a wolf had sacrificed herself and Adriane hadn't been able to stop it.

Emily ran to the downed wolf, healing stone blazing.

Keening howls sliced over the preserve as the wolves sensed the loss of their fallen pack mate.

Adriane felt the evil spirit meld with the tree, sinking its venom into the rich veins. She grabbed at the demon, twisting her magic around it like a rope. Dawnrunner's brave act had weakened the creature.

The warrior held up her jewel and met Moonshadow's steely eyes.

"Fire!" Adriane ordered.

Five jewels erupted with magic, encasing the tree in a glittering force field. The wolves surrounded the tree, giving all they had left to help the mages.

The demon shrieked, thrashing the oak's wide branches.

"Orenda, come back to us." The warrior flattened

her palms on the tree, moving tendrils of golden magic into the demon.

The contact burned like fire. She could feel the energy of Ravenswood pulsing through the demon as the Spider Witch threaded each tree into her horrible spell.

Tweek's magic had felt like this at first, too, all swirling and dark, but she had found the pure elemental spark within him. She focused harder, desperately trying to touch the gentle forest sylph.

But Orenda was being controlled like a puppet, forced to destroy everything she had spent years building.

Adriane cried out. No trace of Orenda's pure blue, gold, and green magic remained. Utter blackness had consumed the sylph. The witch had wormed her way into the heart of Ravenswood and extinguished its light—Orenda was no more.

"It's too late." The warrior slumped to the ground, eyes glazed with tears. Once again, she had failed.

"Keep firing!" Kara's jewel blazed with red, pink, and white fire.

The trapped demon shrieked in anger as the force field closed around it.

There was only one place the demon could go now—and there was only one thing left for Adriane to do.

The warrior rose, eyes sparking. Magic crashed through her, but it didn't matter. Rage and sorrow burned inside. The mistwolves had come to her for help, to make their stand. Now Dawnrunner had paid for that trust. Chain's words rang in her head, mocking her. How many more would suffer before this was over? How many more would she betray?

This was her fault. She had to make it right.

With all the strength she had left, she reached out and grabbed the demon, tightening her golden wolf magic around its very core.

"Adriane!" Emily's cry drifted away.

Brilliant dragon magic reached out to her, but she ignored it.

"Where is she?" Zach's worried voice floated from a million miles away.

The faint cries of her friends faded as she fell.

Chain's wolfish laughter echoed ahead of her in the swirling gloom.

Then everything went black as Adriane plummeted into the oblivion between worlds.

# Chapter 14

**H**er feet hit solid ground, crunching the thick layer of leaves and twigs on the forest floor.

What happened? Was she still in Ravenswood?

She turned. A stand of oaks was behind her. One of the trees had an ornately carved door leading right into it.

That's very curious, she thought.

She opened the door and cautiously stepped inside. Following a long, winding tunnel, she finally emerged in a strange garden. Giant flowers bloomed beside golden geometric hedges.

Raucous laughter floated to her left. She recognized her friends' voices. It sounded as if they were having a party! She darted around large hedges and found herself in a clearing.

Her friends were all sitting at a long table—plates, teacups, confetti, balloons, and party gear piled high atop the fringed purple tablecloth. A giant cake with pale green frosting tilted precariously in the center.

*"Twinkle, twinkle little cat,"* Lyra sang from her seat at the head of the table, fake cat ears on her baseball cap. Teacups and saucers clattered as the group turned around to stare.

Adriane gaped, openmouthed.

*"How I wonder where you're at."*

"Who are you?" Adriane ran a hand over the table. It felt real enough.

"That's the mad catter, silly," Ozzie said, floating in an orange and blue porcelain teapot.

"Who are you supposed to be?" Adriane asked Ariel. The owl perched on the table, wearing a sea captain's hat.

"The mad hooter, of course," Ozzie said.

Drake held a dainty teacup in his huge paws, trying unsuccessfully to drink.

"What is going on here?" Adriane asked, dumbfounded.

"What is going on here?" Ozzie demanded, scrolling over a long sheet of paper that fell to the ground in waves. "You are down for two!"

Zach stood up, straightening his finely tailored pinstriped suit and wide red silk tie. "Everyone is supposed to bring a guest," he announced. "You can't come here all by yourself."

"Shhhhh!" Emily, her hair a mass of wild red ringlets, turned wide eyes to the boy. "She's always alone, she doesn't have anybody."

"Where is your hat?" Kara demanded. Her

golden hair was pulled into pigtails with two giant pink velvet bows that matched her frilly, doll-like dress. "You can't just come to our party looking like that."

"Listen to me!" Adriane exclaimed.

"I'm all ears." With a dramatic bow, Zach swept the cat ears off his head.

Adriane reached for the dragon's warm magic. "Drake, what's going on?"

*"Tea party!"* Drake snorted a burst of fire over his cup, making it boil.

This wasn't the spirit world, Adriane realized. She had fallen into the dream state. It shouldn't surprise me, she thought dully.

"I have to find Dreamer," she said, backing away from the bizarre scene.

"Who?"

Everyone looked at one another, confused.

"He's not on the list," Ozzie announced, cramming the scroll in the spout of the teapot.

"Dreamer!" Adriane cried. "My pack mate."

"Mistwolf?" Tweek leaped up and pirouetted across several muffins. "Don't be ridiculous. No one's seen one of those in years."

"They died out long ago," Emily added. "Thanks to you."

"What?" Adriane backed away in horror. "Don't even say that."

"That puppy was so cute!" Kara squealed.

"Where is he?" the warrior demanded.

"How should we know?" Zach asked. "You're the one who lost him."

"This is crazy," Adriane muttered. Things were getting hazy, her head was swimming. She had to get out of here, figure out what to do.

She ran to a path on the opposite side of the clearing, dodging between bushy branches laden with pastel marshmallows. She sped around a triangular hedge and stopped dead.

*"It's her again!"* Lyra exclaimed. A huge cowboy hat was crammed on her head.

Adriane's pulse pounded. "How did I get back here?"

"I know, I know!" Emily raised her hand in the air excitedly. The rainbow feathers sprouting from her wide-brimmed green hat swayed. "Every path leads here."

"Twingo!" Tweek, a mossy fedora on his head, twirled across the table.

Adriane stood staring.

"You can't do anything right." Kara adjusted her pink beret, giving Adriane a scornful look. "You are such a loser."

Adriane flopped into a large armchair at one end of the table. Orenda was dead, Dreamer lost, the magic of Ravenswood gone. Some earth warrior she was. She shook her head. This was surreal. She couldn't think clearly.

Suddenly, she gasped. "Where are your jewels?"

"What jewels?" Emily asked, looking over her sparkly plastic rings.

"Like this." Adriane held up her wrist—and stopped cold. Her wolf stone had vanished. Even her bracelet's tan line had disappeared completely. As if she'd never had it at all.

"I . . . I have to go," she whispered.

"Where?" Kara asked.

"How?" Emily asked.

"When?" Ozzie and Zach chorused.

"Hooo?" the mad hooter asked.

"I can world walk away from here right now." Adriane sprang to her feet. "Just watch me!"

She stepped forward, concentrating, and walked right into the table.

Everyone clapped.

"There's no place to go—you might as well stay here." Zach smiled.

"Nothing to do but eat cake." Ozzie dove into the green frosting.

"Just sit down and try to be normal like the rest of us," Kara said haughtily.

Somewhere inside, Adriane knew this was all wrong, but she just couldn't focus. Besides, they were right.

She slumped back down. She could walk away, but she could never leave—just keep going round and round, always ending up where she started. Destined to repeat everything again and again, all her mistakes, all her failures.

She might as well just give up. Move to Woodstock and paint fruit. There was nothing at Ravenswood for her now. She was never meant to have magic, or friends, or a real home. Why had she ever thought she didn't have to be alone?

She hung her head and closed her eyes, cutting off the jabbering noise of the party. This was just a dream. She wasn't alone. There had to be someone who could help her.

"Hey!" a familiar voice called out. "What's happening, dudes, and how come I wasn't invited?"

Adriane opened her eyes. A second Kara walked into the clearing, surveying the rainbow garden.

"Soooo . . . slacking off, are we?"

Oh, this is just great! Adriane thought. Of all the friends, I gotta pull in her!

*"Who are you?"* the catter called out, now wearing a thick wool hat with the earflaps pulled down.

"The question is . . ." The blazing star inspected the scene. "Who are *you*?"

*"We know who we are."* Lyra looked around. *"Don't we?"*

"What are you doing here?" The second Kara walked to Adriane's overstuffed chair. "Get up."

"Leave me alone." The warrior was suddenly exhausted.

"Say," the first Kara said, sizing up Kara Two. "You look very familiar."

Kara Two smiled. "You're quite beautiful."

"So true." Kara One giggled, pigtails swinging. "I wish I had hair like yours. Oh, I do!"

"But your fashion sense is, like, last Halloween."

"Oh, you wish you had these shoes!" Kara One wiggled her pointy green elf shoes.

"Yeah." Kara Two chuckled. "Next time I visit Saturn."

"Well, I have everything you have, and more." Kara One crossed her arms and pouted.

Kara Two tapped her chin thoughtfully. "Except for one teeny, tiny, eentsy, beensy, little thingy."

"What?"

"You're not real." Kara Two swung her glittering unicorn jewel.

"Get out!"

"She just got here," Ozzie complained, adjusting his giant polka-dot sombrero.

"Do they ever shut up on your planet?" With a brilliant flash of unicorn magic, the entire party freeze-framed. "Now, let's go!" Kara ordered Adriane.

The warrior yawned, eyes barely able to stay open. "It doesn't matter—I'll just end up here again."

"You have to find the power crystal."

"How'd you get in my dream, anyway?" Adriane asked.

"I have some experience in the astral planes."

Kara swirled her sparkling jewel in her fingers. "Not to mention this little power booster thing I like to call my network of friends. Came in quite handy in the Fairy Realms."

"Yeah, yeah, you saved everyone. Good for you."

Kara placed her hands on her hips. "So, you just going to sit here and sulk and leave the heavy lifting to your buds, or what?"

"I can't do anything."

"Adriane, this isn't real! We all need you."

The warrior eyed her suspiciously. Since when did the perfect blazing star need Adriane?

"This is only the dream state," Kara insisted. "You have to go all the way to the spirit world."

"It's too late." Adriane hung her head.

"Listen to me." Kara knelt in front of Adriane, taking the warrior's hands in hers. "Dawnrunner is okay."

Adriane looked up sharply. "Dawnrunner."

Kara nodded. "She was knocked around, but Emily helped her."

"Dreamer." Adriane's eyes widened.

Kara nodded. "If you don't go now, he and the rest of the mistwolves won't be so lucky. And we are going to lose Ravenswood."

"I don't even have my jewel."

"You mean that jewel?" Kara pointed at Adriane's wrist.

A small pinpoint of light shimmered. Adriane

squinted, looking harder, and the golden glow flashed brighter. The wolf stone appeared like magic.

"Now, come back to your real friends," Kara urged, releasing a sparkle of magic. It floated gently around the wolf stone, making it glow brightly.

Adriane felt the gentle touch of the healing stone, the strength of the dragon stone, the warm, fuzzy ferret stone, and the steadfast love of the animals. Her friends were all there, sending her their magic.

"Adriane, there isn't much time." Kara stood, gently pulling the warrior to her feet.

Adriane's heart thudded. Maybe it wasn't too late. Looking at Kara—the real Kara—Adriane knew her friend was telling the truth.

"Your dream is a total fashion disaster, anyway," the blazing star quipped. She held up her unicorn jewel, sending glittering magic sweeping over her and Adriane. "You ready?"

Adriane took a deep breath, held up her gem, and nodded.

Kara and Adriane faced each other and began to vanish.

"Hey, Barbie."

"Yeah, Xena?"

"Thanks."

In a flash of shining light, Adriane stepped into the spirit world.

She stood on cliffs of silver. A wide chasm gaped below her, seething with brilliant strands of wild magic.

A banshee whine wailed over the chasm. Like a whirling dervish, the ghostly demon spun, sending magic storms coursing through the air.

Adriane moved toward the edge of the cliff. "Storm," she called out.

The wolf's fragile connection with the crumbling spirit trail was fading fast. Wild magic swirled, picking away strands of mist. Storm was barely there.

Wolf stone blazing, Adriane sent the magic of her friends to Storm, praying she could hold the mist together.

The demon cackled, its mocking laughter echoing through the void. "The more magic the better," it sneered, voice raspy and unfamiliar.

That was not Orenda. It could only be the Spider Witch.

"Give me back my wolves!" Adriane ordered.

She jumped back as the glittering spirit trail shuddered beneath her feet, buckling in on itself. Without a pack mate to balance her, there was no way she could fight the witch. But Storm's and Dreamer's lives depended on her.

The wolf stone flashed wildly. Magic was seething inside of her, struggling to break free.

"The path to magic is not always through your friends," the witch said softly. "Free the wolf inside."

Adriane's blood boiled. But she was terrified to let

go. Would she be consumed by the savage beast, like Chain? Would she lose herself forever if she gave in?

Suddenly the air shifted as bands of magic tore apart. Something flew above the demon, flashing in and out of light and shadow—a multifaceted jewel.

The power crystal!

With a terrifying howl, the demon lunged, blackened hands swiping at the crystal. Using all the magic of Ravenswood, the demon reached toward the glittering prize, drawing it closer.

Adriane focused on the awesome crystal and raised her wolf stone. But a black blur flew through the air, knocking her aside.

Dreamer growled viciously, his emerald eyes completely veiled by burning bloodred fire. Pain lanced through her as Chain twisted inside Dreamer, devouring the pup's magic.

"Let him go, Chain!" the warrior commanded.

*"You cannot save him, warrior."* The black wolf's proud face stretched into a ghastly grin. *"You never could."*

Trapped beneath Chain's overbearing presence, Dreamer struggled to reach his pack mate. Adriane raised her wolf stone, mustering healing power and sending it to help Dreamer. She held out her other hand and fired a second beam of magic—to keep Storm alive.

"You cannot match our strength, warrior." The witch laughed.

Adriane's eyes widened as she realized what the witch was saying. "*You* are bonded to Chain?"

"Bonded?" the witch cackled. "Chain is *my* paladin!"

Dreamer suddenly lunged for the crystal, jaws opened wide. Adriane instinctively aimed her stone to stop him.

"Go ahead," the witch ordered, eyes blazing. "Do it!"

Dreamer's eyes flashed emerald as he tried to fight Chain's grip, but the ghost wolf was too strong.

Adriane screamed—her magic stretched beyond the breaking point.

*"You must save the crystal of Avalon,"* Storm called, her mist wavering. *"Or the mistwolves will be lost."*

Wisps of glittering white pulled weakly around the warrior's magic. Her first pack mate was nearly gone.

What was she going to do? She couldn't help Dreamer without letting go of Storm. But without her magic, Storm would be lost forever.

She looked at the wolves, her heart ripping in two. She could only save one. No matter what she did, she was going to betray one of her pack mates.

# Chapter 15

The Dark Sorceress drew in the pure magic of Avalon and breathed deeply, as if tasting its power for the first time. Overwhelmed with the rush, she barely noticed the black wolf that had materialized in the murky chamber, the dazzling power crystal in his jaws.

The Spider Witch saw him, though. "Give it to me," she commanded eagerly.

Eyes glinting blue and green, Chain wore Dreamer's face like a mask. The wolf advanced and carefully dropped the large gem in the witch's out-stretched hand.

"Ravenswood is mine!" she cried, holding the prize high above her head. The magic of Avalon cast gleaming halos onto the lair's rough stone walls.

Across the chamber, the sorceress's animal eyes gleamed. Silver hair blew back from her face as the magic washed over her, reawakening her power. Yet there was something not quite right.

The crystal had been tainted by the touch of an animal.

"I suggest you examine the crystal a little more closely," she said, retreating from the cascading light.

The witch's eyes sparked with anger. The crystal was vibrating, rattling in her hands. Concentrating, she held the jewel tightly as tendrils of glittering mist shimmered around the faceted edges.

Suddenly the crystal began to rock furiously as a low hum emanated from its sparkling center. The noise got louder, until it crescendoed into a chorus of terrifying howls.

The witch turned to the black wolf. "What's happened to it?"

With a golden flash, the mist pulled together.

A dark-haired girl stood in the chamber, her dark eyes burning. Upon her wrist, the wolf stone pulsed dangerously.

Adriane looked around. "What a dump."

Surprised by the girl's sudden appearance, the Spider Witch stepped back, tightening her grip on the shuddering power crystal. "You can't possibly think you can walk in here and take the crystal."

The warrior advanced, her wolf stone blazing like a sun. "I brought a few friends."

Adriane whirled, slamming rings of golden fire into the witch. The crystal flew out of the evil witch's clutches. In a flash, it vanished as glittering streams of misty light coursed through the chamber. The magical mist assumed ghostly forms as the spirit pack poured out. Hundreds of wolves sparkling black, blue, silver, red, gold, and white filled the chamber.

*"The spirit pack!"* Chain's voice echoed from Dreamer as the wolf snarled, furiously yapping and biting at the air.

The Dark Sorceress watched intently. So, the spirit pack had been trapped inside the power crystal. A hidden smile twisted her lips. Her theories had been correct all along. She had used the mistwolves before to lure the magic of Avalon. There was no doubt now that *their* magic was connected to the very source of all magic.

"Chain, kill the wolf!" the Spider Witch shrieked.

"I don't think so," Adriane said coolly.

Hundreds of wolves descended on Dreamer, howling as they enveloped him in ghostly blue light. Adriane could feel the Spider Witch's spell twisting at Chain. She understood now: The wolf was not the witch's true paladin, but a prisoner. Just like Orenda.

Chain's anguished howl tore through the chamber as his glowing form separated from Dreamer and was pulled into the swirling wolf storm. With a last yelp, Dreamer was free.

*"Your spell has been broken,"* the voices of the ancient wolves snarled.

With a loud rip, the top corner of the Ravenswood tapestry fell, strands of webbing unraveling.

The witch bolted toward the weaving. Her robe fluttered, then fell to the floor.

Adriane was stunned.

The Spider Witch's head and torso had warped into a swollen spider abdomen from which eight thick spider legs protruded. The faceted yellow eyes of an insect had monstrously distorted her face. Hair writhing like it was alive, the Spider Witch climbed up the tapestry, frantically trying to re-weave it. More spiders emerged, crawling over her heavy legs.

The spirit pack, now thousands strong, swirled in the room, a maelstrom of wolf power.

Wisps of Ravenswood's tangled magic disintegrated into smoke as the witch's spell broke apart. Adriane caught the remnants of the demon fluttering in the air before it vanished.

"No!" The witch staggered. The weaving unraveled, sending her tumbling to the floor.

With a booming crash, the ceiling crumbled to smoking rubble, leaving a gaping hole. Through it, the spirit pack swirled upward, streaming into the dark sky overhead.

Adriane and the witch saw the floating crystal at the same time. With a shrill cry, the Spider Witch lunged, clawing at it with all her might.

Adriane whipped golden fire through the air, ensnaring the crystal.

"Help me!" the witch cried frantically.

Adriane flicked her eyes to the shifting shadows.

"Impressive, warrior." The Dark Sorceress stood before her, eyes glowing with hunger. "The magic of the mistwolves is truly breathtaking."

"Choke on it," Adriane snarled, wolf stone flashing.

The sorceress raised her arms, trying to pull the spirit pack to her.

Dreamer at her side, Adriane wrapped a shield of wolf fire around the escaping pack.

The ghost wolves howled, disappearing into the night skies.

Red fire crackled from the power crystal as the Spider Witch lashed out.

Adriane staggered back, but kept her jewel trained on the pack. In that moment, the witch pulled the crystal into her hands. Clutching the prize, the Spider Witch scurried from the chamber.

"I see you have a new mistwolf," the Dark Sorceress sneered. "Used up the other one already, did we?"

"You will never take their magic!" Adriane cried, swinging the fire directly at the sorceress, pounding at her in a frenzy of strikes.

Palms held out, the sorceress did her best to deflect the blows. But she was not at full strength. She could not stand against the warrior and the power of the spirit pack.

"I want the crystal!" Adriane ordered, arms raised, black wolf crouched by her side.

"It's out of my hands, so to speak."

Adriane moved to the door but stopped short. A

huge shadow fell across the stone floor. An immense insect, oily wings shimmering upon its back, blocked the way. Like a giant beetle, black armor covered its torso. Green insect eyes gleamed as antennae twitched, sending out secret signals.

With a hiss, its black wings sprang open. Hundreds of spiders charged into the room, shrieking hungrily.

Wolf fire shot toward the creatures, slicing through thick abdomens and legs.

"Bug off!"

Adriane swung a circle of fire around her and Dreamer as more spiders spilled into the chamber.

Suddenly, the lair rumbled, shaking the very foundations of the castle. Adriane felt the magic of the power crystal tickling along her skin as if she were walking through spiderwebs.

"What is that witch doing with the crystal?" Adriane demanded.

"She's a spider," the sorceress said, smirking. "Think about it."

Adriane looked at the destroyed weaving, its strands now littering the floor.

"Too bad you won't be able to save your new wolf." The sorceress smiled, vampire teeth gleaming, eyes focused on the wolf stone. "There's no way out. Losing two wolves—that's got to hurt."

Adriane's heart pounded. It was like her nightmare come to life, but this time she was not going to fail her pack mate, either of them.

Adriane looked skyward to be sure the spirit pack had all escaped. She knew Storm was bravely leading them onto the spirit trail. Now, she had to flee this chamber of horrors and make her stand at Ravenswood, surrounded by her friends. But she had one thing to do first.

Following a slight gesture of Adriane's hand, Dreamer drew close to her side.

"Who did *you* lose?" She stared at the sorceress then gave her pack mate a nod. Dreamer went first, shimmering to mist and vanishing. "Think about it."

Adriane centered her elemental magic, feeling the bright power of the wolf stone wash over her. She had been afraid of the wolf within, but fear had blinded her. Standing on the cliffs of the spirit world, torn between Storm and Dreamer, she had looked into the heart of the power crystal and finally understood. The spirit pack touched every wolf, balancing raw power with ancient magic. Embracing the magical essence rather than the pure animal, Adriane had made her choice. She had released the wolf inside, diving into the power crystal itself.

In a flash, Adriane faded to mist and joined her pack mates.

Welcomed by the spirits of the mistwolves, Adriane

and Dreamer flew onto the glowing spirit trail. Wolf power, past, present, and future, surged through Adriane. It filled her entire being—the knowledge, experience, love, and strength that was at the very core of every mistwolf. This was her magic, too, as much as it was Dreamer's and Storm's.

*"Run with us, wolf sister."*

The voices of the wolves fell gently in her mind.

The spirit trail melted away. Mighty trees sprang up, surrounding them in lush greens, browns, and golds. The smell of the forests filled Adriane's senses.

*"My heart soars to see you, warrior."*

A silver wolf moved to her side, strong and full of magic. Stormbringer.

Adriane smiled at her pack mate.

Fiery reds, ocean blues, brilliant yellows, and deep forest greens curled and danced, flowing across the sky.

The pack came to the trail's end, where sand and sea met, where worlds joined. Their vision of the past shimmered before Adriane's eyes. Great crystalline towers rose, catching glints of light. Giant interlocking rocks set in an immense jigsaw puzzle led the way to the crystal city floating in an ocean of time. Creatures of untold beauty and power inhabited the city.

"What is this place?" Adriane asked, awestruck.

*"Avalon,"* the wolves said.

*"As it was."*

*"As it will be again."*

The vision splintered, replaced with a dark, mist-shrouded island.

"What happened?" Adriane asked.

*"Avalon was destroyed."*

The spirit pack swirled around her, many wolves speaking in one voice.

*"The magical creatures fled to Aldenmor. Mistwolves lost touch with the spirit trail, reverting to savagery. Pack leaders came to believe bonding with humans was harmful."*

"What happened to Chain?" Adriane asked.

*"The wizard Gardener was trying to rebuild Avalon. He won the trust of the wolf, Chain—but they were not meant to bond."*

Adriane listened intently.

*"The path to Avalon can only be found by humans and magical animals working together, even though there are those that will try otherwise. Gardener fought the Spider Witch. As she fell into the Otherworlds, she bound Chain to her. Gardener could not protect his pack mate."*

Adriane nodded. Stormbringer pressed close to her side.

*"Chain sent a clear message to the pack: Humans do not belong with mistwolves."*

"So Moonshadow took the pack into hiding, afraid humans would destroy them all."

Several ghost wolves faced Adriane and Storm, silver eyes shining. *"Your bond with Storm changed the course of the spirit trail forever. You have taken the first step to restoring Avalon."*

Adriane reached out in wonder, her wolf stone flaring as her magic touched the magnificent spirits. "Not all humans betray their pack mates."

*"Take from the past and lead us into the future, warrior."*

A bright beacon blinked in the distance.

*"The pack calls you."*

"We must go to them."

*"May you always run free."*

Adriane burst into the glade in a blaze of golden light. To one side, Dreamer stood, his midnight-black fur gleaming. On her other side stood the great silver mistwolf Stormbringer, her golden eyes shining as the wolf saw the friends she had left behind months ago.

"Storm!"

"Dreamer!"

The mages, animals, and mistwolves rushed forward as Adriane threw her arms around both pack mates, happy tears falling down her cheeks. She hadn't thought she would ever feel Storm's solid, reassuring presence again. And now she was really here, standing in the forests of Ravenswood, where she belonged—alive!

"I don't believe it!" Emily cried as she and Kara hugged Storm.

"Welcome back!" Ozzie beamed, shoving in to hug Storm's chest.

"Woohoot!" Ariel tooted, swirling around the wolf as Lyra nosed in to greet her friend.

*"It is good to see everyone again,"* Storm said, lips turned up at the corners in a wolfish grin.

*"You honor us."* Moonshadow bowed before Storm. *"The spirit pack runs strong."*

*"The magic of Avalon flows through us all."* Dawnrunner came up beside Adriane, sky blue eyes shining brilliantly.

Adriane hugged the alpha female as the wolf nuzzled her cheek. The entire pack surrounded her, everyone eager to welcome back Storm and Dreamer.

*"You have grown strong,"* Stormbringer said to Dreamer, nudging his nose with her own.

*"Pack mates grow strong together,"* Dreamer said.

Adriane looked at both of her pack mates, old and new. "Storm, I—"

*"The pack takes care of its own,"* the silver wolf said, rubbing against Dreamer in a sign of affection.

The warrior smiled, relieved.

Colored bubbles suddenly burst in the air above them.

"Look!" Ozzie jumped up and down, pointing. "Something's coming through!"

*Splat! Splooie! Sparf! Sploof! Sploot!*

Five worried mini dragons plummeted from the sky, falling on the mages.

"Kaaraa!" Goldie squeaked, hugging the blazing star's neck with her bright yellow wings.

Purple Barney peeled himself off Zach's shoulder and stood nose to nose with Drake. "Ooo."

Red Fiona whizzed happily around Emily, nearly colliding with orange Blaze, who barreled straight into Ozzie.

"Hi, Fred!" Adriane hugged the blue dragonfly that landed on her shoulder.

"Finally!" Goldie scowled at Kara.

"How do you expect me to do anything without my favorite mini?" Kara scratched her little friend between her golden wings. "I missed you, too."

"Adriane, you did it!" Emily smiled, arms draped around Storm.

"You saved them all," Zach exclaimed. "Dreamer, Storm, the spirit pack, the wolves of Aldenmor—all the mistwolves!"

"And Ravenswood is totally web free, too," Kara pronounced, unicorn jewel glittering.

Drake nosed Adriane, puffing proudly, as the d'flies circled her head squealing and chirping.

"Aaaaggg." Tweek suddenly tottered past, leaning on a mossy rock as twigs dropped from his torso.

"Now what?" Kara demanded. "Possessed by the Ghost of Christmas Past?"

Adriane scanned the forests nervously.

Moonshadow and Dawnrunner sniffed at the air.

*"Something is different here,"* Dreamer said.

"What's wrong?" Emily asked, suddenly sensing danger.

"The spirit pack was trapped in the power crystal." Adriane blinked as her wolf stone sputtered on her wrist, the bright light burning her eyes. "I freed them, but the witch got the crystal."

*"She is using our magic against us,"* Moonshadow snarled.

"That's ridicu—Gah!" Ozzie's jewel sparked, sending him flying backward.

"Ozzie!" Emily ran her healing stone over the ferret, but the gem crackled in a shower of sparks.

The mistwolves growled, scanning the forest.

"What's happening?" Zach asked, blue eyes wide as his dragon stone pulsed erratically.

With a subtle flick of her wrist, Dreamer and Storm flanked Adriane, standing strong on either side. The warrior reached with her wolf senses, gently touching the forest. The trees lived, but there was no magic flowing through their roots.

"Can't you feel it?" she asked.

"I don't feel—anything," Kara gasped.

"It's gone!" Emily cried.

The warrior nodded grimly. "Orenda is dead."

"No sylph, no magic," Tweek wheezed.

The mages looked at one another, the horrible realization sinking in: The magic of Ravenswood was gone.

# Chapter 16

Lightning crackled atop the Rocking Stone as droplets of dark, oily rain began to fall.

Emily tried to send healing magic into the gathering puddles of dark magic, but her gem sparked and fizzled. "What's wrong with our jewels?"

"Your jewels are tied to Ravenswood," Tweek answered. "Theoretically"—Tweek stuck loose twigs back into his mass—"if the witch controls Ravenswood, she could control your jewels as well."

Dank droplets fell, drenching the trees and seeping into the forest floor.

*"It's spreading fast,"* Dawnrunner said, her golden white coat streaked with black rain.

Adriane and the spirit pack had destroyed the Ravenswood tapestry and broken the spell, but it had served its purpose, creating a demon to attract the power crystal. Now the Spider Witch was going to complete the rest of her plan.

"She's using the power crystal to weave her own magic into Ravenswood," Adriane exclaimed.

"Our friends in the Fairy Realms said she's going

to try to re-weave the entire magic web!" Kara said, remembering what the Goblin Prince had told her about the Spider Witch's plan.

"She been after the preserve all along," Zach realized. "If her plan is to re-weave the web, she's starting with Ravenswood."

The rain fell harder, darkening the sky as if night had fallen. Everything felt completely unbalanced as the magic seeped deeper, lulling the forest into a dark dream.

"What are we supposed to do?" Kara asked.

Adriane frantically wiped oily rain from her arms and legs. She hadn't come this far to lose it all now.

Suddenly Dreamer stood tall, eyes flashing as he raised his nose in the air.

*"Pack mate."*

"What you got?"

*"Magic."*

"Show me."

The black mistwolf sniffed the ground and trotted to a sheltered hollow. Storm ran after him, using her magic to protect him from the toxic rain.

Lightning flashed, illuminating the trees in ghostly light.

The group gathered around Dreamer as he started to dig through a pile of charred twigs. Adriane felt the magic burn him as he nosed aside slabs of shriveled bark.

Suddenly Dreamer stood back.

There, poking through the sodden ashes, was a lone flower—a puffy dandelion sparkling with bright colors, like a sphere of tiny magic gems.

Emily ran over for a closer look. "It's a rainbow flower!" the healer gasped. "Phelonius spread these all over the preserve last summer."

"A phelower!" Kara exclaimed.

Phelonius was the first fairy creature the girls had ever met. He had appeared when Adriane and Emily had discovered their jewels. Along with Ozzie, the mages helped the giant bear-like creature get home to Aldenmor. They'd heard nothing from him since.

"LOooOkie!" The five dragonflies swarmed around the bright bloom, scattering the puffy seeds in a poof of activity. The ground shimmered. Clear, pristine puddles remained where the twinkling bits had fallen.

Adriane's wolf stone flashed bright gold. "Yes!"

"Here it is." Tweek held up his HORARFF, projecting an image of the rainbow flower. "*Flora rainbowpufficus* produces large quantities of raw magic, which can be harvested in a variety of ways. They are elemental in nature."

"If we can get the seeds to grow and bloom, we can replace the magic of Ravenswood!" Adriane exclaimed.

"Easier said than done," Tweek sighed, leaning against Storm. "There's something I'm just not seeing, if I could just put my twig on it—"

"What do we need, a Miracle-Gro spell?" Kara asked.

Tweek's quartz eyes practically bulged out of his grassy head. "Twingo!"

The little E. F. took off, scurrying back through the glade to the Rocking Stone.

Everyone raced after him.

Tweek studied the glowing symbols on the tower's base. "Of course!"

"What?" Ozzie demanded.

The E. F. grabbed Ozzie, pressing his nose to the stone. "Look!"

"Gah!"

"These symbols. It's not a message—they're directions!"

"You mean this is a recipe for growing rainbow flowers?" Ozzie guessed.

"Precisely!" Tweek pointed a twig at a flower-shaped symbol.

"So that's what Phel was doing," Emily exclaimed. "Making sure we'd always have magic in Ravenswood."

"Let's go for it!" Kara called out.

"Inconceivable!" Tweek faced the mages. "Each one of you must add elemental magic needed to make the pufficus."

"Hurryupicus!" Ozzie shook Tweek.

"Earth can't thrive without water, air, fire, or time," Tweek explained. "Each element must work together in harmony, strengthening all the others. Only together do you have the power to save Ravenswood."

"We can do this," Adriane declared. "We have to!"

The warrior led her friends back to the glade. Everything they had learned about magic would be put to the test.

"Everyone team up with your magical animals and form a circle," Tweek shouted, racing after the group.

The mages and animals ringed the seedlings twinkling upon the forest floor. The five dragonflies flew about excitedly, each landing on a mage's shoulder.

The E. F. nodded, looking the group over. "Zach and Drake are a powerful time combination, Kara has Lyra and her paladin for fire, Adriane has the mistwolves for earth, and you two—"

Emily and Ozzie stood in the circle with only Fiona and Blaze.

The two d'flies looked at each other and zipped over to Kara.

"Fine!" Ozzie called out.

Ariel fluttered over the group, landing on Emily's arm.

"Thank you," Emily said, nuzzling the white owl.

"We'll all help Emily and Ozzie," Kara instructed, unicorn jewel sparkling with diamond light.

Tweek waved his twigs at the mages. "But you still have to figure out how to work together."

"I know, spellsinging!" Kara said, twirling her unicorn jewel confidently.

The mages had learned music was a powerful way to combine their magic.

"A spellsong could harmonize your different types of magic," Tweek agreed.

Adriane nodded. "It's time we did a little magic weaving of our own."

"Me, me, me, me," Goldie sang.

"You, you, you," Fred sang back.

Wolf stone glowing, Adriane stepped toward Emily, Kara, Zach, and Ozzie. The mages joined hands and paws, jewels sparkling with intertwining magic. With a rousing cheer, they broke apart and walked to their animal friends, jewels raised and ready.

Tweek looked to Emily. "First up, we need water."

"We're on it." Emily stepped to the center of the circle, Ariel perched on her arm.

The animals of Ravenswood gathered with the mistwolves and Drake ready to send the healer magic.

"Go, Emily!" the animals cheered.

Emily closed her eyes in concentration. Then she started to sway, arms moving in a dance.

*Shimmering, showering*
*Droplets like jewels*
*Fountain of sky*
*Awake, and renew*

Emily sang, spinning in a circle, her long red hair flying around her. Fiona, Blaze, Goldie, Barney, and Fred sparkled in the air as they danced with Ariel. The lake bubbled and churned, shooting arcs of water in rhythm with Emily's soaring spellsong.

Petals of green and blue blossomed from the rainbow stone, sinking into the black clouds overhead. Everyone in the circle gave magic to the healer, as streaks of purple and turquoise raced through the clouds.

*Turning and turning*
*This circle of friends*
*One world, one home*
*Begins where it ends*

Glittering rain fell, diamond white and pure as a spring shower.

"Wonderful!" Adriane swayed to Emily's song, feeling the seedlings springing to life as they drank in the sweet, clean water.

Cheers rang across the glade as Emily, the d'flies, and Ariel took a bow.

"The seedlings need the heat of fire to bloom," Tweek instructed.

"Sun team!" Kara and Goldie shimmied into the center of the circle with Lyra. The blazing star shut her eyes, concentrated, and called upon the magic of fire. "Starfire, I need you." The unicorn jewel flared with bright firemental magic. "We all need you."

In a meteoric *whoosh*, a bolt of fire streaked across the sky. Iridescent orange-and-red flames twisted together and formed a magnificent stallion with strong muscles and flowing mane and tail.

Everyone gaped in awe at the amazing creature that stood before them.

*"Blazing star."* The firemental stallion bent his head over Kara's shoulder as she hugged him, unicorn jewel instantly covering her in a protective shield.

"You came for me," she said, barely holding back tears of joy.

*"I am for you."*

With a swift leap, Kara swung up onto his back. The incredible stallion reared up on his hind legs, flames licking the air.

Lyra and Goldie flapped their golden wings and hovered on either side of the blazing rider.

Kara hugged Starfire's flaming neck. "Let's rock!"

*Gleaming, streaming*
*Star shining bright*
*Color the land*
*With your blanket of light*

Prisms of light streamed from the unicorn jewel, forming a bright rainbow. The fire stallion's hooves burned brightly as he raced into the air, pulling the rainbow after him in a curving arc.

Goldie and Lyra followed Starfire, looping and weaving around the growing rainbow.

As the sun team reached the top of the rainbow, the clouds parted. Bright sunlight spilled over the forest like a golden curtain. Small seedlings burst through the soil, dazzling bright points of color in the grass.

"Excellent!" Adriane said, sensing the flowers reaching for the firemental magic.

Everyone cheered as Starfire landed, Kara's arms held high. The rainbow stretched across the brilliant blue sky.

Tweek nodded. "The flowers need time to grow and bloom."

"I am the germinator!" Zach exclaimed, stepping into the circle as Drake stomped forward, Barney on his head.

The boy held his dragon stone high in the air. Drake threw back his head and roared, sending a burst of flame into the sky. Red waves of magic swirled from Zach's jewel, rippling over the seedlings.

*Hours to days*
*Morning to night*
*Everything blooms*
*In its own perfect time*

Rainbow flowers popped up like popcorn, blooming and spreading as Zach's dragon magic fast-forwarded the flowers' growing cycle. Sparkling puffs blossomed everywhere until there were hundreds shining across the floor of the glade.

Adriane felt the flowers, heavy with magic, swaying on their stems. "Okay, they're ready." She hugged Drake's neck and high-fived Zach.

"We need wind to scatter the seeds," Tweek directed.

A flock of baby quiffles shoved Ozzie forward.

"Go, Ozzie!"

Ozzie closed his eyes tight, ferret stone glowing bright orange. Slowly he started floating up from the ground, until he was nose to nose with Starfire.

Ozzie opened his eyes. "What are you looking at?"

The stallion looked down.

"Gah!"

The ferret plummeted to the ground. Quickly springing to his feet, he adjusted his ferret stone and tried again.

*Wings all a-flutter*
*Trees bend and sway*
*The whistle of wind*
*Brings new life today*

A gentle breeze ruffled the quiffles' head feathers as the d'flies fluttered over Ozzie's head.

"We need more," Adriane called out, sensing the magic coming loose from the flowers. "Come on, Air Team. You're almost there!"

The mages and animals directed all their magic toward the ferret stone.

Ozzie's fur sparked and frizzled as the breeze increased. He bore down harder, sending a stiff wind sweeping across the grass. The rainbow seeds came loose and floated through the air in a twinkling cloud.

"I think I'm getting the hang of this!" Ozzie exulted.

"Fuzzy rocks!" a quiffle cheered.

"HelP!" Ozzie's stone glowed as a huge gust of wind ripped through the preserve, sweeping him off his feet and tumbling him into the trees.

"Excellent!" Tweek approved, then turned to Adriane. "The last step is weaving the magic into the earth."

Adriane hugged Fred as the mistwolves moved in around her. With a nod, the warrior stepped forward. "We're ready."

She could feel the melody building in the heart of her powers, her senses tingling with the magic floating across the glade.

"It's the Dreamer team!"

The pack gathered around the warrior, sending her the power of their renewed magic. Storm stood at her right side, Dreamer to her left, balancing the wave of glowing golden wolf light spreading out from her jewel.

The wolves howled softly, a low whine that rose and fell in pitch. Moving to the earth beat, the sound became a song—the song of Orenda.

*Rhythm of life*
*Spirit of song*
*Growing together*
*Our hearts beat as one*

Thunder rumbled and Dreamer cocked his ears, listening to the mighty growls. Adriane closed her eyes, letting the magic rush through her as the spirit pack, thousands strong, swept across the sky.

Releasing her inner wolf, she joined her pack mates.

Warrior and wolves shimmered and vanished. A cloud of glowing mist hovered where they had stood a second before.

Suddenly Adriane was everywhere at once. The mistwolves swept over the entire preserve, seeking the magic that floated in the air. Adriane held on tight, her essence interwoven with the pack. They were united in a single consciousness, with one purpose: to save the forest. Clear and focused, she sank down into the earth, pulling the magic with her.

*Turning and turning*
*This circle of friends*
*One world, one home*
*Begins where it ends*

Adriane weaved the magic deep into the earth. A pulsing rhythm pounded in time with her heart, enveloping her with the full power of the earth symphony. Every tiny flower, every creature, every tree was a crucial part of the song. But none of it would flourish unless all living things were in balance, supporting one another in harmony—like her circle of friends.

Deeper she went, treasuring the miracle of life at the very core of earth magic. With Storm and Dreamer by her side, a sphere of swirling light enveloping them all, Adriane wove mist back to solid form.

In the middle of the light stood a sylph, her flowing, fairy form surrounded by flowering vines. She greeted Adriane and the wolves with a radiant smile. The angelic beauty of her delicate features contrasted sharply with the craggy roots that spread from her arms and legs.

"Remember this song," the ancient creature said, her voice resonant with the power of the earth.

Adriane listened in wonder.

"It is who you are."

The melody floated through her senses. The

sylph's song held the essence of every living thing in Ravenswood, from the oaks bordering Wolf Run Pass, to the rivers rolling through the deep ravines, to the wide, grassy expanse of the portal field.

In the soaring notes, Adriane heard the echoes of wolf howls. Each refrain flowed into the next, telling of a vast network of forests woven together, of worlds connected.

Adriane felt her pack mates at her side and understood.

"I am alone but also part of the pack, many wolves with one voice."

The fairy creature nodded, sudden sadness washing over her deep eyes. The melody wavered, notes falling flat.

"What's wrong?" Adriane asked.

"Without a forest spirit, the magic will not last."

Adriane faltered. Without Orenda, the magic of the rainbow flowers could not sustain Ravenswood. The final piece was still missing.

*"I am ready."* Storm stepped forward, head held high.

The sylph regarded Adriane, eyes full of compassion. "The mistwolf is a part of us."

"Storm?" Adriane's heart wrenched as she realized what her pack mate was about to do.

*"This has always been my path, warrior,"* Storm said, her warm golden eyes full of love.

Adriane knelt nose to nose with the silver wolf. "But I just got you back," she whispered, fighting back tears.

*"And now I am going home."*

"Home." Adriane smiled, finally realizing the truth.

Dreamer bowed low. *"I will keep her safe."*

*"So will I."*

Adriane hugged Storm, holding on tight. She would remember this moment forever. "I love you, Storm."

*"I am with you, Adriane,"* Storm said to her pack mate. *"Now and forever."*

The sylph reached out. Stormbringer walked to her, silver fur dissolving to starlight. Adriane gazed into her bonded's golden eyes. Then, the wolf vanished.

The mist shone in the center of the glade, separating and transforming back to warrior and wolf. The rest of the pack stood around Adriane and Dreamer, howling joyfully.

"You did it!" Zach cried, hugging her as Drake danced from foot to foot.

A huge cheer erupted. Her friends gathered around, laughing, hugging, and crying.

Around them, the forest spread out majestically, trees and grass shimmering with vibrant greens and browns. A gentle breeze ruffled the sun-bright leaves. Magic flooded through the preserve, clean and pure.

Ravenswood stood stronger than ever.

Emily looked around, concerned. "Where's Storm?"

"She's right here." Adriane smiled, wolf stone glowing bright silver. "Home."

# Chapter 17

"**I**t's a symphony," Adriane said.

"How so?" her father, Luc, asked, clearly pleased.

Emily, Kara, Adriane, and Zach marveled over a series of swooping stainless-steel circles and squares, playing with the light like a mirror.

"Different elements working together to make something beautiful," Adriane responded.

They stood in a wide gallery lined with large, frosted windows. Luxuriant light played over the serene sculptures.

"I've never seen anything like it, Mr. Charday," Zach said.

"It's amazing," Emily added.

"Minimal but elegant." Kara's blue eyes were narrowed in concentration. "Very power style."

"They're awesome!" Adriane declared proudly as her dad slung his arm around her shoulder. "I'd love to see how you make these."

Luc smiled warmly. "We can work on them this summer . . . if you'd like."

"Sure, that would be great," she answered.

"Wonderful show."

Everyone turned at the sound of Gran's voice. Her bright purple dress swayed as she walked confidently across the gallery with Willow, her dark eyes full of renewed strength.

"She's wearing me out," Willow said. "You'd think it was me who just got out of the hospital yesterday."

"I haven't felt this good in years," Gran said, dark eyes dancing.

"I've been showing off the big story." Willow held up a copy of the *Stonehill Gazette*. "You guys are front page."

**"WOLF COMES HOME!"** was the headline atop a picture of Dreamer surrounded by kids from Stonehill Middle School.

"The school started a petition to keep Ravenswood open," Emily said.

"There're over one thousand names on it!" Kara added.

"They're even sending it out to other schools in the area," Adriane said excitedly. Tiff, Molly, Heather, Marcus, Joey, Kyle, and the gang had really pulled through.

"Dreamer's famous!" Gran read. "The official mascot of Ravenswood."

Luc shook his head. "To think he escaped the zoo and walked over a hundred miles to get back to the preserve."

"Wow!" Kara exclaimed. "Uh, I mean . . . poor little guy couldn't bear to be without us."

"Ravenswood is clearly where Dreamer belongs." Willow faced her daughter. "You've both made a good home there."

"Mrs. Windor doesn't seem like the kind of woman who gives up," Luc said thoughtfully.

Gran snorted. "Windor has no choice. She's been outvoted again, since Dreamer got such good publicity for the preserve."

Luc looked over at a well-dressed man waving to him.

"Willow, I want you to meet the museum director," Luc said, nodding to him.

"I'll be right there," Willow said as Luc walked away.

"Kara, let's show Zach the rest of the exhibits," Emily suggested.

"Cool." Kara and Emily slipped their arms into Zach's, pulling the boy into another room full of paintings.

Grandmother, mother, and daughter—three generations—regarded one another.

"Adriane, your grandmother and I have been talking," Willow said, breaking the silence.

"And we think it's best for you to stay where you are," Gran finished.

"Yes!"

"I've never seen you happier, and your friends love you very much," Willow said.

"Yeah, they're okay." Adriane smiled.

Willow clasped her daughter's hands. "Whatever this connection is that you have with Ravenswood, I think it's a good thing. It's almost as if you have an angel there, looking out for you. I just couldn't hear her."

"Maybe you just didn't listen," Adriane said.

"Maybe I couldn't understand what was being said." Willow took Adriane in her arms. "You are a wild spirit, baby girl. Don't ever let it be tamed."

Adriane closed her eyes, hugging her mother tightly.

❧   ❧   ❧

Sunset washed over the forest, kissing the trees with waves of red, orange, and purple. Adriane stood with the wolves near the lake in the glade. Moonshadow lifted his head and howled, a long wail that echoed into the sky. Dawnrunner, Dreamer, and the other wolves joined in the chorus. They were welcoming the new spirit of Ravenswood.

Across the glade, her friends stood listening to the wolf song.

"How's it going?" The warrior stepped forward, the wolf stone upon her wrist shining luminous silver edged with gold—Storm's colors.

"Your jewel is amazing!" Tweek inspected her wrist. "Stormbringer is a powerful paladin."

Kara twirled her pink and white unicorn jewel and regarded the warrior. "You know, I think Adriane's jewel is really another color."

"What do you mean?" Adriane asked, anxiously studying her jewel.

"Every time she gets near Zach, she turns completely red."

"I do not!"

Zach walked up as the girls giggled. "The preserve looks great."

Adriane flushed red as a tomato.

"You can feel her here." He smiled at Adriane, gesturing to the lush trees and sparkling lake.

"Zach, there's a big school dance coming up before summer break," Kara said slyly.

"I've never been to one of those," Zach exclaimed, looking at the warrior.

Adriane blushed again. "It's a date."

"All right!" The boy beamed.

"Oh me, me, me, me." Tweek twirled by, his HORARFF zipping through images. "We have a lot of work to do."

"Tweek, was Avalon really destroyed?" asked Emily.

"From what the spirit pack told Adriane, it would seem so."

"I saw the island," Kara said thoughtfully. "But it was all under mist."

"Even if Avalon was destroyed, the magic still runs

strong. And that means it can be rebuilt." Tweek regarded the mages as the animals of Ravenswood gathered around. "There are several ways to control the magic of Avalon, theoretically. The Dark Sorceress tried to control it through magical animals. The Spider Witch wants to re-weave the entire web. But the only sure way is by returning the nine crystals."

"Eight," Kara said sadly.

"Yes, one was destroyed. Two are with the Fairimentals. And now one is in the Spider Witch's hands."

"So what's next?" Adriane asked.

"We go after the other five," Ozzie said adamantly. "Then figure it out."

"We'll have to be ready." Tweek tottered back and forth. "We have two Level Ones"—he looked to Emily and Zach—"two Level Twos . . ."

Adriane and Kara smiled at each other, Dreamer and Lyra standing proudly by their sides.

"And something else entirely." Tweek looked at the ferret.

"Hey!" the ferret protested.

"Ozzie is very important. A clear case of elemental transformation."

"Transformation—now *that* is interesting," Ozzie said.

"Precisely. You think the Fairimentals just picked any elf to turn into a rodent?"

"Weasel," Kara said.

"Mammal," Emily added.

"Whatever!" Tweek hobbled about. "What I mean is, you have powerful magic, Ozzie."

Ozzie scratched his chin, pondering the revelation.

*"The mistwolves will return to Aldenmor and protect the Fairimentals,"* Moonshadow said.

Adriane nodded, jewel sparking.

*"You take care of Dreamer,"* Dawnrunner said.

Leaning down, Adriane rubbed her head against the wolf.

*"Pup, you sure are a pawful of trouble!"* Moonshadow growled at Dreamer.

*"I learned from the best."* Dreamer stood and stretched, his black fur glistening in the fading sun. He smiled the relaxed grin of a confident wolf, opening his mouth and letting his scarlet tongue loll out.

"Just wait until you have pups of your own," Adriane told Moonshadow.

*"That time is coming soon."* Dawnrunner's eyes twinkled as she snuffled in his ear.

Moonshadow's eyes opened wide.

Everyone cheered.

The pack leader leaped happily around his mate. Zach grabbed his wolf brother and pulled him down so that he half jumped, half fell into the grass.

"Let's get wigjiggy with it!" Ozzie shuffled and leaped, landing on his rump.

Emily and Kara danced with Ozzie, Zach, Drake, Lyra, and Ariel. The dragonflies zipped overhead, careening and twirling in joyous celebration.

Adriane hugged Dreamer, her wolf stone shining like moonlight. She let her pack mate join the joyous romp as she turned and walked across the glade.

Adriane had never felt like she belonged anywhere. Torn between different schools, between the wolf pack and her friends, she'd never fit in completely with any group. Storm had made her feel strong and connected to her magic. When Storm was lost, Adriane had lost herself, too.

Now Storm would be there for her, a paladin who would always come when Adriane needed her most. But Dreamer would be by her side every day, and she intended to make the most of it. They both had so much to learn about their magic. Her bond with Dreamer would never be like her bond with Storm, but that was how it should be. Dreamer was unique. He held a special place in her heart that was his alone.

She reached out to the forest and felt Storm's loving presence all around her.

The last of the day's pink glow filtered through the trees, reflecting off her jewel. A million facets of brilliant love turned in the silver light.

Since losing Storm, Adriane had kept her heart locked in a cage. Now, she was moving on. She had allowed the wolf in her to run free, and in doing so she had unlocked a part of herself. She didn't know what would happen or where she'd be tomorrow. But she was strong; she was fierce. She was a warrior.

Sparkling black eyes raised in laughter to the starry skies. Once again, she had followed her heart—but this time she had found herself.

# Epilogue

**M**oonlight spilled through the trees, casting a silver glow on the dark-haired girl and the black wolf. They moved in sync, running through the lush forest.

*"It's coming from the portal field."* Dreamer's eyes reflected twinkling stars.

Awakened in the night, they had both felt it: strong magic in Ravenswood.

A breeze whispered through the preserve. Adriane could feel Storm watching her, keeping her safe.

Breaking through the thick trees, Adriane came to a stop, Dreamer at her side.

All was still across the field. Mist rose from the forest floor, veiling the trees in a primeval swirl.

Adriane slowly stepped through the tall grass, scanning the trees at the field's edge.

Her stone sparked, and she suddenly reeled, sensing the powerful magic nearby. Dreamer growled low, pointing toward the source.

Hidden in a thick grove of oaks, a shadow moved.

"Who's there?" Adriane called out warily.

Teeth bared, Dreamer crouched, ready to lunge.

Starlight spilled over the lone figure's ragged coat as it stumbled forward, eyes flashing red.

Adriane gasped.

Mrs. Beasley Windor stood hunched, her face twisted into a menacing leer.

Adriane swung into position, jewel flaring with power. "What are you doing here?" the warrior demanded.

Like a puppet, the repulsive figure shuffled toward them. "I believe we have some unfinished business, warrior."

That wasn't Windor's voice. It was the voice of the Dark Sorceress.

"Stay where you are!" Adriane ordered, silver fire coiling around her wrist.

"Your wolf looks quite healthy," Windor sneered, drool hanging from her lip. "As does your jewel."

"Let Windor go," Adriane commanded.

"How else was I supposed to get to you? Your dreamcatcher is stronger than ever."

"What do you want?"

Mrs. Windor lumbered closer to Adriane and Dreamer. "I have something for you."

A brilliant gem lay in her open hands.

Adriane stepped back, the power crystal bathing her tanned face in light. "What kind of trick is this?"

"No trick, warrior." Windor held out the power

crystal. "You have no idea what I risk to bring this crystal to you."

"I'm touched." Adriane could not keep her eyes off the amazing crystal.

"She's insane, you know." The sorceress's voice grated against Windor's throat.

"Takes one to know one."

"We are both served by keeping the power of Avalon out of the witch's hands."

Adriane broke her gaze away. "I don't believe you."

Windor stood in the stark light of the moon.

"You have done what I have only dreamed about," the sorceress said softly. "Taken the magic of the mistwolves. But the path to Avalon is far more dangerous than you can imagine. You think your animals can balance the magic, but each time you use it, there is a price to pay." Windor's eyes glared fire, burning into Adriane's soul. "You cannot have magic without loss. *That* is the only balance."

Adriane listened intently—she had known the dizzying loneliness, the aching and grieving of what it meant to lose what she loved most.

"You asked me what I have lost in my quest for magic," the sorceress hissed. "Everything—even my own sister."

Moonlight cast shimmering beams over the demented figure.

"Why are you telling me this?" Adriane finally asked.

"There may be a way for us to work together to rebuild Avalon."

"You *are* insane!"

It was hard to believe this was coming from the enemy who had nearly destroyed the mistwolves, her friends, and the entire world of Aldenmor.

Yet the crystal was the real thing, she knew it.

"Go ahead, take it." The sorceress's voice oozed like honey.

Dreamer growled as Adriane cautiously stepped forward and grabbed the crystal. "I don't know what you're up to, but whatever it is, my friends and I will be ready."

"We'll see." The sorceress's smile cracked Windor's face into a ghoulish grin.

With a flash, Windor blinked. Horrified, she looked around and took off, screaming into the night.

Adriane took a deep breath, her hands closing around the warm facets of the power crystal.

"Into the great unknown," she murmured, kneeling by Dreamer's side.

Her pack mate nodded, his emerald eyes bright with magic. Dreamer scanned the portal field one last time, then trotted back toward the cottage.

The warrior followed her pack mate into the dark forest, the magic of Avalon lighting her way.

Coming Soon!

Avalon   Quest for Magic # 4

# Heart of Avalon
**By Rachel Roberts**

Avalon needs a healer!

Time is running out—the evil Spider Witch has begun reweaving the magic web, and the fate of Avalon depends on the mages working with their animal friends to recover the missing power crystals.

Yet unless Emily can bond with one special animal, she cannot advance to Level 2 mage like her friends, Kara and Adriane.

When the healer is mysteriously whisked away to a deserted tropical island on Aldenmore, she meets a strange, shapeshifting creature. The creature holds the secret not only to evolving Emily's healing magic, but also to finding the path to Avalon.

But is Emily up to the challenge?

Can the healer find her one true magical animal and fulfill her destiny to heal Avalon?

# KIND News Online

Be a kid in Nature's Defense!
Visit KIND News Online at

**www.kindnews.org**

The website for kids who care about people,
animals and the earth.

---

**Experience even more of the magic:**

**Become an Avalon Clubhouse member!**

To find out more, visit **www.avalonclubhouse.com**

Or write to:
Avalon Clubhouse
P.O. Box 568
Lowell, MA 01853

(Check with your parent or guardian before visiting
any website!)